THE ISLE OF BLOOD

Also by Rick Yancey

THE MONSTRUMOLOGIST: THE TERROR BENEATH
THE CURSE OF THE WENDIGO

THE MONSTRUMOLOGIST

THE ISLE OF BLOOD

WILLIAM JAMES HENRY

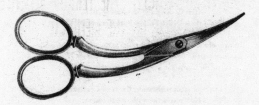

Edited by Rick Yancey

SIMON AND SCHUSTER

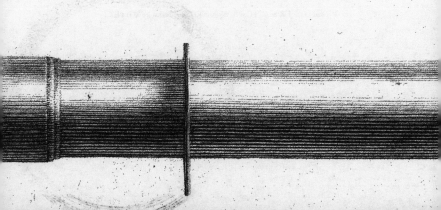

First published in Great Britain in 2011 by Simon and Schuster UK Ltd
A CBS COMPANY

Simon & Schuster UK Ltd
1st Floor, 222 Gray's Inn Road, London WC1X 8HB

Originally published in the USA in 2011 by Simon & Schuster Books For Young Readers,
an imprint of Simon & Schuster Children's Publishing Division,
1230 Avenue of Americas, New York, NY 10020.

www.simonandschuster.co.uk

Text Copyright © Rick Yancey 2011
Book Design by Lucy Ruth Cummins

A CIP catalogue record for this book is available from the British Library.

ISBN 978-0-85707-017-3

3 5 7 9 10 8 6 4 2 1

Printed in the UK by CPI Cox & Wyman, Reading, Berkshire RG1 8EX

For Sandy

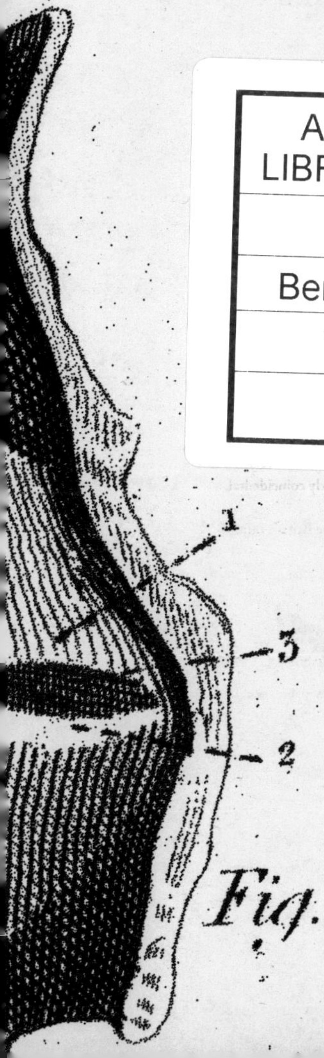

Fig. 36

"There was red rain in the Mediterranean region, March 6, 1888. Twelve days later it fell again. Whatever this substance may have been, when burned, the odor of animal matter was strong and persistent."
—(*L'Astronomie*, 1888)

"[The object that fell from the sky] was a circular form resembling a sauce or salad dish bottom upward, about eight inches in diameter and one inch in thickness, of a bright buff color, with a fine nap upon it similar to that of milled cloth.... Upon removing the villous coat, a buff-colored pulpy substance of the consistency of good soft soap, an offensive, suffocating smell appeared; and on near approach to it ... the smell became almost insupportable, producing nausea and dizziness. A few minutes' exposure to the atmosphere changed the buff into a livid color resembling venous blood."
—Professor Rufus Graves,
The American Journal of Science, 1819

"Seek a fallen star," said the hermit, "and thou shalt only light on some foul jelly, which, in shooting through the horizon, has assumed for a moment an appearance of splendour."
—Sir Walter Scott, *The Talisman*, 1825

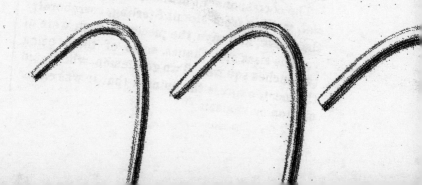

FLESH DESCENDING IN A SHOWER.

AN ASTOUNDING PHENOMENON IN KENTUCKY—FRESH MEAT LIKE MUTTON OR VENISON FALLING FROM A CLEAR SKY.

LOUISVILLE, March 9.—The Bath County (Ky.) *News* of this date says: " On last Friday a shower of meat fell near the house of Allen Crouch, who lives some two or three miles from the Olympian Springs in the southern portion of the county, covering a strip of ground about one hundred yards in length and fifty wide. Mrs. Crouch was out in the yard at the time, engaged in making soap, when meat which looked like beef began to fall around her. The sky was perfectly clear at the time, and she said it fell like large snow flakes, the pieces as a general thing not being much larger. One piece fell near her which was three or four inches square. Mr. Harrison Gill, whose veracity is unquestionable, and from whom we obtained the above facts, hearing of the occurrence visited the locality the next day, and says he saw particles of meat sticking to the fences and scattered over the ground. The meat when it first fell appeared to be perfectly fresh.

The correspondent of the Louisville *Commercial*, writing from Mount Sterling, corroborates the above, and says the pieces of flesh were of various sizes and shapes, some of them being two inches square. Two gentlemen, who tasted the meat, express the opinion that it was either mutton or venison.

—The New York Times, March 10, 1876

PROLOGUE

September 2010:
"Contact"

Everyone has someone.

More than three years had gone by since the director of the nursing home had handed over to me the thirteen leather-bound notebooks belonging to the deceased indigent calling himself William James Henry. The director did not know what to make of the journals, and, frankly, after reading the first three volumes, I didn't either.

Headless humanoid killing machines running amok in late-nineteenth-century New England. The "philosopher of aberrant biology" who studies and (when necessary) hunts down such creatures. Microscopic parasites that somehow give their hosts unnaturally long lives—if they don't "choose" to kill them instead. Midnight autopsies, madmen, human sacrifice, monsters in underground lairs, and a monster hunter who may or may not have been the most famous serial killer in history. . . . There was no question that Will Henry's strange and disturbing "diary" had to be a work of fiction or the carefully executed, highly organized delusions of a man whose reason had clearly come undone.

Monsters are not real.

But the man who wrote about them certainly was real. I had spoken to the people who had known him. The paramedics who had taken him to the hospital after a jogger discovered him unconscious in a drainage ditch. The social workers and policemen who worked his case. The staff and volunteers at the assisted-living facility who had bathed and fed him, who had read to him and eased his passing at the ripe old age (according to Will Henry) of 131. And, of course, I had in my possession the journals themselves, which *someone* had written. The question was—has always been—one of identity, not veracity. Who was William James Henry? Where did he come from? And what unfortunate circumstance brought him to that drainage ditch, half-starved, those handwritten notebooks—besides the clothes on his back—his sole possession?

Everyone has someone, the director of the facility had told me. Someone knew the answer to those questions, and I took it upon myself to find that person, publishing the first three volumes of the journal under the title *The Monstrumologist* in the fall of 2009. The second set, called *The Curse of the Wendigo*, was published the following year. Though the subject matter was just this side of outlandish,

I hoped the author had incorporated at least some of the truth about himself and his past. A reader might recognize something in the tale about a relative, a coworker, a long-lost friend, and contact me. I was convinced someone some-where knew this poor man calling himself Will Henry.

My motivation went beyond mere curiosity. He had died alone, with nothing and no one, and had been laid to rest in a pauper's grave with the poorest of the poor, forgotten. My heart went out to him, and I wanted, for reasons I still do not entirely understand, to bring him home.

Soon after *The Monstrumologist* was published, I began receiving e-mails and letters from readers. The vast majority were cranks claiming to know who Will Henry was. More than one offered to tell me—for a price. A few offered well-meaning suggestions for further research. Some, predict-ably, accused me of being the author. A year went by, then two, and I was no closer to the truth. My own research had resulted in no significant progress. In fact, at the end of two years, I had even more questions than when I'd begun.

Then, in late summer of last year, I received the follow-ing e-mail from a reader in upstate New York:

Dear Mr. Yancey,

I hope you don't think I'm some kind of nut or con artist or something. My daughter was assigned your

book to read for her language arts class, and she came
to me last night very excited because we happen to
have a relative whose name really was Will Henry.
He was the husband of my father's great-aunt. It's
probably just a crazy coincidence, but I think you
might be interested, if you really didn't just make up
the stuff about finding the journals.

Sincerely,
Elizabeth Reed[1]

A few e-mails and a phone call later, I was on a flight to
New York to meet Elizabeth in her hometown of Auburn.
After some pleasant conversation and several cups of coffee at a local diner, she took me to Fort Hill Cemetery.
My guide was a vivacious, outgoing middle-aged woman
who had come to share my fascination with the mystery
of Will Henry. She agreed with me—as would any reasonable person—that his story had to be more fiction
than fact, but her very real family connection to a man by
that name was no fabrication. It was that connection that
brought me to New York and to that cemetery. She had
e-mailed me a picture of the tombstone, but I wanted to
see it with my own eyes.

It was a beautiful afternoon, the trees decked out in all

[1]At her request, the name has been changed to protect her identity.

their autumnal glory, the sky a cloudless, brilliant blue. And, three years and three months after first reading those haunting opening lines (*These are the secrets I have kept. This is the trust I never betrayed . . .*), I was standing at the foot of a grave, before a granite marker that read:

LILLIAN BATES HENRY

1874–1950

Beloved Wife

Parting is all we know of heaven,

And all we need of hell.

"I never knew her," Elizabeth said. "But my father said she was quite a character."

I could not take my eyes off the name. Until that moment I had had nothing tangible except the diaries and a few old newspaper clippings and other questionable artifacts tucked within the yellowing pages. But here was a name etched in stone. No. More than that. Here was a *person*, literally right at my feet, whom Will had written about.

"Did you know him?" I asked hoarsely. "Will Henry?"

She shook her head. "I didn't know either of them. He disappeared a couple years after her death, before I was born. There was a fire. . . ."

"A fire?"

"Their house. Will and Lilly's. A total loss. The police suspected arson, and so did the family."

"They thought Will Henry set it, didn't they?"

"My family didn't like him very much."

"Why?"

She shrugged. "Dad said he was . . . kind of odd. But that isn't the main reason."

She dug into her purse. "I brought a picture of her."

My heart quickened. "Is Will in it?"

She pulled out a faded Polaroid photograph and tipped it slightly to reduce the glare from the bright sun overhead.

"It's the only one I could find in Dad's things. I'm still looking, though; maybe I'll find some more. It's from her seventy-fifth birthday."

I did the math quickly. "That would be in '49—her next to last."

"No, it was her last. She died before her next birthday."

"Is that Will sitting on her left?" He looked to be about the right age.

"Oh, no. That's her brother, Reggie, my great-grandfather. Will is sitting on her other side."

The photograph was more than sixty years old and was slightly out of focus, but the man on Lilly's right struck me as being at least twenty years younger than her. Elizabeth agreed.

"That's the main reason the family didn't like him, according to Dad. Lilly told everyone he was ten years younger, but he looks twice that in this picture. Everyone thought he married Aunt Lilly for her money."

I could not tear my eyes away from the blurry image. A lean face, dark deep-set eyes, and a stiff, somewhat enigmatic smile. *These are the secrets I have kept.*

"Children?" I asked.

She shook her head. "They never had any. And Dad said they *never* met any of Will's relatives. He was a total mystery-man. No one was even sure what he did for a living."

"I guess you know what I'm going to ask next."

She laughed brightly. It sounded oddly tinny in the setting.

"Did he ever talk about working for a monster hunter when he was younger? He didn't—at least in none of the stories I've heard. The problem is, anyone who might have heard a story like that is dead now."

We were silent for a moment. I had a thousand questions and couldn't get a grip on a single one of them.

"So their house burns down and Will disappears, never to be heard from again," I finally said. "That would be—when? Two years after she died, so 1952?"

She was nodding. "Around that time, yes."

"And fifty-five years later he turns up again in a drainage ditch a thousand miles away."

"Well," she said with a smile. "I never said I had *all* the answers."

I looked at the gravestone. "She was all he had," I said. "And maybe when she died he went a little crazy and burned down the house and lived on the streets for the next five decades?"

I laughed ruefully and shook my head. "It's weird. I'm closer to the truth now than I've ever been, and it feels like I'm farther away."

"At least you know he was telling the truth about her," she tried to comfort me. "There really was a Lilly Bates who was around thirteen years old in 1888. And there really was a man named William James Henry."

"Right. And everything else he writes about could still be a product of his imagination."

"You sound disappointed. Do you *want* monsters to be real?"

"I don't know what I want anymore," I confessed. "What else can you tell me about Lilly? Besides Reggie, were there any other brothers or sisters?"

"Not that I know of. I know she grew up in New York. The family was pretty well off. Her father—my great-great-grandfather—was a big-time financier, right up there with the Vanderbilts."

"Don't tell me. After she died and the house burned down, they found her bank accounts cleaned out."

"No. They hadn't been touched."

"Some gold-digger Will was. You'd think the family might have changed its mind about him."

"It was too late," she replied. "Aunt Lilly was dead, and Will Henry was gone."

✳

That was it, I thought on the plane ride back to Florida. The thing I wanted. I knew monsters were not real, and was fairly certain there had been no serious scientists called monstrumologists who chased after them. It wasn't about the journals, though I had to admit they fascinated me; it was the *why* behind the *what*. It was Will Henry himself.

I went back to the journals. Monsters might not be real, but Lilly Bates had been. Buried in the folios were clues that might lead me to Will Henry, to the *why* I was so desperate to understand. Sprinkled in those pages were verifiable facts, a jigsaw puzzle of the real intermingled with the bizarre. His life—and this strange record of it—demanded an explanation, and I was more determined than ever to discover what it was.

We are hunters all. We are, all of us, monstrumologists, Will Henry writes in the transcript that follows. I can say that he's absolutely right, at least in my case. And the monster I hunt is not unlike the creature that almost destroyed him and his master. Pellinore Warthrop had his grail—and I have mine.

R. Y.
Gainesville, FL
April 2011

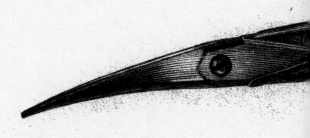

It is no longer possible to escape men.
Farewell to the monsters,
Farewell to the saints.
Farewell to pride.
All that is left is men.

—Jean-Paul Sartre

Fig. 37

FOLIO VII
Objet Trouvé

"BEAUTY IS NOTHING BUT THE BEGINNING OF TERROR."
—RAINER MARIA RILKE, *DUINO ELEGIES*

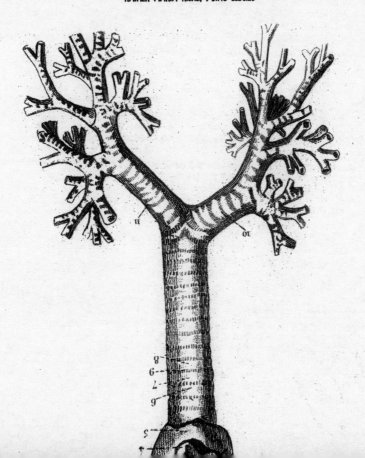

ONE

"A Very Dangerous Poison"

After several years of service to the monstrumologist, I approached him with the idea of recording, in the interest of posterity, one or two of his more memorable case studies. I waited, of course, until he was in one of his better moods. Approaching Pellinore Warthrop while he wallowed in one of his frequent bouts of melancholia could be hazardous to one's physical well-being. Once, when I made that ill-advised approach, he hurled a volume of Shakespeare's tragedies at my head.

The moment presented itself at the delivery of the day's mail, which included a letter from President McKinley, thanking Warthrop for his service to the country upon the satisfactory conclusion of "that peculiar incident in the Adirondacks." The doctor, whose ego was as robust as any of Mr. P. T. Barnum's sideshow strong men, read it aloud three times before entrusting it to my care. I was his file clerk, among other things—or, I should say, as well as *every* other thing. Nothing outside his work could brighten the monstrumologist's mood more than a brush with celebrity. It seemed to satisfy some deep yearning in him.

Beyond elevating his moribund spirits and thus ensuring—momentarily, at least—my physical safety, the letter also provided the perfect entrée for my suggestion.

"It *was* quite peculiar, wasn't it?" I asked.

"Hmmm? Yes, I suppose." The monstrumologist was absorbed in the latest issue of the *Saturday Evening Post*, which had also arrived that day.

"It would make quite a tale, if someone were to tell it," I ventured.

"I have been thinking of preparing a small piece for the *Journal*," replied he. The *Journal of the Society for the Advancement of the Science of Monstrumology* was the official quarterly of the Society.

"I was thinking of something for more widespread consumption. A story for the *Post*, for example."

"An interesting idea, Will Henry," he said. "But wholly impractical. I made a promise to the president that the matter would remain strictly confidential, and I've no doubt that, if I should break my vow, I might find myself locked up in Fort Leavenworth, not exactly the ideal place to pursue my studies."

"But if you published something in the *Journal* . . ."

"Oh, who reads *that*?" he snorted, waving his hand dismissively. "It is the nature of my profession, Will Henry, to labor in obscurity. I avoid the press for a very good reason, to protect the public *and* to protect my work. Imagine what the publication of that affair would do—the firestorm of panic and recriminations. Why, half the state of New York would empty out, and the rest would appear on my doorstep to hang me from the nearest tree."

"Some might say your actions were nothing short of heroic," I countered. If I could not appeal to his reason, I would plead to his ego.

"Some *have*," he replied, referring to the president's letter. "And that must be enough."

But not *quite* enough; I knew what he meant. More than once he had seized my hand at his bedside, staring beseechingly at me with those dark backlit eyes nearly mad with desperation and sorrow, begging me to never forget, to bear his memory past the grave. *You are all I have, Will Henry. Who else will remember me when I am gone? I will sink into oblivion, and the earth shall not note or care at my passing!*

"Very well. Another case, then. That matter in Campeche, at Calakmul . . ."

"What is this, Will Henry?" He glared at me over the magazine. "Can't you see I am trying to relax?"

"Holmes has his Watson."

"Holmes is a fictional character," he pointed out.

"But he is based on someone real."

"Ah." He was smiling slyly at me. "William James Henry, do you have literary ambitions? I am astounded."

"That I might have literary ambitions?"

"That you have any ambition at all."

"Well," I said, taking a deep breath. "I do."

"And all this time I had allowed myself to hope you might follow in my footsteps as a student of aberrant biology."

"Why couldn't I be both?" I asked. "Doyle is a physician."

"*Was*," he corrected me. "And not a very successful one at that." He laid down the magazine. I had at last gotten his full attention. "I will confess the idea intrigues me, and I would have no objection to your trying your hand at it, but I retain the right to review anything you set to paper. Beyond my own reputation, I have the legacy of my profession to protect."

"Of course," I said eagerly. "I wouldn't dream of publishing anything without obtaining your approval first."

"But nothing of our difficulties in the Adirondacks."

"I was actually thinking of that case from a few years ago—the incident in Socotra."

His face darkened. His eyes burned. He leveled a finger at my face and said, "Absolutely not. Do you understand? Under no circumstances are you *ever* to do such a thing. The temerity, Will Henry, to even suggest it!"

"But why, Dr. Warthrop?" I asked, taken aback by the ferocity of his reaction.

"You know very well the answer to that question. Oh, I should have guessed it. I should have known!" He rose from his chair, shaking with the force of his passion. "I see it now, the true fount of your ambition, Mr. Henry! You would not immortalize but humiliate and degrade!"

"Dr. Warthrop, I would do nothing of the kind—"

"Then, I ask you, of all the cases we have investigated, why did you choose the one that casts me in the worst possible light? Ha! See, I have caught you. There is only one reasonable answer to that question. Revenge!"

I could not hide my astonishment at his accusation. "Revenge? Revenge for what?"

"For your perceived mistreatment, of course."

"Why do you think I have been mistreated?"

"Oh, that is very clever of you, Will Henry—parsing my words to mask your perfidy. I did not confess to mistreating you; I pointed out your *perception* of mistreatment."

"Very well," I said. There were very few arguments anyone could win with him. In fact, I had never won *any*. "You pick the case."

"I don't *wish* to pick the case! The entire idea was yours to begin with. But you've shown your hand in this, and rest assured I will disavow anything you dare to publish under the guise of preserving my legacy. Holmes had his Watson, indeed! And Caesar had his Brutus, didn't he?"

"I would never do anything to betray you," I said evenly. "I suggested Socotra because I thought—"

"No!" he cried, taking a step toward me. I flinched as if expecting a blow, though in all our years together he had never struck me. "I forbid it! I have labored too long and too hard to banish the memory of that accursed place from my mind. You are never to speak that name again in my presence, do you understand? Never again!"

"As you wish, Doctor," I said. "I shall never speak of it again."

And I didn't. I dropped the matter and never brought it up again until now. It would be extremely difficult—no, impossible—to immortalize someone who denied the very facts reported. Years passed, and as his powers waned with them, my duties expanded to include the composition of his papers and letters. I took no credit for my efforts and received none from the monstrumologist. He ferociously edited my work, striking out anything that, in his opinion, smacked of poetic indulgence. In science, he told me, there is no room for romantic discourse or ruminations upon the nature of evil. That he himself was a poet in his youth drenched the exercise in irony and pathos.

It has often puzzled me, what pleasure he derived from denying himself those very things that gave him pleasure. But I am not the first to point out that love is a complicated thing. It is true the monstrumologist loved his work—it was, besides me, all he had—but his work was merely an extension of himself, the firstborn fruit of his towering ambition. His work may have brought him to that strange and accursed island, but it was his ambition that nearly undid him.

It began on a freezing February night in 1889 with the arrival of a package to the house on Harrington Lane. The delivery was unexpected but not unusual. Having been an apprentice to the monstrumologist for almost three years, I was accustomed to the midnight knock upon the back door, the furtive exchange of the portage charge, and the doctor acting like a boy on Christmas morn, his cheeks ablaze with feverish anticipation as he bore his present to the basement laboratory, where the box was unwrapped and its foul contents revealed in all their macabre glory. What was unusual about this particular delivery was the man who brought it. In the course of my service to the monstrumologist, I had seen my fair share of unsavory characters, men who, for a dollar and a dram of whiskey, would sell their own mothers—willing mercenaries in service to the natural science of aberrant biology.

But this was not the sort who stood shivering in the alleyway. Though bedraggled from a journey of many miles, he wore an expensive fur-lined coat that hung open to reveal a tailored suit. A diamond ring glittered on the little finger of his left hand. More striking than his regalia was his manner; the poor fellow seemed nearly mad with panic. He abandoned his cargo on the back stoop, pushed his way into the room, seized the doctor by his lapels, and demanded to know if this was number 425 Harrington Lane and if he—the doctor—was Pellinore Warthrop.

"I am Dr. Warthrop," said my master.

"Oh, thank God! Thank God!" the tormented man cried in a hoarse voice. "Now I've done it. It's right out there. Take it, take it. I've brought you the blasted thing. Now give it to me! He said you would—he said you had it. Quickly, before it's too late!"

"My good man," replied the doctor calmly. "I would gladly pay the charge, if the price is reasonable." Though he was a man of substantial means, the monstrumologist's parsimony soared to near operatic heights.

"The price? The price!" The man laughed hysterically. "It isn't you who'll pay, Warthrop! He said you had it. He promised you would give it to me if I brought it. Now keep his promise!"

"Whose promise?"

Our uninvited guest let loose a banshee howl and doubled over, clutching his chest. His eyes rolled back into his head. The doctor caught him before he hit the floor, and eased him into a chair.

"Damn him to hell—too late!" the man whimpered. "I am too late!" He wrung his hands in supplication. "Am I too late, Dr. Warthrop?"

"I cannot answer that question," replied the doctor. "For I have no idea what you're talking about."

"He told me you would give me the antidote if I

brought it, but I was delayed in New York. I missed the train and had to wait for the next one—more than two hours I had to wait. Oh, God! To come all this way only to die at the end of it!"

"The antidote? The antidote to what?"

"To the poison! 'Bring my little gift to Warthrop in America if you wish to live,' he told me, the devil, the fiend! So I have, and so you *must*. Ah, but it is hopeless. I feel it now—my heart—my heart—"

The doctor shook his head sharply and with a snap of his fingers directed me to fetch his instrument case.

"I will do all within my power," I heard him say to the poor man as I scampered off. "But you must get a grip on yourself and tell me simply and plainly . . ."

Our tormented courier had fallen into a swoon by the time I returned, eyes rolling in his head, hands twitching in his lap. His face had drained of all color. The doctor removed the stethoscope from the case and listened to the man's heart, bending low over the quivering form, his legs spread wide for balance.

"Galloping like a runaway horse, Will Henry," the monstrumologist murmured. "But no abnormalities or irregularities that I can detect. Quickly, a glass of water."

I expected him to offer the distressed man a drink; instead Warthrop dumped the entire contents of the glass over his head. The man's eyes snapped open. The mouth formed a startled O.

"What sort of poison did he give you?" demanded my master in a stern voice. "Did he say? Answer!"

"Tip . . . tipota . . . from the pyrite tree."

"Tipota?" The doctor frowned. "From what kind of tree?"

"Pyrite! Tipota, from the pyrite tree of the Isle of Demons!"

"The Isle of Demons! But that is . . . extraordinary. Are you quite certain?"

"Bloody hell. I think I would remember what he poisoned me with!" the man sputtered vehemently. "And he said *you* had the antidote! Oh! Oh! This is it!" His hands clawed at his chest. "My heart is exploding!"

"I don't think so," said the doctor slowly. He stepped back, studying the man carefully, dark eyes dancing with that eerie backlit fire. "We still have a few moments . . . but only a few! Will Henry, stay with our guest while I mix up the antidote."

"Then, I am not too late?" the man inquired incredulously, as if he could not dare to allow himself to hope.

"When was the poison administered?"

"On the evening of the second."

"Of this month?"

"Yes, yes—of course this month! I would be as dead as a doornail if it had been last month, now, wouldn't I!"

"Yes, forgive me. Tipota is slow-acting, but not quite *that* slow-acting! I shall be back momentarily. Will Henry, call me at once should our friend's condition change."

The doctor flew down the stairs to the basement, leaving

the door slightly ajar. We could hear jars knocking against each other, the clink and clang of metal, the hiss of a Bunsen burner.

"What if he's wrong?" the man moaned. "What if it is too late? My eyesight is failing—that's what goes just before the end! You go blind and your heart blows apart—blows completely apart inside your chest. Your face, child. I cannot see your face! It is lost to the darkness. The darkness comes! Oh, may he burn for all eternity in the lowest circle of the pit—the devil—the fiend!"

The doctor bounded back into the room, carrying a syringe loaded with an olive-green-colored liquid. The dying man jerked in the chair upon the doctor's entrance and cried out, "Who is that?"

"It is I, Warthrop," answered the doctor. "Let's get that coat off. Will Henry, help him, please."

"You have the antidote?" the man asked.

The doctor nodded curtly, pulled up the man's sleeve, and jabbed the needle home.

"There now!" Warthrop said. "The stethoscope, Will Henry. Thank you." He listened to the man's heart for a few seconds, and I thought it must be a trick of the light, for I spied what appeared to be a smile playing on the doctor's lips. "Yes. Slowing considerably. How do you feel?"

A bit of color had returned to the man's cheeks, and his breathing had slowed. Whatever the doctor had given him was having a salutary effect. He spoke hesitantly, as if he could hardly believe his good fortune. "Better, I think. My eyesight is clearing a bit."

"Good! You may be relieved to know that . . . ," the monstrumologist began, and then stopped himself. It had occurred to him, perhaps, that the man had already suffered enough distress. "It is a very dangerous poison. Always fatal, slow-acting, and symptom-free until the end, but its effects are entirely reversible if the antidote is administered in time."

"He said you would know what to do."

"I'm quite certain he did. Tell me, how did you come by the acquaintance of Dr. John Kearns?"

Our guest's eyes widened in astonishment. "However did you know his name?"

"There is only one man I know—and who knows me— who would play such a fiendish prank."

"*Prank?* Poisoning a man, hurling him to the threshold of death's doorway, for the purpose of delivering a *package*— that's a prank to you?"

"Yes!" the doctor cried, forgetting himself—and what this suffering soul had been through—for a moment. "The package! Will Henry, carry it down to the basement and put on a pot for tea. I'm sure Mr.—"

"Kendall. Wymond Kendall."

"Mr. Kendall could do with a cup, I think. Snap to now, Will Henry. I suspect we're in for a long night."

The package, a wooden box wrapped in plain brown paper, was not particularly heavy or cumbersome. I toted it quickly to the laboratory, placed it on the doctor's worktable, and returned upstairs to find the kitchen empty. I could hear the rise and fall of their voices coming from the parlor down the hall while I made the tea, my thoughts a confusion of dreadful anticipation and disquieted memory. It hadn't been quite a year since my first encounter with the man named Jack Kearns—if that was his name. He seemed to have more than one. Cory he had called himself, and Schmidt. There was one other name, the one he'd given himself in the fall of the previous year, the one by which history would remember him, the one that best described his true nature. He was not a monstrumologist like my master. It was not clear to me then *what* he was, except an expert in the darker regions of the natural world—and of the human heart.

"He was renting a flat from me on Dorset Street in Whitechapel," I heard Kendall say. "He was not the usual kind of tenant one finds in the East End, and clearly he could afford better, but he told me he liked to be close to his work at the Royal London Hospital. He seemed very dedicated to his work. He told me he lived for nothing else. Do you know, the funny thing is, I liked him; I liked Dr. Kearns very much. He was quite the conversationalist . . . a marvelous, if slightly skewed, sense of humor . . . very well-read, and he'd always been on time with his rent. So when he came up two months late, I thought something must have happened to him. This is Whitechapel, after all. Dr. Kearns kept very late hours, and I was afraid he might have been waylaid by ruffians—or worse. So more out of concern for his welfare than the arrears, I decided to check up on him."

"I take it you found him well," offered the doctor.

"Oh, he was the picture of soundness and good cheer! The same old Kearns. Invited me in for a spot of tea as if nothing were amiss, told me he had been distracted lately by a particularly troublesome case, a yeoman with the British Navy who was suffering from some mysterious tropical fever. Kearns seemed completely taken aback—though touched—by my concern for his welfare. When I brought up the matter of the rent, he expressed his mortification, blaming it on this case of his and assuring me I would have it, plus interest, by the end of the week. So soothed was I by his silver-tongued rationale, and also a bit embarrassed to intrude upon his important work, I actually apologized for coming to collect what was rightfully mine. Oh, he is the devil's own progeny, this Dr. John Kearns!"

"He has a way with words," the doctor allowed. "Among other things. Ah, but here is Will Henry with the tea."

The monstrumologist was standing by the mantel when I entered, running a finger contemplatively up and down the nose of the bust of the ancient Greek philosopher Zeno. Our guest reclined on the divan, his lean face still flushed from his ordeal. He reached for his cup with a quivering hand.

"The tea," he murmured. "It must have been the tea."

"The medium for the poison?" asked the doctor.

"No! He injected that once I had come to my senses."

"Ah, you mean he slipped you some sort of sleeping draft."

"That must have been the case. There can be no other explanation. I thanked him for the tea—oh, how he must have relished my appreciation!—and was no more than two steps from the door when the room began to spin and all went black. When I awoke, many hours had passed—night had fully come on—and there he was beside me, smiling ghoulishly.

"'You've had a bit of a spell,' he said.

"'I fear so,' said I. I felt utterly drained and entirely help-less, emptied of all vitality. Just turning my head to look at him required every ounce of strength in my body.

"'Lucky for you it struck in the presence of a doctor!' he observed with a perfectly straight face. 'I thought something was the matter when I first saw you, Kendall. A bit green around the gills. Of course, you've probably been working too hard exploiting the poor and downtrodden, collecting rents on hovels a rat would be ashamed to call home—a case of slumlord exhaustion is my guess. I would suggest you consider a holiday in the countryside. Get some fresh air. The atmosphere of these neighborhoods is absolutely putrid, infused as it is with the funk of human suffering and despair. Take a trip. A change of scenery would work wonders.'

"I protested vehemently these offensive remarks. I am no

slumlord, Dr. Warthrop. I provide a necessary service, and only once or twice have I put someone out for not paying the rent. So complete was my outrage, I would have struck him for these repugnant jibes upon my character, but I could not raise my hand even an inch from the bed.

"'I am exceedingly glad you dropped by,' he went on in that maddeningly chipper tone of his. 'God himself must have sent you—God, or something very much like him. You see, I can't trust it to the mails, and I can't go myself—I must take my leave of this blessed isle tomorrow—and finding a reliable courier in this milieu has proved more difficult than I anticipated. You simply cannot rely upon anyone from the ghetto—but I don't have to tell *you* that. And now here you are, Kendall! Delivered unto me like the best of presents—wholly satisfactory and completely unexpected. The answer to a prayer of a man who never prays! It is serendipitous to say the least, don't you think?'"

Kendall paused, sipped his tea, and stared silently for a moment into space. He possessed the haunted look of a man who had barely escaped a brush with death's angel, which, literally, he had.

"Well, I will confess I didn't know what to think, Dr. Warthrop. What was I to think? In an instant and without warning, all my faculties had been stripped from me, and now I lay dizzy, my thoughts a blur, paralyzed upon his bed, with him leering down at me. What was a man to think?

"'It is a small matter,' he went on. 'A trifle, really. But it should be delivered sooner rather than later. If it is what I suspect it is and represents what I think it represents, he'll want it quickly. Delay might cost him the entire game and he would never forgive me.'

"'Who?' I asked. Understand, I was quite beside myself at this point, for it had at last dawned on me that *he* was the cause of my sudden and mysterious affliction. 'Who would never forgive you?'

"'Warthrop! Warthrop, of course. The monstrumologist. Now, don't tell me you've never heard of him. He's a very dear friend of mine. You might call us brothers, in a spiritual sense of course, though we couldn't be more different from each other. He's entirely too serious, for one, and he possesses a curious romantic streak for someone who fancies himself a scientist. Has a savior complex, if you want my opinion. Wants to save the whole bloody world from itself, while my motto has always been "live and let live." Why, the other day I killed a large spider, quite without thinking it through—and afterward I was consumed with remorse, for what had that spider ever done to me? What makes me, by virtue of my superior intellect and size, any better than my eight-legged flatmate? I did not choose to be a man any more than he chose to be a spider. Are we both not equal players in the grand design, each fulfilling the role given to us—until I violated the sacred covenant between us and the one who made us? It's enough to tear a man's soul in twain.'

"'You're mad,' I told him; I could not help myself.

"'To the contrary, my dear Kendall,' the monster replied. 'It is your great good fortune to be in the company of the sanest man alive. It has taken me years to rid myself of all delusion and pretense, the cloak of self-righteous superiority with which we humans drape ourselves. In this sense the spider is *our* superior. He does not question his nature. He is not burdened by the sense of self. The mirror is nothing to him but a pane of glass. He is pure, as sinless as Adam before the fall. Even Warthrop, that incorrigible moralist, would agree with me. I've no more right to kill the spider than you've to judge me. *You*, sir, are the hare at this tea party; *I* am Alice.'

"He withdrew for a moment while I lay as if a two-ton boulder pressed down upon me, barely able to draw the next breath. When he returned, he was holding the syringe in his hand. I will confess, Dr. Warthrop, I'd never known fear like that. The room began to spin again, but not from any sleeping draft—from sheer terror. Helplessly I watched as he tapped the glass and pressed upon the plunger. A single drop clung to the needle's tip, glistening like the finest crystal in the lamplight.

"'Do you know what this is, Kendall?' he asked softly, and then he chuckled long and low. 'Of course you don't! I wax rhetorical. It's a very rare toxin distilled from the sap of the pyrite tree, an interesting example of one of the Creator's more maleficent flora, indigenous to a single island forty nautical miles from the Galápagos Archipelago, called the

Isle of Demons. I love that name, don't you? It's so . . . evocative. But now I wax poetical.'

"He drew close—so close I could see my own reflection in the dark, blank pools that were his eyes. Oh, those eyes! If I ever should see them again in a thousand years, it would be too soon! Blacker than the blackest pit, empty—so *empty* of . . . of *everything*, Dr. Warthrop. Not human. Not animal. Not *anything*.

"'It's called *tipota*,' he whispered. 'Remember that, Kendall! When Warthrop asks you what I've stuck you with, tell him that. Tell him, "It is tipota. He poisoned me with tipota!"'"

My master was nodding gravely, but did I detect a hint of amusement in his eyes? I wondered what in this horrible tale the monstrumologist could find the least bit comical.

"He slipped a piece of paper into my pocket—yes! Here it is; I still have it."

He held it up for the doctor to see.

"Your address—and the name of the poison, lest I forget it. Forget it! As if I will ever forget that accursed name! He told me I had ten days. 'More or less, my dear Kendall.' More or less! He proceeded to lecture me—hovering there with that horrid needle glistening an inch from my nose—on how prized this poison was; how the czar of Russia kept a stash of it in the royal safe; how it was valued by the ancients ('They say it was what *really* killed Cleopatra'); how it was the method of choice of assassins, preferred because it was so slow-acting, allowing the perpetrator to be miles away by the time the victim's heart exploded in his chest. *That* ghastly speech was followed by an extended description of the poison's effects: loss of appetite, insomnia, restlessness, racing thoughts, palpitations, paranoid delusions, excessive perspiration, constipated bowel in some cases or diarrhea in others—"

The doctor nodded curtly. He had grown impatient. I knew what it was. The box. The package was pulling on him, beckoning him. Whatever Kearns had entrusted to this loquacious Englishman, it was valuable enough (at least in the monstrumological sense) to risk killing a man over its successful delivery.

"Yes, yes," Warthrop said. "I am familiar with the effects of tipota. As acquainted, if not as intimately, as—"

Now it was Kendall who interrupted, for he was more *there* than *here*, and ever would be, lying helpless upon Kearns's bed while the lunatic leaned over him, leering in the lamplight. I doubt the poor man ever fully escaped that dingy flat in London's East End, not in the truest sense. To his death he remained a prisoner of that memory, a thrall in service to Dr. John Kearns.

"'Please,' I begged him," Kendall continued. "'Please, for the love of God!'

"Ill-chosen words, Dr. Warthrop! At the mention of the deity's name, his entire manner was transformed, as if I had profaned the Virgin herself. His ghoulish grin disappeared, the mouth drew down, the eyes narrowed.

"'For what, did you say?' he asked in a dangerous whisper. 'For God? Do you believe in God, Kendall? Are you praying to him now? How odd. Shouldn't you rather pray to me, since I now hold death literally an inch from your nose? Who has more power now—me or God? Before you answer "God," think carefully, Kendall. If you are right and I stab you with my needle, does that prove you right or wrong—and which answer would be worse? If right, then God surely favors me over you. In fact, he must despise you for your sin and I am merely his instrument. If wrong, then you pray to nothing.' He shook the needle in my face. 'Nothing! And then he laughed."

As if in counterpoint he paused in his narration and cried bitter tears.

"And then he said, the foul beast, 'Why do men pray to God, Kendall? I've never understood it. God loves us. We are his creation, like my spider; we are his beloved. . . . Yet when faced with mortal danger, we pray to him to spare us! Shouldn't we pray instead to the one who would destroy us, who has sought our destruction from the very beginning? What I mean to say is . . . aren't we praying to the wrong person? We should beseech the devil, not God. Don't mistake me; I'm not telling you where to direct your supplications. I'm merely pointing out the fallacy of them—and perhaps hinting at the reason behind prayer's curious inefficaciousness.'"

Kendall paused to angrily wipe clean his face, and said, "Well, I suppose you can guess what he did next."

"He injected you with tipota," tried my master. "And within a matter of seconds, you lost consciousness. When you awoke, Kearns was gone."

Our tormented guest was nodding. "And in his stead, the package."

"And you made straightaway to book your passage to America."

"I considered going to the police, of course . . ."

"But doubted they would believe such an extravagant tale."

"Or admitting myself into hospital . . ."

"Risking that they would not know the antidote for so rare a toxin."

"I had no choice but to do his bidding and hope he was telling the truth, which it seems he was, for I am feeling myself again. Oh, I cannot tell you what agony these last eight days have been, Dr. Warthrop! What if you were away? What if those two hours' delay in New York had been two hours too much? What if he'd been wrong and you knew not the antidote?"

"Well, I was not; they weren't; and I did. And here you are, safe and sound and only slightly worse for wear!" The doctor turned quickly to me and said, "Will Henry, stay with our guest while I have a look at this 'trifle' of Dr. Kearns.' Mr. Kendall might be hungry after his ordeal. See to it, Will Henry. If you'll excuse me, Mr. Kendall, but Jack did say delay might cost the entire game."

With that the monstrumologist fled from the room. I heard his hurried footfalls down the hall, the creak of the basement door, and then the thunder of his descent into the laboratory. An awkward silence ensued between my companion and me. I felt slightly embarrassed over the doctor's abrupt and disrespectful departure. Warthrop was never one to observe the strict protocols of proper Victorian society.

"Would you care for something to eat, sir?" I asked.

Kendall drew a heavy breath, the color high in his cheeks, and said, "I just vomited and shat my way across the entire Atlantic Ocean. No, I would *not* like something to eat."

"Another cup of tea?"

"Tea! Oh, dear God!"

So we sat for a few moments with but the ticking of the mantel clock for company, until at last he dozed off, for who knew how long it had been since he last had slept? I tried—and failed—to imagine the unimaginable terror he must have felt, knowing that with each tick of the clock he'd drawn closer to the final doorway, that one-way ingress into oblivion, every delay dangerous, each moment lost perilous. Did he consider himself lucky—or did he think it more than luck?

And then it occurred to me that he'd never given an answer to Kearns's question: To whom should we pray? With a shudder I wondered to whom he had prayed—and who, precisely, had answered.

TWO

"I Have All That I Need"

I crept from the parlor to the basement door, reasoning that, though unbidden, I would be slightly less useless by the doctor's side. The laboratory below was ablaze in light, and I could hear the soft, unintelligible exclamations of the monstrumologist. I will confess even I, who thought daily of running away from the house on Harrington Lane as fast as his thirteen-year-old legs could carry him, who more than once wished he could be anywhere in the world other than at the side of a monstrumologist before the necropsy table, who nearly every night prayed to the same holy being—about whose efficacy and existence the unholy Kearns had scoffed—that he might be delivered, somehow, some way, into a life more like the one that had been snatched from him nearly three years before, even I felt the pull of the box, felt the by now familiar morbid regard for all loathsome things . . . the citizens of our night-mares . . . the denizens of our darkest dreams. *What is in that package? What has been delivered this night?*

I will not say my descent was eager, but it was swift and not entirely owing to my sense of duty. I *did* want to see what was in that box. Dreaded it and desired it. More than any-thing else, dread and desire were my chief inheritance from the monstrumologist.

I caught the word "Magnificent!" as I came down. The doctor was bent over his worktable with his back toward me, hiding the open box from view. The twine and brown paper wrapping, hastily ripped away, lay in a wad on the floor. The bottom step whispered the smallest of groans beneath my foot, and he whirled around, pressing the small of his back against the tabletop and spreading his arms wide to obscure what was on the table.

"Will Henry!" he cried hoarsely. "What the devil are you doing? I told you to stay with Kendall."

"Mr. Kendall is asleep, sir."

"I've no doubt that he is! He's been injected with a ten percent solution of morphine."

"Morphine, Dr. Warthrop?"

"And a bit of food coloring for effect. Perfectly harmless."

I struggled to grasp his meaning. "It wasn't the antidote?"

"There is no antidote for tipota, Will Henry."

I gasped. Warthrop had lied, and I had never known him to tell a deliberate falsehood. In fact, he reserved his most vehement contempt for that very practice, calling it the worst sort of buffoonery and foolishness—and the monstrumologist was not the sort of man who suffered fools gladly.

What could be the explanation? To placate a doomed man? To give him a measure of peace upon his final moments on earth? Had his lie been indeed an act of mercy?

The doctor glanced over his shoulder at the table. He turned back to me with an icy glare. "What?" he demanded. "What are you staring at?"

"Nothing, sir. I only thought you might need—"

"I have all that I need at the present, thank you. Return at once to Mr. Kendall, Will Henry. He should not be left alone."

"How . . . how long does he have?"

"That is very difficult to say—there are so many variables—thirty, perhaps forty, years."

"Years! But you said there was no anti—"

"Yes, I did, and no, there isn't, because there is no such thing, Will Henry. 'Tipota' is the Greek word for 'nothing.'"

"It is?"

"No, I am lying to you. It is actually the Greek word for 'stupid child.' Yes, it means 'nothing' in Greek, and there is no such thing as a pyrite tree. Pyrite's other name is 'fool's gold.' And there is no Isle of Demons near the Galápagos. When Kearns instructed Kendall, 'Tell him it is tipota,' he meant it literally."

"You mean it was . . . it was all a *joke*?"

"More of a trick. He needed Kendall to believe he was

poisoned in order to ensure the package's delivery. Now, if you're quite finished standing there with your jaw hanging open like the most disagreeable of mouth-breathers, please do as I requested and attend to our guest."

I did not obey immediately. My astonishment outweighed my loyalty.

"But his symptoms . . ."

"Are all attributable to the psychological distress produced by his belief that he had been poisoned."

"So you knew the whole time? But why didn't you—"

"Tell him the truth? Do you think the poor fool would have believed me if I had? He doesn't know me from Adam. Might not he think I was part of Jack's fiendish plan and keel over from a heart attack brought on by the enormity of his fear and the finality of all hope? There was a good possibility of that, and it was something Kearns probably anticipated, making his game all the more wickedly delicious. Imagine it, Will Henry! The lie sends him all the way here . . . and then the truth kills him! No, I saw through it at once and took the only moral path available to me—and so, even saints may sin that God's will be done!"

He pointed up the stairs. "Snap to, Will Henry."

So I did, though there wasn't much *snap* in my *to*. He called after me, "Shut the door behind you and *do not come down again*."

"Yes, sir. I will, Dr. Warthrop—and I won't."

I kept the first promise, at least.

I sat in the parlor with our unconscious guest, restless and bored. I was not accustomed to being dispensed with, after being told ad nauseam by my master how indispensable I was. I was suffering also from the dreadful notion that Warthrop might be wrong, that there *was* such a poison as tipota and at any moment Kendall would keel over; I did not wish to watch a man's heart explode in our parlor.

But as the minutes ticked by, he continued to breathe—and I to stew. Why had the monstrumologist so abruptly dismissed me? What was in that box that he did not want me to see? He had never seemed particularly concerned about exposing me to the most disgusting and frightening of biologic phenomena—or to their handiwork. I was, like it or not, his apprentice, and had not he himself often said, "You must become accustomed to such things"?

Ten minutes. Fifteen. Then the crash and rattle of the basement door flying open, the thunder of his footsteps down the hall, and Warthrop barreled into the room. He went straight to the divan and hauled Kendall upright.

"Kendall!" he shouted into the man's face. "Wake up!"

Kendall's eyes fluttered open, closed again. I noticed the doctor had donned a pair of gloves.

"Did you open it, Kendall? Kendall! Did you touch what was inside?"

He grabbed the unconscious man by the wrists, turned Kendall's hands this way and that, and then bent low to sniff his fingers. He pulled up Kendall's eyelids and squinted deep into the unseeing orbs.

"What is it?" I asked.

"At least three have touched it. Was one you, Kendall? Was it you?"

The man answered with a soft moan, deep in his drug-induced dream. Warthrop snorted with frustration, turned on his heel, and marched from the room, pausing at the door to bark at me to remain where I was.

"Watch him, Will Henry, and call me at once if he wakes. And, do not touch him under any circumstances!"

I thought he would race back to the basement, but he fled in the opposite direction, and presently I heard him in the library, yanking old weathered tomes from the shelves and depositing them on the large table with thunderous wallops. I could hear him muttering to himself in agitation, but could not make out the words.

I crept down the hall to the library door. He was standing with his back to me, hunched over a leather-bound book. He stiffened suddenly, sensing my presence, and whirled around.

"What?" he cried. "What do you want now?"

"Did you—Could I—"

"Did I *what*? Could you *what*?"

"Is there anything I can do for you, sir?"

"I told you already what you could do, Will Henry. Yet here you are. Why are you here, Will Henry?"

"I thought you might want me to—"

"Interrupt my work? Hector me with your incessant sycophantic sniveling? It is not as if I asked you to construct a perpetual motion machine or juggle teacups while you stood on your pointy little head. My distinct memory is that I asked you to watch Mr. Kendall—that is all and nothing else—but you seem incapable of following even that simple injunction!"

"I'm sorry, sir," I said, fighting back the dueling desires to flee and to throw myself upon the floor in a childish fit. I backed out of the doorway and returned to the parlor. Kendall had not moved a muscle, but mine were moving quite freely, particularly the ones around my mouth.

"I hate him," I whispered to my incognizant witness. "Oh, how I hate him! 'Snap to, Will Henry, snap *to*.' Why don't *you* snap to, Warthrop—straight to hell!"

It was so *unfair*! I had not asked for this. My father had gladly served the monstrumologist, but my own servitude was more of the involuntary kind, the result of tragic circumstances with which I, at thirteen, had yet fully to come to terms. If not for the man who had just unfairly and savagely upbraided me, my father and mother would still be alive and I would not know a scintilla of the dark and dusty interior of 425 Harrington Lane. Perhaps the monstrumologist was not directly responsible for their deaths, but monstrumology certainly was. Oh, that accursed "philosophy"! That noisome "science" that had doomed my parents—and now me.

The acrid stench of rotting flesh . . . the sightless orbs

of some foul creature staring up at me from the necropsy table . . . the unutterable horror of Pellinore Warthrop cleaning human flesh from bloody fangs as he whistled with the happiness of a man lost in the thing he loves . . .

While the boy he'd inherited, the boy who had watched his parents perish in a fire for which he, Warthrop, had supplied the metaphorical match, stood in half-swoon close by, ever the faithful, indispensable companion, feet like ice in blood-flecked shoes on a cold stone floor . . .

And little by little that boy's soul, his human animus, growing cold, going numb, atrophying . . .

Wer mit Ungeheuern kämpft, mag zusehn, dass er nicht dabei zum Ungeheuer wird.

Do you know what this means?

I do.

Year after year, month after month, day after day, hour after hour, minute after minute, second after second, in the company of the monstrumologist, something chews at the soul, like the churning surf shapes the shoreline, eroding the edifice, exposing the bones, revealing the skeletal structure beneath our sense of human exceptionalism.

When I first came to live with him, it was part of our dissection protocol to have a bucket by the table so I might unload the contents of my stomach—it was inevitable. After a year at his side, the pail was no longer necessary. I could reach my hands into the putrid remains of an organism's corruption as casually as a young girl plucks daisies in the meadow.

I could feel it as I held vigil in that parlor, the loosening of something bound tight inside me, an unraveling that both thrilled and terrified. I had no name for it, not then, not at thirteen, this thing unwinding inside me. It was part of me—the most fundamental part, perhaps—and it was apart from me, and the tension between them, the *me* and *not-me*, could break the world in half.

Wer mit Ungeheuern kämpft . . .

I don't mean to speak in riddles. I am an old man now. The old speak plainly; it is our prerogative.

If I would speak plainly, I would call it *das Ungeheuer*, but that is only *my* name for the *me/not-me*, the unwinding thing that compelled and repulsed me, the thing in me—and the thing in *you*—that whispers like thunder, *I AM*.

You may have a different name for it.

But you've seen it. You cannot be human and *not* see it, feel its pull, hear it whisper like thunder. You would flee from it, but it is *you*, and so where might you run? You would embrace it, but it is *not-you*, and so how might you hold it?

You see, more than a starving man wants bread, I wanted to see what was in that box, whatever it might be. That desire made me more my master's progeny than my own father's; I was Pellinore Warthrop reincarnate, but unalloyed by any poetic compunctions. In me it was pure hunger, a desire untainted by platitudes or petty human morals.

But within that thing inside unwinding, *das Ungeheuer*, also dwelled the loathing—the counterbalancing force of revulsion that screamed for me to remain in the parlor with Kendall.

My charge had moved not a muscle in nearly an hour and did not look as if he would for several more. If I remained a moment more, *my* heart might explode. By that point I did not merely *want* to look at Kearns's special gift. I *had* to look.

I crept down the hall and peeked into the library, where I spied the monstrumologist seated at the table, his head resting on his folded arms. Softly I called his name. He did not move.

Well, thought I, *he's either sleeping or he's dead. If the former, I dare not wake him. If the latter, I cannot!*

I shuffled quickly and quietly to the basement door, hesitating but half a breath before making the descent.

And within me, the unwinding.

Just one little look, I promised myself. I reasoned it must be a very curious prize indeed for my master to be so secretive about it. And, to be honest, my pride was wounded. I interpreted his caginess as a lack of trust—after all we had been through together! If he could not trust me, the one person in the world who endured him, whom could he trust?

A black cloth covered the worktable. Beneath it lay the prize of Dr. John Kearns; I could see the outline of the box in which it had arrived. Now, why had the monstrumologist covered it? To hide it from prying eyes, obviously—and there was only one pair of eyes in the house that would pry.

My anger and shame doubled. How dare he! Had I not

proved myself time and again? Had I not *always* been the model of unquestioning loyalty and steadfast devotion? And *this* was my recompense? The gall of the man!

I did not gingerly lift one corner and furtively glance at what lay beneath. I *flung* back the black cloth; it snapped angrily in the cold atmosphere as it fell away.

THREE

"The Answer to a Prayer Unspoken"

I gasped; I could not help it. I might have perversely prided myself on my transformation from naïve boy to world-weary apprentice to a monstrumologist, morbidly happy with the carapace that had grown around my tender sensibilities, but *this* laid me bare, exposing the aboriginal protohuman that still dwells within us all, the one who regards in terror the vast depths of the evening sky and the unblinking eye of the soulless moon. The doctor's word for it had been "magnificent." That was not the word I would have chosen.

From a greater distance and in weaker light, it might have resembled a bit of ancient earthenware—a large clay serving bowl, perhaps—though one fashioned by a blind man or a potter still learning the craft. It was, for lack of a better word, *lumpy*. The sides bulged; the rim was uneven; and the bottom was slightly convex, causing it to lean precariously toward one side.

But the distance was not great and the light not weak; I saw close up and clearly the material with which this odd container was constructed. I'd learned enough anatomy from Warthrop to identify some of the things that constituted this confusing morass of remains, woven together with mind-boggling intricacy—there a proximal phalanx, here a mandible snapped in half, but others were as mysterious—and nearly meaningless—as pieces of a jigsaw puzzle scattered to the four corners of a room. Rip a human being apart, shred him into pieces no larger than the length of your thumb, and see how much of him you can recognize. Is that a tuft of hair—or a muscle's stringy sinew turned black? And that blob of purplish substance there—a piece of his heart, or perhaps a chunk of his liver? The difficulty was compounded by the interweaving of the various parts. Imagine an enormous robin's nest fashioned not from twigs and leaves but from human remains.

Yes, I thought, *not a bowl. A nest. That's what it reminds me of.*

It puzzled me at first, how the monstrous artisan, whoever—or *whatever*—he was, had managed to achieve it. Lifeless tissue rots quickly when exposed to the elements, and without some bonding agent the entire gruesome sack would no doubt have collapsed into a chaotic mass. The thing *did* glisten like fired clay in the harsh electrified lighting of the laboratory. Perhaps that's how my first impression of it was formed, for it was coated in a slightly opaque, gelatinous substance resembling mucus.

In his mad rush to confront Kendall—*Did you open it, Kendall? Did you touch what was inside?*—the doctor had abandoned his notes. At the top of the page was this notation:

London, 2 Feb '89, Whitechapel. John Kearns.
Magnificum???

Below this line was a word I did not recognize, for my studies in the classical languages had languished under the doctor's care. He had written it in large block letters that dominated the page:

Τυφωεύς

The rest of the page was blank. It was as if, once he had committed that one word to paper, he could think of nothing else to write.

Or, I thought, there was nothing else he *dared* to write.

This was deeply troubling, more so than what he had hidden beneath the black cloth. Though still a boy, I could, as I've confessed, endure with stoic fortitude the grotesque manifestations of nature's villainous side. This was far worse;

it shook the foundations of my devotion to him.

The man with whom—*for* whom—I lived, the one for whom I had risked my life and would again without hesitation at the slightest provocation, the man whom in my mind I called not "the monstrumologist" but "*the* monstrumologist," was acting less like a scientist and more like a conspirator to a crime.

There remained but one thing to do before I made good my escape from the basement.

I did not want to, and nothing required that I do it. In fact, every good impulse in me urged an expeditious retreat. But there are thoughts we think in the forward part of our brains, and then there are those whose origins are much deeper, in the animal part, the part that remembers the terrors of the open savanna at night, the oldest part that was there before the primordial voice that spoke the words "*I AM*."

I did not *want* to look into that glistening sack of dismembered remains; I *had* to look.

Leaning on the edge of the table for balance, I went onto my tiptoes to peer inside. If function followed form, there could be but one purpose for this strange—and strangely beautiful—objet trouvé.

"Will Henry!" a sharp voice cried behind me. In two strides he was upon me, pulling me back as if from a precipice, whipping me round to face him. His eyes shone with fury and—something I rarely witnessed—fear.

"What the devil are you doing, Will Henry?" he shouted into my upturned face. "Did you touch it? Answer me! *Did you touch it?*"

He grabbed my wrists as he'd done Kendall's and brought my fingertips close to his nose, sniffing noisily, anxiously.

"N-no," I stammered. "No, Dr. Warthrop; I didn't touch it."

"Do not lie to me!"

"I'm not lying. I swear I didn't; I didn't touch it, sir. I was just—I just— I'm sorry, sir; I fell asleep, and then I woke up, and I thought I heard you down here . . ."

His dark eyes searched mine intently for several agonized moments. Gradually some of the fear I saw reflected there faded. His hands dropped to his sides. His shoulders relaxed.

He stepped around me to the table and said briskly, sounding more like his old self, "Well, what's done is done. You've seen it; you might as well lend a hand. And to answer your question—"

"My question, sir?"

"The one you did not ask. It is empty, Will Henry."

He set to work methodically, his excitement betrayed only in his eyes. Oh, how those dark eyes danced with delight! He was wholly in his unholy element now. This was his raison d'être, the world of blood and umbrage that is monstrumology.

"Hand me the loupe, and I'll need you to hold the light for me, Will Henry. Close now, but not too close! Here, put on these gloves. Always wear gloves. Don't forget."

He slipped on the loupe and cinched the headband tight. The thick lens made his eye appear absurdly large in proportion to his face. He leaned over the "gift" from John Kearns while I directed the light upon its glistening irregular surface.

He did not move the object; we rotated around it. He stopped several times in our circuit around the table, bringing his nose dangerously close to the surface of the thing, transfixed by minutiae invisible to my naked eye.

"Beautiful," he murmured. "So beautiful!"

"What is?" I wondered aloud. I couldn't help myself. "What is this thing, Dr. Warthrop?"

He straightened, pressing his hands against the small of his back, wincing, for he had been stooping for nearly an hour.

"This?" he asked, his voice quavering with exhilaration. "This, William Henry, is the answer to a prayer unspoken."

Though I hardly understood what he meant, I did not press him to elaborate. Monstrumologists, I had learned, do not pray to the same gods we do.

"Come along," he cried, turning abruptly on his heel and racing up the stairs. "And bring the lamp. The morphine should be wearing off soon, and it's imperative that we eliminate Mr. Kendall as a suspect."

A suspect? I wondered. *A suspect of* what?

In the parlor the doctor crouched before the supine man, who was now groaning, arms crossed over his chest, eyes rolling beneath the fluttering lids. Warthrop pressed his gloved fingers against the man's neck, listened to Kendall's heart, and then pried open both of the man's eyelids to stare into his jittery, unseeing eyes.

"Beside me, here, Will Henry."

I went to my knees beside him and shone the light into Kendall's jerking orbs. The doctor bent very low, so close, their noses almost touched, creating the absurd tableau of a kiss suspended. He murmured something; it sounded like Latin. "*Oculus Dei!*"

"What are you looking for?" I whispered. "You said he wasn't poisoned."

"I said he wasn't poisoned by *Kearns*. There are three distinct sets of fingerprints infixed in the sputum coagulate. *Someone* has handled it—three 'someones,' apparently—and I doubt John was one of them. He knows better."

"It's poisonous?"

"To put it mildly," the doctor answered. "If the stories have an ounce of truth."

"What stories?"

He did not turn from his task, but he sighed heavily. The doctor was like most men in this at least. He was not adept in performing two things at once.

"The stories of the *nidus*, Will Henry, and of the *pwdre ser*. Now you are going to ask, 'What is a *nidus*?' and 'What is *pwdre ser*?' But I beg you to hold your questions for now; I'm trying to think."

After a moment he stood up. He regarded his accidental patient for another moment or two. Then he turned and stared silently at me for another two or three.

"Yes, sir?" I said with a tremulous little gulp. The heavy silence and his unreadable expression unnerved me.

"I don't see that we have a choice, Will Henry," he said matter-of-factly. "I don't know for certain he's touched it, and the stories may be nothing more than superstition and tall tales, but it's better to err on the side of caution. Run upstairs and strip the bed in the guest room, and we're going to need some sturdy rope. I should give him another dose of morphine, I suppose."

"Rope, sir?"

"Yes, rope. Twenty-four or -five feet should be enough; we can cut it to fit. Well, what are you waiting for? Snap to, Will Henry. Oh, and one more thing," he called after me. I paused at the door. "Just as a precaution . . . get my revolver."

FOUR

"It Is Human to Turn Round"

In another half hour it was done. Wymond Kendall lay spread-eagled upon a bare mattress, stripped to his undergarments, bound by wrists and ankles to the four posters, and beside him was the monstrumologist, who had decided to postpone another dose of morphine, though he kept the syringe close—in case, he confessed, his faith in the probity of our species was misplaced.

Kendall moaned deep in his throat. Then his eyes fluttered open. Warthrop rose from his chair, his hand dropping casually into his coat pocket, where I'd seen him slip the gun. He offered the disoriented soul what I call the Warthropian smile—thin-lipped, awkward; more of a grimace than a grin.

"How are you feeling, Mr. Kendall?"

"I am cold."

He tried to sit up. That he could not came home to him slowly, the realization exposed in his expression, which was nearly comical in its glacial shift from shock to unalloyed terror. He jerked hard on the ropes. The bedposts creaked. The frame shook.

"What is the meaning of this, Warthrop? Release me! Release me at once!"

It was too much for the poor man to bear. In less than a fortnight he'd found himself in the same position he'd been in at the beginning of this strange and unexpected nightmare. It must have seemed to him that he had escaped one madman only to be captured by another.

"I have no intention of harming you," my master tried to reassure him. "What I've done is for your own protection— as well as my own. I will gladly release you when I am satisfied that neither of us is in danger."

"Danger?" the panicked victim squeaked. "But you gave me the antidote!"

"Mr. Kendall, there is no antidote for the danger of which I speak. You must tell me the truth now. Though all men lie, and most men more than they should or even must . . . the truth in this instance could literally set you free."

"What are you talking about? I've told you the truth; I've told you everything exactly as I remember it. Dear God, how could I invent such a tale?"

Spittle flew from his lips. Warthrop took a step back

and calmly held up his hand, waiting for the man to calm himself before the doctor continued.

"I'm not accusing you of *ad*mission, Kendall; I am accusing you of *o*mission. Tell me the truth. Did you touch it?"

"'Touch it? Touch what? What did I touch? I didn't touch anything."

"He told you not to touch it. I'm sure he did. He couldn't suffer his courier to touch it and risk it being lost or destroyed. He must have warned you not to touch it."

"Are you talking about the package? You think I opened it? Why would I open it?"

"You couldn't bear it. The not knowing. Why would Kearns go to such bizarre lengths to send me this package? What was in it that was so valuable he was willing to commit murder rather than see it go undelivered? You were terrified; you didn't want to open it, but you *had* to open it. Your desire is understandable, Mr. Kendall. It is human to turn round, to stare into Medusa's face, to tie ourselves to the mainmast to hear the sirens' song, to turn back as Lot's wife turned back. I am not angry at you for looking. But you did look. You did touch it."

Kendall had begun to cry. His head rocked back and forth on the bare mattress. He twisted his arms, his legs, and I heard the rope scratching against his flesh.

The monstrumologist snatched the lamp from my hand and brought it close to the tormented man's face. Kendall recoiled; his right arm jerked as he instinctively attempted to cover his eyes.

"You are sensitive to light, aren't you, Mr. Kendall?"

Warthrop handed the lamp back to me. The doctor grasped Kendall's right index finger with his gloved hand, and the man winced in pain, teeth clamping down hard on his bottom lip to stifle the sob of pain.

"This was the hand, wasn't it? The hand that touched the thing inside the box. The hand that touched what no hand should touch."

The doctor rolled the man's fingers within his loosely closed hand.

"Your joints ache terribly, don't they? All over, but particularly in this hand. You've been telling yourself it's the cold or the tipota, perhaps, or both. It is neither."

He closed his fist around the base of Kendall's fingers and said, "They're growing numb, aren't they? The numbness began at the tips of the ones with which you touched it, but the numbness is spreading. You are telling yourself the rope is cutting off the circulation or the room is very cold. It is neither."

Warthrop released his hand. "I cannot say with any reasonable certainty how badly you will suffer, Mr. Kendall. As far as I know, yours is the first verifiable exposure known to science."

"Exposure, you say? Exposure to what?"

"The Welsh call it *pwdre ser*. The rot of stars."

"Star rot? What the bloody hell is that?"

"A rather poetic description of a substance that is neither rot nor from the stars," the doctor said. His voice had assumed that maddening dry, lecturing tone I'd heard a thousand times before. "It is actually part of the digestive system, like our own saliva, but unlike our saliva, it is highly toxic."

"All right! All right, damn you, yes, yes, I touched it—I did touch it! I reached into that blasted box and gave it a pinch, but that was all! I didn't take it out and cuddle with it—just a little touch, a tiny poke to see what it was! That's all. That's all!"

The doctor was nodding gravely. His expression was one of profound pity.

"That was probably enough," he said.

"Why am I bound to this bed?"

"I have told you."

"Why have you taken my clothes?"

"So I may examine you."

"What is the thing in the box?"

"It is called a *nidus ex magnificum*."

"What is it for?"

"Its name explains its function."

"Where does it come from?"

"Well, that is the riddle, isn't it, Mr. Kendall? What did John Kearns say?"

"He didn't."

"He's a viper, I would agree, but as far as I know his

sputum is not venomous or even particularly sticky; he did not make the *nidus*. Did he happen to mention by any chance where the maker might be?"

"No. No, he did not. I told you . . . everything he said. . . . Ah, God, the light. The light burns my eyes."

"Here, I shall lay this cloth over them. Is that better?"

"Yes. Please untie me."

"I wish I could. Would you like something to eat?"

"Oh, God, no. No. My stomach. Hurts."

"Mr. Kendall, I'm going to extract a small sample of your blood. Slight pinch. . . . Good. Will Henry, another vial please. Where's the other one? Did you lose it? Ah, there it is. . . . Slow, deep breaths, Mr. Kendall. Would you like another shot of morphine for your nerves?"

"I want you to untie me from this bloody bed."

"Will Henry, will you turn off the light please? And close the door." The doctor removed the cloth. "Mr. Kendall, I want you to open your eyes. Do you see me clearly?"

"Yes. Yes, I can see you."

"Really? I can't see you. The room is pitch dark. Tell me, how many fingers am I holding up?"

"Three. Why?"

"It is called *Oculus Dei*, Mr. Kendall. I do not know who gave it that colorful sobriquet."

"What does it mean?"

"The eyes of God."

"I *know* that. I did manage to pick up a bit of Latin in

school, Dr. Warthrop. I am asking what it *means*."

The monstrumologist did not know the answer, or if he did, he kept it to himself.

He drew me into the hall and shut the door.

"An extraordinary development, Will Henry, and not without its fair share of irony. He *is* poisoned—not by Kearns's hand but by his own . . . literally!"

"Is he going to die?"

Warthrop confessed he did not know. "We are in uncharted waters, Will Henry. No victim of *pwdre ser ex magnificum* has ever been recovered, much less studied." Though his expression was grave, his voice betrayed his excitement. "He may die; he may fully recover. I have some hope. After all, his exposure was minuscule, and there are some anecdotal reports that suggest *pwdre ser* loses some of its potency over time. It could depend upon the age of the *nidus*."

"Shouldn't we . . . Would you like me to fetch a doctor, sir?"

"To what purpose? Mr. Kendall is not suffering from a head cold, Will Henry. The unfortunate fool has managed to find his greatest fortune by coming to the one person who best understands his misfortune. Ha! Now I must have a look at this sample. Stay with him until I return, Will Henry. Do not leave. Under no circumstances is Mr. Kendall to be left alone. And do not doze off or allow your mind to wander! I expect to know everything he does or says while I am away. Do not touch him; do not allow him to touch you. And pay attention, Will Henry. You are a witness to history!"

"Yes, sir," I responded dutifully.

"I shan't be long. Here, just in case, you had better have this."

He pressed the revolver into my hand.

"Who is there?" Kendall cried upon my stepping back into the room. The doctor had covered his eyes again before leaving and turned back on the light.

"It's me. Will Henry," I answered.

"Where is the doctor? Where is Warthrop?"

"He's downstairs in his laboratory, sir."

"Trying to find a cure?"

"I . . . I don't know, Mr. Kendall."

"What do you mean?" he cried. "Is he a doctor or isn't he?"

"He is but he isn't."

"What? What did you say? He is but he isn't?"

"He is not a medical doctor."

"Not a medical doctor? What sort of doctor is he, then?"

"He is a monstrumologist, sir."

"A monster . . ."

"Monstrum . . ."

"Monstrum . . ."

"—ologist."

"Ologist?"

"Monstrumologist," I said.

"Monstrumologist! That's the most absurd thing I've ever heard of. What sort of nonsense is that?"

"It's a scientist," I said. "A doctor of natural philosophy."

"Oh, good Christ!" he moaned loudly. "I have been kidnapped by a *philosopher*!" His chest heaved. "Why am I tied to this bed? Why aren't you taking me to hospital?"

I made no reply. I did not think it would serve any purpose to tell him the truth. I caressed the barrel of the doctor's gun nervously. Why *was* Kendall tied to the bed? Why had the monstrumologist given me the gun?

"Hello?" he called.

"I'm here."

"I can't feel my hands or feet. Be a good lad and help me."

"I—I can't untie you, Mr. Kendall."

"Did I ask you to untie me? Just loosen the knots a bit. The rope's cutting into my skin."

"I will ask the doctor when he comes back."

"Comes back? Where did he go?"

"He's in the laboratory," I reminded him.

"I am a British citizen!" he cried shrilly. "My uncle is a member of Parliament! I will prosecute your 'doctor' for assault and battery, kidnapping, false imprisonment, and torture of a foreign national! They'll hang him for certain, and *you* with him!"

"He is only trying to help, Mr. Kendall."

"Help? By stripping me bare and tying me up? By refusing to take me to a proper doctor?"

The revolver's skin was cold beneath my fingers. Where was the dawn? The sun would rise soon; it had to.

"I'm cold," he whimpered. "Can't you at least put some covers on me?"

I gnawed on my bottom lip. The man was shivering uncontrollably, teeth literally chattering in his head. What should I do? The doctor hadn't forbid covering him, but I was sure if he'd wanted him covered he would have done it himself. It would clearly ease his suffering, if only by a little—and wasn't that my duty, my simple human obligation?

I laid down the gun and pulled the coverlet from the closet. As I bent to spread it over his quivering form, I caught a whiff of a familiar odor, one that I had smelled many times before—the cloyingly sweet smell of putrefying flesh.

I raised my head, bringing my eyes to the level of his right hand, and saw that the skin had gone from a rosy red to a light gray. It seemed almost translucent. I imagined I could see right down to his bones.

The hand that had touched *it*, the thing that Warthrop had called *beautiful*, was beginning to decompose.

"I am dying."

I swallowed hard and said nothing.

"*Squeezed*, that's how I feel. Like a giant fist squeezing me, every inch, down to my very bones."

"The doctor will do everything he can," I promised him.

"I don't want to die. Please. Please don't let me die."

His rotting fingers clawed uselessly at the empty air.

FIVE

"The Singular Cure"

He slipped into semiconsciousness—not awake, not quite asleep.

Dawn came. The doctor did not come with it. He didn't appear until an hour later. I jumped in my chair when the door opened; I was exhausted, my nerves shot.

"Why did you cover him?" he demanded.

"I didn't touch him. He was cold," I added defensively.

Warthrop peeled off the coverlet and let it drop to the floor.

"It was my mother's. Now I shall have to burn it."

"I'm sorry, sir."

He waved my apology away. "As a precaution—the precise toxicity of *pwdre ser* is unknown. How long has he been out?"

"About an hour and a half."

"'About'? Haven't you been keeping notes?"

"I—I didn't have anything to write with, sir."

"Will Henry, I thought I had impressed upon you the urgency of this case, one of the most—if not *the* most—important discoveries in the history of biology—aberrant or otherwise. We must be meticulous. We must not allow our personal failures or biases to compromise our observations. . . . When did this grayish discoloration begin to manifest itself?"

"Shortly after you went downstairs," I answered, my face hot with shame. I had not noted the hour. "It started with his hand—"

"Which hand?"

"His right hand, sir."

"Hmmm. Stands to reason. It's spreading rapidly, then."

It had, I told him. A slaty tide swamping hands, then arms, then torso, groin, legs, feet. Kendall's face was a paper-thin gray mask stretched drum-skin tight over protruding bone.

"What has he reported?"

"He said he's going to have you arrested and hanged."

Warthrop sighed loudly. "About his symptoms, Will Henry. His symptoms."

He was bending over the bed, listening to Kendall's heart through his stethoscope.

"He said he was cold and that it felt like a giant fist was squeezing him."

The doctor told me to bring over the lamp. With great

care he slowly removed the cloth covering Kendall's eyes and peeled up one eyelid. The orb jittered in its socket as if maddened by the onslaught of light.

"The pupil is grossly dilated. The iris has completely disappeared," he observed.

He dropped his gloved fingers to Kendall's cheek and pressed gently. The skin ripped apart at his touch, exposing the dark gray bone beneath. A viscous mixture of pus and blood dribbled from the fissure. The noxious stench of decay wafted around our heads.

"Both dermal and epidermal layers are in active decay, the tissue having begun to liquefy. . . . Early stages of imperfect osteogenesis noted in the zygomatic bone," Warthrop breathed. "Forming non-arthric osteophytic structures . . ."

He ran his hands over the rest of the face, over the arms, the chest and abdomen, down the legs. He had learned his lesson; he did not press hard. His touch was whisper-soft.

"Additional osteophytic growths noted in the elbows, wrists, knuckles, knees, hips. . . . We'll need to take some measurements of these, Will Henry. . . . Acute myositis throughout. . . ." He glanced down at my notes. "*M-y-o*, Will Henry, not *m-i-o*. . . . Myositis is the inflammation you see here in the skeletal, or voluntary, muscles. At this rate, in a few hours our Mr. Kendall will begin to resemble a circus strong man—a *skinless* one, I should say."

He peered at Kendall's right hand, then the left.

"Note the abnormal thickness and dark yellow color of

the nails," he said. He tapped one with his own gloved fingernail. "As hard as steel! The condition is called onychauxis." Taking pity on me, he spelled it out.

He looked over at me, eyes shining with that unnerving backlit glow.

"A precise parallel to the stories in the literature, Will Henry," he whispered. "He is . . . *becoming*. And it's happening faster than I first assumed."

"And you don't think a hospital . . ."

"Even if I did think it, the nearest hospital is in Boston. It would be over before we got there."

"He's dying?"

Warthrop shook his head. What did that mean? Did it mean Kendall was dying? Or did it mean the monstrumologist did not know for certain?

"Is there a cure for it?" I asked.

"Not according to my sources, which are not very reliable. There is, of course, the singular cure that ends all ailments."

Only a monstrumologist, I thought, would characterize death as a cure for anything. I watched him pick up the syringe loaded with morphine and roll it back and forth in his open palm. It would ease the poor soul's suffering; it might give him the smallest measure of peace. But the drug also might interfere with the progress of Kendall's *becoming* and thus compromise Warthrop's scientific inquiry.

It would, in short, desecrate the temple.

Without comment the monstrumologist laid down the syringe. He seemed to tower ten feet above the writhing form in the bed, and his shadow fell hard upon that pile of bones wrapped loosely in its sack of gossamer skin.

He told me to rest; he would hold vigil for a while.

"You look terrible," he observed dispassionately. "You need to sleep. Probably should find yourself something to eat, too."

I glanced toward the bed. "I'm not very hungry, sir."

He nodded. It made sense to him. "Where is my revolver? You haven't lost it, have you? Thank you, Will Henry. Now off to bed, but *first* I'll need you to take care of this."

He handed me a slip of paper, a note jotted down in his nearly illegible scrawl.

"A letter for Dr. von Helrung," he explained. "You may want to recast it in your own hand first, Will Henry. Send it by express mail marked 'personal' and 'confidential.'"

"Yes, sir."

I started out. He called after me, "Straight there and back, and be quick if you want any sleep this day."

He motioned toward the bed.

"It appears to be accelerating."

The letter to the head of the Society for the Advancement of the Science of Monstrumology was brief and to the point:

'PERSONAL AND CONFIDENTIAL'

Von Helrung—

I have, under the most unusual of circumstances,
come into possession of an authentic *nidus ex
magnificum*, by way of Dr. Jack Kearns, whom I
believe you've met. Expect me in New York within
the week. In the interim direct our friends in London
to make *discrete* inquiries into Kearns's whereabouts.
He is working—or did work—at the Royal London
Hospital, Whitechapel, and resided in the same
district, in a flat on Dorset Street owned by a
Mr. Wymond Kendall, Esq.

—Warthrop

I went straight to the post office, resisting all temptations
along the way, Mr. Tanner's shop in particular, where the fragrance of fresh scones hung warm in the bitter air. The wind
was sharp upon my cheek, the day bright and bracingly cold,
the snow faultlessly white—dazzlingly white, unblemished,
pure. My heart ached for the snow.

I paused but once and then only for a moment. There,
white upon white in the beneficent snow, my former schoolhouse, and children playing in the drifts. A battle raged for

the highest ground, the defenders screeching, hurling down their hastily packed cannonade upon the heads of their attackers. A little ways off, a squadron of fallen angels had left its impression, and nearby a passable likeness of the headmaster, complete with cap and cape and walking stick.

And their cries were thin, their laughter high and hysterical in the biting wind.

There was a boy I recognized. He was shouting something from the top of the little hill, crouched behind the ramparts of the fort, taunting the assault force below, and I remembered him. The slightly pug nose. The shaggy blond hair. The splash of freckles across cheeks. I remembered everything about him, his high-pitched voice, the gap between his teeth, the color of his eyes, the way he smiled first with those eyes. You could see the smile coming a year before it arrived. I remembered where he lived, what his parents looked like. He had been a friend, but I could not remember his name. What was his name? He had been my friend, my best friend, and I could not remember his name.

The doctor was standing in the kitchen when I came in, eating an apple.

"You're late," he said. He did not sound angry, not his usual self at all. He said it casually, a knee-jerk response to my entering the room. "Did you stop somewhere?"

"No, sir. Straight to the post office and back."

It struck me then, and with a heart in which fear and hope

intertwined in an obscene embrace, I asked, "Is he dead?"

"No, but I had to eat something. Here, you should too."

He tossed an apple at me and bade me follow him upstairs. I slipped the apple into my coat pocket; I had no appetite.

"The sclerosing bone dysplasia has exacerbated," he called over his shoulder as he took the steps two at a time. "But his heart is as strong as a horse's, his lungs are clear, his blood super-oxygenated. The edema of the muscular tissue continues unabated, *and*—" He stopped suddenly and whirled about, causing me to almost smack face-first into his chest. "This is the most remarkable thing, Will Henry. Although his dermis continues to deteriorate and slough off, he hasn't lost more than a teacup's worth of blood, mostly around the wrists and ankles, so I took the precaution of loosening the bindings a bit."

I followed him into the room. Immediately my hand flew up to cover my nose; the smell was truly overwhelming. It dropped scorching into my lungs. Why hadn't he opened the window? The monstrumologist seemed oblivious to the reek. He continued to chomp on his apple, even as tears of protest coursed down his cheeks.

"What?" he demanded. "Why are you staring at me like that? Don't look at me; look at Mr. Kendall!"

He didn't nudge me toward the bed. I took that step myself.

He did not grab my chin and force me to look.

I looked because I wanted to look. I looked because of the tight thing unwinding, *das Ungeheuer*, the me/not-me, Tantalus's grapes, the thing you cannot name. The thing I knew but did not understand. The thing you may understand but do not know.

I flung myself from the room and managed a dozen shuffling steps down the hall before I collapsed. Everything inside gave way. I felt empty. I was nothing more than a shadow, a shell, a hollow carapace that had once dreamed it was a boy.

A shadow fell over me. I did not look up. I knew I would find no comfort from the bearer of that shadow.

"He's dying," I said. "We have to *do* something."

"I am doing all within my power, Will Henry," he responded gently.

"You aren't doing anything! You're not trying to cure him."

"I have told you there is no—"

"Then, find one!" I screamed at him. "You said it yourself, there is no one else. You're the one. You're the one! If you can't help him, then nobody can, and you *won't*. You won't because you *want* him to die! You *want* to see what the poison does to him!"

"May I remind you that I am not the one who exposed him? He did that to himself," he said. He squatted beside me and placed his hand upon my shoulder. I heaved myself away from him.

"What he is, that's what you are inside," I told him.

"There is but one way to end his suffering," he said, the gentle tone abandoned; his voice, like his shadow upon me, was hard.

He pulled the revolver from his pocket and thrust it toward me. "Here. Would you like to do it? For I cannot. Simply because there is no hope for *him*, Will Henry, that doesn't mean I have to give up all hope for *me*."

"There is no hope—for either of you."

He dropped the revolver to the floor. It lay between us. His shadow and the gun lay between us.

"You're tired," he said. "Go to bed."

"No."

"Very well. Sleep on the floor. It makes no difference to me!"

He scooped up the revolver and left me alone with my misery. I don't know how long I lay there in that hall. It mattered no more to me than it did to the monstrumologist where I slept. I do not remember climbing the stairs into the loft, but I do remember throwing myself upon the bed fully clothed and watching the snow-laden clouds through the window over my head. The clouds were the color of Mr. Kendall's rotting skin.

I closed my eyes. There in the darkness inside my own head, I saw him, gray-skinned, black-eyed, hollow-cheeked, sharp tusks of bone tearing through papery flesh, a corpse whose galloping heart refused to stop.

My stomach rumbled loudly. When was the last time I'd eaten? I could not remember. I pulled from my pocket the apple that the monstrumologist had given me. Its skin was the color of Mr. Kendall's bloody teeth.

When I see gray now, I think of rotting flesh.

And red is not the color of apples or roses or the dresses that pretty girls wear in summertime.

That is not the color of red at all.

SIX

"An Interesting Phenomenon"

Sometime later—though it was not much later—his hand fell upon my shoulder. Above me was the window and, above the window, the clouds with their bellies full of snow.

"Will Henry," the monstrumologist said. His voice was cracked and raw, as if he'd been screaming at the top of his lungs. "Will Henry."

"What time is it?" I asked.

"A quarter past three. I did not wish to wake you . . ."

"But you woke me anyway."

"I wanted to show you something."

I rolled onto my side, away from him.

"I don't want to look at him again."

"It isn't Mr. Kendall. It's this." I heard the crinkle and crunch of papers in his hand. "A treatise by a French scientist named Albert Calmette, of the Pasteur Institute. It's concerned with the theoretical possibility of developing antivenin, based on the vaccine principles of Pasteur. The theory applies to certain poisonous snakes and arachnids, but it could have applications in our case—Mr. Kendall's case, I mean. It may be worth a try."

"Then, try it."

"Yes." He cleared his throat. "The chief obstacle is time, in that Mr. Kendall doesn't have much of it left."

I rolled onto my back, and the form of the monstrumologist swung into view. He looked exhausted. He swayed like a man trying to keep his balance on the yawing deck of a ship.

"Then, you had better get to work."

"It means you will have to sit with Mr. Kendall."

I sat up, swung my feet over the side of the bed, and tugged on my shoes.

"I will sit with him."

Before he allowed me into the room, the doctor uncapped a small vial filled with a thick, clear liquid and shook several drops of the substance onto his handkerchief.

"Here. Tie this round your face," he instructed me, and then proceeded to tie the knot himself. My senses were assaulted by a sweet, musky fragrance that reminded me of rubbing alcohol, though without the biting astringency.

"What is it?" I asked.

"Ambra grisea, or ambergris, the aged regurgitation of the sperm whale," the monstrumologist answered. "A common ingredient in perfume. I often wonder, though, how common it would be if ladies in particular knew where it came from. You see, ambergris is normally expelled through the whale's anus with fecal matter, but—"

"Fecal matter?" My stomach rolled.

"Shit. But sometimes the mass is too large to pass, and the material is regurgitated through the mouth."

"Whale vomit?"

"In a manner of speaking, yes. The ancient Chinese called it 'dragon's spittle.' In the Middle Ages people carried balls of it around, believing it could ward off the plague. It's quite pleasant, though, isn't it?"

I agreed that it was. The doctor smiled with satisfaction, as if he had just imparted an important lesson.

"All right. Quietly now, Will Henry."

We stepped into the bedroom. Despite the gift of regurgitated whale shit, I could smell Kendall's decay. It stung my eyes. The taste of it tingled upon my tongue. I had expected it, though that had done little to prepare me for it. All other expectations, to my surprise, were not met.

First, Warthrop had taken his mother's coverlet and put it back where he had found it. Mr. Kendall was covered from feet to neck.

That was not all. Mr. Kendall himself had changed. I had expected more of the agonized writhing, the grunts and throaty moans of someone in extreme mental and physical distress. Instead he was so still, so quiet, that for the briefest of moments I thought he might have finally succumbed. But no, he lived. The covers rose and fell, and upon closer examination I saw that his eyes roamed beneath their half-closed lids. Most astonishing of all (given the astonishing circumstances) was the smile. Wymond Kendall was smiling! As if lost in a pleasant dream, he smiled.

"Mr. Kendall . . . is he—"

"Smiling? Yes, I would call that a smile. The stories say that in the final stages the victim experiences moments of intense euphoria, an overwhelming feeling of bliss. It's an interesting phenomenon; perhaps once in the bloodstream *pwdre ser* releases a compound structurally similar to an opiate." He stopped, laughed softly—at himself?—and said, "I should get to work on the antivenin. Call me at once should his condition change."

And with that the monstrumologist left me alone with Kendall. He would not have done so, I have told myself many times over the course of my long life, if he had known what Kendall had become—if he had known that Kendall was not Kendall anymore—that he was no more human, or more sentient, than a dime-store mannequin.

I have told myself that.

The room is cold. The light is gray. The even exhalations of the once-human thing on the bed are the only things the boy can hear—metronomic, the ticking of the human clock, lulling him to sleep.

He is so tired. His head lolls. He tells himself he won't fall asleep. Just rest his eyes for a moment or two . . .

In the gray light in the cold room, to the rhythmic breath of the thing becoming—sleep.

Sleep now, Will Henry, sleep.

Do you see her? In the white behind the gray, in the warm beyond the cold, in the silence past the ticking of the clock—she is baking a pie, an apple pie, your favorite. And you at the table with your tall glass of milk, swinging your legs, not long enough yet for your feet to touch the floor.

It must cool first, Willy. It must cool.

A strand of hair loosed from her bun falling down her graceful neck, and her new apron, and a dab of flour upon her cheek, and how long her arms seem reaching into the oven, and the whole world smelling like apples.

Where is Father?

Away again.

With the doctor?

Of course with the doctor.

I want to go.

You do not know what you're wishing for.

When will he be home?

Soon, I hope.

He says one day I shall go with him.

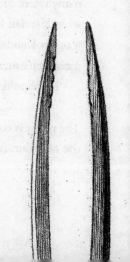

Does he?

One day I will.

But if you go, who will keep me company?

You can come too.

Where your father goes, I have no desire to follow.

The fire that engulfs her has no heat. Her scream makes no sound. The boy sits in his chair with his short legs swinging and his tall glass of milk, and he watches the flames consume her, and he is laughing while his mother burns, and the world still smells like apples.

And then his father's voice, calling him:

Will Henry! Will Henreeeeeeee!

I bolted from the chair, stumbled toward the bed, turned, lunged through the doorway into the hall, and started down the stairs. It was not my father's voice—not the dream voice—but the doctor's calling me, as he had a hundred times before, in desperate need of my indispensible services.

"Coming, sir!" I called, pounding down the stairs to the main floor. "I'm coming!"

We met in the front hall, for as I raced down, he ran up, and both of us were winded and slightly wild-eyed, regarding each other with identical expressions of comic confusion.

"What is it?" he asked breathlessly.

And I, with him: "What is it?"

"Why are you asking me 'What is it?' What is it?"

"What, Dr. Warthrop?"

"I asked you that, Will Henry."

"Asked me what?"

"What is it!" he roared. "What do you want?"

"You—you called for me, sir."

"I did no such thing. Are you quite all right?"

"Yes, sir. I must have . . . I think I fell asleep."

"I would not advise that, Will Henry. Back upstairs, please. We mustn't leave Mr. Kendall unattended."

The room was still very cold. And the light gray. And there was the whisper of snow now against the windowpane.

And the bed, empty.

The chair and the Louis Philippe armoire and the dead embers and the little rocking chair and the littler doll in that chair and her littler still black, unblinking china eyes and the boy frozen on the threshold, staring stupidly at the empty bed.

I backed slowly into the hall. The hall was warmer than the room, and I was much warmer than the hall; my cheeks were on fire, though my hands were numb.

"Dr. Warthrop," I whispered, no louder than the snow against the pane. "Dr. Warthrop!"

He must have fallen, I thought. *Got loose of the ropes somehow and fell out of bed. He's lying on the other side, that's all. The doctor will have to pick him up. I am not touching him!*

I turned back. My turning took a thousand years. The stairs stretched out below me for a thousand miles.

To the landing, another millennia. There was the beating

of my heart and my hot breath puffing my makeshift mask, and the smell of ambergris and, above and behind me, the gentle protest of the top step, creaking.

I stopped, listening. The passing of the third millennia.

I was patting my empty pockets for the gun.

Where is the gun?

He had forgotten to give it back to me, or, as he would undoubtedly say, I had forgotten to ask him for it.

I knew I should keep going. Instinctively I understood where salvation lay. But it is human to tie ourselves to the mainmast, to be Lot's wife, turning back.

I turned back.

SEVEN

"Would You Live?"

It launched itself from the top step, a reeking sepulcher of jutting bone and flayed skin and crimson muscle dripping purulence, a yawning mouth festooned with a riot of jagged teeth, and the black eyes of the abyss.

The once-Kendall slammed into me, its shoulder driving into my chest, and the black eyes rolled in their sockets, like a shark's eyes when it attacks, in the ecstasy of the kill. I punched blindly at its face; my knuckles knocked against the sharp, bony growths that had erupted from the rubbish of its flesh, bone meeting bone, and my entire arm sang with pain.

The creature seized my wrist and flung me down the last flight of stairs as easily as a boy tosses a stick. I landed face-first with a loud wallop at the bottom, making no more noise than that, for the fall knocked all the breath out of me. In the space of a heartbeat, I rolled onto my back, and it was upon me, so close I saw my own face reflected in its soulless eyes. Its face was not that of a human being. I have looked at that face a thousand times; I keep the memory of it in a special cabinet of curiosities, and I take it out from time to time, when the day is bright and the sun warm and the evening very far away. I take it out and hold it. The more I hold it, you see, the less I'm afraid of it. Most of the skin is gone, torn or sloughed off, exposing the underlying musculature, the marvelously complex—and marvelously beautiful—underpinning. Pointed horns of calcified tissue protrude from the skull, scores of them, like the thrust-up roots of cypress trees, from the cheekbones, the forehead, the jaws and chin. It has no lips. Its tongue has putrefied and broken apart; just the base remains. I saw the brown stringy mass spasm as the open mouth came down at me. The rest of the tongue he swallowed; the lips, too. The only thing in Mr. Kendall's stomach was Mr. Kendall.

At the last instant before he landed on top of me, I brought up my hands. They broke easily through him; my fingers tangled with his ribs. If I'd had my wits about me, I would have thought to push just a bit more, find his heart and squeeze until it burst. Perhaps, though, it was a matter of timing, not acumen. There was no time to think.

In the time it took for me to realize that this inhuman face would be the last face I would see, the bullet punched through the back of his head, blowing out an apple-size hole as it came out the other side before burying itself in the carpet not quite a quarter inch from my ear. The body jerked in my hands. I felt—or thought I felt—the protest of his heart, an angry push against my fingers wrapped tight around his ribs, the way a desperate prisoner grasps the bars of his cell, before it stopped beating. The light did not go out of his eyes. There hadn't been any light in them to begin with. I was still trapped in those eyes—sometimes I think I am trapped still—in their unseeing sight.

Warthrop heaved the body away—once he had freed it from my maddened grip—tossed the gun aside, and knelt beside me.

I reached for him.

"No! No, Will Henry, no!"

He lunged out of my reach; my bloody fingertips brushed his coattails.

"Do . . . not . . . touch—anything!" He held up his hand as if to demonstrate. "Are you injured?"

I shook my head. I still had not found my voice.

"Do not move. Keep your hands away from your body. I will be right back. Do you understand, Will Henry?"

He scrambled to his feet and raced toward the kitchen. It is human, the compulsion to do the very thing you've been cautioned not to do. The handkerchief was still tied around my face. I felt as if I were slowly being suffocated, and all I desired was to yank it down.

A moment later he was back, wearing a fresh pair of gloves, and he tugged the mask down as if he knew without my telling him the immediate cause of my distress. I took a long, shuddering breath.

"Don't move, don't move, not yet, not yet," the monstrumologist whispered. "Careful, careful. Did he hurt you, Will Henry? Did he bite or scratch you?"

I shook my head.

Warthrop studied my face carefully, and then, as abruptly as he returned, he abandoned me again. The hall began to fade into a gray mist. My body was going into shock; suddenly I was terribly cold.

In the distance I hear the plaintive cry of a train's whistle. The mist parts, and on the platform stands my mother and me, holding hands, and I am very excited.

Is that it, Mother? Is that the train?

I think it is, Willy.

Do you think Father has brought me a present?

If he has not, then he is no longer Father.

I wonder what it could be.

I worry what it could be.

Father has been gone very long this time.

Yes.

How long has it been, Mother?

Very long.

Last time he brought me a hat. A stupid hat.

Now, Willy. It was a very nice hat.

I want him to bring me something special this time.

Special, Willy?

Yes! Something wonderful and special, like the places he goes.

I do not think you would find them so wonderful and special.

I would, and I will! Father says he will take me with him one day, when I'm old enough.

Gripping my hand tightly. And, in the distance, the growl and huff of the locomotive.

You will never be old enough for that, William James Henry.

One day he will take me. He promised he would. One day I will see places other people only dream about.

The train is a living thing; it screeches angrily, complaining of the rails. Black smoke blows grumpily from its stack. The train glares contemptuously at the crowd, the self-important conductor, the porters in their neat white jackets. And it is huge, throbbing with power and restrained rage. It is a huffing, growling, enraged monster, and the boy is thrilled. What boy wouldn't be?

Look now, Willy. Look for your father. Let's see who will be the first to spot him.

I see him! I see him! There he is!

No, that isn't him.

Yes, it— Oh, no, it isn't.

Keep looking.

There! There he is! Father! Father!

He has lost weight; his dusty clothes, rumpled from travel, hang loosely on his lean frame. He hasn't shaven in weeks and his eyes are weary, but he is my father. I would know him anywhere.

And here he is! Here is my Will. Come here to me, boy!

I soar a thousand feet into the air; the arms that lift me are thin but strong, and his face turns beneath me, and then my face is pressing into his neck, and it is *his* smell beneath the grime of the rails.

Father! What did you bring me, Father?

Bring you! Why do you suppose I brought you anything?

Laughing, and his teeth are very bright in his stubbly face. He starts to set me down so he may embrace his wife.

No! Carry me, Father.

Willy, your father is tired.

Carry me, Father!

It's all right, Mary. I shall carry him.

And the shrill, startling shriek of the monster, the last angry blast of its breath, and I am home at last, in my father's arms.

Warthrop lifted me from the floor, grimacing from the effort of holding me as far from his body as possible.

"Hold your hands up, Will Henry. And hold them still!"

He carried me into the kitchen. The washtub sat on the floor by the stove, half-filled with steaming hot water. I saw the teakettle on the stove, and I realized, with an odd pang of sadness, that it was the kettle I'd heard whistling, not a train. My mother and father were gone again, swallowed by the gray mist.

The monstrumologist placed me on the floor before the tub and then sat behind me, pressing his body close. He reached around and grasped my arms firmly, just below the elbows.

"This is going to burn, Will Henry."

He leaned forward, forcing me toward the steaming surface, and then plunged my bloody hands into the solution, a mixture of hot water and carbolic acid.

I found my voice then.

I screamed; I kicked; I thrashed; I pushed back hard against him, but the monstrumologist did not yield. Through my tears I saw the crimson fog of Kendall's blood violate the clear solution, spreading out in serpentine tendrils, until I could no longer see my hands.

The doctor pressed his lips against my ear and whispered fiercely, "Would you live? Then hold! Hold!"

Black stars bloomed in my vision, went supernovae, flickered, and died. When I could bear it no longer, at the precise moment when I teetered upon the edge of unconsciousness, the monstrumologist pulled out my hands. The skin had turned a bright, sunburned red. He held them up, turning them this way and that, and then his body stiffened against mine. He gasped.

"Will Henry, what is this?"

He pointed at a small abrasion on the middle knuckle of my left index finger. Fresh blood welled in its center. When I didn't answer immediately, he gave me a little shake.

"*What is this?* Did he bite you? Is it a scratch? Will Henry!"

"I—I don't know! I fell down the stairs. . . . I don't think he did."

"Think, Will Henry! Think!"

"I don't know, Dr. Warthrop!"

He stood up, and I fell backward, too weak to rise, too frightened to say any more. I looked into his face and saw a man squeezed tight in the crushing embrace of indecision, caught between two unacceptable courses.

"I don't know enough. God forgive me, I don't know enough!"

He seemed so large standing over me, a colossus, one of the Nephilim, the race of giants who bestrode the world when the world was young. His eyes darted about the room, as if he were looking for an answer to his impossible dilemma, as if somewhere in the kitchen would be the sign that would show him the way.

Then the monstrumologist became very still. His restless eyes came to rest upon my upturned face.

"No," he said softly. "Not God."

He stepped away quickly, and before I could crane my neck around to see where he had gone, he returned, carrying the butcher knife.

He leaned over, reached out, grabbed my left wrist, yanked me from the floor, dragged me to the kitchen table, slapped my hand upon it, shouted, "Spread your fingers!" pressed his left hand hard over the top of mine, brought high the knife, and slammed it down.

EIGHT

"The One Thing That Keeps Me Human"

Would you live?

The smell of lilacs. The sound of water dripping in a basin. The touch of a warm, wet cloth.

And a shadow. A presence. A shade beyond my shaded eyes.

Would you live?

I float against the ceiling. Below me is my body. I see it clearly, and sitting next to the bed, the monstrumologist, wringing out the washcloth.

Then he covers me. I cannot see his face. He is looking at my other face, my mortal face, the one belonging to the boy in the bed.

He sits back down. I can see his face now. I want to say

something to him. I want to answer his question.

He rubs his eyes. He runs his long fingers through his hair. He bends forward, rests his elbows on his knees, and covers his face with his hands. He remains like this but for a moment, and then he is on his feet, pacing to the end of the bed and back again. The lamp flings his shadow upon the floor, and the shadow crawls up the wall as he approaches and then trails behind him as he turns.

He collapses into the chair, and I watch him reach out and lay his hand upon my forehead. The gesture seems absentminded, as if touching me might help him to think.

Above, I watch him touch me. Below, I feel it.

The light burrows deep into my eyes, brighter than a thousand galaxies. Behind the light his eyes, darker than the deepest pit.

His fingers wrapped around my wrist. The press of the cold stethoscope against my chest. My blood flowing into chambers of glass.

And the light digging into my eyes.

What did you bring me, Father?
I brought you a seed.
A seed?
Yes, a golden seed from the Isle of Bliss, and if you plant it and give it water, it will grow into a golden tree that bears lollipops.
Lollipops!

Yes! Golden lollipops! And peppermints and horehound drops and lemon drops. Why are you laughing? Plant it; you'll see.

I see him standing in the doorway. He has something in his hand.

Ropes.

He drops the ropes into the chair. Reaches into his pocket.

Revolver.

He sets the gun on the table by the chair. Do I see his hand shaking?

Gently he fishes out my arm from beneath the covers, picks up a length of rope—there are three—and ties a knot around my wrist.

I float above him. I cannot see his face. He is looking down at the face of the boy.

He whirls away from the bed; the free end of the rope tumbles over the edge.

Then he turns back, sweeps the ropes lying in the chair onto the floor, and sits down. For a long moment he does not move.

And then the monstrumologist takes the other end of the rope, ties it to his wrist, leans back in the chair, and closes his eyes to sleep.

Where did you go this time, Father?
I've told you, Willy. The Isle of Bliss.
Where is the Isle of Bliss?

Well, first you must find a boat. And not just any boat will do. You must find the fastest boat in the world; that is, a boat with a thousand sails, and when you've sailed for a thousand days, you will see something that the world hasn't seen in a thousand years. You'll swear the sun has fallen into the sea, for every tree on that island is a golden tree, and every leaf a golden leaf, and the leaves shine with a radiance all their own, so even in the darkest night the island seems to burn like a lighthouse beacon.

"I have been thinking about your father for some reason," the monstrumologist said to the boy. "He saved my life once. I don't think I ever told you."

The room seemed so empty; I had gone to a place he could not go. It didn't matter really whether I could hear him. His words were not meant entirely for me.

"Arabia, the winter of '73—or it may have been '74; I can't recall now. Late one night our camp was ambushed by a hostile and extremely violent pack of predators—by that I mean *Homo sapiens*. Bandits. Lost three of our porters— and our guide, a very pleasant bedouin by the name of Hilal. I felt badly about Hilal. He thought the world of me. Even tried to give me one of his daughters—either in marriage or as a slave, I was never quite sure because I was never completely comfortable in the language. At any rate, one moment he was talking to me, smiling, laughing—he was very jolly. Few nomads are glum, Will Henry; if you think about it, you will understand why. And the next moment his head was hacked clean off his shoulders. . . .

"Afterward I told his widow, 'Your husband is dead, but at least he died laughing.' I think she took some comfort in that. It is the second-best way to die, Will Henry." He did not say what the best way was.

"At any rate, your father pulled me from harm's way. I would have stood my ground, if only to avenge Hilal's death, but I'd been badly wounded in the thigh and was losing a great deal of blood. James threw me over the saddle of his pony and rode all night to the nearest village. Rode that horse until it collapsed, and then carried me the rest of the way."

I want to go, Father. Will you take me there, to the Isle of Bliss?

It's a very, very long way from here, Will.

I don't care. We'll find a ship of a thousand sails to carry us there.

Oh, now, those ships are very difficult to come by.

You found one.

Yes, I did. I did find that ship.

"I was laid up for two weeks—the wound had become infected—slipping in and out of delirium, and all the while your father was by my side. At one point, though, I saw Hilal sitting beside me, dimly, as if through a veil or mist, and I knew to the marrow of my bones that I had come to the lip of the stage, as it were. I was not surprised to see him sitting there, and I was not in the least afraid. I was

actually happy to see him. He asked me what I wanted. 'What do you want, Sheikh Pellinore Warthrop? Ask and it will be done.'

"And of all the things I might have asked, I asked him to tell me a joke. And he did, and the devil of it is, I can't recall it now. It still bothers me. It was a very funny joke. My difficulty is that I have no memory for jokes. My mind does not tend in that direction."

He was playing with the knot around his wrist. His wan smile faded, and suddenly he was angry—intensely angry.

"It is . . . unacceptable. *Intolerable.* I will not tolerate it, do you understand? You are forbidden to die. You did not will your parents' death; you did not ask to come here—it is not your debt; you should not have to pay."

Here, here, now. Do not cry. You're still very young. You'll have years and years to find it. Until then I shall be the ship of a thousand sails. Climb aboard me back, me matey, and I shall bear thee to that fabled isle!

"I will not suffer you to die," he said fiercely. "Your father died because of me, and I cannot afford your death too. The debt will crush me. If you go down, Will Henry, you will drag me down with you." Tugging on the rope.

I see it, Father! The Isle of Bliss. It burns like the sun in the black water.

"Enough!" he cried. "I forbid you to leave me. Now snap to, get up, stop this foolishness. I have saved you. So snap *to*, you stupid, stupid boy."

He brought back the hand connected to mine and slapped me hard across the cheek.

"Snap to, Will Henry!" *Smack!* "Snap to, Will Henry!" *Smack!* "Snap to, Will Henry!" *Smack, smack, smack!*

"Would you live?" he shouted. "Then, choose to live. *Choose* to live!"

Gasping, he fell back toward the chair; the rope connecting us yanked on his arm. Roaring his frustration, he pulled his wrist free of the knot and flung the rope onto my body.

He was spent. All fear, all anger, all guilt, all shame, all pride—gone. He felt nothing; he was empty. Perhaps God waits for us to be empty, so he may fill us with himself.

I say this, because next the monstrumologist said this:

"Please, do not leave me, Will Henry. I would not survive it. You were nearly right. What Mr. Kendall was, I am always on the brink of becoming. And you—I do not pretend to understand how or even *why*—but you pull me back from the precipice. You are the one. . . . You are the one thing that keeps me human."

NINE

"The Final Disposition"

You are the one thing that keeps me human.

In the months that followed—well, *years* to be completely accurate—the monstrumologist never wavered in his disavowal of saying those words. I must have been delirious; he never said anything like it; or, my favorite, he said something entirely different and I misheard him. This was more like the Pellinore Warthrop I had come to know, and somehow I preferred the familiar version. It was predictable and therefore comforting. My mother, as devout as any New England woman of Puritan stock, loved to speak of the days "when the lion lies down with the lamb." Though I understand the theology behind it, the image does not bring me peace; it makes me feel sorry for the lion. It strips him of his essence, the fundamental part of his being. A lion that doesn't behave as a lion is not a lion. It isn't even the lion's opposite. It's a mockery of a lion.

And Pellinore Warthrop, like that lion—or its Creator!— is not mocked.

"I do not deny affirming what I have often said, Will Henry, and that is that, *in general*, your services have proven more indispensable than not. I have never pretended otherwise. I believe in acknowledging debts where debts are owed. One must take care, however, not to extrapolate anything . . . well, *excessive* from it, for lack of a better word."

And then he would brusquely change the subject.

I forbid you to leave me.

It seemed quite sudden to me, my acquiescence to his demand. One moment I could see myself and see him and see the room—and more, much more. I saw . . . everything. I saw our house on Harrington Lane; I saw our town of New Jerusalem; I saw New England. I saw oceans and continents and the earth spinning round the sun. I saw the moons of Jupiter and the Milky Way and the unfathomable depths of space. I saw the entire universe. I held it in the palm of my hand.

And the next moment I was in the bed, my head splitting, my left hand throbbing. And Warthrop was sound asleep in the chair beside me. I cleared my throat; my mouth was desert-dry.

He came awake at once, a wild look in his eyes, as if he were seeing a ghost.

"Will Henry?" he croaked.

"I'm thirsty," I said.

He said nothing at first. He continued to stare until his stare unnerved me.

"Well, then, Will Henry, I shall fetch you a drink of water."

After I drank some water and sipped some lukewarm broth, he placed the tray on the bedside table (the gun was gone, as were the ropes) and said he needed to change the dressing on my injury.

"You don't have to look—unless you'd like to. It's a clean cut, a really extraordinary amputation considering the circumstances."

"If it's all the same to you, Dr. Warthrop . . ."

"Of course. You'll be happy to know there's no sign of infection. The operation was not performed under the most sanitary of conditions, as you know. I expect a full recovery."

"It doesn't feel like it's gone."

"That's common."

"What's common?"

"Hmmm." Examining his handiwork. "Yes, it's healing up quite nicely. We are extremely fortunate it is your left index finger, Will Henry."

"We are?"

"You're right-handed, are you not?"

"Yes, sir. I suppose that is fortunate."

"Well, I'm not saying you should feel *grateful*."

"But I do feel grateful, Dr. Warthrop. You saved my life."

He finished putting on the fresh bandage in silence. He seemed troubled by the remark. Then he said, "I would like to think so. The plain truth is that it may have been for nothing. You don't know if Mr. Kendall was the author of your injury, and I do not know what, if anything, might have happened if he were. When faced with the unknown, it's best to take the most conservative approach. That's all well and good as theories go, but the end result is that I took a butcher knife and chopped off your finger."

He gave my knee an awkward pat and stood up, wincing, pressing his hands into the small of his back.

"Now, if you'll excuse me, I must have a bath and a change of clothes. Don't try to get up yet. Use the bedpan if you need to void your bladder or relieve your bowels. What are you smiling about?" he asked crossly. "Did you think I would allow you to wallow in your own excrement?"

"No, sir."

"I fail to see what is humorous about a bedpan."

"Nothing, sir. It's the idea of you emptying one."

He stiffened and said with great dignity, "I am a natural scientist. We are accustomed to dealing with shit."

He returned at the setting of the sun, asked how I was faring, and informed me it would not be a bad thing if I tried to get out of bed.

"You will be dizzy and sore, but the sooner you become

ambulatory the better. We've much to do before we leave for New York."

"What is there to do, Dr. Warthrop?" I assumed he meant the packing, a chore that always fell to me.

"I would have done it already, but I didn't want to leave . . . I thought it best, when you regained consciousness . . . Well, I could not be two places at once," he finished impatiently.

I was, I nearly told him. I bit back the words. He would scoff at the notion of my disembodied spirit observing him from the ceiling.

"You would have done what already?"

"Mr. Kendall, Will Henry. We must . . ." He paused as if searching for the right word. "Resolve this issue of Mr. Kendall."

We must resolve this issue of Mr. Kendall.

By this the monstrumologist did not mean notifying the family of his demise or making arrangements for returning the body to its native England for burial.

I don't know why I would think for an instant that it did. How would one go about explaining to his loved ones—or to the British authorities, for that matter—a badly decomposed corpse with a fresh gunshot wound to the head? There was also the sticky matter of the potential virulence of the contagion. As Warthrop put it, "It could be the spark that lights a conflagration that would make the plague seem like a campfire in comparison."

No, we spent the entirety of that first evening of my recovery in the basement laboratory, dismembering Wymond Kendall.

The monstrumologist wanted samples of every major organ, including the brain (he was very excited to have a look at Mr. Kendall's brain), which he removed in toto after sawing off the top of his head. I was forced to hold it—an awkward proposition given the thick bandages on my left hand—while the doctor severed the medulla. I had never held a human brain before. Its delicacy surprised me; I thought it would be much heavier.

"The average human brain weighs approximately three pounds, Will Henry," the doctor said in response to my startled expression. "Compare that to the total weight of our skin, around six pounds, and you have a fact that is as compelling as it is unnerving."

He took the three-pound seat of Kendall's consciousness from me and said, "Observe the frontal lobe, Will Henry. The sulci—these deep crevices you see covering the rest of the brain—have all disappeared. The thinking part of his brain is as smooth as a billiard ball."

I asked him what that meant.

"Well, we may assume it is not a congenital defect, though he did not strike me as all that bright—more gyri than sulci— Sorry, a bit of anatomical tomfoolery there. We may assume it is a manifestation of the toxin. This aligns perfectly with the literature, which claims the victim, in the final stages, becomes little more than a beast, incapable of reason but fully capable of a murderous, cannibalistic rage. Certain indigenous tribes of the Lakshadweep Islands report whole villages wiped out by a single exposure to the *pwdre ser*, until the last man standing literally eats himself to death."

The doctor laughed dryly, absently caressing the smooth tissue of Kendall's brain, and added, "I mean he eats *himself* to death. When everyone else is dead or has run off, he turns upon himself and feeds from his own body, until he has either bled to death or contracted an infection. Well, you've seen the contents of Mr. Kendall's stomach; I don't believe he swallowed his tongue by accident."

He directed me to fill a large specimen jar with form-aldehyde, into which he then carefully lowered the brain. As I was heaving the jar onto the shelf, my eye was drawn to a nearby container, one I had not seen before. It took a moment for me to recognize what floated inside the amber fluid.

"Is that . . ."

"It is," he answered.

"You kept it?"

"Well, I didn't want to just throw it out with the trash."

"But why did you—What are you going to do with it?"

"I thought I'd rip a page from Mrs. Shelley's book and construct another boy, one who won't pester me with questions, who refrains from getting seriously injured at the most inopportune time, and who does not see it as his mission in life to judge my every decision as if appointed by God to be my conscience." His attendant smile was quick and humorless. "It's an important piece of evidence. Forgive me. I thought that would go without saying. When I have the time—which at the moment I most certainly do *not*—I'll perform a thorough analysis to determine whether you were actually infected."

I stared at my finger floating in the fluid for a long moment. It is exceedingly odd to see a piece of yourself apart from yourself.

"If I wasn't, I don't want to know," I said.

He started to say something, and then stopped himself. He nodded curtly. "I understand."

The monstrumologist next opened up Mr. Kendall's torso to remove the major organs. He found numerous sacklike growths—"omental cystic lesions," he called them—lining the interior of the stomach. He gently pressed into one with the tip of his scalpel, and it popped open with a barely audible *pompf!*, spilling a clear, thick fluid with the consistency of mucus.

After the organs had been preserved and properly labeled, it was time to address, in Warthrop's words, "the final disposition."

"The bone saw, please, Will Henry. No, the large one there."

He began by removing Mr. Kendall's hollowed-out head. "The ground is much too hard for us to bury the body," he said as he sawed through the neck. "And I can't afford to wait until the spring thaw. We'll have to burn it, Will Henry."

"What if someone comes looking for him?"

"Who? He fled quickly, in a state of extreme fear. Perhaps he told no one. But let's assume that he did. What do they know? They know he was coming; he did not have the opportunity or the means to inform them what happened once he arrived. Should the authorities ask questions, I can always say I never met the man, that he may have set out to find me but in the end failed in his quest."

He dropped the severed head unceremoniously into the empty washtub beside the necropsy table, the same washtub into which he had plunged my bloody hands. The head landed with a frightening clang and rolled to one side, the right eye open (the left had been removed by the monstrumologist for study) and seeming to stare directly at me.

"There is one bright spot in this distasteful turn of events," the doctor opined as he separated Mr. Kendall's right leg from his torso. "We have removed all doubt as to the authenticity of Dr. Kearns's 'present.' We have in our possession the second greatest prize in monstrumology, Will Henry."

"What is the first greatest?" I asked.

"The 'first greatest'? Really, Will Henry."

"The thing that made it?" I guessed. "The ... *magnificum?*"

"Very good! *Typhoeus magnificum,* named for the father of all monsters—also called the Unseen One."

"Why is it called that?"

He looked up from his work and stared at me as if all my sulci had given way to gyri.

"It is called the Unseen One, Will Henry," he said slowly and carefully, "because it has never been seen.

"Practically everything about it is a mystery," he told me. He was cutting through the glenohumeral joint that connected Mr. Kendall's humerus to his scapula. My job for this portion of the "disposition" was literally to hold the corpse's hand, to keep the arm perpendicular to the legless torso. "From class to species, from mating habits to habitat, from life cycle to precise form. We aren't even sure if it's a predator. The stories—and they are nothing more than that, folktales passed on from generation to generation—say it is unequivocally predacious, but they are just that—stories and folktales, not credible observation. The only real physical evidence we have of the *magnificum* are the *nidi*, its nests, and *pwdre ser*, which first were thought to be its droppings and are now considered, as I told Mr. Kendall here"—he nodded to the washtub by his feet—"to be part of the digestive system, its saliva or venom, produced in its mouth or some other glandular organ." He pulled the blade free and said, "There, Will Henry. Give his arm a tug and see if it comes free. Oh, good! Give Master Henry a hand!"

He laughed. I did not. His macabre attempts at humor were getting on my nerves.

"Well, don't just stand there with it. Put it in the tub with the rest. We are running out of time. I think I should cut the torso in half, at the seventh thoracic vertebra. What do you think?"

I confessed I did not have an opinion; I was only thirteen, and this was my very first dismemberment.

The monstrumologist nodded. "That is true."

We divided Mr. Kendall's remains, separating the longer pieces (like his thighs) from the smaller (his hands), the former to be burned in the alley, the latter in the library fireplace.

"What about the bones?" I asked. "What will we do with them?"

"Keep them, of course. I'd like to reconstruct the skeleton, once I have a little time. Ideally we should use acid, but I haven't enough for the job and it's not as quick as fire. Time is of the essence now, Will Henry, if we have any hope of tracking down the *magnificum*."

We were standing in the alley by the ash barrel, our feet buried in four inches of freshly fallen snow. The brunt of the storm had passed, but a few fat flakes spun down lazily, glowing in the amber light of the streetlamp, like the golden leaves of my father's island, the one that he had promised to show me, the one he never did.

Warthrop doused the remains in kerosene. He struck the match and held it until the flame scorched his fingers, then dropped it to the ground.

"Well, I suppose something should be said. A few

appropriate words. I know some might say that Wymond Kendall reaped what he sowed, that curiosity killed the cat, that he should have minded his own business and kept his nose out of monstrumology's business. And there would be an equal number who could justly say he is an innocent victim of a vicious madman, the tragic consequence of man's inhumanity. What do *you* say, Will Henry?"

"No one deserves *that*," I answered.

"Ah. I think you've touched on the heart of the matter, Will Henry. Half the world prays they will be given what they deserve, and the other half that they will not!" He looked down at the tangled jumble of parts, a *nidus* not yet made. . . . That would be one way to look at it.

"I did not know you, Wymond Kendall," said the monstrumologist to the dismantled man stuffed into the ash barrel. "I do not know if your life was happy or sad, if you ever loved anyone more than yourself, if you enjoyed the theater or books or were interested in politics. I do not know if you were querulous or kind, vindictive or forgiving, pious or profane. I know next to nothing about you, and I am the one who has held your brain in the palm of his hand. I hope, before your light went out, you made peace with your past, that you forgave those who trespassed against you, and that, more important by far, you forgave yourself."

He struck a second match and tossed it into the barrel. The flames leapt upward, smoky and dark-edged, and there was intense heat and the acrid smell of burning hair and the sizzle of water boiling out of flesh and the spinning of golden snow. Without thinking, the monstrumologist and I shuffled closer to the barrel, for the night was very cold, and the fire was very warm.

TEN

"I Am the One"

We departed the next morning for New York. I fell asleep on the train, waking upon our arrival at Grand Central Depot with my head in the crook of the doctor's arm, dizzy and disoriented and feeling sick to my stomach. I'd had a horrible dream in which the monstrumologist had been demonstrating to a group of school children the proper method of removing a brain from a human body—*my* body.

We dropped our luggage at the Plaza Hotel (save for the doctor's black valise, into which Warthrop had packed, with exquisite care, the *nidus ex magnificum*) and left immediately for the Society's headquarters. As our hansom rattled south along Broadway, the monstrumologist cradled the valise in his lap like an anxious mother with her newborn child. He chided our driver over the slightest delay and eyed every passerby, cart, and carriage suspiciously, as if they were bandits intent on separating him from his precious cargo.

"I am loath to part with it, Will Henry," he confessed to me. "There is only one other of its kind in the world—the Lakshadweep *nidus*, named after the place of its discovery in 1851, the Lakshadweep Islands off the Indian coast. If something should happen to it . . ." He shuddered. "Tragic. It must be safeguarded at all costs, and if I cannot trust him, then no one can be trusted."

"Dr. von Helrung?" I guessed.

He shook his head. "Professor Ainesworth."

He was very old, the curator of the Monstrumarium, very cross most of the time, and very hard of hearing. He was also quite vain, a fault that prohibited him from admitting to his near-deafness, which in turn produced his foul temper. Constant disagreement over what was said rendered the old man altogether disagreeable. He had a habit of shaking the head of his cane (fashioned from the bleached skull of a long-extinct creature, a noisome little beast called an *Ocelli carpendi* that he had nicknamed Oedipus) in the face of any who dared raise their voice to him. Since raising one's voice was the *only* way to talk to him, there was not a single monstrumologist—Warthrop included—who had not been the recipient of what one wit had dubbed "the full Adolphus." The heavy chin thrusts forward; the bushy white eyebrows meet over the bridge of the bulbous, slightly pink, pockmarked nose; the muttonchops bristle and contort in cottony confusion, as a cornered cat's fur; and then up comes the gnarled fist clutching the walnut cane, at the end of which, waving an inch from your nose, the *carpendi's* two-inch fangs and the sightless glare of its oversize ocular cavities.

We found Professor Ainesworth in his musty basement office, perched upon a tall stool behind the massive desk upon which Everests of paper rose halfway to the ceiling. This after we negotiated the serpentine path through books, boxes, and crates—shipments waiting to be catalogued and stocked in the Society's house of curiosities on the corner of Twenty-second Street and Broadway. On the wall behind the irascible old man hung the Society's coat of arms, inscribed with the motto *Nil timendum est*—"fear nothing."

"There are no children allowed within the Monstrumarium!" he shouted at my master without preamble.

"But this is Will Henry, Adolphus," replied Warthrop in a loud but respectful tone. "You remember Will Henry."

"Impossible!" shouted Adolphus. "You can't be a member until you're eighteen. I know that much, Pellinore Warthrop!"

"He is my assistant," protested the monstrumologist.

"You watch your language with me, Doctor! He'll have to leave immediately." He shook the head of his cane at me. "Immediately!"

Warthrop placed a hand on my shoulder and said in a voice

only slightly softer than a shout, "It's Will Henry, Adolphus! You remember—last November. You saved his life!"

"Oh, I remember very well!" cried the old Welshman. "He's the reason we have the rule!" He wagged a gnarled finger at my face. "Poking around in places where children shouldn't poke, weren't you, little man?"

The doctor's fingers squeezed the back of my neck, and I, as if his puppet, nodded quickly in response.

"I will keep him under the strictest supervision," promised the doctor. "He shan't stray an inch from my sight."

Before Professor Ainesworth could protest further, Warthrop placed the black valise on the desk. Adolphus grunted, popped the clasps, pried open the top, and peered inside.

"Well, well," he said. "Well, well, well, *well!*"

"Yes, Adolphus" returned the doctor. "*Nidus ex—*"

"Oh-ho, do you really think so, Dr. Warthrop?" interrupted the curator, clicking his teeth. He shoved his gnarled hands into a pair of gloves and reached inside the bag. The doctor stiffened reflexively, perhaps apprehensive that the arthritic hands might damage his precious cargo.

Adolphus pushed the empty bag aside with his forearm and gingerly lowered the gruesome nest onto the desktop. He produced a large magnifying glass from his coat pocket and proceeded to inspect the thing up close.

"I have already thoroughly examined the specimen for—," began the doctor, before Ainesworth cut him off.

"Have you now! Hmmmm. Yes. Have you? Hmmmm-mmmm."

His eye, magnified comically large by the glass, roamed over the specimen. His false teeth clicked—a nervous habit. Adolphus was quite proud of his dentures and somewhat emotionally—as well as biologically—attached to them. They'd been fashioned from the teeth of his son, Alfred Ainesworth, who had been a colonel in the Union army. He'd fallen in the battle of Antietam, and his teeth had been rescued after his death and sent to Adolphus, who thenceforward proudly—and literally—sported a hero's smile.

"Of course, I would not have brought it to you for safekeeping were I not unequivocally certain of its authenticity," said the monstrumologist. "There is no one else in whom I place more trust or hold in higher admir—"

"Please, please, Dr. Warthrop. Your incessant chattering is giving me a headache."

I cringed, waiting for the explosion. But none came. Beside me Warthrop was smiling as benignly as Buddha, completely unfazed. No one in my experience had ever talked to my master with such impertinence, with such condescension and disdain—in short, the way he usually spoke to me. Many times I had witnessed eruptions that would rival Krakatoa in their ferocity over the smallest slight, the most trivial of untoward looks, so I expected "the full Warthrop," as it were.

The curator pinched a bit of the sticky resin between his

gloved thumb and forefinger and tugged it free. He rolled it into a tiny ball and sniffed it, bringing it dangerously close to the end of his nose.

"Not bad," he opined. "Not bad—very close. More—what is the word?—*pungent* than the Lakshadweep *nidus*, but that is to be expected. . . . But what is this? There are *fingerprints* here!" He looked across the desk at Warthrop. "Someone has touched it with his bare hands!" Then his gaze shifted to the bandaging on my left hand. "Well, of course! I might have guessed."

"I didn't touch it," I protested.

"Then, what happened to your finger?" He turned to the monstrumologist. "I am surprised and disappointed, Dr. Warthrop. Of all who desire to apprentice under you, and I know there are many, you choose a liar and a sneak."

"I did not choose him," the doctor replied, brutally honest as always.

"You should send him away to an orphanage. He's no good to you or himself. He'll get both of you killed one day."

"I shall take my chances," Warthrop returned with a wan smile. He nodded to the *nidus* between them; it was not an easy task, keeping Professor Ainesworth on track. "You'll note it is nearly identical in every aspect—well, except, perhaps, the smell, which of course I had no means to compare to the Lakshadweep *nidus*."

"Do you know he tried to bribe me!" the old man barked suddenly with a shake of his cane.

Startled, the monstrumologist asked, "Who? Who tried to—"

"Mr. P. T. Barnum! That old blackguard offered me seventeen thousand dollars for it—just to *borrow* it for six months, so he could put it on display right alongside Tom Thumb and the Feejee Mermaid!"

"The Lakshadweep *nidus?*"

"No, Warthrop, my toenail clippings! Gah! You were fairly clever once. What in heaven's name happened to you?" *Click, click, click* went the teeth of his son. "I refused, of course. Denied I even knew what he was talking about. How he heard about it, now that's a mystery. He used to chum around with that unsavory Russian monstrumologist. What was his name?"

"Sidorov," said my master. Apparently he needed to hear only the words "unsavory" and "Russian" to know the answer.

"Shish kebob? No, no—"

"Sidorov!" shouted Warthrop, his patience at last wearing thin.

"Sidorov! That's the one. Thick as thieves, those two, and they were, too—thieves, I mean. I suspect it was Sidorov who told him about the *nidus*. It was my idea, you know."

"I'm sorry, Professor. Your idea?"

"To boot him! Kick him out upon his rapacious two-faced arse!"

"Whose two-faced arse? Barnum's?"

"Sidorov's! 'He's a schemer,' I told von Helrung. 'Up to

no good. Expel him! Strip him of his credentials!' I had it on good authority Sidorov was an agent of Okhranka." Adolphus looked at me, muttonchops aquiver. "The czar's secret police. I'll wager you didn't know *that*, which is why I say monstrumology is no business for children! Really, Warthrop, you should be ashamed of yourself. If you're lonely for companionship, why don't you just get a dog? At any rate, you can hardly blame him."

"Blame . . . Will Henry?"

"The czar! If I were him, I would want a monstrumologist in *my* secret police! Anyway, that's how Barnum got wind of it, is my guess. Whatever happened to him, do you know?"

"Barnum?"

"Sidorov!"

"Back in Saint Petersburg, the last I heard," said the doctor, and then hurried on. "Professor Ainesworth, I promise you, I am no friend to Mr. P. T. Barnum or Anton Sidorov or the czar. I've come here today—"

"Without an appointment!"

"Without an appointment—"

"*And* unannounced!"

"And unannounced, yes . . . in order to entrust to your care this rare and altogether incredible addition to our— *your*—collection of extraordinary finds and irreplaceable oddities. It would, in short, be an honor if you would secure it in the Locked Room with its cousin, the Lakshadweep *nidus*, which you have so admirably protected over the years from the likes of Barnum and Sidorov and the treacherous Russian secret police."

Old Adolphus's eyes narrowed. His teeth clicked. He pursed his lips and stroked his muttonchops.

"Are you attempting to flatter me, Dr. Warthrop?"

"Shamelessly, but with all sincerity, Professor Ainesworth."

Down the narrow poorly lit halls of the Monstrumarium we followed him, past darkened chambers wherein thousands of samples and specimens, artifacts and esoterica, relating to the field of monstrumology were housed. The Monstrumarium was the premier research facility of its kind in the world, a treasure trove of rare curiosities from every continent— the kind of rare curiosities that would make a proper lady blush and a grown man faint. The facility's name literally meant the "house of monsters," and that it was. Within the Monstrumarium were enough grotesqueries to fill fifty of P. T. Barnum's sideshow tents—things that did not seem possible—or seemed possible only in our worst nightmares. Stored within those musty rooms were the things your parents told you were not real, floating in jars of formaldehyde or mummified behind thick glass, dismembered in drawers, disemboweled, flayed open, hanging from hooks, or stuffed like trophies borne back from a safari in hell.

In all the Monstrumarium there was but one locked room. It had no name; most monstrumologists simply referred to it as "the Locked Room." An irreverent wag had christened it the *Kodesh Hakodashim* ("Holy of Holies"), for here was kept that portion of the collection deemed too precious—or too dangerous—to be left unsecured. There were some things—well, as you already know, there still *are* things—that must have escaped our benevolent Creator's notice in his haste to make the world in only six days. All other explanations are simply unthinkable.

Admittance to the Locked Room was restricted to only two classes of organisms—those that posed the highest risk to human life and those fools who would pursue them.

I feel shame for saying that; I should not call the doctor a fool. Without question he was the most intelligent man I have ever met, and there are many descendants of those whose lives he saved who would argue that his life's work was considerably less than foolish. But wisdom and sacrifice were never enough for the monstrumologist. He wanted recognition, to be held in the highest esteem by his fellow man (it was the only kind of immortality in which he could bring himself to believe), but, tragically, he had chosen the wrong profession. There are those who labor in darkness that the rest of us might live in the light.

"He doesn't like you very much," I said to the monstrumologist in the cab afterward.

"Adolphus? Oh, no. He dislikes human beings as a general principle; he expects to be disappointed by them. Not an unwise position to take, Will Henry."

"Is that why he's so mean?"

"Adolphus isn't mean, Will Henry. Adolphus merely speaks plainly. The old *should* speak plainly; it is their prerogative."

Our knock upon the door of the von Helrung brownstone on Fifth Avenue was answered by the great man himself, who threw his short, thick arms around my master without preamble. The snow flitted and fussed about them with confounding complexity, a fitting metaphor for their complicated relationship.

Von Helrung was more than Pellinore Warthrop's former teacher in the dark arts of monstrumology; he was friend, surrogate father, and sometimes rival. Three months before, the conflict between them over the future of monstrumology had nearly torn their friendship asunder. If von Helrung had been a less forgiving man, the two might never have spoken again, but the master loved his pupil as a father his son. I will not say Warthrop loved him—that is a very insubstantial limb upon which to venture, indeed!—but he was fond of von Helrung, and my master had lost so much already. Discounting me (and I think the doctor probably would have), the old monstrumologist was the only friend Warthrop had left.

"Pellinore, *mein Freund*, how wonderful to see you again! And here is William, too—dear, brave Will Henry!" He pulled me into his chest and proceeded to crush the air from my lungs. Leaning over, he whispered into my ear, "Every day I pray for you, and God in his mercy must hear. But what is this?" He had noticed my bandaged hand.

"An accident," Warthrop said tersely.

"Dr. Warthrop chopped off my finger with a butcher knife."

Von Helrung's brow knotted up in confusion. "By accident?"

"No," I answered. "That part was on purpose."

The old man turned to my master, who shook his head impatiently and said, "May we go inside, von Helrung? We are quite cold and careworn, and I'd rather not talk about such things on your front stoop."

Von Helrung ushered us into the well-appointed parlor, marvelously cluttered in the Victorian style, cupboards and cabinets groaning with oddities and knickknacks, overstuffed chairs and settees and sofas, and a mantel the surface of which could not be seen for all the bric-a-brac. The doctor's tea was ready, and for me von Helrung had thoughtfully arranged for a glass of Mr. Pemberton's delightful concoction, that remarkable confection of fizzy delight called Coca-Cola. I particularly enjoyed the first sip, that tickling sensation upon the tip of my nose.

Von Helrung settled into his wingback chair, clipped off the end of a Havana cigar, and rolled it back and forth over his wide tongue.

"I shall guess the circumstances of young Will's 'accident.'"

His expression was stern; he clearly was not pleased with my master for allowing such a calamity to happen. His bright blue eyes shone beneath his bushy white eyebrows. "The child was allowed to handle your special delivery from Dr. John Kearns."

"Not precisely," replied the doctor. "The child was 'handled' by the one who handled it."

He then proceeded with the story from the beginning, the midnight call of Wymond Kendall and the astonishing gift he'd borne from England. Von Helrung did not interrupt him, though occasionally he injected an *ach!* or winced in revulsion or grew misty-eyed with wonder and pity.

"*Pwdre ser*—the rot of stars!" he said softly at the conclusion of the doctor's tale. "So the stories are true. I never quite believed them, for I did not *wish* to believe them. That the Creator of all things could create such a thing! Is it not unbearable, Pellinore, even for us, who devote our lives to this work, the import of its existence? What kind of God is this? Is he mad or is he malicious?"

"I like to refrain from burdening myself with questions that cannot be answered, *Meister* Abram. Perhaps he is neither mad nor malicious but adores all his creatures equally— or is indifferent to all equally."

"And you do not find either possibility appalling?"

"They are only appalling in the context of human arrogance. Now you are going to argue that we were given dominion over the earth and all its creatures, as if that sets us apart from the very creation to which we belong. Tell that to Wymond Kendall!"

The monstrumologist returned to the reason for our visit. He found philosophical discussions like this distasteful—not precisely beneath him, but useless in the sense that the unanswerable was a waste of his time.

"What have you learned about Jack Kearns?" he asked.

Von Helrung shook his head. "Vanished, Pellinore. His flat abandoned, his offices at the hospital cleaned out. He is gone, and no one seems to know where he might have fled."

Now Warthrop was the one shaking his head. "Impossible. He must have told someone."

"My sources assure me he did not. The hospital staff, his former patients, neighbors—they all know nothing. Or I should say, all they can say is that one day Herr Kearns was there; the next he was not. The only person he seems to have confided in is the man you immolated in your fireplace."

"Kearns didn't tell Kendall where he had obtained the *nidus*; I asked."

"And I believe him. He would not have told poor Mr. Kendall."

The doctor nodded. "That is the true prize. More valuable than the *nidus* is where it came from. How did he get hold of it? Did someone give it to him, and if so, who? And why?"

The ember of the old monstrumologist's cigar had perished. He placed the expired stogie on the ashtray beside him and spoke somberly to my master. "There is something rotten here, *mein Freund*. Kearns is no monstrumologist—he would have no *scientific* interest in *nidus ex magnificum*—but he is also no fool. He must know how valuable it is."

Warthrop nodded again. His head bobbed in counterpoint with his foot tapping nervously upon the carpet. "There is more than one bounty being offered for a *nidus*," said the doctor. "I've heard that the Ottoman sultan Abdul Hamid has a standing offer of twenty thousand ducats."

Unable to contain his ardor, the younger monstrumologist leapt to his feet and commenced to pace.

"Think of it, von Helrung. The first credible *nidus* to be found in a generation! And in pristine condition—no more than a few months old, I would guess. Do you understand what this means? We are close—closer than we have ever been." His voice fell to a whisper. "*Typhoeus magnificum*, *Meister* Abram—the Unseen One—the ultimate prize—the Holy Grail of monstrumology! And this time it may be within my grasp—"

"*Your* grasp?" interrupted von Helrung softly.

"Our grasp. I meant ours, of course."

Von Helrung nodded slowly, and I noted a sorrowful look in his eyes when he spoke.

"Many are called, dear Pellinore, but few are chosen. How many have been lost searching for our version of the Questing Beast? Do you know?"

My master waved the questions away impatiently. Von Helrung pressed on. "And how many more come back in humiliation and defeat, reputations ruined, their careers in ashes?"

"I hardly see what that matters," answered the doctor angrily. "But yes, I do happen to know. Six, counting Lebroque."

"Ah, Lebroque. I forgot about him, *armes Schwein*. And who was that talkative little Scotsman, the one with the lisp?"

"Bisset."

"*Ja, Bithet*." Von Helrung chuckled. "All arms and chest and the bluster to match!"

"A dilettante," said Warthrop dismissively. "The rest quixotic adventurers."

"But not Lebroque."

"*Especially* Lebroque. He allowed his ambition to blind him—"

"Ambition will do that," allowed von Helrung. "And worse." He rose and went to my master's side, placing a pudgy hand on his forearm and gently braking his restless pacing.

"But you are exhausting your old master. Please, Pellinore, sit so we might reason together and decide upon our course."

The doctor pulled free from the old man's grasp and said, "I already know the course. I will leave for England tomorrow."

"England?" Von Helrung was taken aback. "Why do you go to England?"

"To find Jack Kearns, of course."

"Who has vanished like the mist, leaving no trace of himself behind. How will you find him?"

"I will begin by looking under the largest rock on the continent," answered the doctor grimly.

Von Helrung chuckled. "And if he isn't there?"

"Then I shall move on to the smaller rocks."

"And once you find him—*if* you find him—what if he refuses to tell you what you want to know? Or worse, doesn't *know* what you want to know?"

"Know, know, know," Warthrop savagely mimicked. "You wish to know what I know, *Meister* Abram? I *know* Jack Kearns wanted me to have the *nidus*. He took great pains to make sure I received it quickly. He also wanted me to know he was leaving England—quickly. There can be only one explanation: He knows where the *nidus* came from. *And that is why he let it go.* There is only one thing on earth more valuable than an authentic *nidus ex magnificum*, and that is the *magnificum* itself. The *nidus* is a great prize, but the Unseen One is *the* prize, the prize of *all* prizes." Warthrop was nodding vehemently. "It is the only explanation."

"But why send anything to you at all? What was the reason for it? Surely he would want no one to know that the prize of prizes was within his grasp, least of all Pellinore Warthrop."

The doctor nodded. "It *has* been troubling me a bit. Why did he do it? The only thing that makes sense only makes sense if you know John Kearns."

Von Helrung thought for a moment. "He is taunting you?"

"I think so. In the cruelest manner possible. You know Kearns, *Meister* Abram. You know as well as I the depravities to which he will stoop."

My master then waved the thought away. He did not wish to dwell on Jack Kearns or what drove him. He was too much in the grip of his own demons.

"He is a cruel man," he said. "Some might say a monster of a man. But that is no concern of mine."

"Listen to you; listen! My former pupil! Father in heaven, forgive me for my transgressions, for I have failed you—and my dear student! Pellinore, we are men before scientists; it is the human monster we should *most* concern ourselves with!"

"Why?" the doctor said sharply. "What of monstrous men? I can't think of anything more banal. I have no doubt—no doubt whatsoever—that once it has obtained the means to do so, the species will wipe itself off the face of the earth. There is no mystery to it. It is in our nature. Oh, one might delve into the particulars, but really, what might we say about the species that *invented* murder? What *can* we say?"

Forgetting myself for a moment, I said, "You sound like him."

Warthrop whirled on me. "What did you say?"

"What you were saying . . . It sounded like something Dr. Kearns would say."

"Just because a man is a homicidal maniac doesn't make him *wrong*," the monstrumologist snarled.

"No," said von Helrung softly, his bright eyes flashing dangerously. "It merely makes him evil."

"We are scientists, von Helrung; such concepts are alien in our vocabulary. In India it is a sin to kill a cow. Are we Westerners evil for slaughtering them?"

"Human beings, *mein Freund*," replied von Helrung, "are not cows."

Warthrop did not have a ready retort for that, and he listened silently as his old friend begged him to reconsider. Rushing off to England would be premature. Kearns was gone, and, after all, the quest was not for Kearns but for the place where the *nidus* had been fashioned.

Warthrop hardly listened. He, the caged lion, might have been pacing the floor, but not so his passion—nothing could contain that.

"There are those who live their entire lives in ignorance," he shouted into the frightened face of his former mentor. "With no inkling of their purpose, who, if pressed, could not answer why they were even born. Many are called, you said. True, and most are deaf! And the majority of them are blind! I am neither. I have heard the call. I have seen the way. I am the one. *I am the one.*"

He was in the fever's full grip. It was the call of destiny— *his* destiny—the reason he had sacrificed so much, endured so much, lost so much. This was fate, to a man who did not believe in fate. This was deliverance, to a man who did not subscribe to any notion of personal salvation. This was redemption, to a man for whom the idea of redemption was a bit of useless esoterica.

Ah, Warthrop! How often you cautioned me to control my passions, lest my passions control me. What now? Do you contain the fire or does the fire contain *you?* I see it clearly now—not so much then.

Von Helrung saw it, though. Saw it and was powerless against its infernal force. In all his years as master instructor in the art of monstrumology, never had he a finer pupil— and he had taught dozens. Warthrop was his crowning achievement—a monstrumologist without compunction, a scientist without the slightest bias or qualm. And yet! Sometimes our greatest strength is also our greatest weakness: The flame that lit up Pellinore Warthrop's genius was the same inferno that drove him pell-mell toward the abyss.

Von Helrung saw that abyss, and von Helrung was afraid.

ELEVEN

"What Do You Know of My Business?"

Von Helrung, who knew where the true *Monstrum horribilis* of the case lurked, said, "The call has come, then, and you must answer, but you must not answer alone."

"Well, of course. Will Henry is coming with me."

"Of course," echoed von Helrung. His brilliant blue eyes fell upon me. "Will Henry."

"Will Henry . . . what? Do not underestimate him, von Helrung. I would trade a dozen Pierre Lebroques for one William James Henry."

"No, no, you misunderstand, Pellinore. The boy has proved indispensable to you, his father's untimely demise a tragic blessing. But your right hand, as it were, has been grievously wounded on his left—"

"He lost a finger. A finger! Why, I once had a Sherpa

who guided me across the Himalayas with his small intestines hanging out his gut—in winter!"

"There are many fine monstrumologists who would leap at the chance to—"

"Undoubtedly!" Warthrop laughed harshly. "I am certain I'd have enough volunteers to outnumber the entire *magnificum* population by ten to one. Do you think I am a complete fool?"

"I do not suggest we place an advertisement in the *Journal*, Pellinore," returned von Helrung with exaggerated patience, as a forbearing father to a wayward child. "What of Walker? He is a worthy scientist, and quintessentially British. He won't breathe a word to anyone."

"Sir Hiram—that simpleton? He's always been more concerned about advancing his own interests than those of science."

"An American, then. You always were fond of Torrance."

"True. I have a soft spot for Jacob, but he is too headstrong. And a libertine. I'd never get him out of the pubs."

"Caleb Pelt. Now come, Pellinore, I know you respect Pelt."

"I do respect Pelt. And I happen to know that Pelt is in Amazonia and is not expected back for another six months."

Von Helrung straightened, puffed out his thick chest, and said, "Then, I shall go with you."

"You?" Warthrop started to smile and caught himself when he realized the old man was deadly serious. He nodded gravely instead. "A perfect choice, if only the *nidus* had come to us fifteen years ago."

"I am not so old that I cannot handle myself in a pinch," said the Austrian stoutly. "My knees are not what they were, but my heart is strong—"

The monstrumologist laid a hand on his old friend's shoulder. "The strongest heart I have ever known, *Meister* Abram, and the truest."

"You cannot take the burden solely upon your shoulders," von Helrung pleaded with him. "Some burdens, dear Pellinore, are impossible to put down once—"

The jangling of the bell interrupted him, and caused my master to whirl toward the door in alarm.

"You are expecting someone?" he demanded.

"I am, but upon his insistence, not my invitation," replied von Helrung easily. "Do not be concerned, *mein Freund*. I have told him nothing—only that I expected you today. He wants very badly to meet you, and I am softhearted, as you know; I could not refuse."

Barely had our host cracked open the door than his caller pushed his way into the vestibule. He did not pause, not even long enough to hand his hat and gloves to von Helrung, but barreled into the parlor to practically hurl himself at the doctor.

He was young, in his early twenties, I guessed, tall, athletic of build, fashionably attired (a bit of a dandy was my first impression of him), dark of hair and lean of face. With his high, angular cheeks and sharp, slightly hooked nose, he might have been considered handsome in a patrician sort of way—the "lean and hungry look" so common among the privileged classes. He seized my master's hand and pumped it vigorously, squeezing hard enough to make Warthrop wince.

"Dr. Warthrop, I cannot begin to express my profound delight to finally meet you, sir. It is truly a . . . well, an honor, sir! I hope you'll forgive my intruding like this, but when I heard you were coming to New York, I simply could not allow the opportunity to pass!"

"Pellinore," said von Helrung. "May I introduce my new student, Thomas Arkwright, of the Long Island Arkwrights."

"Student?" Warthrop frowned. "I thought you had retired from teaching."

"Herr Arkwright is very persistent."

"It's all I've really cared about, Dr. Warthrop," said Thomas Arkwright of the Long Island Arkwrights. "Since I was no older than your son here."

"Will Henry is not my son."

"No?"

"He is my assistant."

Thomas's eyes grew wide with wonder. He appraised me with new respect.

"I don't think I've ever heard of an apprentice so young. What is he, ten?"

"Thirteen."

"Awfully small for thirteen," Thomas observed. He flashed me a quick, slightly patronizing smile. "You must be very clever, Will."

"Well," said the doctor, and then he said no more.

"I feel positively old now, terribly behind in my studies," joked Thomas. He turned to Warthrop. "I never would have applied, if I had known you already had an apprentice."

"Will Henry is not precisely my apprentice."

"No? Then, what is he?"

"He is . . ." The doctor was staring down at me. In fact, all three men were staring at me. The silence was heavy. What was I exactly to Pellinore Warthrop? I squirmed in my chair.

At last the monstrumologist shrugged and turned back to Thomas. "What did you mean when you said you never would have applied?"

"Why, to apprentice under you, Dr. Warthrop."

"It is true," admitted von Helrung. "I am not Thomas's first choice."

"I don't recall receiving your application," said my master.

Thomas seemed crestfallen. "Which one? I sent twelve."

"Really?" Warthrop was impressed.

"No, not really. Thirteen, actually. Twelve somehow sounded less desperate."

To my shock the monstrumologist laughed. It happened so seldom, I thought he had gagged on a crumpet.

"And I never answered any of them?" Warthrop turned toward me with a frown, one eyebrow arching toward his hairline. "Will Henry arranges the mail for me, and I cannot recall receiving even one from you."

"Oh. Well. Perhaps they were misplaced somehow."

Again a weighty silence slammed down. My face grew hot. In truth I did arrange the doctor's correspondence. And, in truth, I could not recall the name of Thomas Arkwright; I was certain I had never seen it before. But to protest would only convince my guardian of my guilt.

"So the saying is true, all is well that ends well," put in von Helrung at last, with a consoling pat upon my shoulder. "I have a new student, and you, Pellinore, you have your . . ." He searched for the proper description. "Will Henry," he finished, with an apologetic shrug.

Thomas begged to take his leave shortly thereafter. He'd only interrupted Dr. Warthrop to express his undying admiration; he knew the doctor had pressing business and he did not wish to delay him.

"What do you know of my business?" asked the monstrumologist sharply, with an accusatory glance toward von Helrung—*You* did *tell him!*

"I know nothing of the present matter. Professor von Helrung has been quite annoyingly coy about it," said Thomas, running to his mentor's rescue. "I know it is urgent—monstrously urgent, if I may make a play on the word. The rest of it I can only guess at. You are here in New York to entrust to Professor Ainesworth a *nidus ex magnificum*, which has recently come into your possession from overseas—England, I would guess." He shrugged apologetically. "But that is all I can guess."

Thomas Arkwright waited for the monstrumologist's reaction with a slightly smug expression, for he did not *guess* that he was correct; he *knew* he was.

"That is a remarkable 'guess,' Mr. Arkwright," said Warthrop, glowering at von Helrung. He clearly thought he had been misled and betrayed.

"Not all that remarkable," replied Thomas. "I know you have been to the Monstrumarium—that's easy. The smell floats about you like a foul perfume. And I know you went straight there from the depot, for you are still in your traveling clothes, which suggests your errand was of the utmost exigency—not a moment to lose."

"You are correct so far," allowed my master. "But that much, as you said, is easy. What of the rest?"

"Well, you didn't go to *get* something from the old man. The Monstrumarium has not been called Fort Adolphus for nothing. You must have *brought* something—and not just any something, but a something that could not sit even for a moment in your hotel untended, being too large a something to secure upon your person. In other words, a very special something, a something so rare and valuable you had to secure it at once, without delay."

Clearly intrigued, the doctor nodded quickly and flicked his finger at him, a gesture he had given me innumerable times—*Go on, go on!*

"So it is quite rare, this prize you brought—*extremely* rare, and that leaves but a handful of monstrumological curiosities. And out of that handful only one or two might compel a scientist of your stature to drop everything and rush straight to the Monstrumarium after a long journey by stage and rail. *Nidus ex magnificum* is the obvious choice and, since no *nidus* has ever been discovered in the New World, in all likelihood it came from Europe—"

"Hah!" cried the monstrumologist, holding up his hand. "The scaffold of your reasoning grows unsteady, Mr. Arkwright. Why would you assume my special something came from Europe, since the only authenticated something comes from the Lakshadweep Islands in the Indian Ocean?"

"Because I know you too well—or *of* you too well, I should say. If you knew the origin of the something, you would not be in New York. You would have sent the something to Dr. von Helrung to place in the Locked Room, and been on the first boat out."

"Why England, though?"

"England is a guess, I will admit that. I passed on France. The French contingent of the Society has never cared much for us Yanks—less so after that unfortunate incident last fall involving Monsieur Gravois, for which, I hear, they blame you, unfairly in my opinion. The Germans would *never* trust a *nidus* to an American—even if his name is Pellinore Warthrop. The Italians—well, they *are* Italians. England was the most logical choice."

"Extraordinary," murmured Warthrop with an appreciative nod. "Truly extraordinary, Mr. Arkwright! And precisely right in all details; I shan't mislead you." He turned to von Helrung. "My congratulations, *Meister* Abram. My loss seems to be your gain."

The Austrian monstrumologist smiled broadly. "He reminds me of another promising student from many years ago. I confess in my dotage I sometimes forget myself and call him Pellinore."

"Oh, I hope not!" said my master with uncharacteristic humility. "I wouldn't wish that upon anyone—or the world. One is enough!"

Thomas did not take his leave until the doctor and I departed for our hotel; I suppose he forgot in the excitement of the moment his humble desire not to delay the great man in his important scientific pursuits. The great man himself seemed to forget the pressing matters before him, utterly absorbed in a conversation that revolved entirely around him or that singular extension of himself called monstrumology.

And Arkwright appeared to be an expert on both. With alacrity he demonstrated an encyclopedic knowledge of all things Warthropian—his sickly childhood in New England; the "lost years" in the London boarding school; his tutelage under von Helrung; his early adventures in Amazonia, the Congo, and "that ill-fated expedition to Sumatra"; his invaluable contributions to the *Encyclopedia*

Bestia (more than a third of the articles were written or cowritten by Warthrop); his championing of the cause to the broader world of the natural sciences. The monstrumologist drank deep the sycophantic draft until he was positively drunk. It had taken thirty-odd years, but at last it appeared he had met someone who admired Pellinore Warthrop as much as he did.

Indeed, the atmosphere in the room was so saturated with Warthrop that I found it difficult to breathe. Von Helrung noticed my discomfort and proposed, sotto voce, a foray into the kitchen for a raid on the pantry. I gladly accepted the commission, and we charged the larder, conquering two platefuls of sweet pastries and two steaming cups of hot chocolate.

"He is very bright," said von Helrung, meaning Thomas Arkwright. "But one can look into the sun for only a moment, and then . . . blindness! Frequent respites are called for, but you must know what I mean, Will. Pellinore is the same."

I nodded slowly, avoiding his gaze. He understood at once, and said quietly and with great compassion, "It is hard, I know, to serve him. Men like Pellinore Warthrop—one must exercise the utmost caution or be subsumed by their brilliance. The fate of your father, I'm afraid. In the presence of men like Warthrop, the lesser light is consumed by the greater."

"How does Thomas know so much about him?" I asked. In the space of a half hour, I had learned more about the monstrumologist from a stranger than I had after two years of living with him.

"From me primarily. The rest from any and all who will talk about him."

"Well, he doesn't know everything about him," I said. "He didn't know the doctor already had an apprentice."

"Yes, that did strike me as strange. He *does* know; I told him upon our first meeting a fortnight ago. Perhaps he forgot."

"Or he's lying."

"Is this wise, Will? Given the choice, should we not always choose the good motive over the bad? It probably wasn't important to him, so he forgot." Not important to him! I pushed my plate away; I had lost my appetite.

"No, no, eat, eat!" he said, sliding the plate back. "You are far too slight for a boy of ten."

"I'm thirteen," I reminded him.

"Then you are *much* too thin. A growing boy is like an army, *ja?* He travels upon his stomach! I must speak to Pellinore about it. I do not imagine he cooks very much."

"He doesn't cook at all. We used to have a cook," I added, "but the doctor fired her. She boiled one of his specimens."

It was true. A delivery had arrived at the kitchen door the night before he sacked her, and the cook, a kindly old woman named Paulina, who was nearly blind (Warthrop considered this deficiency a plus), had mistaken it for an order she had placed with Mr. Noonan the butcher. That evening we unknowingly dined upon the carcass of the rare *Hallux turpis* of Cappadocia, which Paulina had transformed into a hearty stew. The doctor fired her, of course, the moment he realized, to his horror, that he had consumed one of monstrumology's most sought after prizes. Afterward, after he had calmed down, he acknowledged that it wasn't a total loss to science. We had discovered that *Hallux turpis* tasted remarkably like chicken.

"I do everything for him," I said with an uncomfortable knot of pride and resentment in my heart. "All the cooking and cleaning, and the washing, and I write his letters and run the errands and keep his files, and take care of the horses, of course, and assist him in the laboratory—that too. Especially that."

"Well! I am surprised you have time for your studies."

"My studies, sir?"

"You do not go to school?"

"Not since I came to him."

"Then, he tutors you, yes? He must tutor you. No?"

I shook my head. "No, I don't think so."

"You don't think so!" He clucked in disapproval.

"He doesn't sit me down with books and pencils and teach me lessons—nothing like that. But he does try to teach me things."

"Things? What things does he try to teach you, Will? What have you learned from him?"

"I've learned . . ." What had I learned? My mind went blank. What had the monstrumologist taught me? "I've learned that half the world prays they will be given what they deserve, and the other half that they will not."

"*Mein Gott!*" cried my teacher's former teacher. "I do not know whether to laugh or cry at your answer! But that is the way of truth."

He went to the stove and returned with the pot of hot chocolate, topped off my cup, and then filled his to the brim, lowering his nose close to the mud-colored surface to breathe in the aroma; the steam painted his cheeks rosy. He looked at me through the steam, and smiled.

"I love chocolate. Don't you?"

For the briefest of moments, I wanted to throw my arms around him and hug him tight.

"Dr. von Helrung, sir?"

"*Ja?*"

I lowered my voice. I did not think about it; it seemed appropriate somehow. "What is *Typhoeus magnificum?*"

His smile disappeared. He pushed his cup away and folded his hands on the tabletop. I had the sense of the space shrinking between us, until I was but a hairsbreadth from his transcendent visage.

"That is hard to say—very hard. Only his victims have seen him, and, forever mute, they keep his secrets.

"We know he lives, for we have held the *nidus* in our

hands, and we've seen—*you* have seen, ah, too much!—the victims of his terrible venom. But his form is hidden from us. There are stories . . . that he stands twenty feet tall, that his teeth are mobile like a spider's, which he uses to fashion his ungodly nest, that he swoops down from the blackest sky borne on wings ten feet across to snatch his prey, carrying them past the highest clouds to rip them apart, and the leavings fall back to earth in a rain of blood and spit, what is called the *pwdre ser*, the rot of stars." He shuddered violently and breathed deep the soothing scent rising from his mug.

"It sounds like a dragon," I said.

"*Ja*, that is one of his faces; he has many more, as many as there are those who have suffered his wrath. And so we call him the Faceless One and the One of a Thousand Faces.

"We are the sons of Adam. It is in our nature to turn and face the faceless, to name the nameless thing. It drives us to greatness; it brings us to ruin. I only pray Pellinore understands this. Many brave men have sought it, all have failed, and now I do not know what I fear more—that the dragon will go unseen or that Pellinore will find it."

"Why is it so hard to find, though?" I asked.

"Perhaps it is like the devil himself—never seen, always there!" He laughed softly, breaking the somber spell. "The world is large, dear Will, and we, no matter how much we would like to pretend otherwise, we are quite small."

TWELVE

"The Most Terrifying Monster of All"

"Will Henry, you're quiet tonight—even for you," observed my master in the cab ride back to the Plaza.

"I'm sorry, sir."

"Sorry for what?"

"For being quiet."

"It wasn't a criticism, Will Henry. It was merely an observation."

"I'm tired, I suppose."

"That is not something one supposes. Are you tired or are you not?"

"I am tired."

"Then, say so."

"I just said so."

"You don't strike me as tired. More like angry." He

turned away. His angular profile flitted in and out of shadow as we rattled down the granite street. The fresh snowdrifts glittered diamond-bright in the glow of the arc lights lining Fifth Avenue.

"It's Mr. Arkwright, isn't it?" he asked. On those infrequent moments when the monstrumologist decided to take actual note of my existence, he missed very little.

"Dr. Warthrop, he lied to you."

"What do you mean?" He turned from the window. Light and shadow warred upon the landscape of his face.

"He knew you had an apprentice. Dr. von Helrung told him."

"Well, he must have forgotten."

"And he never applied to you. I would have seen the letters."

"Perhaps you did."

The implication that I was lying could not have hurt more than if he had physically struck me.

"I am not making an accusation," he went on. "I just don't know why Mr. Arkwright would lie about it. To me, more striking than his mental acuity—which is truly extraordinary—is his sincerity. Truly a remarkable young man, Will Henry. He will make a fine addition to our ranks one day. There is very little of import that escapes his notice."

"He forgot you already had an apprentice," I pointed out, not without a note of triumph.

"As I said, *of import*—" He stopped himself and took

a deep breath. "Anyway, I'm surprised to hear you use the word 'apprentice.' I was under the impression you detested monstrumology."

"I don't detest it."

"So you love it?"

"I know how important it is to you, Dr. Warthrop, so I . . ."

"Ah, I see. It is not monstrumology you love, then." He considered the white world outside the cab. The wheels crunched in the newly fallen snow. The snap of our driver's whip was muffled in the hard wind coming over the East River.

"Oh, Will Henry," he cried softly. "I should never have taken you in. It was not what either of us desired. I should have known little good would come of it."

"Don't say that, sir. Please don't say that." I reached over to touch his arm with my wounded hand, and then withdrew. I did not think he would approve of my touching him.

"Oh, no," he said. "It is an unfortunate habit of mine to say things that probably shouldn't be said. Little good can come of this, Will Henry; I have known it for quite some time. What I do will kill me one day, and you will be abandoned again. Or worse, what I love will kill—"

His gaze fell to my left hand, and then he continued. "I am a philosopher in the natural sciences. Matters of the heart I leave to the poets, but it has occurred to me, as a failed poet myself, that the cruelest aspect of love is its inviolable integrity. We do not *choose* to love—or I should say, we cannot choose *not* to love. Do you understand?"

He leaned very close to me, and my world became the dark fire burning in his eyes. I was overcome with dizziness, as if I teetered on the very edge of a lightless abyss.

"I shall put it this way," he said. "If we monstrumologists were serious at all about our vocation, we would give up the study of biological aberrations to concentrate on the most terrifying monster of all."

In my dream I am standing before the Locked Room in the Monstrumarium with Adolphus Ainesworth, and he is fumbling with his keys.

The doctor said you'd want to see this.

But I'm not allowed.

The doctor said.

He unlocks the door, and I follow him inside.

Now, let's see . . . Where did I put it? Ah, yes. Here it is!

He's pulling a container the size of a shoe box from its niche, setting it upon a table.

Go on, open it! He wanted you to see.

My fingers are trembling. The lid doesn't want to come off. Is the box quivering, or is it my hand?

I can't open it.

There is something in the box. It is alive. It vibrates against my fingers.

Thickheaded boy! You can't open it because you're asleep!

You want to know what's in the box, you have to wake up. Wake up, Will Henry, wake up!

I did as he commanded, breaking the surface between my dream and the dark room with a startled cry, my heart racing in panic; for a moment I could not remember where I was—could not remember *who* I was . . . until a voice beside the bed reminded me.

"Will Henry."

"Dr. Warthrop?"

"You were dreaming, I think."

"Yes . . . I was."

The light in the hall was on; it was the only light. It streamed across the floor and up the wall beside the bed. The monstrumologist stood on the side opposite the light.

"What was your dream?" he asked.

I shook my head. "I—I don't remember."

"'Between the sleeping and the waking, it is there. . . . Between the rising and resting, it is there. . . . It is always there.'"

There was the bar of light on the floor and the column of light on the wall, but the bar and the column bled their substance into the room; I could see his face dimly, but I could not read his eyes.

"Is that from a poem?" I asked.

"From a very anemic attempt at one, yes."

"You wrote it, didn't you?"

His hand rose, fell. "How is your hand?"

"It doesn't hurt."

"Will Henry," he gently chided.

"Sometimes it throbs a little."

"You must hold it above your heart."

I tried it. "Yes, sir. It does help. Thank you."

"Do you still feel it? As if the finger were still there?"

"Sometimes."

"I had no choice."

"I know."

"The risk was . . . unacceptable."

He sat on the edge of the bed. More light upon his face, nothing more illuminated. Why had he been standing in the dark, watching me?

"You do not know this, of course. But afterward I took the rope, and I was going to tie you up—only as a precaution . . ."

I opened my mouth to say, *I know. I saw you.* But he held up his finger to stop me.

"I couldn't do it. It was the wise thing to do, but I couldn't do it."

He looked away; he would not look at me.

"But I was very tired. I had not slept in . . . how long? I didn't know. I was afraid I would fall asleep and you might . . . slip away. So I tied the other end of the rope to my arm. I bound you to me, Will Henry. As a precaution; it seemed the prudent thing to do."

He was flexing his long fingers, curling them into fists, uncurling them. Fist. Open hand. Fist. Open hand.

"But it wasn't. It was absolutely the worst thing to do.

Perhaps the stupidest thing I have ever done. For if you did slip away, you would have dragged me into the abyss with you."

Fist. Open hand. Fist.

"I may not have the poet's gift for words, Will Henry, but I do have his love of irony. Until that night our roles had been reversed. Until that night it had not been me who'd been bound and by virtue of those bindings been in danger of being dragged into the abyss."

He reached down and slowly unwound the wrappings on my wounded hand. My skin tingled; the air seemed very cold against the exposed flesh.

"Make a fist," he said.

I complied, though my fingers were very stiff; the muscles along the back of my hand seemed to groan in protest.

"Here." He picked up his teacup from the table beside the bed. "Take the cup. Drink."

My hand was shaking; a drop plopped upon the covers as I brought the cup, shaking, to my lips.

"Good."

He took the cup with his right hand and held out his left.

"Take my hand."

I pressed my palm into his. My whole body was trembling now. This man whose every nuance I could instinctively read had become a cipher.

The doctor said you'd want to see this.

"Squeeze. Squeeze my hand, Will Henry. Harder. As hard as you can."

He smiled. He seemed pleased.

"There. Do you see?" Holding my hand tight. "Part of it's gone, but it's still your hand."

The monstrumologist released me and stood up, and my fingers ached from his grip.

"Go back to sleep, Will Henry. You need your rest."

"So do you, sir."

"It is not your place to worry about me."

He strode to the doorway, into the bar of light, and his shadow stretched across the floor and climbed up the wall. I lay back and closed my eyes. Two breaths, three, four, and then slowly opened them again, but not very much, just enough to peek.

He had not moved from the doorway. He had not left me. Not yet.

My hand throbbed; his hold had been strong. I felt a maddening itch where my index finger should have been. I flexed my thumb into empty space to scratch it.

FOLIO VIII
Exile

PARTING IS ALL WE KNOW OF HEAVEN,
AND ALL WE NEED OF HELL.
—EMILY DICKINSON

THIRTEEN

"The Space Between Us"

Warthrop had booked out passage for the next morning on the SS *City of New York*, the swiftest ship in the Inman Line. As first-class passengers we could expect to endure the most trying of passages—subsisting in a private suite comprising a bedroom and separate sitting room, decorated in the most gaudy of Victorian excesses, with hot and cold running water and electric lighting; forced to take our evening meals at tables shabbily draped in crisp white linen and decorated with crystal vases laden with fresh flowers every evening, under the great glass dome of the first-class dining saloon; trapped for hours in the walnut-paneled library with its eight hundred volumes; or being constantly pestered by the obsessively attentive staff and crew, white-jacketed and always, according to the doctor, at your elbow, ever eager to deliver the most mundane of services.

"Think of it, Will Henry," he had said in our rooms at the Plaza, before bidding me a good night for the first time, before I'd dreamed of the Locked Room and the box, before his shadow had hung on the wall.

"It took our forebears more than two months to cross the Atlantic, two months of deprivation and disease, scurvy, dysentery, dehydration. It shall take us less than a week, in regal splendor. The world is shrinking, Will Henry, and by no miracle, unless we alter our definition of what makes a miracle."

His eyes had been misty, his tone wistful. "The world grows smaller, and little by little the light of our lamps chases away the shadows. All shall be illuminated one day, and we will wake with a new question: 'Yes, *this*, but now ... *what?*'" He laughed softly. "Perhaps we should turn back and go home."

"Sir?"

"It will be a seminal moment in the history of science, Will Henry, the finding of the *magnificum*, and not without some ancillary benefit to me personally. If I succeed, it will bring nothing short of immortality—well, the only concept of immortality that I am prepared to accept. But if I do succeed, the space between us and the ineffable will shrink a little more. It is what we strive for as scientists, and what we dread as human beings. There is something in us that longs for the indescribable, the unattainable, the thing that cannot be seen."

And then he fell silent.

And the next morning he was gone.

Something was wrong; I knew it the moment I woke. I understood instantly—not in the trivial sense, not intellectually, but with my heart. Nothing had changed. There was the bed in which I lay and the chair in which he'd sat watching me and the large dressing table and the wardrobe and even his teacup on the table. Nothing had changed; everything had changed. I jumped from the bed and raced down the hall into the empty sitting room. Nothing had changed; everything had changed. I stepped over to the windows and threw back the curtains. Eight stories below, Central Park glistened, a white landscape ablaze in sunlight beneath a cloudless sky.

His trunk. His valise. His field case. I ran to the closet and yanked open the door. Empty.

Everything had changed.

I was getting dressed when the knock came. I would have been dressed already, but I was having trouble with the buttons on my trousers. I'd never realized how helpful my finger had been in the procedure. For one irrational moment I was sure the doctor had returned to fetch me.

Ah, good. You're up. I went downstairs for some breakfast before we board. What is it, Will Henry? Did you really think I would leave without you?

Or, what was more likely:

Snap to, Will Henry! What the devil are you doing? Why

is your fly hanging open like that? Come along, Will Henry. I will not miss the most important crossing of my life on account of a thirteen-year-old's inability to dress himself! Snap to, Will Henry, snap to!

It was not the doctor, though. You have deduced that by now.

"*Guten Morgen*, Will! I am sorry to be so late, but my carriage dropped an axle, and my driver—he is a *Dummkopf*. He couldn't fix a broken smile. I would fire him, but he has a family, which unfortunately is part of *my* family, being a third or fourth cousin, I cannot remember—"

"Where is Dr. Warthrop?" I demanded.

"Where is Warthrop? What, did he not tell you? Surely he told you."

I grabbed my coat and muffler from the rack, and the hat he had given me—the only thing he'd ever given me.

"Take me to him."

"I cannot, Will."

"I am going with the doctor."

"He is not here—"

"I know he isn't here! That's why you're taking me to him!"

"No, no, he is not *here*, Will. His ship departed an hour ago."

I stared up into von Helrung's kind face, and then punched him as hard as I could in his round belly. He grunted softly from the punch.

"I thought he told you," he gasped.

"Take me," I said.

"Take you where?"

"To the docks; I must go with him."

He leaned over, placing his square, pudgy hands upon my shoulders and looking deeply into my eyes.

"He has left for England, Will. The ship is not there."

"Then, I will take the next ship!" I shouted. I pulled free from his grasp and pushed past him, into the hall, throwing my muffler round my neck, yanking on my hat, fumbling with the buttons of my coat. The floor vibrated with the heaviness of his tread as he followed me to the elevator, where he caught up with me.

"Come, *Kleiner*. I will take you home."

"I don't want you to take me home; my place is with him."

"He would have you safe—"

"I don't want to be safe!"

"And he charged me with your safety until he returns. Will. Pellinore has left, and where he has gone you cannot follow."

I shook my head. I was confounded to the core of my being. The sun vanishes in the wink of an eye and the universe collapses; the center cannot hold. I searched for the answer in his kindly eyes.

"He went without me?" I whispered.

"Do not worry, dear Will. He will come back for you. You are all he has."

"Then, why did he leave me behind? Now he doesn't have anyone."

"Oh, no; do you think his *Meister* Abram would allow such a thing? *Nein!* Thomas is with him."

I was speechless. Thomas Arkwright! It was too much. I remembered the doctor's words in the cab the night before: *Truly a remarkable young man, Will Henry. He will make a fine addition to our ranks one day.* That day, it seemed, had come . . . at my expense. I had been discarded—and for what? What had I done?

Von Helrung was pressing my face against his chest. His vest smelled of cigar smoke.

"I am sorry, Will," he murmured. "He should have at least told you good-bye."

It is not your place to worry about me.

"He did," I answered. "But I didn't hear him."

And after this my exile.

"Here, this will be your room, and you see, it is a very comfortable bed, much larger than the bed you're used to, I'll wager. And look, here is a nice chair for you to sit in by the fireplace, very cozy, and a lamp for you to read by, and here is the chest for your clothes. And look out there, Will. There is Fifth Avenue, such hustle and bustle and the goings on and doings. Here, look at that man on the bicycle! He's going to hit that truck! Now, you must be hungry. What would you like? Here, let's put your bag on the bed. Would you like to sit on the bed? It has a feather mattress and feather pillows; it is very soft. So you are hungry, *ja?* My chef is excellent, from France—doesn't understand a word of English—or German—but he understands food!"

"I'm not hungry."

"But you must be. Why don't you put down your bag? I will send up your food. You can eat here, by the little fire. I thought later I would show you the library."

"I don't want to read anything."

"You're right. It's too fine a day to sit inside. Perhaps the park later, *ja*? Or we could—"

"Why did the doctor take Arkwright with him?"

"Why? Well, for the obvious reasons. Arkwright is young and very strong and quite clever." He changed the subject. "But come, you *must* eat. You're withered halfway down to nothing, Will."

"I'm not hungry," I said again. "I don't want to eat or read or go to the park or anything else. Why did you let him go without me?"

"One does not 'let' Pellinore Warthrop do anything, Will. Your master, he does all the 'letting.'"

"You could have stopped Mr. Arkwright from going."

"But I wanted him to go. I could not allow Pellinore to go alone."

It was absolutely the worst thing he could have said, and he knew it.

"I will go now," he said meekly. "But I expect you downstairs for lunch. I will instruct François to whip up something extra special for you, *très magnifique!*"

Von Helrung hurried from the room. I dropped my carpetbag onto the floor, lay down face-first upon the bed, and willed myself to die.

It did not take long for my shock at being cast aside to change to shame (*Arkwright is young and very strong and quite clever*), or shame to confusion (*Do not underestimate him, von Helrung. I would trade a dozen Pierre Lebroques for one William James Henry*), and then harden into a white-hot ember of rage. Sneaking off like that without a word of explanation, without even a farewell—fond or otherwise! The bravest man I'd ever known, a coward! How dare he, after all we'd suffered together, after my saving his life more than once. *You are the one thing that keeps me human.* Yes, I suppose I am, Dr. Warthrop, until you find someone to keep you human in my place. It dumbfounded me; it shook me to the foundations of my being. It did not matter that he had promised to return for me. He had left me; that's what mattered.

Too much time had passed. I'd been too long with him. For two years he had bound me to him, a mote of dust caught in his Jovian gravity. I didn't even know what the world looked like without the Warthropian lenses through which to view it. Now they were gone, and I was blind.

"We shall see how Mr. Arkwright likes it," I told myself with bitter satisfaction. "'Snap to, Mr. Arkwright! Snap *to!*' Let's see how he likes being laughed at and scolded and mocked and ordered around like a coolie. Have at it, Mr. Arkwright, and welcome to it!"

I refused to eat. I could not sleep. All of von Helrung's efforts to coax me out of the room failed. I sat in the chair by the fireplace and sulked like Achilles in his tent, while the war of day-to-day life raged on without me. On the evening of the third day von Helrung shuffled in bearing a tray of hot chocolate and pastries and a chessboard.

"We will have a nice game of chess, *ja*? Now, do not tell me Pellinore failed to teach you. I know him better."

He had. Chess was one of the monstrumologist's favorite diversions. And, like many who excelled at the game, he never seemed to tire of utterly humiliating his opponent—that is, me. In the first year of our tenancy together, he wasted more than a few hours trying to instruct me in the finer aspects of strategy, attack, counterattack, and defense. I never bested him, not once. He might have chosen generosity over ruthlessness and allowed me to win a game or two, to build up my confidence, but the doctor never had much interest in building up anything in me other than a strong stomach. Besides, destroying an eleven-year-old boy in six moves—in a game he had been playing longer than the boy had been alive—lifted his spirits, like a fine wine at dinner.

"I don't feel like playing."

He was setting up the board. It was a set made from jade, the pieces carved into the shapes of dragons. The dragon king and queen wore crowns. The dragon bishops clutched shepherd crooks in their talons.

"Oh, no, no. We shall play. I shall teach you as I taught Pellinore. Better, so you can beat him when he comes back." He was humming happily under his breath.

I hurled the board against the wall. Von Helrung gave a soft cry, mewling as he picked up the dragon king, who had lost his crown; it had broken off when the piece had hit the floor.

"Dr. von Helrung . . . I'm sorry . . ."

"No, no," he said. "It is nothing. A gift from my dear wife, may her sleep go undisturbed." He snuffled. Not knowing how to comfort him, and feeling mortified by my childishness, I awkwardly dropped my hand upon his shoulder.

"I worry too, Will," he confessed. "The days ahead will be dangerous for him, and dark. Remember that when the tide of self-pity threatens to overwhelm you."

"I know that," I replied. "It's why I should be with him. He doesn't need me to cook or clean or take his dictation or care for his horse or any of that. Those things anyone can do, Dr. von Helrung. He needs me for the dark places."

On the morning of the seventh day, a telegram arrived from London:

ARRIVED SAFE. WILL ADVISE. PXW.

"Four words?" von Helrung moaned. "That is all he has to say?"

"An overseas cable costs a dollar a word," I told him. "The doctor is very stingy."

Von Helrung, who was not nearly as wealthy as my master, or as penny-pinching, returned this reply:

REPORT AT ONCE ANY FINDINGS.
HAVE YOU MET WITH WALKER?
ANXIOUSLY AWAITING YOUR REPLY.

That reply was long—very long—in coming.

After two weeks had passed with no discernible improvement in my condition, von Helrung summoned his personal physician, a Dr. John Seward, to have a look at me. For an hour I was poked and prodded, thumped and pinched. I had no fever. My heart and lungs sounded good. My eyes were clear.

"Well, he's underweight, but he is small for his age," Seward told von Helrung. "He could also use a good dentist. I've seen cleaner teeth on a goat."

"I worry, John. He's eaten little and slept less since he came."

"Can't sleep, hmmm? I'll mix up something to help." He was staring at my left hand. "What happened to your finger?"

"Doctor Pellinore Warthrop chopped it off with a butcher knife," I replied.

"Really? And why would he do that?"

"The risk was unacceptable."

"Gangrene?"

"*Pwdre ser.*"

Baffled, Seward looked at von Helrung, who laughed nervously and waved his hand in a vague circle.

"Oh, the children, *ja?* So robust, their imaginations!"

"He cut it off and put it in a jar," I said, as von Helrung, standing slightly behind Seward, violently shook his head.

"Did he? And why did he do that?" Seward asked.

"He wants to study it."

"Couldn't he have done that when it was still attached to your hand?"

"My father was a farmer," von Helrung announced loudly. "And one day a cow would get sick, she would lie down, and no coaxing would bring her back up. 'There is nothing to be done, Abram,' my father would tell me. 'When an animal gives up like that, it has lost its will to live.'"

"Is that it?" Seward asked me. "Have you lost your will to live?"

"I live here. I don't want to be here. Is that the same thing?"

"It could be melancholia," surmised the young doctor. "Depression. That would account for the loss of appetite and the insomnia." He turned to me. "Do you ever have thoughts of killing yourself?"

"No. Other people sometimes."

"Really?"

"No, not really," von Helrung put in. *Nein!*

"And I have."

"You have . . ."

"Killed other people. I killed a man named John Chanler. He was the doctor's best friend."

"You don't say!"

"I do not think that he did!" von Helrung barked in a voice just shy of a shout. "He has bad dreams. Very bad dreams. Terrible nightmares. Ach! He is talking about the dreams. Aren't you, Will?"

I lowered my eyes and said nothing.

"Well, I can't find anything physically wrong with him, Abram. You may want to consult an alienist."

"To confess, I have been thinking of bringing in an expert in the field."

The "expert" arrived at the Fifth Avenue brownstone the following afternoon—a soft knock on the door, and then von Helrung poked his mane of white hair into the room, saying over his shoulder to someone in the hall, "*Gut*, he is presentable."

I heard a woman's voice next. "Well, I should hope so! You did tell him I was coming, didn't you?"

He stepped lightly to one side, and in charged a dynamo draped in lavender, wearing a fashionable bonnet and carrying a matching umbrella.

"So this is William James Henry," she said in a refined East Coast accent. "How do you do?"

"Will, may I present my niece, Mrs. Nathaniel Bates," said von Helrung.

"Bates?" I repeated. I knew that name.

"Mrs. Bates, if you please," she said. "William, I have heard so much about you, I cannot help but feel we've known each other for years. But stand up and let me get a look at you."

She took my wrists into her gloved hands and held my arms out from my sides, and puckered her lips in disapproval.

"*Much* too thin—and how old is he, Uncle? Twelve?"

"Thirteen."

"Hmmm. *And* short for his age. Stunted growth for lack of proper nutrition, I would say." She squinted down her nose at my face. She had bright blue eyes like her uncle's. And, like his, they seemed to shine by their own soulful light, insightful, a bit wistful, kind.

"I would not speak ill of any *gentleman*," she said. "But I am not impressed with the rearing abilities of Dr. Pellinore Warthrop. Uncle, when was the last time this child had a bath?"

"I don't know. Will, how long has it been since you've bathed?"

"I don't know," I answered.

"Well, here is the problem as I see it, William, and that is, if one cannot remember the last time one had a bath, it is probably time to take one. What is your opinion?"

"I don't want to take a bath."

"That is a desire, not an opinion. Where are your things? Uncle Abram, where are the boy's belongings?"

"I don't understand," I said to von Helrung, somewhat pleadingly.

"Emily has generously proffered an invitation for you to stay with her family for a few days, Will."

"But I—I don't want to spend a few days with her family. I want to stay here with you."

"That is not going so well, though, is it?" Emily Bates asked.

"I'll eat. I promise. I promise to try. And Dr. Seward, he gave me something to help me sleep. Please."

"William, Uncle Abram is many things—some of them wonderful and some I would rather not think about—but he hasn't the first idea how to raise a child."

"But that's what I'm used to," I argued. "And no one is going to raise me. No one has to. The doctor will be coming back soon and—"

"Yes, and when he does, we will give you back, safe and sound and *clean*. Come along now, William. Bring whatever you have; I'm sure it isn't much, but that can be remedied too. I will wait for you downstairs. It's very warm in here, isn't it?"

"I'll walk you down," von Helrung offered. He seemed anxious to remove himself from my presence.

"No, that's all right. Good-bye, Uncle Abram." She kissed both his cheeks, adding, "You've done the right thing."

"Oh, I pray so," he murmured.

And then we were alone.

"I will explain . . . ," he began, and then shrugged. "She is right. I know nothing about children."

"I'm not going."

"Your . . . situation demands a woman's touch, Will. You've been without one for far too long."

"That isn't my fault."

His eyes flashed. For the first time he lost patience with me. "I do not speak of fault or blame. I speak of remedy. True, I pledged to Pellinore I would watch after you in his absence, but I have other responsibilities that I can no longer neglect." He puffed out his chest. "I am president of the Society for the Advancement of the Science of Monstrumology, not a nursemaid!"

He saw my expression at this hurtful remark, and his softened immediately. He placed his hands on my shoulders.

"Of course you will be the first to know should I hear anything from Europe. The first to know, the moment I know it."

"I don't want to go," I said. "I don't want to leave you. I don't want to stay with your niece's family, and I don't—I don't want a bath."

He smiled. "You will like her, I think. Her heart is fierce, like someone else's you know."

FOURTEEN

'The Thing That Cannot Be Seen'

And so it was in the winter of my thirteenth year that I came to live with Nathaniel Bates and his family, in their three-story townhouse facing the Hudson on the Upper West Side of Manhattan. Nathaniel Bates was "in finance." I didn't learn much of anything else about him during my sojourn there. He was a quiet man who smoked a pipe and was never seen without a tie and never went outside without his hat, and whose shoes were always polished to a dazzling finish and who never had a hair out of place, and he always seemed to have a newspaper tucked under his arm, though I never saw him read one. He communicated, as far as I could tell, by means of monosyllabic grunts, facial expressions (a look over his pince-nez with his right eyebrow raised meant he was displeased, for example), and the occasional bon mot, delivered with such deadpan sincerity that one always laughed at one's own peril.

Besides their daughter, the Bateses had one other child, a boy of nine named Reginald, whom they called Reggie. Reggie was small for his age, spoke with a slight lisp, and seemed completely enthralled with me from the moment I stepped through the door. My reputation, it seemed, had preceded me.

"You're Will Henry," he announced. "The monster hunter!"

"No," I answered honestly. "But I serve under one."

"Pellinore Warthrop! The most famous monster hunter in the world."

I agreed that he was. Reggie was squinting at me through his thick spectacles, his face lit up by the great man's glow reflecting off me.

"What happened to your finger? Did a monster bite it off?"

"You could say that."

"And then you killed it, right? You chopped off its head!"

"That's close," I answered. "Dr. Warthrop shot it in the head."

I thought he might faint from excitement.

"I want to be a monster hunter too, Will. Will you train me?"

"I don't think so."

Reggie waited until his mother turned her back, and then he kicked me as hard as he could in the shin.

Their daughter I had already met.

"So here you are, and Mother was right, you've lost a finger," said Lillian Bates. I'd just finished my bath—the first in weeks—and my skin felt too loose on my bones, and my scalp burned from the lye. The robe I wore was her father's and I was lost in it, overly warm, dizzy, and extremely sleepy.

For her part Lilly seemed taller, thinner, and not in the least uncomfortable in her own skin. It had been only a few months since I'd last seen her, but a girl matures faster than her male counterparts. I noticed she had started wearing makeup.

"How did you lose your finger?" she asked.

"Pruning the rosebushes," I answered.

"Do you lie because you're ashamed, or do you lie because you think it's funny?"

"Neither. I lie because the truth is painful."

"Mother says your doctor left you."

"He's coming back."

She crinkled her nose at me. "When?"

"Not soon enough."

"Mother says you may be staying with us for a long time."

"I can't."

"You will, if Mother says. Mother always gets her way." She did not seem particularly happy about the fact. "I believe you are her new project. She always has a *project*. Mother is a firm believer in causes. She is a suffragette. Did you know that?"

"I don't even know what a suffragette is."

She laughed, a tinkling of bright, shiny coins thrown upon a silver tray. "You never were very bright."

"And you were never very nice."

"Mother didn't say where your Dr. Warthrop went."

"She doesn't know."

"Do *you* know?"

"I wouldn't tell you if I did."

"Even if I kissed you?"

"*Especially* if you kissed me."

"Well, I have no intention of kissing you."

"And I have no intention of telling you anything."

"So you *do* know!" She smiled triumphantly at me. "Liar." And then she kissed me anyway.

"It is a pity, William James Henry" she said, "that you are altogether too young, too timid, and too *short*, or I might consider you attractive."

Lilly's faith was not misplaced. I was her mother, Emily's, next project. After a restless, unendurably long night in the same room as Reggie, who pestered me with questions and entreaties for monster stories, and who exhibited an alarming disposition toward midnight flatulence, Mrs. Bates bundled me up and trotted me to the barber's. Then she took me to the clothier's, then to the shoemaker's, and finally, because she was as thorough as she was determined, to the rector of her church, who questioned me for more than an hour while Mrs. Bates sat in a pew, eyes closed, praying, I suppose, for my immortal soul. I confessed to the kindly old priest I had not been to church since my parents had died.

"This man who keeps you . . . this—what did you call him? Doctor of 'aberrant biology'? He is not a religious man?"

"I don't think many doctors of aberrant biology are," I answered. I remembered his words the day before he abandoned me:

There is something in us that longs for the indescribable, the unattainable, the thing that cannot be seen.

"I would think it'd be the norm for such men, given the nature of their work."

I didn't offer a contrary opinion. I really had nothing to say. What I saw, in my mind's eye, was an empty bucket sitting on the floor beside the necropsy table.

"Look at you!" cried Lilly when we arrived back at the house on Riverside Drive. She had just gotten home herself. She had not yet changed out of her uniform and had had no time to apply makeup. She looked as I remembered her, a young girl close to my own age, and somehow that made my palms begin to itch. "I hardly recognize you, Will Henry. You look so . . ." She searched for the word. "Different."

Later that evening—much later; it was not easy in the Bates home to have time to oneself—I happened to glance in the bathroom mirror and was shocked by the image of the boy captured there. But for the slightly haunted look in his eyes, he bore little resemblance to the boy who had warmed himself by a fire fed with the chopped-up remains of a dead man.

Everything was different.

Each morning there was a full breakfast, for which we were expected to arrive promptly at six. No one was allowed to start this meal—or any meal—until Mr. Bates picked up his fork. After breakfast Lilly and Reggie went off to school, Mr. Bates went off to his job "in finance," and Mrs. Bates went off with me. She was appalled at the staggering extent of my ignorance in the most elemental aspects of a proper childhood. I had never been to a museum or a concert or a minstrel show or the ballet or even the zoo. I had never attended a lecture, seen a play, watched a magic lantern show, been to the circus, ridden a bicycle, read a book by Horatio Alger, skated, flown a kite, climbed a tree, tended a garden, or played a musical instrument. I hadn't even played a single parlor game! Not charades or blindman's bluff, which I'd heard of, and not deerstalker or cupid's coming or dumb crambo, which I had not.

"Whatever did you do at night, then?" she inquired.

I did not wish to answer that question; I was honestly concerned she might arrange to have the monstrumologist arrested for endangering a child.

"Helped the doctor."

"Helped him with what?"

"Work."

"Work? No, I am speaking of *afterward*, William. After the work was finished for the day."

"The work was never finished."

"But when did you have time for your studies?"

I shook my head. I did not understand what she meant.

"Your schoolwork, William."

"I don't go to school."

She was flabbergasted. When she discovered I had not been inside a classroom in more than two years, she was furious—so furious, in fact, that she brought up the matter to her husband.

"William has informed me that he has not attended a single day of school since the death of his parents," she told him that evening.

"*Humf!* You seem surprised."

"Mr. Bates, I am mortified. He's treated no better than one of that man's horrid specimens."

"More like one of his instruments, I'd say. Another tool in his monster hunting kit."

"But we must do something!"

"*Humf.* I know what you're going to suggest, but we've no right, Emily. The boy is our guest, not our responsibility.

"He is a lost soul placed in our path by the Almighty Father. He is the Jew beaten by the side of the road. Would you be the Levite or the Samaritan?"

"I prefer being Episcopalian."

She dropped the subject, but only for the time being.

Emily Bates was not the kind of "expert in the field" who allowed a boil to fester.

I did not see much of Lilly on school days. Her afternoons were devoted to piano and violin lessons, ballet classes, shopping trips, trips to the salon, visits with friends. I saw her at breakfast, at the evening meal, and afterward when the family gathered in the parlor, where I learned all the games in the Bates family repertoire. I detested charades, because I was awful at it. I had no cultural context upon which to draw. But I liked card games (old maid and old bachelor, our birds and Dr. Busby) and I Have a Basket, at which I excelled. When my turn came round, I could always name what was in my "basket," no matter what letter fell to me. *A* was easy: *Anthropophagi. V?* Why, I have a *Vastarus hominis* in my basket! What about *X?* That's a hard one, but not too hard for me. Look here. It's a *Xiphias!*

The weekends were a different story. Hardly an hour passed without her company. Bicycling in the park (after an afternoon of instruction; I never got very good at it), picnics by the river when the weather warmed, hours in the library at the Society's headquarters on the corner of Broadway and Twenty-second Street (when we could sneak away; Mrs. Bates took a dim view of all things monstrumological), and, of course, many hours at her great-uncle's brownstone. Lilly adored Uncle Abram.

She had not given up her dream to become the first

female monstrumologist. Indeed, she possessed an almost encyclopedic knowledge on the topic, from monstrumology's colorful history to the even more colorful practitioners of the craft, from its catalogue of malevolent creatures to the intricacies of its Society's governing charter. She knew more about monstrumology from studying on her own than I did after living two years with the greatest monstrumologist since Bacqueville de la Potherie, a rather embarrassing fact she delighted in pointing out at every opportunity.

"Well," I said one Saturday afternoon while we sat among the dusty stacks on the fourth floor of the old opera house, my patience giving way, "maybe I'm just stupid."

"I have often wondered."

"Doing it isn't the same as reading a book about it," I shot back.

"The only thing the same as reading a book is . . . reading a book!" She laughed. "If you'd chosen books instead, you'd still have a finger."

Like her mother, she had Abram von Helrung's eyes, as blue as a mountain lake on a sunny autumn day. If you sank beneath the azure surface, you would drown for wanting to stay.

"Where did Dr. Warthrop go?" she asked suddenly. She popped this question at least four times a week. And I always gave the same answer, which was the truth:

"I don't know."

"What is he looking for?"

I had searched in the library for a picture of it. There was a very long entry in the *Encyclopedia Bestia* (cowritten by Warthrop), but no picture and no description of *Typhoeus magnificum*, except an extensive footnote detailing the various fanciful—that is, unverifiable—depictions of the Unseen One. It was a dragonlike creature, as von Helrung had mentioned, that took its victims "higher than the tallest mountain peak" before ripping them apart in its frenzy; it was a giant troll-like beast that flung pieces of its prey with such force that they fell from the sky miles from where their owners had lost them; it was an enormous wormlike invertebrate—a cousin of the Mongolian Death Worm, perhaps—that spat its venom with such velocity that it blew apart the human body, vaporizing it into a fine mist that came down again as the phenomenon called "red rain."

The article mentioned the circumstances surrounding the discovery of the Lakshadweep *nidus* in 1851, the theories about the *magnificum*'s range (most monstrumologists agreed it was limited to the remote islands of the Indian Ocean and parts of Eastern Africa and Asia Minor, but that belief was based more on native traditions and stories than on hard scientific evidence), and the sad stories of the men who went looking for the Faceless One, the ones who returned empty-handed and the ones who did not return at all. Particularly poignant (and alarming) was the tale of Pierre Lebroque, a well-respected aberrant biologist—though somewhat of an iconoclast—who, after a five-month expedition in which no expense was spared (his party included five elephants, twenty-nine coolies, and a trunk-load of gold coins to bribe the local sultans), returned a raving lunatic. His family was forced into the painful decision of committing him to an asylum, where he lived out the remainder of his days in unrelieved torment, shouting the incessant refrain, "*Nullité! Nullité! Nullité!* That is all it is! Nothing, nothing, nothing!"

"He is searching for the Questing Beast," I told her.

I suppose we cannot help it. We are hunters all. We are, for lack of a better word, monstrumologists. Our prey varies depending on our age, sex, interests, energy. Some hunt the simplest or silliest of things—the latest electronic device or the next promotion or the best-looking boy or girl in school. Others hunt fame, power, wealth. Some nobler souls chase the divine or knowledge or the betterment of humankind. In the winter of 1889, I stalked a human being. You might be thinking I mean Dr. Pellinore Warthrop. I do not. That person was me.

Go on, open it! the curator said. *He wanted you to see.*

Every night the same dream. The Locked Room. The old man jangling keys. And the box. The box and the boy and the stuck lid and the unseen thing moving inside the box and the old man scolding, *Thickheaded boy! You can't open it because you're asleep!*

And the thickheaded boy starting awake, sweating under warm covers in a cold room, teetering on the edge of it, *das*

Ungeheuer, the center not holding, the *me* unwound, only the *not-me* awake now, echoing the cry of a madman, "*Nullité! Nullité! Nullité!* That is all it is! Nothing, nothing, nothing!"

Sometimes the woman down the hall heard him crying, and no matter the hour she rose from her bed and slipped on her robe and went down the hall to his room. She sat with him. "Hush now. Shhhh. It's all right. It's only a dream. Hush now. Shhh." A mother's refrain. She smelled of lilacs and rosewater, and sometimes he forgot and called her Mother. She did not correct him. "Hush now. Shhh. It's only a dream."

Or she would sing to him songs he'd never heard before, in languages he did not understand. Her voice was beautiful, a rich velvet curtain, a river over which the demons could not cross. He did not know a mortal voice could sound so heavenly.

"Do you mind my singing to you, William?"

"No, I don't mind. I like the way it sounds."

"When I was young girl around Lilly's age, it was my great ambition to sing opera upon the professional stage."

"Did you?"

"No, I never did."

"Why not?"

"I married Mr. Bates."

I was pursuing the one I had lost, the boy I was before I came to live with him. For a while—a very long while—I thought I was hunting for the monstrumologist. He was, after all, the one who had dropped off the face of the earth.

I thought I saw him one night at the opera. Mrs. Bates took Lilly and me to a production of Wagner's *Das Rheingold*, which had premiered at the Metropolitan Opera House the previous month.

"I hate the opera," Lilly complained. "I don't understand why Mother drags me to it."

We were sitting in a private box high above the orchestra when I thought I spotted him in the crowd. I *knew* it was him. I did not question why the monstrumologist would be attending the opera—that did not matter. It was him. The doctor had come back! I started to stand; Lilly tugged me back into the chair.

"It's Dr. Warthrop!" I whispered excitedly.

"Don't be silly," she whispered back. "And don't say his name in front of Mother!"

I thought I saw him a second time, in Central Park, walking a Great Dane. When he drew close, I realized he was twenty years older and twenty pounds heavier.

Whenever I saw von Helrung, I asked the same question:

"Have you heard from the doctor?"

His answer on the seventeenth day was the same as his answer on the twenty-seventh:

"No, Will. Nothing yet."

On the thirty-seventh day of my exile, after hearing those words again, *No . . . nothing yet*, I said to him, "Something is wrong. He should have written by now."

"It could be that something is wrong—"

"Then, we must do something, Dr. von Helrung!"

"Or it could mean everything is very *right*. If Pellinore has picked up the trail of the *magnificum*, he would not take the time to write two words. You have served the man; you know this to be true."

I did. When the fever of the hunt was upon him, nothing could distract him from his goal. But I was troubled.

"You have friends in England," I said. "Can't you ask them if they know where he's gone?"

"Of course I can—and I will, if circumstances dictate, but not yet. Pellinore would never forgive me if I allowed that particular cat out of the bag."

I returned on a blustery afternoon in early April to ask a special favor.

"I want to work in the Monstrumarium."

"You want to work in the Monstrumarium!" The old monstrumologist was frowning. "What did Emily say?"

"It doesn't matter what she says. She isn't my guardian and she isn't my mother. I don't need her permission to do anything."

"My dear little Will, I suspect the sun itself needs her permission to shine. Why do you want to work in the Monstrumarium?"

"Because I'm tired of sitting in the library. I've read so much, it feels as if my eyes are bleeding."

"You have been reading?"

"You sound like Mrs. Bates. Yes, I do know how to read, *Meister* Abram. Well? I'm sure Professor Ainesworth could use some help."

"Will, I don't think Professor Ainesworth cares much for children."

"I know. And he cares even less for me. That's why I'm coming to you, Dr. von Helrung. You're the president of the Society. He has to listen to you."

"Listen, yes. Obey . . . Well, that's something altogether different!"

His hope for success was not high, but he decided to humor me, and together we descended to the old man's basement office. The meeting went well only in the sense of its outcome; the rest bordered on the disastrous. At one point I actually feared Adolphus might bash von Helrung's head in. *I do not need any help! He will sabotage my system! The Monstrumarium is no place for children! He will get himself hurt! He will get me hurt!*

Von Helrung was patient. Von Helrung was gentle. Von Helrung was kind. He smiled and nodded and expressed his utmost respect for and admiration of the curator's achievements, the finest collection of monstrumological relics in the world, and not *merely* that but the creation of the most unique cataloguing system in the Western hemisphere. He intended to propose at the next congress that a section of the Monstrumarium be named in his honor—the Adolphus Ainesworth Wing.

The professor was not mollified.

"Stupid! Too wordy! It should be the Ainesworth Wing—or better, the Ainesworth *Collection*."

Von Helrung spread his hands apart as if to say, *Whatever you like*.

"I do not like children," said the curator, scowling at me over his spectacles. "And I especially do not like children who meddle in dark places!" He pointed a crooked finger at von Helrung. "I don't know what it is about this boy. Every time I look up, there he stands at the side of another monstrumologist. What happened to Warthrop?"

"He has been called away on urgent business."

"Or he's *dead*."

Von Helrung blinked rapidly several times, then said, "Well, I am not sure. I don't think so."

"That's the most urgent business there is, when you think about it," Adolphus pronounced in my general direction. "Death. Sometimes I will be sitting here, just sitting here working away, and I will think about it, and then I will jump up from my chair and think, 'Hurry, Adolphus. Hurry, hurry! *Do* something!'"

"You should not worry yourself over such things," said von Helrung.

"Did I say I was worried? Bah! I have been surrounded

by death for forty-six years, von Helrung. It isn't the dead that worry me." Then, turning to me and glowering, he barked, "What are you good at?"

"I can organize your papers—"

"Never!"

"Maintain the files—"

"Won't happen!"

"Take down dictation—"

"I have nothing to say!"

"Sort the mail—"

"Absolutely not!"

"Well," I said wearily. "I'm handy with a broom."

Spring. Blooms break forth from the startled earth. The sky laughs. The trees, abashed, dress themselves in verdant green. And the heavens are lush with stars. *Redeem the time*, the stars sing down. *Redeem the dream.*

And the boy waking in the land of broken rocks, the dry land wet with spring rain, waking in the place where two dreams cross—the dream where seeds grow into trees of gold and the dream of the box that he cannot open.

"I shouldn't tell you this," Lilly said. "I really shouldn't tell you."

I shall be the ship of a thousand sails.

"Last night I heard them talking about you."

Go on, open it! He wanted you to see.

"And Father did not say yes, but he did not say no."

I want to go, Father. I want to go.

"*I say no,*" she said. "I've kissed you now, three times."

And the stars sing down, *Redeem the time, redeem the dream*, in the land of broken rocks where two dreams cross.

"And that's a horrid thought, kissing my own brother!"

I don't want you to take me home. My place is with him.

"Well, William, what do you think?" asked Mrs. Bates.

"I think the doctor will be very displeased when he comes back."

"Dr. Warthrop, *if* he comes back, will not have a say in the matter. He has no legal claim to you."

"Dr. Warthrop, *when* he comes back, won't care about legal claims."

"*Humf!*" grunted Mr. Bates. "Cheeky."

"I've no doubt of that, William. But he would acquiesce to your wishes, I think. What is your wish?"

My prey was in sight. I had but to stretch forth my hand and seize it. The boy with the tall glass of milk in the kitchen that smelled like apples and no darkness, no darkness anywhere, no bodies in ash barrels, no blood caked on the soles of his shoes, no screaming of his name in the deadest hours of the night, no unwinding thing that compelled and repulsed, that whispered like the thunder, *I AM*. Just the laughing sky, and trees adorned in gold and the abundance of stars that sing down and the boy with his milk and the smell of the earth, the undiminished whole of it, like apples.

FIFTEEN

"What You See, My God Sees"

The curator of the Monstrumarium tapped my chest with the sneering head of his cane and said, "You are to touch *nothing*. Ask first. Always ask first!"

I followed him through the snarl of dimly-lit passageways crammed floor-to-ceiling with unopened yet-to-be catalogued crates, walls festooned with cobwebs and coated in fifty years' worth of grime, his cane going *click, click, click* on the dusty floor, the smell of preserving solution, the tartness of death upon the tongue, deep pools of shadow, feeble haloes of yellow gaslight, and the awful loneliness of being just one small person in a vast space.

"It may not look it, but there's a place for everything, and everything is in its place. If a member should happen to ask you for help in finding something, *do not help*. Find me. I am not hard to find. I am usually at my desk. If I am not at my desk, tell them to come back another time. Tell them, 'Adolphus is not at his desk. That means he is somewhere in the Monstrumarium, has gone home for the day, or is dead.'"

We paused by an unlabeled door—the *Kodesh Hakodashim*. He was absently shaking his key ring. It was my dream, down to the jangling of the keys.

"No one is to go in here," he said. "Off-limits!"

"I know that."

"Don't talk back! Better, don't talk! I do not like chattering children."

Or quiet children, I thought.

"It's the *nidus*, isn't it?" Adolphus Ainesworth asked suddenly. "The 'urgent business.' Hah! Warthrop's gone after the *magnificum*. Well, well. Doesn't surprise me. Always the tilter at windmills. But what about you, Sancho Panza? Why didn't you go with him?"

"He took another in my place."

"Another *what*?"

"Dr. von Helrung's new pupil, Thomas Arkwright."

"Arse wipe?"

"Arkwright!" I shouted.

"Never met the man. His pupil, did you say?"

"He must have introduced you to him."

"Why must he? Yesterday was the first time I've seen the old fart in six months. He never comes down here. Anyway, what do I care about von Helrung's pupil or anybody else's for that matter? Here is the thing, Master Henry. You should never get friendly with a monstrumologist, and I can tell you why. Would you like to know why?"

I nodded. "Yes, I would."

"Because they aren't around for very long. They die!"

"Everyone dies, Professor Ainesworth."

"Not like monstrumologists, they don't. Now, look at me. I could have been one. Was asked more than once when I was younger to apprentice for one. Always said no, and I shall tell you why. *Because they die.* They die in droves! They die like turkeys on Thanksgiving Day! And their demise is not the usual untimely type. You know what I mean. A man falls off a boat and drowns. Or a horse kicks him in the head. That's an accident; that's natural. Being torn limb from limb by something *you went looking for*, that's *un*natural; that's monstrumological."

In the Monstrumarium, in the hall outside the Locked Room, jingling his keys.

"'Tis a pity," Adolphus said pensively. "I didn't like Warthrop very much, but I could tolerate him. Not many men know what they're about. He did and made no apologies for it. Most men have the face they show the world and the other face, the face only God sees. Warthrop was Warthrop down to the marrow of his bones. 'What you see, my God sees,' was his motto." He sighed and shook his withered pate. "'Tis a pity."

"You shouldn't say that, Professor Ainesworth. We

haven't heard from him yet, but that doesn't mean—"

"He went hunting the *magnificum*, didn't he? And he's Pellinore Warthrop, isn't he? Not the kind of man to limp home with his tail between his legs. Not the kind to give up, ever. No, not him. No, no, no. You won't be seeing your boss anymore, boy."

Standing outside the Holy of Holies, jingling his keys.

I found von Helrung in his offices on the second floor. The head of the Monstrumologist Society was shuffling about in a pair of old slippers with a watering can, tending to his philodendrons on the dusty windowsill.

"Ah, Master Henry, has Adolphus sacked you already?"

"Dr. von Helrung," I said, "did you ever bring Mr. Arkwright down to the Monstrumarium?"

"Did I ever—?"

"Bring Mr. Arkwright to the Monstrumarium."

"I do not believe so, no. No, I did not."

"Or send him there for anything?"

He was shaking his head. "Why do you ask, Will?"

"Professor Ainesworth has never met him. He's never even heard of him."

He set down the watering can, leaned against his desk, and folded his thick arms over his chest. He regarded me soberly, bristly white eyebrows furrowing.

"I do not understand," he said.

"The night he met the doctor, Mr. Arkwright said he

knew we'd been to the Monstrumarium because of the smell. 'The smell floats about you like a foul perfume.' Remember?"

Von Helrung nodded. "I do."

"Dr. von Helrung, how would Mr. Arkwright know that it smelled like *anything* if he's never been there?"

My question hung in the air for a long time, a different kind of foul perfume.

"You are accusing him of lying?" He was frowning.

"I *know* he lied. I know he lied about applying to study under Dr. Warthrop, and now I know he lied about knowing we'd been to the Monstrumarium."

"But you *had* been to the Monstrumarium."

"That doesn't matter! What matters is he lied, Dr. von Helrung."

"You cannot say that with certainty, Will. Adolphus, may God bless him, is an old man, and his memory is not what it once was. And he often falls asleep at his desk. Thomas could have explored the Monstrumarium at his leisure, and Professor Ainesworth would know nothing about it."

He cupped my cheek with his hand. "This has been hard for you, I know. All you have in the world, all you understand, all upon which you thought you could rely—poof! Gone in an instant. I know you are worried; I know you fear the worst; I know what terrors may fill the vacuum of silence!"

"Something isn't right," I whispered. "It's been almost four months."

"Yes." He nodded gravely. "And you must prepare

yourself for the worst, Will. Use these days to steel your nerves for that—not to torture yourself over Thomas Arkwright and these perceptions of perfidy. It is easy to see villains in every shadow, and very hard to assume the best of people, particularly in monstrumology—for our view of the world is skewed, by virtue of the very thing we study. But hope is no less realistic than despair. It is still our choice whether to live in light or lie down in darkness."

I nodded. His soothing words, however, brought no solace. I was deeply troubled.

I suppose it is a measure of the depths of my disquiet that I confided my greatest fear to the last person I thought could keep any confidence quiet. It slipped out over a game of chess one afternoon in Washington Square Park. Chess was actually my idea. Perhaps if I practiced more, I reasoned, by the time the doctor returned, I might best him—and wouldn't that be something! Lilly accepted my challenge. She was very competitive, having learned the game from her uncle Abram. Lilly's style of play was aggressive, impetuous, and intuitive, not so different from the girl herself.

"You take so *long*," she complained as I agonized over my rook. He was trapped between her queen and a pawn. "Do you ever just *do* something? Just *do* it without thinking about it? Next to you, Prince Hamlet seems positively impulsive."

"I'm thinking," I answered.

"Oh, you think all the time, William James Henry. You

think too much. Do you know what happens to someone who thinks too much?"

"Do *you?*"

"Ha, ha. I suppose that was a joke. You shouldn't joke. People should know their limitations."

I said good-bye to my rook and advanced my bishop to threaten her knight. She bopped my rook onto its side with her queen.

"Check."

I sighed. I felt her eyes on me as I studied the board. I willed myself not to look up. The breeze tickled the new leaves of the trees; the spring air was soft and smelled of her lavender soap. Her dress was yellow, and she wore a white hat with a yellow ribbon and a large yellow bow. Even with a new wardrobe and a fresh haircut, next to her I felt shabby.

"Still no word from your doctor?"

"I wish you wouldn't say it like that," I said without looking up. "He isn't 'my' doctor."

"Well, if he isn't yours, I'd like to know whose he is. And don't try to change the subject."

"One of the benefits about thinking too much," I said, "is that you notice the little things, things other people miss. You say 'your doctor' like that on purpose, because you know it annoys me."

"And why would I want to do that?" I heard a smile in her voice.

"Because you enjoy annoying me. And before you ask

why you enjoy annoying me, I suggest you ask yourself that question. I don't know why."

"You're in a mood."

"I don't like losing."

"You were in a mood before we started playing."

I moved my king out of danger. She barely glanced at the board before swooping in and capturing my last bishop. Inwardly I groaned. It was only a matter of time now.

"You can always concede," she suggested.

"I shall fight on until the last drop of blood is spilt."

"Oh! How so very un-Will-Henry-like! You sounded very much like a *doer* just then. Like Leonidas at Thermopylae."

My cheeks were warm. I should have known not to become too pleased with myself, though.

"And all this while I thought of you as Penelope."

"Penelope!" My cheeks grew hotter, albeit for an entirely different reason.

"Pining away in your bridal chamber, waiting for Odysseus to return from the war."

"Do you enjoy being mean, Lilly, or is it something you can't help, like a nervous tic?"

"You shouldn't talk to me that way, William," she said, laughing. "I'm to be your big sister soon."

"Not if the doctor has anything to say about it."

"I would think your doctor would be relieved. I was not around him much, but I got the feeling he didn't like you."

She had gone too far, and knew it. "That was cruel," she

said. "I'm sorry, Will. I—I don't know what comes over me sometimes."

"No," I said with a wave of my wounded hand. "It's your move, Lilly."

She moved her knight, exposing her queen to my pawn. A pawn! I glanced up at her. Speckles of sunlight shimmered in her dark hair, a strand of which had come loose from her hat and fluttered, a fitful black streamer, in the soft springtime wind.

"Why do you think you haven't heard from him, Will?" she asked. The quality of her voice had changed, was as soft as the wind now.

"I think something terrible has happened," I confessed.

We stared into each other's eyes for a long moment, and then I was up from the bench and trotting across the park, and the world had gone watery gray, bleached of its springtime vibrancy. She caught up to me before I reached the exit at Fifth Avenue, and pulled me round to face her.

"Then, you must do something," she said angrily. "Not think about how frightened you are or lonely you are or whatever it is you think you are. Do you *really* think something terrible has happened? Because if I thought something terrible had happened to someone I loved, I would not mope around *thinking* about it. I would be on the next boat to Europe. And if I had no money for a ticket, I would stow away, and if I couldn't stow away, I would *swim* there."

"I don't love him. I hate him. I hate Pellinore Warthrop

more than I hate anything. More than I hate *you*. You don't know, Lilly. You don't know what it's been like, living there in that house, and what happens in that house and what happens because I live in that house. . . ."

"Like this?" She gathered my left hand into hers.

"Yes, like that. And that isn't all, not everything."

"He beats you?"

"What? No, he doesn't beat me. He . . . he doesn't *see* me. Days go by, weeks sometimes . . . and then I can't escape him; I can't get away. As if he's taken a rope and tied us together with it. And it's him and me and the rope, and there is no undoing it. That's the thing you don't understand, that your mother doesn't understand, that *no one* understands. He is thousands of miles away—maybe even dead—and it doesn't matter. He's right here, right *here*." I slapped my open palm hard against my forehead. "And there's no getting away. It's too tight, too *tight*."

My knees gave way. She threw her arms around me and held me up. She kept me from falling.

"Then, don't try, Will," she whispered into my ear. "Don't try to get away."

"You don't understand, Lilly."

"No," she said. "I don't. But I am not the one who has to."

SIXTEEN
"Be Still and Listen"

I had discovered it during one of my recent forays into the formidable library of the Monstrumologist Society, a slim volume covered in a fine sheen of dust, some of its pages still uncut, its spine creaseless. Apparently no one had bothered to read it since its publication in 1871. What drew my eye to that little book, out of the sixteen thousand others surrounding it, I do not know. But I remember distinctly the small jolt of recognition when I opened to the title page and saw the author's name. It was like turning the corner in a crowded city and bumping into a long-lost friend you'd given up hope of ever seeing again.

It was late in the day when I found it—no time to read it before the library closed—and there was a strict no-lending policy toward nonmembers. So I filched it. Tucked it under the back of my coat and walked out, right past Mr. Vestergaard, the head librarian, whom most monstrumologists called (behind his back) the Prince of Leaves—a rather weak bit of whimsy, I thought, but a monstrumologist's sense of humor, if he had one at all, tended toward the macabre. Efforts at anything lighter of heart invariably fell flat.

Though the slim volume had been composed when Warthrop was only eighteen—a mere five years older than I when I discovered it—as part of his final examination before the Admitting Committee of the Society, as a dissertation of sorts, the writing was remarkably sophisticated, if characteristically prolix. The title alone made my eyes glaze over: *Of Uncertain Origin: The Case for Interdisciplinary Openness and Intellectual Collectivism Between All Disciplines of the Natural Sciences, Including Studies in the Field of Aberrant Biology, with Extended Notes upon the Development of Canonical Principles from Descartes to the Present Day.*

But I read it—most of it, anyway—because the subject matter wasn't the thing I was after. Reading his words was the nearest I could get to hearing his voice. The Warthropian diction was there, the authoritative tone, the rigorous—some might say ruthless—logic. Every line held echoes of the older Warthrop's voice, and reading them, sometimes aloud, late at night in my room, when the house was quiet and it was just Warthrop's words and me, opened a door for him to return and talk a little while. I caught myself murmuring after certain passages, "Really, sir?" and "Is that so, Dr.

Warthrop?" as if we were back in the library at Harrington Lane and he was boring me with some arcane text written a hundred years ago by someone I'd never heard of, a form of mental cruelty that sometimes lasted for hours.

The night of my near-collapse in Washington Square Park, I picked up the book again, because I could not sleep, and I thought, with a little bit of spite, that the book would have definitely found a wider audience if it had been marketed to insomniacs. I opened it to a random page, and my eye fell upon this passage:

> A thing is either true (real) or it is not. There is no such thing as a half-truth in science. A scientific proposition is like a candle. The candle can be said to have two states or modes—lit and unlit. That is, a candle is either one or the other; it cannot be both; it cannot be "half-lit." If a thing is true, to put it colloquially, it is true through and through. If false, then false through and through.

"Is that so, Dr. Warthrop?" I asked him. "What if the candle has a wick at both ends? One is lit, the other not. Could not one say in that hypothetical circumstance that the candle is indeed both lit and unlit, and your argument false through and through?" I chortled sleepily to myself.

You cannot change the central element of an analogy to make it false, Will Henry, his voice spoke into my ear. *Is this why you're reading this old monograph of mine? To make your-self feel better at my expense? After all I've done for you!*

"And *to* me. Let's not forget that."

How could I? I am constantly reminded of it.

"I'm doomed, like Mr. Kendall. Just doomed."

What do you mean?

"Even when you're gone, I can't get rid of you."

I don't see how that is analogous to Mr. Kendall's fate.

"Once touched, infected. Just tell me, please, if you are dead. If you're dead, there is hope for me."

I'm right here. How could I be dead? Really, Will Henry, was there some childhood accident of which I'm not aware? Did you fall down a flight of stairs, perhaps? Did your mother drop you as an infant or suffer a fall while she carried you in her womb?

"Why do you insult me all the time?" I asked him. "To make yourself feel better at my expense? After all I've done for you!"

What have you done for me?

"Everything! I do everything for you. I wash and cook and launder and run errands and—and everything except wipe your arse!" I laughed. My heart felt thrillingly light, no heavier than a grain of sand. "Arse wipe."

Will Henry, did I hear you call me a name?

"I would never call you a name—to your face. I was remembering something Adolphus said. He mistook 'Arkwright' for 'arse wipe.'"

Ah, Arkwright. That's the perfect alternative to my candle analogy.

"I don't understand."

If you will be still and listen, I will explain. Thomas Arkwright is the candle. He is either who he claims to be or he is not. He cannot be both. Either von Helrung is right or you are. You cannot both be.

"I know that, Dr. Warthrop."

Didn't I just now, no more than thirty seconds ago, ask you to be still and listen? Seriously, Will Henry—perhaps an accident in the stable? Or milking the irascible family cow? Let us assume for a moment that von Helrung is correct. Mr. Thomas Arkwright is who he claims to be, a brilliant young man with a passion for all things monstrumological, who happens to be enamored with a certain doctor of natural philosophy, so enamored, in fact, that he writes not once, not twice, not three times, but a total thirteen times, begging for a position to study with this modern-day Prometheus, this colossus that bestrides the scientific landscape.

What is required for this one proposition to be true? That you, the said Prometheus's arse wiper, were so neglectful of your ancillary duties as file clerk that you missed his application not once, not twice, not three times, but a total of thirteen times. That, or you are simply a liar and destroyed them, lest you be replaced by a more convivial or efficient or passionate arse wiper, one who takes his arse wiping seriously, who considers a finely wiped arse a work of art.

Now, you know, of course, that you are neither neglectful nor deceitful, and the candle, as it were, is as cold as a wedge. What does this mean? It means Arkwright is the liar, though his motives may be pure. In other words, he lies because he actually is enamored with our doctor. It does not mean he has insidious intentions; he is not Iago, but more like Puck. Are you following this so far, or would you like for me to speak more slowly and less polysyllabically?

"I am, Dr. Warthrop. I'm following you, sir."

Excellent! Now to the more recent and infinitely more troublesome development—the second candle, we shall call it. Mr. Arkwright, Adolphus, and the "foul perfume" of the Monstrumarium. Let us assume, for the sake of our argument, that this second candle is lit—in other words that you are correct and von Helrung is wrong. Arkwright is indeed playing false; he has never stepped foot inside Professor Ainesworth's realm; he would no more recognize the "foul perfume" than a blind man would the color blue. On its surface, a rather innocuous slip—almost trivial. Who cares that he pretended to recognize a smell he could not possibly know? Another attempt to impress his idol with his powers of observation, as he tried to impress him earlier by his overabundance of applications. . . . We may stop now, yes? Your troubled heart has been assuaged, so you may sleep and I may go?

"I'm not sleepy," I said. "Don't go."

Very well. I will stay. For your heart should not be assuaged, Will Henry. Your unease is justified, though you cannot articulate why.

"But why can't I, Dr. Warthrop?" My eyes stung with tears of frustration. "I *know* it's important, but I couldn't convince Dr. von Helrung it was. I couldn't say *why*."

That's it precisely, Will Henry! You have been focusing on the wrong question. You've been asking "Why is he lying?" instead of "What does this lie mean?" What does it mean, Will Henry?

"It means . . ." The truth was I did not know what the lie meant. "Oh, I hate myself; I'm so stupid—"

Oh, stop it. Self-pity is like self-abuse—it may feel good in the moment, but the final result is a disgusting mess. I've given you one hint. Here's another: Mr. Arkwright is like the foolish man who built his house upon sand.

"And the rains came and washed the foundation away. So his slip-up about the smell—that's the rain—"

Oh, good God! No, no, Will Henry. Not the rain. Why did you bring up the rain? I didn't even mention it! You are the rain, or would be if you used your head for something other than a hat stand.

I closed my eyes and plugged my ears to remove all distraction. If I was the rain, what was Arkwright? The house? The foundation? Oh, why couldn't Warthrop just tell me and be done with it? Did he enjoy making me feel like a cretin? *Most people do not like to think, Will Henry,* he told me once. *If they did, we would have fewer lawyers.* (He had just been given notice that he was being sued—a common occurrence and occupational hazard.)

Oh, Will Henry, what shall I do with you? You are like the ancient Egyptians, who believed the seat of thought lay in the heart. The foundation is not the object of your jealousy.

"Not Arkwright," I whispered into the dark, for the light had finally come on. "The lie! His *lie* is the foundation, isn't it? And the house is . . ." *Think, think!* To think is to be human, the doctor always said, so be human and *think.* "The house is the conclusion based on the lie . . . the *nidus.* The *nidus* is the house! He *couldn't* have deduced you had the *nidus,* because his deduction began with a lie—that he knew we'd been to the Monstrumarium! He knew about the *nidus* before he walked through the door!"

I bolted upright and swung my legs over the side of the bed. I fumbled in the drawer of the bedside table for the box of matches.

"And there're only two ways he could have known. Dr. von Helrung told him . . ."

Which he said he did not, and we've no reason to assume he did.

". . . or Jack Kearns told him." I lit the match and touched it to the candlewick. "He's working with Kearns!"

Or someone else who knows what Kearns sent me, came Dr. Warthrop's voice again. *Kearns could have told someone, but it is difficult to imagine who and nearly impossible to understand why.*

I was on my feet, tugging on my trousers. "Either way, he's false, but why? What is his game?" I watched the flame sputter in the draft coming from the open window across the room. I could smell the river, and heard, in the distance, a tugboat's throaty call. The voice within had fallen silent. "It was a trick. He tricked you, Dr. Warthrop. You! He needed to come with you to find Kearns, so he lowered your guard and puffed you up with flattery and made you think he was the perfect replacement." Yanking on my shirt, searching for my shoes—what had happened to my shoes? "I have to tell Dr. von Helrung, before it's too late."

And the voice spoke up again, and said:

It is already too late.

SEVENTEEN

"Too Late"

I ran, barefooted, along Riverside Drive, south to Seventy-second Street and then east to Broadway, running as if the devil himself were after me, along a narrow mountain pass and, on either side, the abyss, *das Ungeheuer*, the tightly wound thing unwinding, and the unspooling refrain repeating until the words became a gibbering howl, *It is already too late It is already too late It is already too late It is already too late It is already too late It is already too late It is already too late*, the granite pavement scraping and clawing the soles of my naked feet, the smeared blobs of streetlamps in the early morning mist, and the hellish glow of the ash barrels where you can warm yourself over a dead man's bones, and the bloody footprints left behind; now the park and there the shadows between trees and the wet rocks and the sensuous whisper of leaf brushing leaf and the silence in between, and then Broadway, the glittering blade thrust into the city's heart; along its garish edges shrieks of hysterical laughter from darkened doorways and the smell of stale beer, tramps in doorways, whores hanging from second-story windows of bawdy houses, and the tinny music of the dance hall, the drunken cries of sailors, the white coats of the sanitation workers, the thing unwinding pulling me as if by a silver cord, my blood the breadcrumbs marking the way back, but there is no going back now; *It is already too late It is already too late It is already too late It is already too late It is already too late It is already too late It is already too late*; crossing Fifty-first Street, dodging the manure stacked in steaming piles, and the lights from the burlesque hall splashing on painted faces and the blue coats of the roundsmen swinging their nightsticks, the darkened storefronts, the empty stalls of the fruit peddlers; running on a river of fire, breathing it in, granite striking bone; drawn by a silver cord, and the diminished stars singing down, in the granite defile, singing down, *Redeem the time, redeem the dream*, singing, singing down, between the lightless divide, the vacuity on either side, careening onto Fiftieth, where Broadway's garish light fades and the buildings are dark and a dog furiously barks, maddened by the blood-smell, bloody rock against bloody bone, and the snarling river of fire that I breathe, the river of fire on which I run, a fire fed by blood, river of fire, river of blood, and the unquiet voice, the silver cord, *It is already too late It is already too late It is already too late It is already too late It is already too late It is already too late It is already too late;* praying that we not be suffered to perish in the fire, praying we are not divided like the man in the ash barrel, praying, *Merciful God, let my prayer come unto thee out of the fire. Let my prayer come unto thee between the division, from the fire that bisects the abyss;* turning on Fifth Avenue, six blocks, snap to, snap to!, the sick wet slap of bloody feet on hard pavement, blood black in the yellow streetlights, and do not suffer us to die unrelieved and divided, do not consign us to the ash barrel, headwater of this fiery river upon which I run, where the melting muscles sizzle and the bones sing back to the stars singing down, *And after this, our exile,* and the river eddies at the foot of the brownstone, and I leap onto shore, and the house is ablaze with light, every window a glowing featureless eye; banging on the door that opens at once, suddenly, like the yanking back of a curtain, and I am there.

I fell into the vestibule like a landed trout gasping for air, clutching my stomach, my bare, bloody toes curling on the wooden planks. Von Helrung's kindly face swam into view; he pulled me to my feet and held me for a long time.

"Will, Will, what are you doing here?" he murmured.

"It's the doctor," I managed to get out after several attempts. "Something . . . something is . . . ruh . . . *wrong.*" He would listen to me this time. I would *make* him listen.

To my surprise the old monstrumologist was nodding,

and then I saw his wet cheeks, fresh tears welling in his blue eyes, his cottony white hair worried into tangled knots.

"It is late. I was going to call in the morning. Wait for the morning. But now God has brought you here. *Ja,* it is his will. His will. And his will be done!"

He stumbled away in a gait wobbly like a drunkard's, muttering to himself, "*Ja, ja,* his will be done," leaving me to shiver in the vestibule, sweating, my lungs and feet on fire. A crumpled piece of paper fell from his hand; he did not stop to pick it up. I do not think he realized he'd dropped it.

It was a Western Union telegram; I recognized the yellow paper. He had signed for it but an hour before, around the same time as my lesson with the monstrumologist three miles away on Riverside Drive.

The cable read:

CONFIDENTIAL—

LEAVING LIVERPOOL TOMORROW.
ARRIVING NY THURS. TERRIBLE
NEWS. FAILURE ON ALL FRONTS.
WARTHROP IS DEAD.

It was signed "Arkwright."

EIGHTEEN

"The Best of Us"

Jacob Torrance downed his glass of whiskey, smoothed his neatly trimmed mustache, and then proceeded to drum his fingers aggressively on the arm of the wingback chair. His ruby red signet ring, stamped with the motto of the Society (*Nil timendum est*), sparked and spat back the light. His shoes shone as brilliantly as his ring, and besides the ones in his trousers, there was not a crease anywhere on him; he looked like a man carved out of stone, a Greek statue wearing a perfectly tailored suit. He had the face of a statue too, or rather the face of someone who might model for one—jaw square, chin strong, nose straight, eyes large and soulful, if a little too close together, which gave him a perpetually angry look, as if at any moment he might rear back and bash you in the face.

At twenty-nine Jacob Torrance was one year shy of what monstrumologists called "the magic thirty," a reference to the average life expectancy of a scholar in the field of aberrant biology. (The average life expectancy in the United States at the time was a little more than forty-two years.) Reaching "the magic thirty" meant you had beaten the odds. Usually your colleagues threw you a party. Magic Thirties, as these bacchanals were called, could last for days and were said to rival the debaucheries of Caligula's court in ancient Rome. There was nothing a monstrumologist delighted in more than cheating death, unless it was discovering some creature that delighted in dealing it out. Warthrop's Magic Thirty was celebrated before I came to live with him, but by all accounts it put all others before it to shame; in fact, for years afterward many of his colleagues did not dare set foot inside the city limits of Boston for fear of being arrested.

I had suggested Torrance to von Helrung for his youth and physical prowess. (He was somewhat of a legend in monstrumological circles, nicknamed "John Henry" Torrance by his fellow scientists, after the legendary nail-driving strong man. The doctor had told me a story about Torrance flattening a charging *Clunis foetidus* with a single blow, hitting it so hard in the snout that it dropped dead at his feet.) I'd also suggested Torrance for the simple reason that he was one of the few monstrumologists that Warthrop liked, though the doctor did not approve of Torrance's hard drinking and irreformable philandering. "It is a shame, Will Henry," he told me. "With great gifts there always seem to come great burdens. He would be the best of us, if he only could control his appetites."

Von Helrung was nervously puffing on the expired stub of a Havana cigar. He looked haggard, eyes swollen from lack of sleep, chin stubbly with a three-day-old growth that he rubbed incessantly with the palm of his pudgy hand.

It had not been the best week of his long life. Or my short one.

"Would you like another whiskey, Jacob?" asked von Helrung.

"Do you think I should? Probably shouldn't." Torrance clipped off the ends of his words, bit them hard with his large teeth, as if words had a taste and he liked the way they tasted. He swirled the ice in his glass. "Oh, what the hell."

Von Helrung shuffled to the liquor cabinet. Among the decanters of sherry and brandy, bottles of wine and liqueurs, was a small blue bottle—the sleeping draught prescribed by Dr. Seward. He stared at it for a moment, brow furrowed, bushy white eyebrows nearly touching above his large nose, before he refilled Torrance's glass with whiskey and scuffled back.

"Thanks." Back went the finely sculpted head, the large Adam's apple bobbed once, and the ice tinkled again in the empty glass.

"That's enough," he said to no one in particular. He adjusted the signet ring on his finger and mused, "Maybe

I shouldn't be sitting here when he comes in. Might make him suspicious."

"He may not come," von Helrung said. "He says nothing of coming, only that he arrives Thursday—today." He consulted his pocket watch, snapped it closed. In another minute he would check the time again.

"Then, we'll go to him," Torrance said. "I'm up for a hunt. What about you, Will?"

"He'll come," I said. "He will have to."

Von Helrung shook his head in consternation, a gesture Torrance and I had seen repeated since the evening had begun.

"I do not like this. I have said it before; I say it again. I do not like any of this. Ack! It goes against everything I believe in—or have said I believed in—or *believed* I believed in. It is not the way a Christian gentleman behaves!"

"I'll take your word for it, *Meister* Abram," Torrance returned dryly. "Can't say I've met many of those, and those I have didn't act very Christlike."

He pulled out his Colt revolver, and von Helrung cried, "What are you doing? Put that away!"

"It's only Sylvia," said Torrance slowly, as if speaking to a half-wit. "All right, I'll put her away."

"I never should have trusted him," moaned von Helrung. "I am a fool—the very worst kind of fool—an *old* fool."

"How are you a fool? He came with excellent references and letters of recommendation, and claimed to hail from one of the oldest families in Long Island. Why wouldn't you trust him?"

"Because I am a monstrumologist!" von Helrung replied, striking his breast. "An *old* monstrumologist. And a monstrumologist does not get to be my age without a healthy dose of skepticism. The eyes and ears are not to be trusted! I have spent my career stripping off nature's masks; I should have seen through the ruse. But did I see it? No! It took a child to show the way."

"Don't take it so hard, *Meister* Abram. He fooled Warthrop, too, and Warthrop's no fool." His fingers drummed on the chair arm the cadence of a galloping horse.

At the mention of the doctor's name, von Helrung collapsed into his chair with a loud cry. "Pellinore! Pellinore, forgive me. Thy blood is on my hands!"

"We don't know if he's dead," I spoke up. "Arkwright could be lying about that, too."

"There is only one reason he would say so—because it is so!"

"You said it yourself, Dr. von Helrung," I returned. "Hope isn't any less reasonable than despair. I think he's alive."

"You *hope* that he is."

"Well, he *could* be alive," Torrance put in. "So my money's with Will's. I hate to think of a world without Pellinore Warthrop—be a hell of a lot less interesting place."

He stood up, which seemed to take a very long time—he was well over six feet tall—and opened his powerful arms wide to stretch. "Well, I'm going to find something to eat. I suppose you've sent François home for the evening?"

"*Ja*, and the rest." And then he added bitterly, "We would not want any witnesses, would we?"

"Speaking of that, I think I will stay out of sight till you're ready for me. Wouldn't want the little rat to smell one. That's a shame, about François I mean. That fellow's crepes are the finest I've ever tasted."

"Will, I am sorry," von Helrung said after Torrance had left. "If I had only listened to you—"

He was interrupted by the bell. He closed his eyes and took a deep breath to steel his nerves.

"Our quarry arrives," he said. "Now we screw our courage to the sticking place, Master Henry. How is my expression? I fear the fly will see me for the spider I am!"

He glanced at himself in the mirror by the front door, tugged at his vest, and ran both hands over his mop of white hair. Out of the corner of his eye, he caught me easing into the vestibule.

"What are you doing?" he cried softly. "No, no. Go back to the parlor." He waved frantically toward the room. "Lie upon the divan. You have collapsed in grief! You have lost your master—lost everything. Can you feign tears? Rub your eyes, very hard, make them red."

The bell rang a second time. I scampered back to the parlor, threw myself upon the divan, and practiced a keening wail, softly, but not soft enough, for von Helrung, just before he flung open the door, called out hoarsely, "What is that? What *is* that? *Soft* tears—tears of lamentation. You sound like a hog in the slaughterhouse!"

And then: "Thomas! Thank God you have arrived safely! I was worried."

"Dr. von Helrung—*Meister* Abram—that I've arrived at all is nothing short of a miracle."

"But you look terrible—exhausted. Here, I will take your bags; my staff has left for the evening. And we will retire to the parlor, where you may rest from your long and no doubt dangerous journey."

They stepped into the room. Arkwright started when he saw me, and turned to his host. "Not the boy. I beg you, sir—" He was carrying a worn leather satchel. I recognized it at once, and a dagger pierced my heart. It was the doctor's field case, an heirloom from his father, who'd received it from *his* father. Warthrop would never have willingly parted with it.

"I would prefer that Will remain," von Helrung said stiffly, his jaw tightening. He looked as if he might haul back and coldcock Arkwright; he was not an accomplished actor. "And pray you will indulge me in this, Thomas. The boy has been through much at the side of our fallen friend; I thought he should hear firsthand of his fate."

Arkwright nodded absently, fell into the chair vacated by Jacob Torrance, cradling the doctor's field case in his lap as a toddler clutches a favored toy, and promptly forgot my presence. His sole focus was von Helrung, the "mark" of his confidence game.

Von Helrung took a fresh cigar from the humidor and clipped off the tip. He lit a match after rolling the cut end over his tongue; the flare chased all shadowy crevices from his face. For an instant he looked ten years younger.

"So begin at the beginning, and tell me everything," he said, bluish smoke enveloping his head. "Warthrop is dead?"

"That isn't the beginning," Arkwright objected. "It's the end—and a terrible one. After these months in his company, I am satisfied he was every bit the great man I thought he was before we met. Ten times greater! The loss to science . . . to me personally . . . and to you, of course . . . to all humanity! Incalculable, Dr. von Helrung. A man like Pellinore Warthrop comes along very seldom, perhaps once in a hundred years, and to lose him now, in the prime of life, at the height of his considerable powers—the mind can hardly grasp it."

"Alas, dear Thomas," commiserated von Helrung, "such is the fate of many great men in life, but particularly in monstrumology! At least tell me that God granted him, like his prophet Moses, a glimpse of the promised land before his passing? Did he see—have *you* seen—the Unseen? Did he, before he faced his end, face the Faceless? Otherwise, all has been for naught."

Arkwright slowly shook his head. "He was taken up, von Helrung. Snatched from our camp in the dead of night as if the hand of God had reached down and grabbed him, and then . . ." He made a choking sound, as if he were about to be sick. "And then the rain! The rain!" His body folded up in the chair, crushing the case against his stomach; I heard the faint dull clank of the instruments within. "A rain of *blood*—a red rain of—of—" His voice dropped to a mortified whisper. "*Him.*"

"What?" Von Helrung seemed genuinely horrified. "Do you mean to say his body was torn asunder?"

Arkwright opened his mouth to speak, but no sound came out. He nodded helplessly. Von Helrung sighed loudly and looked over at me.

"So Dr. Pellinore Warthrop makes seven," he said softly. "No—eight now, for your news has torn this old man's heart asunder. He was like a son to me, Thomas—the one with whom I'd cheerfully trade places. Ach, terrible, terrible." He wiped his palm over his forehead, and no one spoke for a few minutes. Then von Helrung looked at Arkwright, and his gaze was hard. "But you escaped. How is this so?"

"The simplest answer, sir. I ran."

"And you did not see it? The thing that took him?"

"It was his turn to keep the watch," Arkwright answered with a note of defensiveness. "I was sleeping. I woke to the snap and pop of the tent canvas, blown by a gale that came straight down, from the very vault of heaven, strong enough to crack the center pole, and then I heard an unearthly roar, like the sound of thunder or the blasting of a thousand pounds of TNT, followed by a screeching loud enough to split a man's head in half. I grabbed my rifle and crawled to the opening—and saw his legs fly straight up as he was *yanked* into the sky, and above . . . a shadow large enough to blot out the stars, as big as a house, and Warthrop ascending like one of the saved on Judgment Day. . . . That is what I saw, *Meister* Abram. And I am satisfied to never see it again for as long as I live!"

"'Satisfied'?" von Helrung asked, watching impassively the tears coursing down Arkwright's cheeks. "No, I suppose anyone would be 'satisfied,' Thomas, though not the one who might have risked all to see the thing that devoured him!"

"It happened too fast! In the wink of an eye, *Meister* Abram—the wink of an eye! And a moment later—he returned . . . raining all around me. I lifted my face to the sky and was soaked to the skin with . . . *him*. With him! And you would judge me for it? You were not there; you were not the shore upon which the flotsam of a human being washed down!"

He slumped over again, rocking back and forth, clutching the doctor's case, caressing it.

"Forgive me, Thomas," von Helrung said kindly. "I do not pass judgment on your actions. It is not to me you must answer in the final days. But you are here and he is not. And so I am glad and aggrieved, relieved and burdened. As you are, I'm certain. Here, though. You haven't finished the tale, and I would hear all of it, how you tracked down Jack Kearns and found the home of the *nidus* maker and all of that, but first a drink to steady your nerves, *ja*? Will Henry, be a dear and fetch a drink for Mr. Arkwright. What would you have, Thomas?"

"A bit of whiskey would be nice, if you have it, with some ice."

I went to the liquor cabinet while von Helrung stationed himself directly in front of Arkwright, who raised the case with both hands, holding it toward von Helrung like a high priest making an offering to his god. "I went back at first light, and found this. I thought you might want it. It's all that's left of him."

"All?"

Arkwright swallowed hard and whispered, "The rest I was able to wash off in the tidewaters of the sea."

His drink was ready. Von Helrung took it from me and handed it to Arkwright, who emptied the glass in a single, shuddering gulp.

"Ahhh."

"Would you like another?" von Helrung asked.

"It *does* help somewhat."

"Then, you shall have another. You deserve it, Thomas. You deserve all you can drink, to the last drop."

When Thomas Arkwright came to, an hour later, he was no longer in Abram von Helrung's cozy parlor on Fifth Avenue. Where he found himself was neither cozy nor on Fifth Avenue.

I wonder what he noticed first. Was it the strange smell of moist air mixed with chemicals and the subtle undertones of decay? Or was it how the world had gone gray—gray walls, gray ceiling, gray floor—and was covered in the grimy residua of the smoke from oil lamps. Or did he notice the dust not yet captured by the walls, lazily floating in the tiny chamber's atmosphere? Perhaps. But I suspect he first noticed the ropes.

"Well, baby's up from his nap," murmured Jacob Torrance.

Arkwright jerked in the chair and, as he was bound tightly hand and foot to it, nearly toppled over. He squinted in the weak light of the single kerosene lamp on the table behind Torrance, who stood in front of him, a six-foot-six hulking shadow, with face hidden and the voice of God's avenging angel come to bring justice to the wicked.

And in me the thing unwinding, a swift, fierce thrill when I saw the fear in Thomas Arkwright's eyes.

"Who are you?" Arkwright asked in a remarkably steady voice. Sound can play tricks in the underground crypts of the Monstrumarium. It careens from the walls, skitters down the serpentine passageways, smacks back and forth, ceiling to floor, wall to wall and back again. Did I hear the faintest trace of an accent far removed from the shores of Long Island?

"I'm the man who's going to kill you," Torrance answered evenly. "Unless Will would like the honor."

"Will!" He peered into the murk until his eyes fell

upon me. I willed myself not to look away. "Where is von Helrung?"

"I killed him," Torrance answered. "No, I didn't. Did I? What do you think?"

"Where am I? Why am I tied to this chair?" The drug still floated in his blood. He was fighting it, willing his tongue to mold the words.

"What, you don't recognize the smell? I thought you'd been here before. And you know why you are tied to that chair. So you're even now: two questions to which you don't know the answer, and two to which you do. You are only allowed five, so I would suggest that you ask one from the first category."

"The last one I don't—I didn't know the answer to. What—what has happened? I really don't understand. . . . Will, can you tell me what's happened?"

"You're asking him because you haven't liked my answers. That isn't my fault."

"Very well, then! I shall ask you: Why do you want to kill me?"

"I didn't say I wanted to. I said I was *going* to. I'm not a monster, you know; I just study them." He shrugged out of his jacket, handed it to me. He pulled out his Colt revolver.

"This is my gun. I named it Sylvia. It's a long story."

He flipped open the cylinder and held it a foot from Arkwright's aristocratic nose.

"She is empty, see?"

He dug into his vest pocket and removed a single bullet. "A bullet," he said, holding it up.

He slid it into a chamber and slapped the cylinder closed. Then with no further preamble he stepped forward and pressed the muzzle against Arkwright's finely formed forehead.

Our captive did not flinch. His gray eyes looked unblinking into Torrance's face. "Go on; pull the trigger. You don't frighten me."

"I don't want to frighten you," Torrance replied. He dropped the gun onto the bound man's lap and said, "I want to tell you a story. It's one of my favorite stories, written by a very good friend of mine who happens to be the world's reigning hot dog-eating champion. He ate two and a half hot dogs, *plus buns*, in sixty seconds. It's hard to make a decent living eating hot dogs, so he turned to writing—which pays a little better but wins not half the glory of achieving two and a half wieners in a minute—plus the buns. It's the buns that's impressive. The story's pretty famous; you've probably heard of it.

"Once upon a time there was a very mean king. He had a beautiful daughter whom, despite the fact that he was very mean, he loved very much. Well, one day this beautiful daughter of his disobeys him and falls in love with a fellow well below her station—a commoner, in other words. This made the mean king very, very angry, and that's a bad spot to be in if you're this princess's paramour. The king threw the poor sucker into the deepest, dankest, darkest dungeon—not too different from this place. He was just going to kill him, but the mean king was an ol' softie when it came to his daughter, who was just as heartbroken as Juliet over her lover's misfortune—that is, his being born out of the wrong womb.

"So the mean king doesn't kill him, but boy, does he set him up good. He plops him down in this big closed-off arena, like a coliseum, the kind the Romans had, and in the arena are two identical doors. Behind one door is a very good-looking woman—not a real looker like the princess, but several degrees from not bad. Behind the other is a ferocious man-eating tiger. The prisoner must choose one door—no coercion, entirely up to him. If he opens the door that hides the lady, he must marry her—the till-death-do-us-part kind of marrying, or the mean king will kill him. If he opens the door to the tiger ... Well, you can picture the outcome.

"Now, you might be thinking, 'Well, I know which one I'd try for!' But wait. Right as he's about to pick, he looks up and sees the princess. Ah, true love will triumph! Good will overcome immoderate meanness! For she does indeed know what is behind each door. And lo, when he looks up at her, she flicks her finger to the right—meaning 'Pick the door on the right; trust me!'

"Now, her lover may have been a commoner and may not have had all the perks of a royal education, but he was no simpleton. He begins to think about it. He begins to wonder how his dear would feel if she had to watch her true love spend the rest of his life in the arms of another, albeit just a notch or two less beautiful, woman. Did that flick of the finger mean, therefore, 'Dinner's served?' Oh, but no, 'Charity suffereth long, and is kind; charity envieth not. . . .' Wish him to be torn limb from limb and eaten before the king and the court and *her*? Impossible! So it must be the lady behind the right door.

"But wait! Did I mention *who* the lady is? She is well-known to the king's daughter, a woman she despises, loathes with all her being, so if it is her behind the right door, the princess will be forced to watch, *for the rest of her life*, this hateful creature have what she, the royal princess, cannot. And her poor lover knows this.

"'Still, I cannot believe she could simply sit there and watch me be *eaten*,' our poor lover thinks. 'So she points to the door that will slay her heart but save my life.' He starts to turn the knob on the right-hand door.

"'But wait!' he thinks. 'What if she is worried that I do not trust her? That would mean she points out the tiger, thinking I will choose the *other* door and thus live. I must choose the door on the left!'

"So he steps to the door on the left. But just as he's about to open it, he thinks, 'But wait! I *do* trust her. Her heart could not bear the sight of my mangled corpse being dragged around the arena by a wild animal, entrails trailing in the sawdust, blood everywhere, a mess. The lady must be behind the right door! *Unless* . . . unless I *shouldn't* trust her. Love may suffer long, but a lifetime is an awfully "long" long. The tiger is behind the right door. I should open the left!'

"Two doors. Behind one, the lady. Behind the other, the tiger. Which should he choose?"

Torrance fell silent. Arkwright, convinced by this point, perhaps, that he was in the presence of a lunatic, said nothing at first, and then, unable to bear the tension any longer, blurted out, "All right, which is it? Which door did he choose?"

"I don't know! The bugger just leaves it there. He can knock off two and a half hot dogs in a minute, but he can't finish a damn story. Anyway, it's the wrong question. The correct question is which will *you* choose—the lady or the tiger?"

Torrance nodded to me. I stepped into the hall and returned with the rolling cart; its wheels had not been oiled since its construction, most likely; they squeaked and squealed as I pushed it into the small chamber. Arkwright's eyes cut to the cart and the large jar sitting on top of it—and then cut away. His shoulders bunched and relaxed; his right leg jerked.

"You know what this is," Torrance said with a flick of his finger toward the thing suspended inside the amber-colored preserving solution. Arkwright did not answer. His face shone with sweat. A nerve beneath his right eye danced.

"Now, where did I put my gloves?" Torrance wondered. "Oh, here they are on the table. You too, Will. Put them on." He picked up the scalpel from the cart and sliced through the wax ring around the lid. "Hold this a moment, please, Will," he said, handing me the scalpel. He unscrewed the lid. The sound was very loud in the closed space.

"All right," Arkwright said loudly. "All right! This really is becoming tiresome. I demand to speak to Dr. von Helrung immediately!"

Torrance set the lid aside, and then reached inside to remove the *nidus*, grimacing a bit, not from fear, I think, but, because his forearms were so large, it was a tight fit. He carefully lowered the nest of woven human remains next to the jar, where it glistened wetly in the lamplight.

"Spatula, Will," Torrance murmured. I handed him the flat-bladed tool, which he used to coax off a dime-size amount of the bonding material, the sticky sputum of *Typhoeus magnificum*.

"What is it?" Arkwright shouted. "What are you doing over there?"

"You know what I'm doing."

"You do not realize it, sir, but you have made a grievous mistake. A grievous mistake!"

"Me? *I* have made a grievous mistake?" Torrance held up the spatula.

"Do you think that frightens me?" Arkwright laughed derisively. "You won't do it. You *can't* do it."

"I can't do it?" Torrance seemed genuinely puzzled.

"No, you can't—because I don't have to tell you anything. I *won't* tell you anything unless you release me. Ha! Now which shall *you* choose? If you do this to me, you will never know."

"Never know what? I don't recall asking you a damn thing."

Arkwright tried to laugh. It came out as a strangled hiccup. His hands were locked around the rear legs of the chair, and they were shaking, and so the chair too was shaking. The very air around Thomas Arkwright shook; the dust particles vibrated in sympathy to his terror.

Torrance continued: "The absorption rate varies depending on the location of the exposure. Exposure to the upper dermis, for example, results in a more prolonged development of symptoms than, say, exposure to the mouth, or eyes, nose—any body cavity, really, such as the ear canal or the anus."

He was speaking in a very dry monotone, similar to the one I'd heard the doctor use, as if he were addressing some unseen classroom of students.

"You're mad," Arkwright said matter-of-factly.

"No," Torrance replied. "I'm a *monstrumologist*. It's a subtle distinction."

Then he continued with his presentation: "And the symptoms . . . Well, I probably don't need to go into all *that*. If you're curious, I suppose Will here could describe them to you—what you may expect in the hours to come. He's seen it up close."

I nodded. I felt light-headed. Blood roared in my ears. And in my heart, the tightly wound thing unwinding.

"Will . . . ," Arkwright echoed. "Will! Will, you can't do this. Don't let him do this, Will! Run and find von Helrung. Quick, Will! Go!"

"I wouldn't appeal anything to Mr. Henry if I were you," said Torrance. "Truth is, all this was his idea."

Arkwright stared at me, dumbfounded. I returned his stare frankly; I did not look away.

"He's the one who figured you out for the stinking liar you are. So I wouldn't be barking orders at Mr. Will Henry, no sir!"

He stepped toward the seated man, and that one step caused Arkwright to jerk violently. The feet of the chair complained against the concrete floor. The gun fell from his lap.

"Dear God, I don't know what you want from me!" he cried, his bravado beginning to break.

"Hear that, Will?" inquired Torrance. "That sound like a Long Island accent to you? Doesn't to me. Sounds English almost."

"I am a British citizen, a servant to the crown of Her Majesty, Queen Victoria, and I will see you hang, sir!"

"I doubt that," Torrance returned easily. He stepped around the chair to stand directly behind Arkwright, moving with startling alacrity for a man his size. He did not hesitate; he did not wait for his prisoner to turn his head; he reached forward with his free hand and pinched shut Arkwright's nose.

The reaction was immediate. Arkwright bucked and twisted, threw his body impotently against the ropes, whipped his head from side to side in a vain attempt to dislodge Torrance's viselike grip. Out of the corner of his eye, before it was covered with the palm of his captor's large hand, he must have seen the gleaming spatula in Torrance's other hand. His lips were clamped tightly together, but he and Torrance knew it could be maintained for only so long. He could hold his breath until he passed out, but what would that accomplish? It would make Torrance's job easier; that's all.

He had little choice. The lady or the tiger? It was a poor analogy.

He opened his mouth and gasped, "My name is not Arkwright." With his nose clamped tight, he sounded like he had a bad head cold.

"I don't care what your name is."

"You *will* hang for this!" he shouted. "You and von Helrung and your little bastard assistant."

"Will isn't my little bastard assistant. Will is Pellinore Warthrop's little bastard assistant."

"Warthrop? Is that it? You want to know what happened to Warthrop? Warthrop is dead. He died on Masirah, the bloody island of Masirah, in the Arabian Sea, just like I told von Helrung!"

Torrance looked across the room at me. I shook my head.

"We don't believe you," he told Arkwright. "Will, lend me a hand here. He keeps jerking around like this, and I'm going to drop the spatula."

I took the implement from him and watched Torrance wrap his huge forearm around Arkwright's neck.

"You've done it now," Torrance whispered. "See, I might hesitate. I'm at the age where the idea of hanging actually gives me pause, but he's just a child, and children think they will live forever. He's got a strong case. He thinks you may have killed Warthrop, you know, and I'm thinking he may be right."

"I didn't kill him!"

"Well, he sure didn't die the way you described it. My money is on Kearns. Kearns killed him."

"No one killed him—no one. I swear to you, no one!" His eyes fell upon me; I was the one who held death itself—and therefore his life—in my hand.

"He's alive," he gasped. "There. He's alive! Is that satisfactory to you?"

"First he's dead; now he's alive," Torrance said. "Next you'll have him appearing in a traveling minstrel show."

He released Arkwright and snapped his fingers at me. He wanted the *pwdre ser*.

Arkwright cried out, "I'm telling you the truth! And I'll tell you what else. The bastard wouldn't be alive if it weren't for me! That's the ironic thing. Warthrop owes his life to me, and you're going to take mine for the debt!"

"Owes you his life," Torrance echoed.

"Yes, his life. They wanted to kill him. Wanted to kill both of us. But I put a stop to it. I stopped them—"

"'Them,'" said Torrance.

"No, no, please. I can't tell you that."

"'*They* wanted to kill him.'"

"They'll kill me. They will hunt me down like a dog and they—"

"'They.'"

"Listen to me!" Arkwright screeched. His eyes were darting back and forth—to me, to Torrance, to me again, back to Torrance. To whom should he appeal? The child who had composed this play, or the actor who was performing it? "If I tell you that, I'm a dead man."

"You're a dead man if you don't."

The lady or the tiger. Perhaps the analogy was not so poor after all.

I could contain myself no longer. "Where is Dr. Warthrop?" I blurted out.

He told us, and the answer held no meaning for me. I had never heard of the place, but Torrance had. He stared at Arkwright for a long moment, and then burst into laughter.

"Well . . . all right, then! I like it. It's . . . Well, it's crazy. But it also makes some sense. Inclines me toward some skeptical belief, Arkwright."

"Good! And now you know where he is and you're letting me go. Aren't you?"

But Torrance had not finished thinking it through. He had reached the crux of it, the two identical doors.

"'They,' you said. 'They wanted to kill him.' There was Kearns and you and *them*. Or was it Kearns and you, and then *them*?"

"I don't even know what you're *saying*. Oh, Christ help me!" His eyes rolled in my direction. "Christ, help me," he whispered desperately.

I thought I understood, and stepped in as Torrance's interpreter. "How do you know John Kearns?"

"I don't know John Kearns from Adam. Never met him, never saw him before, and never *heard* of him before this bloody business began. And I wish I never had!"

"Got it!" Torrance shouted. "It's Kearns, *then* them, and *then* you. Not you *and* Kearns—not you *with* Kearns. You're not with Kearns, and you're not with them. You're with . . ." He stamped his foot. I was reminded of a rambunctious stallion eager to be free of his stall. "Servant to the Crown . . . *Servant to the Crown*! I get it now. That's good."

All was still then. Even the dust seemed to pause in its fitful ballet. There was Arkwright in his chair and Torrance standing behind him and me against the wall, and there was the lamplight and the *nidus* and the spatula, and, glistening on the spatula, *pwdre ser*, the rot of stars that made men rot, and inside each of us *das Ungeheuer*, the thing unwinding that whispers *I AM* with the force to break the world in half, the thing in you and the thing in me, the thing in Thomas and the thing in Jacob, and the two doors, two for each of us.

Jacob chose his door first, reaching down and untying the ropes that bound the hands of Thomas, and Thomas in the chair shivered like a man who opens the front door of his warm house on a cold morning. Jacob chose his door and freed Thomas's hands, and after he had freed his hands and Thomas knew the bracing wind on his face, the blast that meant he was free, that he'd endured, Jacob yanked back Thomas's head, and Thomas howled, and his hands came up, but it was too late because Jacob had opened the door; the door was flung wide, and into Thomas's mouth went the spatula, to the back of his throat, and Thomas gagged.

Torrance stepped back as Arkwright went forward, fighting desperately to stand, but his legs were still bound to the chair and he pitched forward onto the cold floor, and his screams were inhuman slaughterhouse screeches. He scuttled across the floor, the chair's back pushing his chest down and scraping back and forth as he legs jerked and pulled against the ropes, and then he stopped, his back arched, and he emptied his stomach.

What came next could not have lasted more than a minute:

"Will! Will!" Torrance shouted.

A slap across my cheek, hard enough to rock me back on my heels.

"Get. Out. NOW."

I skittered around Arkwright's heaving form.

Sobs and curses were trapped between the chamber walls, echoes smashing against answering echoes, pummeling me, the sound of the world breaking in half.

The amber-colored liquid in the empty jar that sloshed when I bumped into the cart on the way out. Then, behind me, the soft *tink* of the spatula falling to the floor, and then the wobbly wheels complaining as Torrance shoved the cart toward me.

The *nidus* was now in the hall, and right behind it was Torrance, who slammed shut the door and threw home the bolt. He hurled his huge fist against the locked door. He howled with unloosed rage.

I do not think the man on the other side heard him.

"Stupid, stupid, stupid!" *Bang, bang, BANG!* "You stupid, stupid, *stupid* limey bastard!" *BANG!*

I slid down the wall of the passageway. I pressed my hands to my ears. It goes on forever, the unwinding thing; it has no beginning or end, no top or bottom; it is not contained by the universe; before the universe was, it had been; and when the universe has burned itself to a handful of dust, it will still be there, the thing in me and the thing in you, *das Ungeheuer*, the abyss.

"This wasn't the plan! You weren't supposed to really *do* it!" I screamed at Torrance's back as he pounded on the locked door. "You were supposed to make him just *think* you were!"

He whirled on me. I saw his eyes clearly, in the lamplight dark, in the dim hall, white-less. *Oculus Dei*, I thought, the eyes of God.

"Shut up and listen!" he roared. "Just shut your trap and listen to—"

Now, from the chamber, silence, and the man inside sees before him the two doors, *his* two doors, and the man asks himself, *Which will it be, the lady or the tiger?* And he stretches out his hand . . .

Jacob Torrance stiffened when the shot rang out. His gaze flew toward the low ceiling, and then he closed his eyes.

"It's the lady, then," he murmured.

NINETEEN

"Little Good Can Come of This"

Abram von Helrung crossed his arms behind his back and stared out the window to the street below. Beneath him the great city was coming to life. A large gray draft horse clopped along the granite avenue pulling a dray loaded with dry goods. A man on a boneshaker bicycle whizzed along the sidewalk. Two pretty girls with red ribbons in their hair skipped arm in arm across the street, lifting their bare knees high, their high-pitched laughter like the little lame balloon man's whistle, far and wee.

"'Go, for they call you, Shepherd, from the hill,'" he said quietly. "'Come Shepherd, and again begin the quest!'"

He turned from the window and said, "I was ten, and my father took my little sister and me from our little village of Lech to Stubenbach, where a band of Gypsies had arrived with their traveling show. It was just the three of us; my mother refused to go and warned Papa he must watch us with an eagle eye, for the Gypsies were widely believed to steal children. 'Devil-worshippers,' she called them. But my Papa, though only a poor farmer, had the heart of an adventurer, and so we went. There were dancers and acrobats and fortune-tellers—and the food! *Mein Gott*, you had never tasted such food! In the afternoon we were approached by two men, one very old and the other much younger—his son, perhaps—who offered us a peek inside their tent for a small fee. 'Why?' asked Papa. 'What is in your tent?' And the older one answered, 'Come and see.' So Papa paid the fee, and I went inside. Not Papa or my sister. The younger Gypsy said to him, 'Do not take her. She should stay outside.' And Papa wasn't going to leave her and risk her being stolen—or my mother's wrath for suffering her to be stolen. I went in alone. There was a large wooden crate—it reminded me very much of a coffin—and inside the crate was an abomination. It paralyzed me with dread—froze me to the spot. I wanted to look away, but I could not look away. 'What is it?' I asked the old man. 'It is a monster,' he said. 'Slain by my kinsmen in Egypt. It is called a griffin. This one is only a baby. They grow very large, large enough to blot out the sun. Is it not marvelous?'

"It had the body of a lion, the head of an eagle, and a python for a tail. A fake, and not a very good fake. They had sutured the parts together with thick black twine, but I did not come to that conclusion until many years later. I was a child. I saw the beast with a child's eyes, eyes that could not look away. What sort of thing is this and how could it *be*? How could such a thing exist? I remember feeling tightness in my chest, as if a great hand were squeezing the life from my heart. I would run; I would stay. I would turn aside; I would look closer. . . . It held me, and in some strange way that I do not pretend to understand, I held *it*. I still hold it. And it still holds me."

He turned back to the window. The sun broke over the buildings on the eastern side of the street, flooding the avenue with golden light.

"That day was the beginning."

"I was fifteen, and my first monster had the same name as me," Jacob Torrance said. "He came home after a night with his mistress and a bottle of rotgut and started beating my mother with the business end of a joiner's mallet. So I picked up the closest thing at hand—just happened to be his Springfield musket—and blew a hole the size of a turnip through the back of his head. Been killing monsters ever since."

Von Helrung was frowning. "Thomas Arkwright was no monster until you made him one."

"Thomas Arkwright was an agent for the British intelligence service."

"How do you know this? Did Arkwright tell you? No! You *assume* it. You guess at it!"

"Besides Kearns, there are at least two sets of players at

this poker table, *Meister* Abram. Three, counting us. There's the set Arkwright was afraid would kill him if he showed his hand, and the set that was going to hang *us* if we harmed one little hair on his thinning scalp. I don't know who that first set could be, but I'm betting the second is Her Majesty's government. Makes good sense to me. If I were Kearns and knew where the *magnificum* roosted, I could demand a hefty asking price. A *nidus* would fetch a pretty penny, sure, but compare that to having the momma whose one drop of spit turns grown men's brains into jelly. He could expect a king's ransom—or a queen's!"

"Why would the English send a spy to infiltrate our ranks if Kearns holds the key to the *magnificum?*" asked von Helrung.

"Getting to that. Arkwright obviously knew Warthrop had the *nidus.* Will figured that one out all by himself. And the only way he could have known that, is from Kearns. Unless this first set of people, whoever *they* are, told him— or another set we don't know about yet, but I don't think so. I think Kearns told him. Well, not Kearns personally—the British government, the blokes who sent him. And they sent him because they needed Warthrop for something."

"Needed him . . . for what?" Von Helrung appeared confused.

"Not sure. But I'm pretty sure that Jack Kearns had the *nidus,* but he didn't know where it came from. *That's* why they infiltrated our ranks. If you know where it comes from, you don't need an expert monster hunter. You just go straight to the monster. But if you *don't* know where it comes from, then you're up the proverbial beanstalk. So what does our boy Jack do if he has the golden egg but not the goose that laid it? He'll need a goose hunter. And not just any ol' goose hunter. This ain't no ordinary goose; it's *the* goose, the goose of all gooses—eh, *geese*. Not just any goose hunter but the best goose hunter in the world, in the whole *history* of the world. You don't dare play it straight with him. You don't tell him *why* you want it hunted; he's got it in his goose-hunting head somehow that morals apply to monstrumology."

Von Helrung thought for a moment, and then snorted with disgust.

"And Arkwright is sent here to track Warthrop tracking the *magnificum*? It is absurd, Torrance. Once Pellinore discovered the hiding place of the *magnificum*, the British would have no reason to pay Kearns a penny."

"That's where I think the first set of players comes in. Kearns went to someone else, another government—maybe the French, no love lost there—and he's playing them off each other."

"How?"

"I don't know. Maybe Warthrop does. That's the next step. And I say we don't waste time taking it. They'll be expecting Arkwright back soon, and Arkwright isn't coming back . . . soon or any other time."

"Because you killed him," I piped up. I was still furious at him. "You didn't have to do what you did."

"Think so? And anyway, I killed him in only the loosest definition of the word."

"Why did you kill him, Jacob?" von Helrung asked quietly. "What did you fear?"

Torrance said nothing at first; he played with his signet ring. *Nil timendum est.*

"Well, he did threaten to have me hanged, but never mind that. It's like you stepping into that Gypsy's tent, *Meister* Abram. Once we had him tied up, *alea iacta est*, the die had been cast. Stick to Will's plan, and we get arrested—or worse—for the kidnapping and torture of a British officer, and Warthrop rots where they've stuck him until he's older than you."

"And what if they didn't stick him there?" I shouted at him. "What if Arkwright lied? You didn't have to kill him, and you *shouldn't have* killed him. Now we may never find the doctor!"

Torrance stared stone-faced at me for a long moment, and then shrugged. Shrugged! I hurled myself toward him. I was going to pummel him to death with my bare hands. I was going to choke the life out of him. Von Helrung saved his life. He grabbed my arm and yanked me back, pulled my head to his chest and stroked my hair.

"So you are at peace with his self-destruction?" von Helrung asked Torrance. "The one you conveniently staged?"

"Everybody should have a choice when it comes down to it—and, yes, I think I'll sleep well tonight."

"I envy you this once, Jacob, for I will not."

I waited until Torrance had retired to the guest bedroom, to rest from the night's labor, before I approached von Helrung with my request. I call it a request; it was more like a demand.

"I'm coming with you," I told him.

"It is too dangerous," he returned, not unkindly.

"I won't be left behind again. If you try, I'll stow away on the boat. And if I can't stow away, I'll swim there. I am the one who found him out. I have earned the right."

He placed a hand upon my shoulder. "I fear it is more burden than right, *mein Freund* Will Henry."

That afternoon I said good-bye to Adolphus Ainesworth, who was in a very foul mood, even for him.

"I don't care what anyone says," he snarled at me, his false teeth snapping in fury. "Someone has been inside the Locked Room! I always hang my ring with the outside key on the *inside*, and this morning how do you think I find it facing?"

"Toward the outside?"

"*You* took them."

"No, Professor Ainesworth, I did not," I answered honestly. It had been Torrance who'd entered the Locked Room.

"Well, what do I expect? You are a child, and children

are natural-born liars. Some grow out of it; some don't! And what do you mean, you're leaving?"

"I am sailing to England in the morning with Dr. von Helrung."

"Dr. von Helrung! Why is Dr. von Helrung going to England? And why are *you* going to England?" He was a very old man, but his intellect had not faded with his youth. It took only a moment for him to piece the puzzle together. "The *magnificum*! You have found it."

"No, but we've found Dr. Warthrop."

"You've found Dr. Warthrop!"

"Yes, Professor Ainesworth. We have found Dr. Warthrop."

"He isn't dead?"

I shook my head. "No."

"Why are you smiling like that?" He bared his dead son's teeth to mock my grin. "Well, I will be sorry to miss the joyous reunion. His gain is my gain, I will say."

"Sir?"

"I said his gain is my gain!" He leaned across the desk to shout in my face. "Don't you know *I'm* the one who's supposed to be deaf? Well. Good-bye!"

He bent over some papers on his desk and shooed me toward the door with a wave of his gnarled hand.

I paused in the doorway. It occurred to me that I might not see him again.

"I enjoyed working for you, Professor Ainesworth," I said.

He did not look up from his work. "Keep moving, William James Henry. Always keep moving, like the proverbial stone, or you'll end up an old mossback like Adolphus Ainesworth!"

I started into the hall. He called me back.

"You are a slave," he said. "Or you must think you are, not to be asking for your pay. Here," he added gruffly, shoving two crumpled dollar bills across the desk.

"Professor Ainesworth—"

"Take it! Don't be a fool when it comes to money, Will Henry. Be a fool about everything else—religion, politics, love—but never be a fool about money. That bit of wisdom is your bonus for your long *minutes* of heavy toil!"

"Thank you, Professor Ainesworth."

"Shut up. Go. Wait. Why the devil are you going again?"

"To save the doctor."

"Save him from what?"

"Whatever he needs saving from. I'm his apprentice."

As I packed my things that evening, Lilly approached me with her request. Oh, very well, I shall admit it: It wasn't a request.

"I am going with you."

I did not choose the answer von Helrung had given me. I was tired and anxious, my nerves were shot, and the last thing I wanted was a row.

"Your mother won't let you."

"Mother says she won't let *you*."

"The difference is that she isn't my mother."

"She's already been to Uncle, you know. I've never seen her so angry. I thought her head might burst—literally burst and roll off her shoulders. I'm very curious to see what happens."

"I don't think her head will burst."

"No, I meant with you. I've never known her not to get her way."

She flopped onto the bed and watched me shove clothing into my little bag. Her frank stare unnerved me. It always did.

"How did you find him?" she asked.

"Another monstrumologist found him."

"How?"

"I—I am not sure."

She laughed—spring rain upon the dry earth. "I don't know why you lie, William James Henry. You're very bad at it."

"The doctor says lying is the worst kind of buffoonery."

"Then, you are the worst kind of buffoon."

I laughed. It brought me up short. I could not remember the last time I had laughed. It felt good to laugh. And good to see her eyes and smell the jasmine in her hair. I had the impulse to kiss her. I'd never experienced that particular urge before, and the feeling was not unlike standing on the edge of an abyss of an entirely different sort. This was no knot in my chest unwinding; this was the air itself, the whole atmosphere, expanding at speeds unimaginable. I didn't know quite what to do about it all—except perhaps to kiss her, but actually kissing Lilly Bates entailed . . . well, *kissing* her.

"Will you miss me?" she asked.

"I will try."

She found my answer to be extraordinarily witty. She rolled onto her back and howled with laughter. I blushed, not knowing whether to be flattered or offended.

"Oh!" she cried, sitting up and digging into her purse. "I nearly forgot! Here, I have something for you."

It was her photograph. Her smile was slightly unnatural, I thought, though I liked her hair. It had been styled into corkscrew ringlets, which more than made up for the smile.

"Well, what do you think? It's for luck, and for when you get lonely. You've never told me, but I think you are lonely a great deal of the time."

I might have argued; bickering was our normal mode of discourse. But I was leaving, and she had just given me her photograph, and a moment before I'd thought of kissing her, so I thanked her for the present and went on with my packing—that is, rearranging what was already packed. Sometimes, when Lilly was around me, I felt like an actor who did not know what to do with his hands.

"Write me," she said.

"What?"

"A letter, a postcard, a telegram . . . write to me while you're away."

"All right," I said.

"Liar."

"I promise, Lilly. I will write to you."

"Write me a poem."

"A poem?"

"Well, it doesn't have to be a poem, I suppose."

"That's good."

"Why is that good? You don't want to write a poem?" She was pouting.

"I've just never written one. The doctor has. The doctor was a poet before he became a monstrumologist. I bet you didn't know that."

"I bet you didn't know I did know that. I've even read some of his poems."

"Now you're the liar. The doctor said he burned them all."

Being caught in a lie did not faze Lillian Bates. She simply moved on, remorseless. "Why did he do that?"

"He said they weren't very good."

"Oh, that's nonsense." She was laughing again. "If one burned every bad poem that's been written, the smoke would blot out the sun for a week."

She watched as I tugged my hat from the top shelf of the closet. Watched as I turned it in my hands. Watched my face as I ran my finger over the stitching on the inside band: W.J.H.

"What is it?" she asked.

"It's my hat."

"Well, I can see it's a hat! It looks too small for you."

"No," I said. I stuffed the hat into my bag. It had been his first—no, his *only*—gift to me. I was determined never to misplace it.

"It fits," I said.

I had the dream that night—my last night in New York and the last night I would have it.

The Locked Room. Adolphus fumbling with his keys.

The doctor said you'd want to see this.

The box on the table and the lid that won't come off.

I can't open it.

The box trembles. It mimics the beat of my heart. What is in the box?

Thickheaded boy! You know what it is. You've always known what's in the box. It isn't what's inside he wanted you to see: It's the box!

I pick it up. The box trembles in my hand. It beats in time with my heart. I'd been wrong; it was not the doctor's. It belonged to me.

I was not down for breakfast promptly at six the next morning. Mrs. Bates came up to check on me; I heard her hurrying up the stairs, and then the bedroom door burst open and she stood gasping in the doorway. I noticed she was holding an envelope.

"William! Oh, thank God. I thought you had left."

"I wouldn't leave without saying good-bye, Mrs. Bates. That wouldn't be proper."

She beamed. "No! No, it most certainly would not. And here you are, and here is your bag with all your things, and I suppose you have not changed your mind?"

I told her that I had not. An awkward silence came between us.

"Well," I said finally, and cleared my throat. "I'd better go."

"You must say good-bye to Mr. Bates," she instructed me. "And thank him for all he's done."

"Yes, ma'am."

"And, forgive me, William, but really, you must think I've gone mad if you think you're leaving this house with your hair looking like that."

She found the comb beside the washbasin and ran it through my hair several times. She did not seem pleased with the outcome.

"Do you have a hat?"

"Yes, ma'am."

I dug into my bag for the hat with my initials. I heard what sounded like the soft cry of a wounded animal and looked over at her.

"William, I must apologize," she said. "I do not have a bon voyage present for you, but, I will say in my defense, I had hardly any notice that you were leaving. It was literally *sprung* on me at the last moment."

"You don't need to give me anything, Mrs. Bates."

"It is . . . customary, William."

She sat on the bed. I remained standing beside my little bag, turning the hat in my hands. She was tapping the envelope upon her lap.

"Unless you would consider this a gift," she said, nodding to the envelope.

"What is it?"

"It is a letter of acceptance to Exeter Academy, one of the most prestigious preparatory schools in the country, William. Mr. Bates is an alumnus; he arranged it for you."

"Arranged what?"

"Your acceptance! For the fall term."

I shook my head; I didn't understand. The hat turned; the envelope tapped.

"Stay with us," she said. And then, as if she were correcting herself, "Stay with me. I know it may be too soon to call you 'son,' but if you stay, I promise I will love you as my son. I will protect you; I will keep you safe; I will let no harm come to you."

I sat beside her. My hat in my hands, the envelope in her lap, and the absent man between us.

"My place is with the doctor."

"Your place! William, your place is wherever the good Lord decides it is. Have you thought of that? In life there are the silly gifts we give one another and there are the *real* gifts, the gifts beyond all temporal value. It is no accident of circumstance that you've come to me. It is the will of

God. I believe that. I believe that with all my heart."

"If it's God's will," I said, "wouldn't he make sure I *couldn't* leave?"

"You're forgetting his greatest gift, William. That gift does not imprison; it frees. I could refuse to let you go. I could hire a lawyer, report the matter to the police. I could truss you up like a turkey and lock you in this room, but I will not. I will not force you to stay. I am asking you to stay. If you like, William, I will fall on my knees and beg you."

Mrs. Bates began to cry. She cried like she did everything else, with great dignity; there was a stateliness about her tears, a grandness that transcended the mundane—*operatic*, I would call them, and I mean that in the best sense of the word.

I looked down at the hat. A *silly* gift, she had called it. Perhaps it was silly compared to the ultimate gift. What gift would not be? And perhaps *I* was silly to feel any attachment to it or to the man who had given it to me. *Little good can come of this, Will Henry.* I looked at the spot where my finger should have been. That was nothing, the smallest of losses. In the warm kitchen a woman bakes her little boy an apple pie. A man lies upon the floor, spreads his arms, and transforms himself into a ship of a thousand sails.

And in the arena are two identical doors . . .

She reached out and laid her hand upon my cheek. She knew. She never doubted, in the spot where doubt matters, which door I would choose.

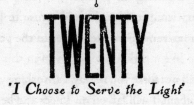

TWENTY

'I Choose to Serve the Light'

Jacob Torrance filled the majority of his time during the six-day crossing with three things: carousing, philandering, and poker—in that order, with the occasional argument with Dr. von Helrung thrown in to break up the monotony. I suppose he slept a bit as well, but he did not share my stateroom. I bunked with the old Austrian monstrumologist, who, I quickly discovered, shed most of his dignity when he put on his nightshirt (he was quite bandy-legged and a little potbellied), though that is true of almost everyone.

I missed one or two of their opening skirmishes. Hardly had Lady Liberty slipped beneath the horizon than I came down with a horrible case of mal de mer, the bane of land-lubbers, forcing me to become more intimately acquainted with a toilet than any person ought to be. Von Helrung put me to bed, gave me some salt crackers, and suggested, very seriously, that the best cure for seasickness was dancing.

"No, it's olives," countered Torrance. "Or gingerroot. You should gnaw on a root, Mr. Henry."

"On every voyage my wife would suffer the same as Will," von Helrung returned. "We would go dancing, and all would be fine."

"So you would like to take Will dancing?"

"It makes more sense for him to dance than to gnaw on a root."

"Maybe he should do both—gnaw on a root while he danced."

"I'd rather not dance or eat," I croaked. "Ever again."

On the second day I was feeling a little better—well enough to try out my sea legs, anyway, and left the stateroom to explore the liner. After an hour of wandering the labyrinthine corridors and miles of decks, I discovered von Helrung and Torrance on the upper promenade, sitting in rocking chairs, the ever-present tumbler of Scotch by Torrance's elbow. He had an annoying habit of smoothing his perfectly trimmed mustache after every sip.

". . . not consistent. Not consistent at all, Jacob," von Helrung was scolding his former student as I approached. So engrossed were they in the debate that my presence at first went unnoticed.

"I'm not saying it *is* there, *Meister* Abram—merely that we should look into it."

"And I ask again, why would Arkwright lie about all things except the most important thing?"

"He wasn't lying about Warthrop," Torrance pointed out. "Well, not on the third go around, anyway."

Von Helrung had received the news via telegram on the morning of our departure. His source had reported that the doctor was indeed where Arkwright had said he was—alive and well, or as well as might be expected, if you were Pellinore Warthrop and woke one day to find yourself in a decidedly un-Warthropian milieu. Von Helrung had been beside himself with joy; he actually danced a little jig on the dock when he read the cable. Perhaps he thought it odd, my somewhat muted reaction, but I had never lost hope, not really. You may call me a mystic or attribute my faith to the magical thinking of a child. Still, whatever one might say of mystics or faith or the thoughts of children, I believed if the doctor were really dead I would know it; I would *feel* it. Though fear for his life had sent me running on a river of blood and fire to save him, when I'd read the words in von Helrung's vestibule, *Warthrop is dead*, I'd known them to be a lie—had known it in the way a child knows things only God himself could have told him.

"But why *there* of all places?" von Helrung had wondered after his impromptu celebratory dance.

"It's perfect!" Torrance had exclaimed. "Can't think of a more perfect place. Perfectly escape-proof and perfectly poetic. Kearns's idea, I'm sure. I will give the man his due. The dirty louse has panache."

"No, it must have been part of the deceit. It is not Masirah," von Helrung was now insisting. "It could not be. Too far north and too close to the mainland. Oman is but ten miles to the west."

Torrance was not going to give up easily, though. It was difficult to tell with Jacob Torrance. I wondered if he really believed everything he said or if he played devil's advocate just for the childish thrill of it.

"But it could work, *Meister* Abram—sparsely populated, surrounded by treacherous currents, a rough and rocky coastline, a rugged inhospitable terrain. It could work." He jiggled the ice in his tumbler. "The general area is right. Maybe our quarry has expanded its territory or migrated northward. It *has* been nearly forty years since the Lakshadweep discovery. Masirah is how far from Agatti? A thousand or so miles? That's an average migration rate of twenty-five miles per year, very reasonable, particularly if the flying version of the *magnificum* turns out to be the right one."

"I am not saying it is false from a monstrumological standpoint, Torrance," von Helrung snapped. "If you are correct and the British government is involved, why would its agent reveal the one thing they would most want hidden, and hide all the rest? No. They choose Masirah for Pellinore to meet his Waterloo because it would seem a reasonable nesting ground to us *and* it was far from the real one."

The old man's face darkened, and he added, "Of course, the entire issue would be moot if you had kept your head in the Monstrumarium."

"I didn't ask Arkwright, because I didn't need to, *Meister Abram*," returned Torrance.

"I see! You are adept at mind reading as well as torture."

"You're just trying to get under my skin. That's all right. The reason I didn't ask Arkwright is Warthrop. I didn't need Arkwright to tell me something I can get straight from the horse's mouth."

"And what convinces you that—"

"Why put the hound back in its kennel unless you've bagged the fox? Warthrop had served his purpose. He'd found the home of the *magnificum*. Now the really interesting question is—"

His head came round; he must have seen me out of the corner of his eye.

"And here he is!" he said. "Like Lazarus three days dead from the tomb. Only Lazarus had better coloring. Stand back there, Mr. Henry, and head for the railing if you're going to be sick again. I've just shined these shoes. Now, where is that steward? My glass is empty and my whistle's dry."

He excused himself and strode off without the slightest sway in his step. The more he drank, it seemed, the sturdier he became.

Von Helrung patted the arm of the rocker Torrance had

vacated, and I sat down. Why people would find it pleasant to sit in a rocking chair on a rolling deck of an ocean liner was perplexing, to say the least.

"Dr. Torrance sounds like him sometimes," I said.

"Warthrop?"

"Kearns."

Von Helrung nodded; his expression was sad. "I am sorry to say I agree with you, *mein Freund* Will. When I was younger, I often wondered if monstrumology brought out the darkness in men's hearts or if it attracted men with hearts of darkness. I think now it is not the nature of monstrumology but the nature of man. The truth makes us uncomfortable, as truth often does. In every heart, there lives a Jack Kearns."

What he is, that's what you are inside, I had told the monstrumologist.

On our final night at sea, unable to sleep and no longer able to endure the rumbling of my roommate's tummy (von Helrung complained regularly of indigestion), I slipped out of the stateroom and headed for the foredeck. The North Atlantic was restless that night; driven by a sharp southwest wind, the waves smashed and ground angrily against the prow. The deck rose and fell, rose and fell, up toward the cloud-covered sky, then down toward the dark, cold water, as if our ship were balanced upon a fulcrum, teeter-tottering between heaven and hell. I spied two gulls flitting in and out of the running lights, but that was the only life—and only light—I saw. There was no horizon; the world was black from top to bottom. I had the vertiginous sense of being very small in an immense space, like a speck of dust floating in the proto-universe, before the sun was born, before the light pushed back the darkness.

The world is large, dear Will, and we, no matter how much we would like to pretend otherwise, we are quite small.

The next day, my exile would end. But that was the only thing that would. If Torrance was right and Warthrop knew where to find the *magnificum*, our rescue was not the end.

I choose to serve the light, he once told me. *Though that bondage often lies in darkness.*

Right now was the time of equilibrium between light and dark, the time between before and after.

I was leaving something behind. It had been within my grasp. I had only had to stretch forth my hand and seize it. Instead I'd watched it burn in the fireplace of the bedroom on Riverside Drive, when the woman who had sung to comfort me in the lightless, unwinding place had tossed an envelope into the flames.

I was approaching something. I thought I understood what it was. *My place is with the doctor,* I had said—a statement of fact, and a promise, too. I thought I knew what to expect after the end of our exile, the doctor's and mine. I understood—or thought I understood—the cost of service to the monstrumologist. I was reminded of it every time I washed my hands.

That night on the foredeck, under the starless sky, in the space between before and after, I looked out and saw darkness. He would go into that darkness in service to the light. And where he went, I would follow.

I thought I knew the cost of service to the one whose path lies in darkness.

I did not.

He thought he knew what he would find in that darkness.

He did not.

Its name is *Typhoeus magnificum*, the Magnificent Father, the Faceless One we cannot help but turn and face. The One of a Thousand Faces that is there when we turn to look, and then looks back at us.

It is the *magnificum*. It lives in that space between spaces, in that spot one ten-thousandth of an inch outside your range of vision. You cannot see it. It sees you. And when it sees you, it does not see *you*. It has no conception of you. There is *magnificum* and nothing else.

You are the nest. You are the hatchling. You are the chrysalis. You are the progeny. You are the rot that falls from stars.

You may not understand what I mean.

You will.

TWENTY-ONE

"A Pleasure to Meet You"

A sallow-faced little man was waiting for us in the lobby of our hotel, the Great Western at Paddington Station, upon our arrival in London. He wore a topcoat of Harris Tweed over a cashmere suit and sported the worst haircut I had ever seen; his hair looked as if someone had hacked at it with a dull knife. I would later learn that Dr. Hiram Walker had been a barber—among other things; he'd once made a go of sheep farming—before entering the field of aberrant biology. He had bid adieu to all of his customers except one: himself. He smoked a pipe, walked with a cane, hummed nervously through his nose, and regarded the world through small, shifty eyes, like a cornered rat. Those eyes lighted for a moment upon the powerful physique of Jacob Torrance with undisguised distaste; clearly he was not pleased.

"Torrance," he said in a nasally British accent. "I did not expect to see you."

"Or you would have brought me a small token of your affection?"

"*Hemmm,*" Walker whined through his alphorn nose. His gaze darted bird-quick to me. "And who is this?"

"This is Will Henry, the son of Warthrop's former assistant, James," answered von Helrung, laying a hand upon my shoulder.

"I am Dr. Warthrop's apprentice," I said.

"Ah, yes. Quite. I seem to remember seeing you about at the last congress. Come to fetch your master, have you?" He turned to von Helrung without waiting for a reply. "The matter has proved more complicated than I first reported, Dr. von Helrung. They are refusing to release him."

A bushy white eyebrow rose slowly toward the old man's hairline. "What do you mean?"

Walker's restless eyes roamed the crowded lobby.

"Perhaps we should find a spot with a bit more privacy. Since receiving your telegram, I've had the unshakable impression that I am being followed."

We went up to our rooms on the third floor, overlooking Praed Street, where von Helrung ordered a pot of tea. Torrance requested something stronger for himself, but his old teacher preferred that his former pupil keep his wits about him.

"Whiskey *is* what keeps them," Torrance protested. He winked at Walker. "The stable to the wild stallion my erudition."

Hiram Walker answered with a disdainful sniff. "I am surprised every time I see you, Torrance."

"Really? And why is that, Sir Hiram?"

"Because it is reasonable to assume you have been killed in a bar fight. And stop calling me that." He sipped his tea and said to von Helrung, "It is outside their protocol to release a patient to anyone outside the immediate family without an order from a magistrate or upon the recommendation of the attending physician."

"But surely you explained to them the circumstances of the case?" asked von Helrung. "He is confined under false pretenses."

Walker shook his head. "I explained nothing. I made only the most general of inquiries, since I do not know the precise circumstances of the case. He was brought there, I was told, by his nephew, a Mr. Noah Boatman—"

Torrance guffawed. "Noah Boatman! Boatman—Arkwright. Ingenious."

"May I continue? Thank you. A Mr. Noah Boatman, who claimed his 'uncle' had suffered a complete mental collapse, brought about by the recent death of his wife, who was mauled to death by a tiger—"

"By a what?" interrupted von Helrung.

"A tiger. A Bengal tiger, while visiting her sister in

India. He believed himself to be, according to the nephew, an American monster hunter by the name of Pellinore Warthrop. His real name was William James Henry, and—*Please*, Torrance, would you be quiet? Von Helrung, perhaps we should order him up some whiskey—a gallon, so he can drink until he passes out. Now, what was I saying?"

"You've told us enough," von Helrung said with a heavy sigh. "The rest is not difficult to guess. *Mein Freund* obliged the devious schemer by insisting he *was* an American monster hunter named Pellinore Warthrop. Thus, by telling the truth he validates the lie!"

"But there is more, Dr. von Helrung. And here it gets rather . . . well, bizarre. Warthrop also claimed, according to my sources, that his 'nephew' is a British double agent in the employ of the Russian secret police."

"'That's it!' cried Torrance, leaping from his chair. Walker flinched, as if expecting a full frontal assault. A bit of tea sloshed from his cup. "'They'll hunt me down like a dog,' he said," Torrance continued. "It's the first set, von Helrung!"

"Who?" asked von Helrung. "Who is the first set?"

"Okhranka! Oh, he's a devil, this John Kearns! Of *course*. I am a fool for not seeing it. No wonder Arkwright was frightened to the point of soiling himself. That explains the fear, and the fact that he was a double agent explains the bravado. I'm guessing now that the Brits don't even know about the *nidus*. It's a Russian job through and through."

"The *nidus?*" Walker echoed, his small eyes widening by half.

"I spoke out of turn," said Torrance, with an abashed look toward von Helrung, whose cheeks had gone ruddy.

"The Russians have recovered a *nidus ex magnificum?*" Walker asked.

"We do not know," von Helrung answered carefully. "There are many unanswered questions."

"So it appears, Dr. von Helrung, most of which belong to me. Who is this Boatman or Arkwright or whatever his name is? Why would he go to such outlandish lengths to falsely imprison Dr. Warthrop? Why was Warthrop in London in the first place? Who is Jack Kearns, and what does he have to do with the Russian secret police?"

Von Helrung was giving Torrance a withering look.

"What?" demanded Torrance. "You never said it was a secret."

"It was Pellinore's wish to pursue the matter . . ." He searched for the word. "Independently."

"Well, sure!" returned Torrance. "That's Warthrop, wanting all the glory for himself."

"The glory for . . . ," Walker asked von Helrung.

Von Helrung sighed. He gazed up at the ceiling and stroked beneath his chin.

"The Russians do not have the *nidus,*" he said finally. "We have the *nidus.* We have the *nidus,* the British have Warthrop, and the Russians have Jack Kearns."

"You're two thirds right, von Helrung," Torrance said. "I don't know if the Russians have Kearns, but I'm willing to bet Sir Hiram a haircut that they have the *magnificum*."

There was nothing von Helrung could do at that point but tell his English colleague everything, from the delivery of the *nidus* on that freezing February morning and the horrific demise of its unwitting courier, to the disappearance of Warthrop and the fate of the traitor responsible for it. He emphasized, with an eyebrow cocked at Torrance, that all else was mere conjecture. We did not know, for example, if the Russians had found the home of *Typhoeus magnificum*.

"Well, it's been what?" asked Torrance. "Over four months now? Plenty of time if Warthrop got it right, which he did."

"And how do you know that, Jacob?" von Helrung demanded. He was beginning to regret, I think, including Torrance in our rescue mission.

Torrance shrugged. "He's Warthrop."

"Let's pray he did," said Walker. "A living *magnificum* would be the crowning achievement of our discipline."

"I don't think the czar gives a tinker's damn about any crowns except his own," Torrance said, and laughed. "If the Russians have it, we won't be seeing it in the Monstrumarium anytime soon!"

Von Helrung was nodding. His expression was very grave. "I'm afraid Dr. Torrance is correct, at least in this particular aspect. If the *magnificum* should fall into the wrong hands . . ." He shuddered. The thought was unbearable.

Not so much to Torrance, though. He seemed intrigued by the possibilities. "It would change everything, gentlemen. It would shift the entire balance of power in Europe—maybe the world. Alexander conquered half of it. Think what he would have done with arrows dipped in monster snot!"

"Must you, Torrance?" whined Walker. "Why did you become a monstrumologist, anyway?"

"Well, I do like to kill things . . ."

"Enough!" cried von Helrung. He slammed his pudgy hand upon the tabletop. "We are forgetting why we are here. We worry first about freeing Pellinore. Then we worry about monster snot." He bore down on Walker. "We cannot go before a magistrate, and we will not convince his doctor. What does that leave us?"

"As I've said, if it's determined he isn't a danger to himself or the public, he may be released to a family member."

"Hmmm," Torrance hummed. "Too bad his nephew is dead."

"We must be careful not to arouse their suspicion, or we shall find ourselves in rooms adjoining Pellinore's," mused von Helrung. "They are convinced of his condition or they would have released him. A ruse might succeed, but there is no way for us to forewarn him. How can he play a part if he cannot read the script?"

"He can't," Torrance said. "But he doesn't have to." He

turned to Walker. "We'll need someone to vouch for us. Someone the superintendent there knows and trusts and who'd be willing to play a supporting role. Got anybody like that in mind?"

Walker thought for a moment, sucking on the extinct tobacco in his bowl. Then he smiled around the tooth-dented stem, his rat eyes glinting wickedly.

"By George, I believe I have."

Walker's bit player was a compact, athletic-looking man in his early thirties, with very dark, short-cropped hair and even darker deep-set eyes. We met up with him the next morning a few miles west of London, outside the gatehouse of the Hanwell Lunatic Asylum.

After introducing von Helrung and me (Torrance, at the urging of von Helrung, had remained behind; I think *Meister* Abram was concerned his presence might turn a delicate situation into a dangerous one), Walker quickly reviewed our hastily drawn-up plan to win Warthrop's immediate release. His friend suggested a few tweaks in our script but overall seemed pleased with the outline of our little scheme.

"I met Warthrop once, you know," he told us. "Must have been '77 or '78, while I was studying at the university in Edinburgh. He'd come to consult with Dr. Bell on some matter or other—I don't know precisely. Bell was very mysterious about it. He cut a striking figure, I remember that—very tall and lean, with the most piercing black eyes that seemed to slice right through you. He shook my hand and said, quite casually, as if he were remarking upon the weather, 'A pleasure to meet you. You have recently returned from London, I perceive.' I was astounded. How had he known that? Bell swore to me afterward he hadn't told him, and I must confess I never quite believed my old professor's denial. I have always meant to ask Warthrop how he knew—"

Von Helrung gently cut off the loquacious Scotsman, saying, "And we are delighted to present you with the opportunity! I am sure Pellinore will remember the encounter. His memory is as prodigious as his powers of observation and deduction. It is a gross injustice that he is here. I assure you, sir, he is no more mad than you or me, and we will be forever in your debt for helping us affect his speedy release from his lonely sojourn behind these walls! Lead, sir, and we shall follow!"

And so he did, through the gatehouse, where the watchman directed us to check in at the clerk's office, located in the main building, a simple—if somewhat imposing—three-story building at the far side of the spacious front grounds. As we walked along the gravel path toward it, my heart began to race as my eyes sought out the doctor. I was excited, apprehensive, and a little frightened. If our impetuous plan should fail, he might never walk out the gates of this place.

I did not see the monstrumologist, but I saw other patients tending shrubbery with pruning shears and watering cans, some carrying loads of laundry and baskets of bread from the washhouse and bakery, and some in leisurely perambulation about the well-tended lawn, deep in earnest conversation or convulsed in carefree laughter, as if they were holiday campers out for a Sunday stroll in the park rather than patients in a lunatic asylum. I did not know it then, but Hanwell was well ahead of its time in the treatment of the mentally ill. Plop a poor soul from an American asylum—Blackwell's Island, for example—into Hanwell, and he might have thought he had died and gone to heaven.

I do not think Warthrop would agree with me, though.

Our coconspirator signed us in at the front office.

"Dr. Hiram Walker, Mr. Abraham Henry, and grandson, to see the superintendent," he informed the clerk. "And please tell him Dr. Conan Doyle is with them."

TWENTY-TWO
'I Would Gladly Die'

"Arthur Conan Doyle! It is indeed a pleasure, sir," the superintendent of Hanwell Lunatic Asylum said as he ushered us into his private office. "I must confess to you that I am quite the ardent admirer of your writing. My wife, too. She will be green with envy when I tell her I've met the creator of the great Sherlock Holmes!"

Conan Doyle accepted the praise humbly; in fact, he seemed almost embarrassed by it, and quickly changed the subject.

"I hope you've had the opportunity to read my note this morning," he said.

"Yes, I have it here somewhere," said the superintendent, rifling through the stacks of papers on his desk. "I shall keep it, if you don't mind, as a memento of . . . Yes, here it is; I have it. Ah, yes, William Henry. A very interesting case."

"This is Dr. Walker, a good friend of mine and Mr. Henry's personal physician," said Conan Doyle. "And this gentleman is Mr. Abraham Henry, William's father, and this is his grandson, William's eldest child, William Jr."

"Billy," von Helrung piped in. "The family calls him Billy, Herr Doctor."

"You are German, Mr. Henry?"

"I am Austrian, but my son William was born in America."

The superintendent was surprised. "But Mr. Boatman claimed your son was a British citizen."

"He is, he is," said von Helrung quickly. "Noah did not deceive you, Herr Doctor. William was born in America but immigrated to this country when he was twenty to study medicine—at the University of . . ." He was drawing a blank. So hasty had been our preparations, we had not thought to fill in every page in Warthrop's fictitious history.

"Edinburgh," Conan Doyle. "A year or so after I left."

"And then he falls in love with a girl here, gets married, and becomes citizen," von Helrung finished with a loud sigh of relief.

"Ah, Annabelle," the superintendent said.

"Who?"

"Annabelle, Mr. Henry's wife, your daughter-in-law."

"Ack! Forgive an old man for the paucity of his faculties. I thought you said something else about . . . something else. Yes, poor, dear Annabelle! He loved her with a love that was more than love, in this kingdom by the sea."

"Yes," the superintendent concurred with a slight frown. "Though Mr. Boatman never mentioned there were children by the marriage. In fact, he told us that he, Mr. Boatman, was the only family William had."

"Well, my grandson Noah is correct, in a manner of speaking."

"In a manner of speaking?"

"I will explain."

"I am anxious that you do," the superintendent replied with a puzzled look toward Conan Doyle, who was smiling noncommittally. The author drummed his fingers nervously on his bowler hat.

Von Helrung tried his best. "Noah's mother—William's only sibling—died tragically at the age of twenty-two, when Noah was but three years old—the consumption. He was her only child. At the time, I was living with my wife, Helena, in Massachusetts, where we had raised William and Gertrude—"

"Gertrude?" The superintendent had begun taking notes. It was not an encouraging development.

"*Ja*, she is William's sister, Noah's mother, and my dear, dead daughter, Helena."

"Helena?"

"I mean Gertrude. She was the spitting image of her mother; often I called her Helena by mistake." He scratched his head, shrugged his shoulders, sighed. "Now I do not know where I am."

Walker chimed in helpfully, "Gertrude has just died."

"Gertrude, yes." Von Helrung nodded somberly. "She was too young. Too young!"

"Then Noah was raised by his father, your son-in-law?"

"For a time, until he died, when Noah was seventeen."

"How did he die?"

"He drowned."

"Drowned?"

"He had too much to drink one night and fell off his fishing boat into the Thames—he'd never recovered from Helena's death, you see—"

"Gertrude," Walker corrected him. "Helena hasn't died yet."

"William's mother is still alive?"

"Oh, no, I just haven't gotten to her yet. My darling wife passed away last year of the dropsy—and that is what began it, I would say."

"Began . . . what?"

"William's slow march into darkness. He was very close to his mother, more so than most sons, I would say. And then when the tiger tore his sweet Annabelle limb from limb!" Von Helrung's lower lip quivered; he tried to force a tear. "Oh, may God have mercy on my boy! May I see him now, Herr Doctor?"

"I'm afraid I'm still a bit confused, Mr. Henry, about the family history. You see this? This is the admission form signed under oath by your grandson, stating Mr. Henry had no living relatives other than himself. It's a discrepancy that must be resolved before we can release him."

"*Hemmm.* If I may." Walker rested a hand on von Helrung's arm. "Noah Boatman has not been in touch with the family in years."

"The blackest of sheep," von Helrung interjected tearfully.

"I would not wish to cast aspersions upon Mr. Boatman's character," Walker went on. "It is entirely plausible he thought he *was* the sole surviving relative, having neither seen nor heard from Abraham in decades."

"But surely he would know about William's children." The superintendent was now looking at me. I squirmed in my chair.

"I was raising the children, in America," von Helrung said hastily.

"*You* were raising them? Why?"

"Because they were . . ." Von Helrung was beginning to panic.

"It is delicate; I hope you can understand," Walker said, stepping into the breach.

"I am trying very hard to, Dr. Walker."

"They are the children of William's first marriage," von Helrung said. Beside him Walker stiffened suddenly, as if someone had just hit him very hard in the back.

"His first marriage?" the superintendent asked.

"In America, before he came here and met Isabel."

"Annabelle," Walker corrected him.

"*Ja.* The children live with us—*me*. My wife is dead of

the dropsy." Von Helrung swung his thick arm around my shoulder. "The dropsy."

"Well," the superintendent said slowly. "I suppose the only way to clear this up is to speak with Mr. Boatman."

"Ahhh! *Mein Gott!*" von Helrung cried out. He slumped forward in his chair.

"You are about to tell me that Mr. Boatman is dead, aren't you?" asked the superintendent.

It was ironic, I later thought, that this was the one nugget of truth in the entire passel of lies.

If not for our recruitment of the superintendent's literary idol, I do not think our ill-conceived and worse-executed plan would have succeeded. The presence of Conan Doyle probably kept us from being booted from the asylum forthwith—or locked up there until a qualified visiting physician could examine us.

"I'm afraid I must share a bit of the responsibility for William Henry's condition," Conan Doyle confessed.

"You, Dr. Doyle?"

"It appears from what Dr. Walker has told me that a portion at least of his delusions are based upon my stories."

"Which portion might that be? I have interviewed the patient at length, and I do not recall . . ."

"Well, his occupation for one. There is not so much difference between a consulting detective and a hunter of monsters—a distinction more than a difference. And, of course," he added casually with a shrug of powerful shoulders (Conan Doyle was a star cricket player and avid golfer), "the name."

"Whose name?"

"Mr. Henry's. Not his real name. The name he chose for himself, Pellinore Warthrop."

"I am sorry, Dr. Doyle. I don't recall seeing that name in your work."

"Because you are not an American. In the States, Holmes's name is Warthrop."

"It is?"

"It's not uncommon to change a character's name to suit the tastes of a particular culture."

The superintendent expressed his surprise. He'd had no idea that Great Britain's Sherlock Holmes was America's Pellinore Warthrop. It seemed to shake him to his existential marrow, for if Holmes were not, well, *Holmes*, then he would not be Holmes!

"Can I see him now?" von Helrung pleaded. "I assure you, sir, he will know me, his father, and if not me, Billy here, his son. We would take him back to America with us, but if you say no, we cannot. Have mercy and do not send us away without at least the chance to say good-bye!"

The superintendent relented then. I doubt he believed for a second one word of our outlandish story, but he was curious now—intensely curious—to see how this bizarre play might end. He rang for the keeper of Warthrop's ward, who appeared a moment later.

"Where is Mr. Henry this morning?" the superintendent inquired.

"In his room, sir, as usual. After breakfast I asked if he'd care for a walk in the garden, but he refused again."

"Did he eat his breakfast this morning?"

"Sir, he hurled it at my head."

"He's in one of his moods today."

"Yes, sir, one of the bad ones."

"Perhaps his visitors will lighten his spirits. Please let him know. We shall be up momentarily." He turned to us. "Last week Mr. Henry ended a hunger strike—his third since coming to Hanwell. 'I would gladly die,' he told me. 'But I will be damned to give you the satisfaction!' I must say, Dr. Walker, your patient has developed a highly sophisticated delusion, the most detailed and intricate that I've ever encountered. A 'philosopher in the natural science of aberrant biology,' he calls himself, a 'monstrumologist,' one of several hundred around the world who devote themselves to the study and eradication of certain malevolent species, upon which he claims to be the foremost expert. He claims to belong to a 'society' of these so-called monstrumologists, based in New York City, the president of which—"

"Is me," finished von Helrung sadly. "I know this story, Herr Superintendent. Alas, I have heard it many times. To William I am not Abraham Henry, humble shoemaker from Stubenbach, but Abram von Helrung, the head of this imaginary society of monstrumologists. And young William here, not William anymore, no! But *Will Henry*, his faithful apprentice who aids him in this mythical monster hunting of his."

"He even includes me in his fantasy," Walker interjected. "I am, it seems, also a member of the Monstrumologist Society, somewhat of a rival, too, substantially more accomplished and therefore a threat to him—"

Von Helrung cleared his throat noisily, and said, "I want to take him home. He is no danger to anyone—unless you happen to be a three-headed dragon! My grandson, God rest his soul, should never have taken upon himself the burden that rightly belongs to the father. I came at once, as soon as I heard he was here. I will leave at once, as soon as I see my boy again. Will you bring me to my boy now, Herr Superintendent, to ease his burden and my own?"

We were escorted to the third floor, where the most dangerous inmates were housed. There were no bars on the doors, but the locks were sturdy and in the rooms the furniture was bolted to the floor. Some rooms were padded for the patients' own protection, but no one was shackled or restrained in any way, another humane distinction of the Hanwell philosophy. It occurred to me that Warthrop could have suffered a fate much worse than confinement in a house of the mad. No doubt it had been torture for him; without question he had suffered to be sane and to have that very sanity cited as the proof of his madness, but he was alive. He was alive.

The keeper of the ward was waiting for us in the hall. The superintendent nodded to him, the keeper threw back the bolt and swung wide the door, and I saw my master seated on the small bed on the other side, wearing a white robe and slippers that seemed to glow in the shaft of light pouring through the window behind him. He was pale and thin and haggard but alive, his exile at its end, alive—the monstrumologist.

FOLIO IX

Das Ungeheuer

I BELIEVE I AM IN HELL, THEREFORE I AM THERE.
—ARTHUR RIMBAUD

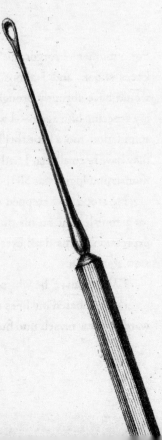

TWENTY-THREE

"My Name Is Pellinore Xavier Warthrop"

For a moment I forgot my lines. My mind went blank, my knees shook, and I almost shouted *Dr. Warthrop!* which would have abruptly brought down the curtain. There was joy at seeing him again—I will not deny that—yet there was trepidation, too, a little thrill of dread. The monstrumologist may have been all that I had in the world, but that meant the monstrumologist was all that I had!

He stood as I stepped forward, a look of nearly comical astonishment on his drawn features, dominated by the expression in his dark eyes—the strange, haunted look of slow starvation.

"Will Henry?" he whispered, hardly daring to believe it.

I remembered my lines then. "Papa! Papa!" I rushed forward. I threw myself into his chest, hard enough to rock him back on his heels, and hugged him with all my might.

"Papa! Papa, you're alive!"

"Well, of course I'm alive. For the love of God, Will Henry . . . Von Helrung, is that you? Good! I was beginning to think you were fool enough to believe—Who is that beside you? Not Walker? Why did you bring Walker? What did you *tell* Walker? *Please*, Will Henry, release me. You are crushing my spine."

"Oh, my son! My son!" von Helrung cried. Now it was his turn to crush my master to his chest. "William! Your father has come for you!"

"I hope not! My father has been dead over fifteen years, von Helrung."

"What? You do not remember me? William, you *must* remember me; I am your father!" Von Helrung was standing between Warthrop and the suspicious superintendent. He seized the opportunity to give the doctor an exaggerated wink. "Your *father, Mein Sohn!*"

Warthrop missed it entirely. Perhaps it was the suddenness with which he had been shoved upon the stage. Perhaps it was the result of a constitution weakened from three attempts at self-starvation. Or perhaps it was the inevitable consequence of caging a man like Pellinore Warthrop—like trying to stuff the sun into a bottle. Whatever it may have been, he refused to step into the part.

"No," he said. He was calm now; the door had at last opened. The rest was simply a matter of walking through the open doorway. "You are Dr. Abram von Helrung, president of the Society for the Advancement of the Science of Monstrumology. The man standing behind you is Dr. Hiram Walker, a colleague of ours of rather mediocre talent, who for some inexplicable reason you've brought along—I pray only to help in affecting my release from this accursed place. The one standing beside Walker I do not know, but his face is vaguely familiar—a physician, I think, and he enjoys the game of golf, I will guess.

"And you . . ." He turned to me. "You are William James Henry, my indispensable assistant, my cross—and my shield. But mostly my cross."

He turned to the superintendent.

"Do you see? I *told* you I was telling the truth!"

"Mr. Henry," the superintendent said. "You do not recognize these people?"

"Yes, I do recognize them. In fact, I just told you who they are!" He snarled in von Helrung's direction, "Do you see what I've been forced to endure for the past one hundred and twenty-six days, seven hours, and twelve minutes? The more I profess the truth, the madder I become!"

He shouted at the superintendent, "My name is Pellinore Xavier Warthrop, of 425 Harrington Lane, New Jerusalem, Massachusetts! I was born in the year of our Lord 1853, the only child of Alistair and Margaret Warthrop, also of New Jerusalem, Massachusetts! I am not now, nor have I ever been—nor do I have any desire to be—a citizen of Great

Britain. You have no right to hold me here against my will, under English law or international law or the higher laws of decency and reason that govern all civilized human beings!"

"If I may," Walker said sotto voce to the superintendent. "Perhaps we should retire to your offices. The patient is becoming a bit agitated—"

"I heard that!" roared the monstrumologist. "Von Helrung, I am, of course, forever in your debt for rescuing me from these imbeciles, but I will *never* forgive you for involving Hiram Walker in my case."

"As I told you earlier," Dr. Walker said to the superintendent with a mealymouthed little grin.

My master took that as the cue for the next movement in his symphony, his curtain-dropping aria: "Upon all that's holy, Walker, if they hadn't confiscated it, I would pull out my revolver and shoot you. I would shoot you point-blank right between those devious little rat eyes of yours. God save me, I can't stand the English! I challenge anyone in this room to name one worthwhile thing that ever came out of the British Isles, besides William Shakespeare, Charles Darwin, and Tiptree jams! England is home to the most unattractive people on earth!" He glared at Walker. "You are the perfect example. You are a very homely man, and don't get me started on your queen—"

"Now, William—," the superintendent vainly tried to interrupt.

"It comes down to natural selection—to Darwin, like

everything else. Isolated for thousands of years upon an island roughly the size of Texas, inbreeding is unavoidable. We may look no further than to Sir Hiram here, who seems to have misplaced his chin. And not only that. I could gather the collective intelligence of the British people in a teacup. Do you require proof? What other civilized nation would place a man in a padded room without the benefit of a trial, without the opportunity to face his accuser, without making *any* effort whatsoever to corroborate his story?" He pointed a quivering finger at the superintendent's nose. "I shall have you sacked. I shall have this abomination you call a hospital razed to the ground, and then I shall spit on its ashes! For my name is *not* William James Henry." He glanced at me.

"It is Pellinore Warthrop," he roared. "And you may take that to your grave, sir, as will I. *As will I.*"

I don't believe the superintendent of Hanwell Lunatic Asylum was entirely satisfied that anyone, in nearly any regard, was telling the truth about the strange case of William "Pellinore Warthrop" Henry. I do believe, however, that on this, the eighth hour of the one hundred and twenty-sixth day, he was heartily sick of the whole thing and ready to wash his hands of it. It was time for the monstrumologist to be someone else's problem, and we were asking for the problem, after all, so the paperwork was handled without delay (Dr. Walker signed for my master's release—the one person in our cabal, besides Conan Doyle, who would not have to sign a fake name.) By the dawn of the ninth hour, we were on the train bound for Paddington.

"Well, as the Bard did say, all is well that ends well!" von Helrung boomed out with forced good cheer. "You are rescued, *mein Freund* Pellinore!"

Warthrop was in no mood to celebrate. He glowered at the two Englishmen seated across from us. Walker could not meet his icy glare, but Conan Doyle replied to it with a convivial smile.

"Arthur Conan Doyle," the author said. "How do you do? We met several years ago in Dr. Bell's office at Edinburgh."

"Yes, of course. Doyle. Are you still penning those clever diversions about the policeman?"

"Consulting detective."

"Hmmm." He turned to von Helrung. "Whose idea was it to make you my father?"

"Well, it is hard now for me to recall," von Helrung replied weakly, avoiding his eyes.

"It was Dr. Torrance's idea, sir," I said.

"Torrance!" The monstrumologist's cheeks turned scarlet. "Do you mean to tell me Jacob Torrance is part of this too?"

"The inclusion of Dr. Torrance was young Will's idea," von Helrung said to deflect the blame. And then he promptly assigned credit. "And thank God Will had it! It was Torrance who—" He realized Conan Doyle was listening, and stopped himself.

"Sir Hiram, Jacob Torrance, a writer of popular fiction

who isn't even a doctor of monstrumology ... Who else have you involved in the most sensitive case to present itself to us in almost forty years, von Helrung? Might I expect Mr. Joseph Pulitzer to be waiting in our rooms at the Great Western?"

"I would watch the manner in which I expressed my gratitude if I were you, Warthrop," warned Dr. Walker. "If not for Torrance, you would still be just another poor, anonymous face in a sea of troubled faces, your presence there wholly unknown, if not forgotten. And if not for myself—"

"I would prefer that you not talk," the doctor said levelly. "It reminds me of all the things I don't like about the English in general and you in particular, Sir Hiram."

"Stop calling me by that name!"

"Speaking of names," Warthrop said to von Helrung. "How in the world did you think you could pass off a surname like Henry as Austrian?"

"We had hopes you would discern our little farce, Pellinore," returned the Austrian stiffly, parrying the thrust. "*Your* obtuseness could have cost us the game!"

"You think I was obtuse? I am not deaf, *Meister* Abram— or should I call you Father Abraham? Neither am I blind. I saw that 'little' wink of yours. Of course I understood I was to play along, but I realized at once the potential downfall of the improvisation. The superintendent—as if he were not enough already—would be immediately, almost certainly, suspicious, for what sort of madness is it that cures itself in the wink of an eye? If I had shouted 'Papa!' to you or 'Son!' to Will Henry, I do not think I would be sitting on this train right now. I think you, me, all of us, would be having a conversation with officials from Scotland Yard. And so it is the greatest irony that the same truth that imprisoned me has now set me free!"

"Truth with a little assistance from *us*." Walker, it seemed, could not help himself.

"May I remind you, Sir Hiram, that they returned my revolver upon my release? I have it right here—"

"Now, Pellinore," chided Warthrop's old teacher. "These last few months have been trying for you, I know, but—"

The doctor laughed harshly. "Do you? 'Trying' is not the word I would use. Don't mistake me; it is very nice there, for a lunatic asylum. The food is surprisingly good; the staff is, on the whole, more humane than inhumane; the rooms are kept clean of bedbugs and lice; and twice a week we are allowed to bathe. It was rather like a long holiday in the English countryside, with one minor difference—*you could never leave*. I tried to escape—six times. Each time I was returned to my cozy room with the hard sheets and the soft walls. Each time I was gently reminded that I was abusing my *privileges* as a 'guest.' That's what they call us madmen, you know. The 'guests.' Rather like the devil calling the damned his 'lodgers.' Ha!"

Conan Doyle laughed out loud. "Oh, this is marvelous! Positively delightful!"

Warthrop rolled his eyes and said to me, "And you—the

last person I expected to see when that door opened. Why are *you* here, Will Henry?"

"He insisted," von Helrung put in on my behalf. "If I had bound him hand and foot and chained him to a dungeon wall, he would have found a way to come, Pellinore."

The monstrumologist closed his eyes. "You should not have come, Will Henry."

And I answered, "You should not have left me, Dr. Warthrop."

TWENTY-FOUR

"The Blindest of Faiths"

Conan Doyle bade us farewell on the platform at Paddington Station, and then moved not an inch from his proximity to Warthrop; he seemed reluctant to part with his company. I'd seen it happen innumerable times over the years. (In my mind I called it the Warthrop Effect or, less frequently, Warthropian Gravity.) Like any object of enormous mass, the doctor's ego was endowed with an attractive force nearly impossible for weaker souls to resist.

"I really should be off," Conan Doyle said after detaining my exhausted and anxious master for several minutes, peppering him with questions ("How did you know I played golf?"), trailing a step or two behind him as we bumped and jostled our way through the crowded station. "Touie is expecting me."

"What is a Touie?" asked Warthrop.

"Touie is my wife, Louisa. She is at home with our new daughter, Mary Louise, born this January. Would you like to see her picture? She is a beautiful child, if I may say so."

Warthrop stopped abruptly at the bottom of the stairs going into our hotel. "At the moment, Doyle, all I desire is a cup of decent tea and a long nap. Perhaps some other—" He spied something over the shorter man's shoulder. He flashed a quick perfunctory smile and abruptly locked his arm around Doyle's, urging him up the stairs. "Come to think of it, fate may have arranged our meeting. Did you know I was a writer in my youth? Poetry, not prose, but your case inspires me, Doyle. A man *can* wear two hats. Perhaps I should pick up the pen again and try my hand at some verse . . ."

Puzzled by the monstrumologist's sudden about-face, I looked down the platform. Loitering near a column midway down were two men, one tall and broad-shouldered, with a shock of flaming red hair. The other was bald and much shorter, as thin and wiry as his companion was burly. Even from forty yards away and through the hazy gray smoke of the station, the redheaded man's eyes seemed to burn with a backlit fire. I knew only one other man whose eyes burned like that. They were the eyes of a man consumed by the singularity of his life's purpose. For Pellinore Warthrop that singularity was the pursuit of monsters. For the man whose gaze pinned me to the steps like a hammer drives home a nail, it was the pursuit of something altogether different.

"What is it, *mein Freund* Will?" murmured von Helrung. He swung his arm around my shoulders and fairly pushed me up the steps. "You look like you've seen a ghost."

"Not a ghost," Walker answered, his high-pitched voice warbling with distress. He, too, had seen the redheaded man looking back at us. "That big chap with the bright red hair and his bald companion by the pillar. For heaven's sake, don't look now, von Helrung! The same two I saw yesterday. I believe they're following us."

"To be honest, things have not been going all that well with the practice," Conan Doyle was gasping to the monstrumologist when we caught up with them in the third-floor hallway. He was struggling for breath because he was also fighting to match the long strides of my master. "But I don't complain. It gives me plenty of time to write. And I'll need to write plenty, what with a new mouth to feed."

Warthrop stopped suddenly just outside the door to our room. Conan Doyle was not expecting it; he walked directly into the doctor's back.

"Oh! Sorry . . ."

The doctor's hand came up and stayed there, the tips of his fingers lightly drumming the air. I'd seen this gesture before and reacted instinctively, stepping quickly to his side.

"Von Helrung," Warthrop whispered. "Are you armed?"

"No."

"Walker?"

"No. Why do you—"

"Doyle, do you carry a firearm?"

"I do not, Dr. Warthrop."

The monstrumologist pulled his revolver from his coat pocket. "Stay here with the others, Will Henry," he said to me before opening the door and stepping inside.

He wasn't gone long, no more than two or three minutes, I guessed, when he called for us to come in.

"Shut the door, Will Henry, and throw the bolt," he instructed me from across the room. His back was to me. He was crouching beside something on the floor, the gun held loosely at his side, his shoulders slightly stooped. I remember vividly how tired he looked—old before his time.

And before him was the recumbent body of Jacob Torrance.

"*Mein Gott!*" whispered von Helrung. "Pellinore, is he—"

"Dead," pronounced the doctor.

Von Helrung cursed under his breath. Walker pressed his hand to his mouth.

"Let's have some light," Warthrop said. "Will Henry, open the curtains, will you? Doyle, you're a physician. You might want to have a look at this."

Conan Doyle joined the doctor beside the corpse while I stepped around it to the windows, and Jacob Torrance's blood bubbled and oozed around the soles of my shoes. I was not going to look. I did not wish to look. I had no intention of looking. But of course I looked. I threw back the curtains, turned around, and, with the golden afternoon sunlight warming my back, beheld what had befallen Jacob Torrance.

"Extremely deep," Conan Doyle was saying. "Nicked the spinal column. This poor man was nearly decapitated."

He had been sliced from ear to ear, the knife—if it had been a knife; perhaps the killer had used a small axe or hatchet—severing the carotid arteries and jugular veins—creating the font that had soaked the carpet . . . and his clothing . . . and the linen tablecloth a foot away . . . and the seat back of the divan. The damask curtains were spotted with the spray from his expiring heart. The room stank with it, the hot coppery smell of fresh blood.

"The body is still warm," Conan Doyle announced with not a little concern. "He has not been dead long; no more than an hour, I would say."

"Considerably less," the monstrumologist replied. He rose, grimacing. I heard his knees pop when he stood. Von Helrung still lingered near the door; Walker was leaning against the wall beside him, a handkerchief pressed against his mouth, his face the color of parchment paper. The sound of his gagging was very loud in the small room.

"We must summon the police," he said from behind his makeshift mask. No one paid any attention.

Warthrop paced the room, moving in a widening circle around Torrance's body, eyes roaming the blood-enriched floor, the blood-specked walls, the furniture, the windows and sills. At one point, about five feet from the corpse, he fell to his hands and knees and crawled along the floor, snuffing and sniffing like a hound hot on a scent.

"There were two of them," he said at the completion of his inspection. "One very tall—well over six feet, right-handed, a cigar smoker, and redheaded. His companion is much shorter—five-six or -seven, in that range, and walks with a pronounced limp—one leg, his right, shorter than the other . . ."

Conan Doyle's face was a study in scarlet. He was blushing like a young swain in the first heady throes of unrequited passion.

"Astounding. Completely astounding," he said hoarsely.

"It's elementary, Doyle," returned the doctor. "A killer is like any artist. He cannot help but leave something of himself in his work. One only needs to know how to separate the work from the one who authored it."

"What I mean to say is I am having the most extraordinary sensation . . ."

"So am I!" called Dr. Walker from across the room. "I am going to be sick!"

Conan Doyle continued, his eyes growing misty. "A man has been brutally murdered; it is terrible! And yet I find myself overwhelmed by an equally terrible sense of wonder. . . . Why, it's as if I have stepped over some mystical threshold and into one of my own stories! And here, before me, the man himself, the same one I created, come to life. Behold the man!"

"Yes, it is similar to one of your stories, with the exception that it is *not* one of your stories, and there is a very real possibility that you are in mortal danger," replied the monstrumologist.

"Do you really think so?" Conan Doyle seemed practically giddy at the prospect.

"And not just you." Warthrop turned to von Helrung. "We must leave this hotel immediately."

Von Helrung nodded. "What about Jacob?"

The doctor smiled grimly. "He'll be staying here."

We grabbed our luggage and hurried downstairs. (The monstrumologist was pleased that I'd remembered to bring his instrument case. "I thought I would never see it again. Bless you, Will Henry, and damn that turncoat Arkwright!") A line of hansoms sat waiting for customers along the curb outside. Before we enlisted any for our escape, however, I was dispatched to spy out the terrain while the men waited inside the lobby. The doctor did not need to tell me what to look for. I had already seen it inside Paddington Station—a shock of red hair and the disconcerting glow of dark, backlit eyes.

"Well?" Warthrop asked upon my breathless return.

"All clear, sir."

He nodded briskly. "Two cabs—von Helrung, myself, and Will Henry in one. Doyle, Sir Hiram will go with you—"

"Would you *please* stop calling me that?" Walker asked. He was leaning against a column, still trying to collect himself. "It's cruel and childish." The British monstrumologist's nickname, bestowed upon him by Warthrop, had originated several years before, at a party at which Walker had been smitten by a certain young woman with ties to the royal family. Trying to impress her, Walker had inadvisably passed himself off as a peer of the realm, and his fellow scientists were not about to let him forget it.

Warthrop ignored him. He said to Conan Doyle, "I suggest you take a circuitous route, and keep an eye open for our redheaded friend and his hairless compatriot. If they do spot us, I think we shall be the ones followed—but then again, they may split up. Pray you get the bald one!"

He seized Conan Doyle's hand in both of his and gave it a quick, hard shake. "It has been my pleasure to see you again, sir. May our next meeting be in more congenial circumstances!"

"The pleasure has been entirely mine, Dr. Warthrop," replied Conan Doyle earnestly. "Touie will not believe the story I have to tell her!"

"I would not divulge too much," cautioned the doctor, his dark eyes twinkling. "She will think you've been drinking."

"The feeling is not so different," admitted the author. "I don't know if you're a spiritual man, but—"

"Not often," said the monstrumologist, urging Conan Doyle toward the lobby doors. "Hardly ever. No—just once. I was three or four, and my mother caught me deep in a conversation with God." He shrugged. "I have no memory of it. God might."

Five minutes later we were inside a hansom cab, on our way to Hyde Park. "Why Hyde Park?" von Helrung wanted to know.

The doctor shrugged. "Why not?"

"I sincerely hope they haven't followed Doyle," Warthrop said. "I am uncertain why you recruited him to join your rescue party, but I would hate for him to pay the ultimate price for his altruism. And, of course, it would be a great loss to literature. I normally don't care much for fiction, but there is something charming about his stories. A kind of grand naïveté—like the British Empire itself—the blindest of faiths that reason will triumph over ignorance, and human intellect over evil."

Von Helrung looked incredulously at my master. Perhaps he was thinking he did not know Pellinore Warthrop half as well as he'd thought.

"We have just discovered our dear colleague butchered in a hotel room, and you wish to discuss literature?"

Warthrop nodded. He either entirely missed von Helrung's point or he didn't care. I did not think it was the former. "It is a pity; for all his faults, I rather liked Torrance. He would have been my choice too, had I been forced to make one, so do not hold yourself to blame, *Meister* Abram. If you want to assign fault, look no farther than the empty bottle of whiskey on the table in the sitting room. He was three sheets in the wind when his murderers came to call. There is no other explanation for how they overcame him so easily." He looked at me. "There are only three real causes of death, Will Henry. The first is accidents—diseases, famines, wars, or like what befell your parents. The second is old age. And the third is ourselves—our slow suicides. Show me a man who cannot control his appetites, and I will show a man living under a death sentence."

Von Helrung was shaking his head vehemently. "*You* are responsible, Pellinore—not for Torrance, God rest his soul, but for Conan Doyle. Should he perish for what he's seen this day, it will be to pay the fine for your impulsiveness. Why did you invite him to our rooms? He was taking his leave of us at the station, and you—"

"Yes, he was," snapped Warthrop. "And I may have saved his life—temporarily, perhaps, but at least I bought him an hour or two to spend with Touie and his newborn babe. You have no understanding of those men you saw on the platform, von Helrung. They are ruthless. They kill without compunction or remorse. I had to act quickly, and I believe I made the best of a very tenuous situation."

"And what of this ridiculous and bizarre charade in the room? What is your excuse for that? You *knew* it was those men we saw in the station, and yet you pretended that you deduced everything, down to the color of the killer's hair! For what reason, Pellinore? In mocking Doyle, you mocked the dead!"

The doctor's countenance darkened. He leaned forward and poked von Helrung in the chest.

"Do not speak to me of mockery, von Helrung. Do you have any inkling of what it's like to be sane and have your very sanity be the thing that binds you? Think about that before you judge me for a harmless bit of whimsy!"

They fell silent after this heated exchange, until we reached our destination, at which point the doctor knocked sharply on the hansom's roof and directed the driver to now take us to Piccadilly Circus. The whip cracked, and we were off again.

"Where are we going?" von Helrung demanded.

"To Piccadilly Circus."

Von Helrung closed his eyes and sighed wearily. "You know what I meant."

The doctor glanced behind us, and then settled back into his seat. "I do."

"They are ruthless, you said. Killers without compunction or remorse, you said. But you fail to say *who* they are or why they pursue us."

"I would think the *why* is obvious. As to *who* . . . The big red-haired one is called Rurick. His bald partner goes by the name Plešec. They are Okhranka, *Meister* Abram, members of the Russian secret police."

Von Helrung absorbed the news with a crestfallen expression. He had not wanted Torrance to be correct. A part of him, I think, clung to the hope that Jack Kearns had but one coconspirator in the affair, the betrayer Thomas Arkwright, and all the rest of it had sprouted in Jacob Torrance's fertile imagination. The truth sickened his heart. He was a scientist, and the essence of science is the quest for truth, a noble thing in and of itself, but no human endeavor—no matter how noble—remains unsullied for long. Monstrumology could be characterized as a contemplation of nature corrupted. The same could be said of us.

"We were duped," my master stated bluntly. "I suppose we could take some small comfort in the fact that we were not the only ones played for fools. Arkwright played us, but the Russians played *him*, and Jack Kearns, I think, has had his fun with all of us."

"It was Jacob's theory that Kearns and the British—and the Russians, too—were using us to find for them the home of the *magnificum*. They had the golden egg—the *nidus*—but not the goose who lays it. That's how Torrance put it."

Warthrop smiled tightly. "I'm going to miss Jake. He had a way with the colorful metaphor. He was partly right, but mainly wrong. We *were* being used, though not by Kearns or the Russians; they had what they wanted. Thomas Arkwright of the Long Island Arkwrights was a wholly

British creation. Arkwright is an officer in the British secret intelligence service."

Von Helrung sighed. "So the British are involved ... *and* the Russians. Who else?"

"No one—well, not counting us, and I would not count us out just yet," Warthrop said grimly. "I didn't want to believe it. When I was first brought to Hanwell, it suited my naïve faith to believe that Arkwright must have been working with the Russians—a double agent, a traitor to his country—and I bravely hung on to that bit of fiction for quite some time. In the first month of my lunatic holiday, I wrote more than forty letters, none of which, apparently, reached their intended recipient. Someone had to be intercepting them, and it is difficult for me to comprehend that the reach of Okhranka extended to the mails of England or the United States. Six of those desperate missives I personally handed to the superintendent. Now, I suppose he could be in the employ of the czar or be a member of Okhranka, but at some point we must put away childish things, *Meister* Abram, and acknowledge that, in matters where something like the *magnificum* is concerned, there are few limits to the perfidy of men and nations—even men like the superintendent and nations like Great Britain."

"Alas, dear Pellinore, I have lived a very long time and have yet to discern *any*."

We rolled to a stop, and the driver called out in a loud voice, "'Ere you are, guv'ner! Piccadilly Circus."

"The Great Western at Paddington Station, driver. And with all alacrity, please!" called Warthrop. He smiled at the driver's muttered curses as we started off again, to the place from which we'd begun.

"We are going in circles," observed von Helrung.

"We were," replied the doctor. "Though tonight no more! For on this night, my old master, the months in the wilderness come to an end. Our long exile is over. I have the answer; I know from whence the wind cometh; I have found the hiding place of the grail."

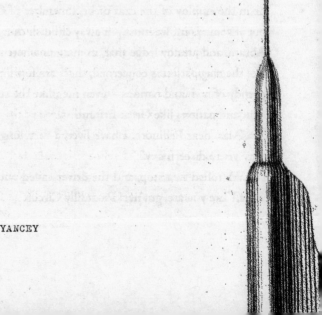

TWENTY-FIVE

"Dvipa Sukhadhara"

Von Helrung turned away from his friend with a pained expression. "You should not call it that."

"Why?" the monstrumologist seemed genuinely puzzled.

"It should not be called that," the old man insisted vehemently. A tear welled in the corner of his eye.

"Where is it?" I asked. "Where did the *nidus* come from?" The central question had gone too long unanswered.

Warthrop's face was glowing with triumph. "The *nidus ex magnificum* was recovered upon the island of Socotra."

Von Helrung looked round and stared at the doctor for a long moment. "Socotra!" he whispered. "The Isle of Blood."

"The Isle of Blood?" I echoed. I could feel the tightly wound thing vibrating to the rhythm of my heart.

"It isn't what you're thinking, Will Henry," said the

monstrumologist. "It is called the Isle of Blood because that happens to be the color of the sap of the Dragon's Blood tree, which grows there—the color of blood. Socotra has other names—better names, if names matter anything to you: the Isle of Enchantment, the Isle of the Phoenix, Tranquility Island, among others. In Sanskrit it is called *Dvipa Sukhadhara*, the 'Isle of Bliss.' Recently it has been dubbed the Galápagos of the East, for the island is so isolated that many of its species, like the Dragon's Blood tree, are found there and nowhere else on earth. . . ."

"Socotra is a British protectorate," von Helrung said.

"Yes," acknowledged Warthrop. "And if it were not, the *nidus* never would have found its way to London's East End and the clutches of Dr. John Kearns. The British have maintained a small presence there since '76, when the treaty was signed with the island's sultan, to protect their shipping routes from India and West Africa."

"So the man who brought the *nidus* to Kearns was a British soldier or seaman?" asked von Helrung.

"No man brought the *nidus* to Kearns. A *man* was brought to Kearns, and that man brought Kearns to the *nidus*, in a manner of speaking. Once I identified the man, I had my answer. I mean, of course, *our* answer."

"And Kearns's answer—to pass on to his client, the czar of Russia! You will forgive this question, and I pray you will answer in the same spirit of goodwill in which I ask it, but, once you supplied the fiends with what they wanted, wouldn't it have been much easier for them to simply kill you? Why risk all by arranging your sojourn in Hanwell Lunatic Asylum?"

"Didn't Arkwright tell you? I am assuming that's how you found me, through Arkwright, when you saw through his story of my untimely demise."

"He did not say."

"You didn't ask him?"

"I could not," answered von Helrung, avoiding the doctor's eyes.

"And why couldn't you?" pressed the doctor. Then he answered his own question. "Arkwright is dead, isn't he?"

Von Helrung did not answer, so I did. "Dr. Torrance killed him, sir."

"Killed him?"

"In a manner of speaking," I answered.

"How does one do something like that 'in a manner of speaking'?"

"Is not that how all things are done in our dark and dirty business—our 'science'?" asked von Helrung bitterly. "*Pour ainsi dire*—'in a manner of speaking'?"

Our cab jerked to a stop in the exact spot from which our journey had started, before the entrance of the Great Western Hotel at Paddington Station. The driver called down to us, "And will this do for His Excellency?"

"Another fiver for another five minutes!" Warthrop

called back. He turned to von Helrung, and in my master's eyes I saw the same backlit fire that had burned in the Fifth Avenue parlor a lifetime ago—*I am the one. I am the one!* The same fire I'd seen burning in another man's eye but two hours past. *Ruthless. Without compunction or remorse.*

"I am going to Socotra," he whispered hoarsely. "I am taking the train to Dover and I am boarding the first steamer out. I will be in Aden in less than a fortnight, and then on to Socotra—if I can find passage; and if I can't find passage, I shall swim there. And if I cannot swim there, I shall construct a flying machine and soar like Icarus to heaven's gate!"

"But Icarus did not soar, *mein Freund*," murmured von Helrung. "Icarus fell."

For the second time, the older man turned away; he would not—or could not—endure that strange, cold fire in his friend's eyes.

"I cannot go with you," the old man said.

"I'm not asking you to go with me."

"I am going with you," I said.

"No, no," von Helrung called out. "Will, you do not understand—"

"I won't be left behind again," I said. I turned and repeated it to the monstrumologist: "I won't be left behind."

Warthrop leaned his head against the seat back and closed his eyes. "So tired. I haven't had a decent night's sleep in months."

"Pellinore, tell Will he is coming home with me. Tell him."

"You should not have left me," I said to Warthrop. "Why did you leave me?" I could contain it no longer. It emptied out of me, and once I was empty, *it* contained *me*. "None of this would have happened if you'd listened to me! Why didn't you listen to me? Why don't you *ever* listen to me? I *told* you he was a liar. I *warned* you that he was false! But it's just like always: 'Snap to, Will Henry! Fetch me my instruments, Will Henry! Sit beside me all night while I moan and cry and feel sorry for myself, Will Henry! Will Henry, be a good boy and sit there and watch Mr. Kendall rot inside his own skin! Hold still now, Will Henry, so I can chop off your finger with this kitchen knife! Snap to, Will Henry! Will Henry! Will Henry! Will Henry!'"

He opened his eyes. He said nothing. He observed my tears. He studied my face, knotted up and burning hot. He watched as it spun out, the unwinding thing that was *me* and *not-me*, and he was able to do this, to stare at me with the attitude of a man watching an ant struggle with a burden five times its size, because I had suffered him to live, because I had brought Jacob Torrance into the truth by way of a monstrous lie.

"How strange, then, that you would wish to come with me."

Meister Abram, who had taught my master everything he knew about monstrumology but had failed to teach him what he, von Helrung, knew best, gathered me into his arms and stroked my hair. I pressed my face into his wool vest and smelled cigar smoke, and in that moment I loved Abram von Helrung, loved him as I had loved no other since my parents' fall into the abyss, loved him as much as I hated his former pupil. *What is it?* I remembered thinking in panic. *What is it?* Why did I want to follow this man? What was it about the monstrumologist that consumed me? What demon of the pit chewed and gnawed upon my soul like Judas's in the innermost circle of hell? What did it look like? What was its face? If I could name the nameless thing, if I could put a face upon the faceless thing, perhaps I could free myself from its ravenous embrace.

We are hunters all. We are, all of us, monstrumologists.

TWENTY-SIX

"It Is Part and Parcel of the Business"

He left us sitting in the cab. He stepped onto the street, swung the door closed, and strode away without a word or backward glance. I pushed against von Helrung's soft belly, but he held tight; he would not let go despite my keening wails, saying, "Hush, hush, dear Will. He will come back; he is making sure those evil men are gone. . . . He will come back."

And he did. Von Helrung was right; he did come back, cautioning me to dry my tears and bring down the curtain on my theatrics, for he did not want to draw attention to ourselves.

"There are no police in the lobby, and the desk clerks are gossiping happily. They haven't discovered Torrance yet, or if they have, the English are even odder than I thought.

Our Russian friends are nowhere to be seen. They have either quit the station or we have drawn them off. Snap— It's time to go, Will Henry."

We cut through the lobby to the station entrance unmolested—an unremarkable sight, a boy hurrying to catch his train, flanked by his father and grandfather, perhaps, three generations on holiday.

"There's a train that leaves for Liverpool in a half hour," Warthrop informed von Helrung. "Platform three. Here is your ticket."

"And Will's?"

The monstrumologist said, "Will Henry is coming with me. I do not know what I will find on Socotra; I may require his services. That is, if he is still of a mind to come with me."

Von Helrung looked down at me. "You know what that means, Will, if you go?"

I nodded. "I have always known what it means."

He pulled me into his arms for one last hug. "I do not know for whom I should pray more," he whispered. "For him to look after you, or for you to look after him. Remember always that God never thrusts a burden upon us that we cannot bear. Remember that there is no absolute dark anywhere, but here"— he pressed his open hand upon my heart—"there is light absolute. Promise *Meister* Abram that you will remember."

I promised him. He nodded, looked at Warthrop, nodded again.

"I will go now," he said.

✳

"Well, Will Henry," the monstrumologist said after von Helrung had melted into the crowd. "It is just the two of us again." And then he turned on his heel and strode off without a backward glance. I hurried after him. It seemed I was always hurrying after him.

Back through the hotel and out the main doors and into a hansom, the very same hansom we had vacated a few minutes before. The driver called down, "Goin' to the Great Western at Paddington, guv'ner?" The remark caught Warthrop off guard; he actually laughed.

"Charing Cross station, my good man! Get us there in twenty minutes or less, and there's an extra shilling in it for you."

"Dr. Warthrop!" I cried as he jumped inside. "Our luggage!"

"I've already made the arrangements; it will be waiting for us in Dover. Now get in! Every minute is precious."

We missed the last steamer to Calais by ten of those precious minutes. Warthrop stood on the quay at Dover and shouted invectives at the ship as it chugged toward the horizon. He shook his fist and roared like Lear against the storm, till I thought the famous white cliffs might splinter and crumble into the sea.

There was nothing to do but wait until morning. We took a room at a lodging house within walking distance of the port. Warthrop drank a pot of tea. He stared out the window. He tried out the bed, pronouncing it too short (most beds were for him; he stood just over six-two in his stocking feet), too lumpy, and entirely too small for both of us to rest comfortably. He sent me to inquire at the desk about a larger room or, in lieu of that, a larger bed—both of which were not available.

The hour grew late. The room grew stuffy. He opened the window, letting in a pleasant sea breeze and the sound of the surf, and we lay down to sleep. He flopped and twisted and poked me in the ear with his elbow and complained of my heavy breathing, of my taking up too much room, of "that strange odor peculiar to adolescents." At last he could abide it no longer. Throwing off the covers, he launched himself from the bed and began to pull on his clothes.

"I can't sleep," he said. "I am going for a walk."

"I'll come with you."

"I would rather you did not." He slipped on his coat, felt something in the right-hand pocket—his revolver. It reminded him of something.

"Oh, very well," he said crossly. "Come along if you must, but please keep quiet so I may think. I need to think!"

"Yes, sir," I said, pulling on my clothes. "I will try not to be a burden to you, sir."

The remark, like the gun, reminded him of something. He seized my left hand and held it in the lamplight to examine my injury.

"It's healed up nicely," he pronounced. "How is the mobility?"

I made a fist. I stretched my remaining fingers wide.

"See?" I asked. "Part of it's gone, but it's still my hand."

We walked out onto the beach, and the stars were very bright and the moon was high and the towering cliffs to the northeast shone pearl white. To our left were the lights of Dover. On our right was the darkness of open water. The wind coming off the water was stronger and colder than the wind that had come through our window. I shivered; I had left my jacket in the room.

The monstrumologist turned abruptly and walked to the water's edge. He stared toward the vaguely defined horizon, the thin line between black and gray.

"*Pour ainsi dire*," he said softly. "How do you kill someone 'in a manner of speaking,' Will Henry?"

I told him what had happened to Thomas Arkwright. He was shocked. He looked at me as if he'd never seen me before.

"And using the *pwdre ser* was *your* idea?"

"No, sir. Frightening him with it was my idea. It was Dr. Torrance's idea to actually use it."

"Still. There was only one person in that room who had witnessed firsthand what *pwdre ser* does to a human being."

"Yes, sir. That's why I suggested we use it."

"That is why you . . . ?" He took a deep breath. "It is a very thin line between us and the abyss, Will Henry," he said. "For most it is like that line out there, where the sea meets the sky. They see it. They cannot deny the evidence of their eyes, but they never cross it. They *cannot* cross it; though they chase it for a thousand years, it will forever stay where it is. Do you realize it took our species more than ten millennia to realize that simple fact? That the line is unreachable, that we live on a ball and not on a plate? Most of us do, anyway. Men like Jacob Torrance and John Kearns . . . Those kinds of men still live on a plate. Do you understand what I mean?"

I nodded. I thought I did.

"The very strange and ironic thing is that I left you behind so you wouldn't have to live on that plate with them."

I thought of the signet ring of Jacob Torrance and lifted my chin defiantly. "I'm not afraid."

"Are you not?" He closed his eyes and drew in deep the smell of the sea.

Early the next morning we boarded the first ship out, and some of Warthrop's anxiety lost its bite, though it still continued to nibble around the edges of his relief to be on our way at last. He paced the foredeck, never looking back at the receding English shore. He was not interested in what lay behind.

But I was. I wanted to hear what had happened, how he'd found the origin of the *nidus ex magnificum*; how, or if, he'd found John Kearns; and the particulars of how he'd been betrayed by Thomas Arkwright. Every time I broached the subject, however, he deflected it with a shake of his head or ignored my entreaties altogether. I came to realize that the affair was an embarrassment to him. It wounded his ego, and his was not the sort of ego that recovered easily from even the slightest scratch.

At Maritime railway station in Calais, we secured berths in a private sleeping car for the passage south to Lucerne, where we would switch trains for the final leg of our overland journey to Brindisi on the Adriatic Sea. The remainder of our expedition to Socotra would be undertaken by boat, an unhappy prospect; the memory of my recent bout of mal de mer was still quite fresh.

The train was a crowded, rolling city of Babel— English, French, German, Italian, Spanish, with a smattering of Egyptian, Farsi, and Hindi thrown in. Every race, religion, and class was represented, from the well-to-do English family on extended holiday, to the poorest Indian immigrant returning to Bombay to visit the family he had left behind. There were businessmen and Gypsies, soldiers and peddlers, old men in wide hats and newborn babes in bonnets. And everywhere the smell of smoke and human sweat, shouts, laughter, singing and music—a din of accordions and violins, harmonicas and sitars. It enchanted and frightened me, this rolling makeshift village, this rich sampling of humanity. While the doctor holed up in our car, leaving it only thrice a day for meal service, I took to wandering the length and breadth of the train. That was far more preferable to enduring the eerie silence that enveloped him like a pall of doom. Warthrop did not complain of my wanderings; he merely observed that I should be careful lest I become exposed to some rare contagion. "A passenger train is a traveling circus of pestilence, Will Henry. A smorgasbord of human meat. Take care you are not placed upon the menu."

I was dispatched on the occasional errand, for tea and pastries (the doctor's profound disappointment that there was not a single scone on board would have been comical, if I had not been the one to bear the brunt of his displeasure) and newspapers, any and all I could find, in any language (the monstrumologist was conversant in more than twenty). He read, he drank copious amounts of Darjeeling tea, he paced the compartment like a caged tiger, or stared out the window, pulling and pinching on his lower lip until it grew fat and red. He muttered under his breath, he started when I opened the door, dropping his hand into his coat pocket, where he kept his revolver—he never ventured anywhere without it. He slept with the light on, he started growing a beard, and he ate constantly and in vast amounts, putting on several pounds on the thirteen-hundred-mile journey to the southern tip of Italy. At one meal service I witnessed him consume two beefsteaks, a half loaf of bread, an entire pie, and four glasses of rich buttermilk. He took note of my wide-eyed astonishment at this gluttonous accomplishment and said, "I am building reserves." I puzzled over this remark. What should I expect in the coming days—famine? Was there nothing to eat on the island of Socotra?

By the time we reached the Italian Alps, the wound to his pride had entered the contraction stage, and late one night, at the precise moment I'd drifted off, he woke me with the question he reserved for those moments.

"Will Henry, are you asleep?"

"No, Dr. Warthrop, I am not." Not *now*, Dr. Warthrop!

"I cannot sleep either. I can't stop thinking about Torrance. He was twenty-nine—less than a year to go until his Magic Thirty. Do you know most monstrumologists become as reclusive as Tibetan monks during their twenty-ninth year? Rarely do they take to the field or engage in any pursuit that might jeopardize their chances of reaching their thirtieth birthday. There was one colleague of mine who spent the last six months of his twenty-ninth year locked in his room with boards over the windows and without even a book to pass the time. He was afraid of cutting his finger on a page and dying of infection."

"Dr. Torrance said he became a monstrumologist because he liked to kill things."

"He was not alone in that, just in his willingness to admit it. But he was a very good scholar and completely fearless intellectually; he was not afraid to tread where wiser men trembled. You could not have chosen a better man to break Thomas Arkwright."

I heard him rise from his bunk. I raised my head and saw

his silhouette against the window and then his face reflected in the glass. His face had changed—the cheeks were fuller, the lower half dark with his new beard—all but the eyes, which still shone with the same cold backlit fire.

"I didn't know what he was going to do," I protested. "It happened so fast—"

He raised his hand. Let it fall. "It is part and parcel of the business, Will Henry. Arkwright's, Torrance's . . . ours. Eventually the luck runs out. I suppose I would feel less conflicted about Arkwright if the man had not worked so hard to save my life."

"That's what he told Dr. Torrance—right before Dr. Torrance killed him. How did he save your life?"

The monstrumologist clasped his hands behind his back and spoke to my reflection in the glass. "By presenting a compelling case that I was more trouble dead than alive."

"It was those Russian agents in Paddington, wasn't it? Rurick and . . ."

"Plešec. Yes. Tailing us from the moment we arrived in London. I am not so disappointed in myself that I did not know—but Arkwright, he should have known. He is a professional, after all. It is hard to conceive of a more conspicuous pair of spies—big Rurick with that red hair, and short little Plešec and his shiny scalp."

He closed his eyes. "I am sure Arkwright thought the worst was over, that all that remained was to convince von Helrung that I had died on the quest. He hadn't had much trouble selling von Helrung everything else—'Thomas Arkwright of the Long Island Arkwrights'!"

"It was me, sir. Arkwright lied about the Monstrumarium, and that meant he lied about everything else. It meant he knew about the *nidus* before he even met you, and that meant—"

His eyes came open and fixed upon my image in the window. "*You* suspected him? Not von Helrung? Not Torrance? You?"

I nodded. "Dr. von Helrung wouldn't listen at first, but then the telegram arrived saying you were dead. I didn't believe it. And Dr. Torrance didn't either, once I explained it to him. He told me I would make a fine—"

"Yes, that troubled me too—Arkwright's seemingly serendipitous arrival upon *Meister* Abram's doorstep around the time Mr. Kendall showed up on ours. I've been kicking myself for missing the many subtle blunders Arkwright committed, but I was understandably distracted and completely focused on the task at hand—finding Jack Kearns and the home of the *magnificum*."

"Did you find him—Dr. Kearns?"

He shook his head. "Kearns vanished the day after he dispatched Mr. Kendall with his special delivery. I am uncertain where he went first—most likely it was Saint Petersburg to make the necessary arrangements—but I am fairly certain where he is now. We will see our old friend on the isle of Socotra."

TWENTY-SEVEN

"An Interesting Dilemma"

Upon their arrival in London, Warthrop and Arkwright had stopped by their hotel only long enough to drop their bags, and then they'd split up—Arkwright to Dorset Street in Whitechapel to locate Kearns's flat and discover what, if any, clues he may have left behind; Warthrop to the Royal London Hospital to question Kearns's colleagues and interview the hospital director, the man responsible for overseeing Kearns's work. Warthrop learned how well-liked Kearns had been, how popular with the staff—particularly the female staff—how admired by the other doctors, what a fine physician he was, in addition to being one of the best trauma surgeons the director had ever seen. No, Dr. Kearns had not given notice or any indication whatsoever he was leaving. One day he was there; the next he was not. My master, posing as an old chum of Kearns's from the States, informed the director he had been asked by Kearns to consult on a most unusual case, one he was certain the director would remember.

"It had been nagging at me since the night we'd met Mr. Kendall," the doctor told me. "The remark about the yeoman with the case of 'tropical fever.' The director remembered the case well. 'Baffling and tragic,' he called it, though he did not recall the man being a seaman. He then went on to describe the symptoms, and I knew I had found the owner of the *nidus*."

"*Pwdre ser*," I whispered.

"Yes. He was in the final stages of exposure when he was brought in—was quite beyond coherent thought or speech. There was nothing on his person to identify who he was, and he refused to give—or could not remember, probably— his own name. The only thing the director recalled the man saying was the words, 'The nest! The bloody human nest!' It obviously piqued Kearns's curiosity. He is no monstrumologist; I've no idea if he had ever heard of the *nidus ex magnificum*, but the sailor's anguished cries and dramatic symptoms probably alerted Kearns that he was dealing with something of a monstrumological nature."

The man died within hours of his arrival at the hospital. Kearns signed the order to have the body cremated, the usual precaution when dealing with an unknown disease.

"And then he did precisely what I would have done," the

monstrumologist said. "What I *did* do that same afternoon. Of course, you already have guessed what that is."

I had not. I decided to try. "You went to the naval department to research recent—"

"Oh, for the love of God, Will Henry! Really. You have been listening, haven't you? Neither Kearns nor the director knew at that point he was a yeoman with the navy."

"But Kearns told Mr. Kendall—"

"Yes, *after* he had found out who he was. That is my question. How did he—and I—find out who this man was?"

I took a deep breath and tried again. "He did not give his name. He had no papers when he was brought— Someone brought him in?"

He smiled. "Much better. Yes, he was brought there by one Mary Elizabeth Marks, who claimed she'd discovered him lying in the gutter a block from her flat, at number 212 Musbury Street, less than a mile from the hospital. She claimed she didn't know him, had never seen him before, was playing the Good Samaritan, et cetera, et cetera. Kearns found her—as I did months later—and it did not take him long—or me—to bully the truth out of her. The patient had been a customer of hers. Miss Marks, you see, makes her living by . . . entertaining young, and not so young, sailors . . . or any other members of the armed forces, or civilians, who enjoy . . . being entertained by ladies who . . . entertain."

He cleared his throat.

"I would rather not know. Yes, she was a lady of the

evening. She stuck to her story at first, until I told her I knew Kearns, and then her whole demeanor changed, from surly to schoolgirl giddy.

"'Oh, you mean *Dr.* Kearns. Now, he's the regular charmer, that one,' she said, giggling. 'An' quite the looker, too!'

"'He is an old friend of mine,' I told her, to which she replied, laying her hand upon my arm, 'Well, any friend of Dr. Kearns', guv'na . . .'

"She confessed that the man had been a regular customer; that he had, in fact, been staying with her in the flat on Musbury Street since his discharge from the navy a week before he became ill; and that she had hidden the truth based on her fear that her landlord would evict her for living with a man outside the sanctity of holy matrimony. She began to cry at the mention of marriage. She had loved Tim; there had been talk of a wedding. I did not understand, she told me, how cruel life had been to her, how her father had beaten and then abandoned her mother, how her mother had subsequently died from consumption, leaving Mary on the streets to beg for food, and later to sell her own body for it. Timothy was to be her savior, and then her savior died."

He shook his head; his dark eyes flashed. "She had kept his trunk with all his things, including oddities and other paraphernalia he had gathered in his travels abroad. Kearns had asked to see them. It might help, he explained to her, in his investigation into the cause of poor Timothy's mysterious demise. You know what he found in that trunk, of course.

"'Now, what is this?' he said. 'It looks like . . . Do you know what he kept saying, Mary, over and over again? "The nest! The bloody human nest!"' Mary Marks was horrified. She claimed to never have laid eyes upon the *nidus*. She said Timothy had never once spoken of it. And so Kearns asked the same question of her that I asked."

He paused. I knew what he was waiting for.

"What had been his last port of call before his discharge?" I ventured.

"Ah, the faintest glimmer. The slightest ray breaking through the clouds! Yes, and you know the answer, though not the particulars, which are few and as follows: Timothy Stowe served as yeoman second-class aboard the HMS *Acheron*, a frigate in the Royal Navy that had just returned from its tour in the Arabian Sea, after resupplying the garrison at the British protectorate of Socotra."

Warthrop hurried back to the hotel to tell Arkwright the news. He was surprised to discover that his companion had not returned.

"I'd been gone for several hours, and his errand should not have taken half as long as mine. I waited more than an hour; by then the sun had begun to set, and still no sign of Arkwright. I began to worry I'd been wrong about Kearns. Perhaps he had not left England after all, and Arkwright had unwittingly walked right into the bear's den. How close I was with that metaphor! Night fell and with it my hope of his speedy return. I decided I had no choice but to go look for him, and that meant beginning with Dorset Street, not a very inviting place in broad daylight, much less on a foggy night."

He sighed, tugging on his bottom lip. "They may have followed me there—as one of them must have followed Arkwright—or they may have anticipated my coming there in search of him. I could not have been twenty yards from the spot where the hansom dropped me off, when a hulking shadow loomed out of the mist. I caught a flash of coppery red hair in the lamplight, saw the arm go up, glimpsed the glint of a pistol's barrel, and then darkness—absolute darkness."

The monstrumologist awoke to the smell of raw sewage and the far-off echoes of water dripping, to fitful shadows jittering in lamplight and cold wet stone pressing against his back. He was bound hand and foot, his hands tied behind his back and connected by a short length of rope to the noose around his neck. "Like a dog's leash tied to its collar, so the slightest movement jerked the loop tight, to bring me to heel, as it were."

On the sewer platform beside him slumped Arkwright, identically trussed up, awake, and, to Warthrop's eye, remarkably calm given the circumstances. "As if it were an everyday occurrence, finding oneself with a noose around one's neck in the city's sewers, with the pockmarked face of a redheaded Russian brute a foot away."

"Good evening, Dr. Pellinore Warthrop," the brute greeted him in a heavy Slavic accent. "*Как у Вас дела?*"

To which Warthrop replied, "*Так себе.*"

"Ha, ha. Did you hear that, Plešec? He speaks Russian!"

"I heard that, Rurick. The inflection is good, but the accent is horrible."

The doctor tried to turn his head to locate their other captor, and was rewarded by a hard yank of the rope against his neck, hard enough, he said, to bruise his Adam's apple. Beside him Arkwright whispered, "Careful, Doctor."

Rurick's reaction was immediate. He pressed the long black barrel of his Smith & Wesson revolver against Arkwright's forehead and pulled back the hammer. Its click was loud and resonant in the hollow space.

"You forget rules. Speak only when spoken to. Tell truth. Break rule one, I shoot you. Break rule two, and Plešec guts you with his knife, make rat fodder out of you."

The short bald Russian called Plešec stepped into Warthrop's view. He was turning a bowie knife in his diminutive hands, the same knife that would be used, months later, to nearly decapitate Jacob Torrance.

"You come looking for Mr. Jack Kearns," Rurick said to the doctor. The monstrumologist did not perceive it as a question, so he did not reply. "You go to hospital"—he turned to Arkwright—"and you go to his flat. Why do you do this?"

"He is an old friend of mine," Warthrop said. "I heard that he had gone missing, and we were—"

"Now I must think that you are deaf and do not hear rule two. Or you are idiot and do not understand rule two. You tell me, Dr. Warthrop. Are you deaf or are you idiot?"

"I am neither, sir, and I demand to know—"

Arkwright cut him off. "We are looking for Kearns because he sent Dr. Warthrop something very valuable."

"And?"

"And we wanted to ask him about it."

"If you seek John Kearns, why do you go see two officers of the British intelligence service, Mr. Arkwright? Do you think they know where he has gone or where he may have gotten this 'valuable thing'?"

Warthrop could not help himself; he turned his head to look over at Arkwright, the attendant pain a fair trade, he thought, for the sight of Arkwright's stoic reaction.

"Those men you saw me with this morning left a note for me at the hotel. They understood Dr. Warthrop and I were in London, and wanted to ask me a few questions. I must say, they were far more civilized in their—"

The one called Rurick gathered a fistful of Arkwright's hair in his massive hand and yanked, pulling the rope tight around his captive's neck as he rammed the forehead against the upraised knees. Arkwright's head snapped back, and his eyes glittered beneath the angry red spot above them.

"You are spy," Rurick snarled down at him. "You seek *magnificum*."

Arkwright did not answer. He did not move. He met the Russian's glare and did not blink.

"We do—," he began.

"Arkwright, *no*," whispered Warthrop.

"But I am not a spy, for the English or anyone else. As I told you, my name is Thomas Arkwright; I am an American from Long Island; and I have accompanied Dr. Warthrop to assist him in his investigation into the disappearance of his friend Jack Kearns."

"Let me cut him," Plešec pleaded with Rurick. "He makes fools of us."

The monstrumologist spoke up. "We do seek the *magnificum*. Kearns sent the *nidus* to me but did not tell me anything else. So I came here to ask him, but he is gone, as you know. And you seem to know everything else, a fact that is puzzling in light of this interrogation or prelude to an execution or whatever it is."

Plešec opened his mouth, closed it again, looked over at Rurick. "Was that rule one or rule two?"

"One. Definitely one," Rurick answered. He stepped forward and pushed the muzzle of the revolver against the doctor's forehead, the same spot he'd picked on Arkwright. The thick, hairy index finger twitched on the trigger, and began to slowly squeeze.

"Don't be stupid, Rurick. Pull that trigger, and you'll be serving the remainder of your enlistment in Siberia rounding up gamblers and two-bit petty thieves. You know it and

I know it, so let us dispense with these childish games and speak together as gentlemen."

The voice was Arkwright's; the accent was distinctly and unmistakably British. The monstrumologist closed his eyes. He was not waiting for the bullet; he was kicking himself for not seeing the truth sooner, for ignoring his misgivings and shoving aside his doubts in his lust for glory.

"It was the only way out," Warthrop confided to me. "He knew if he didn't confess his true identity, we were done for. To cling to his cover created a stalemate that only one thing could break—a bullet into our brains. Well, two things, counting Plešec's knife. So he told Rurick what he already knew to be true: He was not Thomas Arkwright of the Long Island Arkwrights; he was an officer of the British intelligence service, a fact of which I had no knowledge, he assured our captors. He'd been assigned by his superiors to infiltrate the Society for the purpose of discovering the origin of the *nidus ex magnificum* recently delivered to me, courtesy of Dr. Jack Kearns."

"And how do you British know of the *nidus?*" Rurick asked next.

"Well, how do you think? Kearns told us about it," returned Arkwright.

"He tells you of the *nidus* but does not say where it comes from?"

"No, he did not say. He said he didn't know where it

came from. We knew he had it, and we knew he sent it to Warthrop, and we knew he disappeared. That is all we knew."

"So you pay Warthrop to be your bird dog?"

"No. It was our understanding that Dr. Warthrop is one of those rare creatures whose honor cannot be bought. We decided to trick him instead. Play to his ego, which by all accounts is considerably large and substantially playable. My job was to stick with him until he found the origin of the *nidus*."

"Ah. And then you kill him."

"No," Arkwright replied patiently. "We are British. We avoid murder if we can help it. Killing is expensive, risky, and usually results in a plethora of unintended consequences. That is what I'm trying to help you to understand, Rurick. Killing us creates more problems than it solves."

"Not if you have discovered *magnificum*," Rurick argued. He turned to Warthrop. "Do you know where it is?"

The monstrumologist turned from our reflections and sat in the chair beside my bunk. His shoulders swayed in rhythm to the rocking of the train. At that moment its whistle shrieked, a shrill, almost hysterical sound, like a wounded animal.

"It was an interesting dilemma, Will Henry," he said calmly. We might have been sitting by a cozy fire on Harrington Lane discussing a paradox of his favorite philosopher, Zeno of Elea. "A bit more complicated than the question implies. If I lied and said no, the wisest course for the Russians would be to kill me, for the alternative was setting me free to find the answer, a risk Rurick—and his government—could not afford to take. However, if I told the truth and said yes, the decision would be even easier. He knew that his British rivals did *not* know the location of the *magnificum*, a secret they were willing to keep at all costs. He would *have* to kill us. Neither the truth nor a lie would spare my life."

"The lady or the tiger," I said.

"The lady or the what?"

"It's nothing, sir. A story Dr. Torrance told."

"Dr. Torrance told you a story?" He was having some trouble picturing it.

"It doesn't matter, sir."

"Then, why did you interrupt me?"

"Rurick didn't shoot you or Mr. Arkwright, so you must have figured something out."

"Correct, Will Henry, but that is rather like Newton's saying the apple fell, so it must be on the ground! Understand that my problem was compounded by the presence of Arkwright, whom I had just discovered was an agent of Her Majesty's government. If I told the truth and by some miracle we were spared, the British would know where to find the *magnificum*, and that would be only slightly less disastrous than my death."

The answer to his "interesting dilemma" occurred to him with no more than a second to spare. Saying nothing broke rule one. Lying broke rule two. Telling the truth broke no established rule except the law of necessity; the end result would be the same.

He could feel Rurick's sour breath bathing his face. He could hear the incessant *drip, drip* of water and smell the nauseating cocktail of urine and human waste wafting up from the trench below. He looked up into those depthless black eyes, the eyes of a predator, a hunter like himself—into those shining eyes, *his* eyes, and he said the one thing, the *only* thing, that could save his life:

"I do know where it is. The Faceless One hails from an island off the coast of Oman, called Masirah."

"Masirah?" I asked.

"Yes! Masirah, a long-suspected hiding place of the *magnificum*. It was the perfect bluff, Will Henry. Any other answer, as I've demonstrated, would have resulted in our deaths. Our only hope lay in the possibility that the Russians already thought that the origin of the *nidus* was Socotra. If they believed I was wrong about the *nidus*'s origin, they might let us go. In fact, it served their interest to let us go. By the time we discovered the *magnificum* was not on Masirah, their mission to Socotra would be complete. It was perfect in another, albeit secondary, sense. Assuming I was correct and we survived, Arkwright would return to his superiors with the intelligence he'd been tasked to gather: *Typhoeus magnificum* was on the isle of Masirah!"

"But why would the Russians kidnap you and Mr. Arkwright if they already knew where the *magnificum* was? I don't understand, Dr. Warthrop."

He patted my shoulder and whirled from his seat, strode back to the window, and admired his newly whiskered profile in the glass.

"In the affairs of nations, Will Henry, *all* governments, whether democratic or despotic, are desperately interested in two things—obtaining information they wish to protect and protecting information they've already obtained. Rurick's question wasn't 'Where is the *magnificum*?' It was, 'Do you know where the *magnificum* is?' That struck me like a thunderbolt. Not 'Tell me where to find the *magnificum*' but 'Do *you* know where the *magnificum* is?' It tipped his hand; I played my little bluff, and we survived."

Rurick's finger relaxed upon the trigger. He looked over at his bald partner, who wore a thin-lipped smirk and was nodding.

"You are sure of this Masirah?" Rurick asked the doctor.

Warthrop drew himself erect, or as erect as the rope around his neck would allow, and said (Oh, how well I can picture it!), "I am a scientist, sir. I seek the truth and only the truth for truth's sake, without regard to the interests of governments or principalities, religious beliefs or cultural biases. As a scientist, I am providing you a theory based upon all the data at my disposal. Hence it can only be called a theory until it is proven otherwise—in other words, until someone actually finds the *magnificum* on the island of Masirah."

Rurick frowned, trying to wrap his reptilian brain around the doctor's answer.

"So . . . you do not know if it is Masirah?"

"I think it is highly probable."

"Damn it, Warthrop," Arkwright cried out. "For the love of bloody hell, before he blows both our brains out, did the *nidus* come from Masirah?"

"Why, yes. I believe it did."

Rurick and Plešec withdrew to consider their options. There were only two. Warthrop used the time to collect himself. It was not the first time he'd faced down death, but that was one thing to which one never got accustomed. As the Russians whispered urgently—it appeared Rurick still thought the best and simplest option would be murder; his comrade, however, had seen the wisdom of releasing them—Arkwright turned to Warthrop and said quietly, "I can save us both, but you must go along with everything I say."

"Excuse me, Arkwright. It sounded like you just asked me to trust you."

"Warthrop, you do not know these men; I do. They're Okhranka, the Russian secret police, and you could not find a more vicious pair of killers this side of the Ukraine. We've been tracking them for more than a year. Rurick is the real brute, a bloody, soulless predator. He was questioned twice by Scotland Yard for the Whitechapel killings last year. He cannot be reasoned with. If he has been given orders to kill you, *he will kill you.*"

The monstrumologist refused to let go his grip upon the faith he put in reason; he was a scientist, as he'd said; reason was his god. Rurick's hesitation to pull the trigger had convinced the doctor beyond all doubt that he'd been correct. The Russians knew Socotra to be the home of the *magnificum.* But he could not explain his reasoning to Arkwright. To do so would give away the game to the British.

"Then, how do you propose we proceed, in that case, Arkwright?" he asked.

The English spy winked at him. "Leave everything to me."

Warthrop sighed at his reflection. "Well, you know what happened next. Arkwright 'revealed' to them the British plan for handling me once I discovered the location of the *magnificum.* It was, he confessed, not the first time an 'inconvenience' to the Crown had found himself in a home for the insane. Rurick was skeptical, or perhaps just confused, but Plešec caught on at once, thought it a capital idea and quite humorous. In another thirty minutes we were on our way to Hanwell. Rurick pulled Arkwright aside at the gatehouse, stuck his Smith & Wesson into his rib cage, and informed him that he knew where his family lived and he'd better keep his end of the bargain, which meant convincing von Helrung that I had met my maker in pursuit of the *magnificum.* Everyone parted company extremely satisfied, with the exception of the one about to be thrown into a lunatic asylum until the end of his days. Arkwright was pleased that he had walked away with the information he'd sought from us, and with his life; the Russians were satisfied that the secret of Socotra was safe; and both felt that there was nothing more to fear."

A feeling of sadness unexpectedly swept over me, and heart-crushing guilt over the fate of Thomas Arkwright. I had distrusted and then hated him for taking Warthrop from me, had tried and convicted him in my mind for a crime conceived only in my mind, and in the end it was not a "bloody, soulless killer" who had orchestrated his final test, no "mean king" as in Torrance's parable. No, it had been a thirteen-year-old boy consumed with jealousy and self-righteousness, casting himself in the role of protector and avenger of a man who had rejected him for another and exiled him from the rarified atmosphere of his presence.

TWENTY-EIGHT

"The Trouble with Venice"

The doctor was not pleased that his great quest for the ultimate prize in monstrumology would be delayed by a six-hour layover in Venice—despite the fact that it was *Venezia, La Serenissima*, the queen of the Adriatic, one of the most— if not *the* most—beautiful cities on earth.

We arrived around three o'clock in the afternoon on a warm, bright day in late spring, when the westering sun turned the canals into ribbons of gold and the buildings lining their eastern banks shone like jewels. The sweet serenades of the gondoliers leapt from their boats and gamboled merrily after us, along every narrow lane and back alleyway, and golden light pooled in the archways of the little shops and restaurants and the balconies framed in wrought iron overlooking the water.

Ah, Venice! You recline like a beautiful woman in her lover's arms, bare-armed and free of care, your beating heart filled with light undefiled. I wished we could have remained nestled in your dewy bosom sixty times six hours. A boy wanders in a dry land of dust and bones, of bleached, broken rocks and the grinding of the wind in a waterless season. The lamentation of the arid earth, the anguish of the bones and dust and the broken rocks gnawed by the hot wind; this has been his home, this his inheritance . . . and then the boy turns round. He turns round and beholds Venice singing in golden light, and he is entranced, her loveliness all the more heartbreaking for what he has inherited.

The monstrumologist seemed to know every byway and backwater of this floating city, to be familiar with every tiny shop and sidewalk café. "I spent a summer or two here during my European period," was how he put it. Perhaps he was reverting to his days as an aspiring poet; it sounded like something an artist might say of himself, 'my European period.' We ate an early dinner at a café in the Piazzetta di San Marco, near the lagoon, a welcome respite after hiking for two hours in the city with no clear—or so it seemed to me—purpose or destination in mind. The doctor ordered a *caffè* and settled back in his chair to enjoy the mild air, and the beautiful women, who seemed so plentiful in Venice and whose careless laughter echoed between the Libreria and the Zecca like water splashing in the fountain of the piazza.

He sipped his espresso and allowed his eye to roam dreamily over the winsome landscape, his gaze as languid as the water of the *Canalasso.*

"Here is the trouble with Venice," he said. "Once you have seen it, every other place seems dull and tired by comparison, so you are always reminded of where you are not." His eye was drawn to two comely young ladies walking arm in arm along the Molo, where the sun sparked and spat bright flashes of gold upon the blue water. "The same is true about nearly everything else Venetian."

He stroked his new whiskers thoughtfully. "Monstrumology, too. In a different way. You've been with me long enough, Will Henry; you must know what I mean. Would not life seem terribly . . . well, *boring,* without it? I am not saying it has always been enjoyable or even pleasant for you, but can you imagine how mundane and interminably *gray* life would be if you had to give it up?"

"I have imagined it, sir."

He looked closely at me. "And?"

"I was . . . I had my chance to . . ." I could not look at him. "I lived with Dr. von Helrung's niece while you were gone— Mrs. Bates—and she offered to adopt me—"

"Adopt you!" He seemed astounded. "For what?"

My face felt warm. "For my own good, I think."

He snorted, saw my wounded expression, set down his cup, and said, "And you said no."

"My place is with you, Dr. Warthrop."

He nodded. What did that nod mean? He agreed my place was with him? Or was he merely assenting to my decision regardless of his own opinion? He did not say, and I dared not ask.

"I was there, you know," he said. "On the night you were born. Your mother was staying in one of the guest rooms—a matter of convenience. *My* convenience, I mean. I had just received a fresh specimen and required your father's assistance in the dissection. We were in the basement when your mother went into labor two floors above us, so we did not hear her cries until we came upstairs several hours later. James rushed up, came back down again, and then dragged me to her bedside."

I stared at him in disbelief. "I was born at Harrington Lane?"

"Yes. Your parents never told you?"

I shook my head. It wasn't something I would have asked them. "And *you* delivered me?"

"Did I say that? What did I just say? I said I was dragged to your bedside by your agitated father. As I recall, your mother's words were, 'Do not let that man come near me!'" He chuckled. "I had the impression your mother did not like me very much."

"She told Father your work would kill him one day."

"Did she? Hmmm. A prescient remark, though the prediction came true in a roundabout way." He stroked the whiskers on his chin and regarded the statue of Saint Theodore slaying the dragon atop the granite column nearby.

"Did you, Dr. Warthrop?"

"Did I what?"

"Deliver me."

"I am not a midwife, Will Henry. Neither am I a physician. I know how to kill things, cut things up, and preserve things. How do you suppose that qualifies me to bring life into the world?" He would not look at me, though, and I found it very hard to look at him. He crossed his legs and clasped his hands over his upraised knee, the delicate fingers interlaced. Were those the first hands that had held me? Were those the eyes that first saw me and the eyes that I first saw? It was a dizzying thought for reasons I could not articulate.

"Why didn't *you* tell me?" I asked.

"It is not the sort of thing that comes up naturally in conversation," he answered. "Why the look of dismay, Will Henry? I was born in that house too. It does not carry with it—as far as I know—the mark of Cain."

We lingered in the *piazzetta* until sunset. The doctor drank four espressos, the last in a single swallow, and when he stood up, his entire body seemed to vibrate inside his clothes. He strode off without a backward glance, leaving me to keep up the best I could in the burgeoning crowd, passing the magnificent Basilica di San Marco before turning into the Piazzetta dei Leoncini. There I lost him in the throng, then caught sight of him again as he was leaving the square, striding east along Calle de Canonica toward the canal.

He stopped abruptly before an open doorway and stood absolutely still, a striking image after the fury of motion, now as motionless as a statue in the velvet dusk. I heard him murmur, "I wonder if . . . How long has it been?" He looked at his watch, snapped it shut, and motioned for me to follow him inside.

We entered a dimly lit low-ceilinged room crowded with wooden tables, mostly unoccupied, at the rear of which was a small stage. The platform was bare except for an ancient upright piano pushed against the wall. The doctor sat down at a table close to the stage, beneath a dance hall poster that somehow managed to cling to the crumbling plaster of the wall. A basset-hound-faced middle-aged man wearing a stained apron asked us what we wanted to drink. Warthrop ordered another *caffè*, his fifth, to which the *cameriere* replied, "No *caffè*. Vino. Vino or *spritz*." The monstrumologist sighed and ordered a *spritz*. It would sit untouched; Warthrop did not drink alcohol. He asked our sad-faced waiter if someone named Veronica Soranzo still sang at the club. "*Sì*. She sings," he said, and disappeared through the doorway to the right of the stage.

The doctor settled into his chair and leaned his head against the wall. He closed his eyes.

"Dr. Warthrop?"

"Yes, Will Henry."

"Shouldn't we be getting back to the station now?"

"I am waiting."

"Waiting?"

"For an old friend. Actually, three old friends."

He opened one eye, closed it again. "And the first has just arrived."

I turned in my chair and saw a hulking, slump-shouldered man filling the doorway. He wore a rumpled overcoat that was much too heavy for the clement weather, and a battered felt hat. It was not by his hair—the hat hid most of that—but by his eyes that I recognized him. I gasped and blinked, and he was gone.

"Rurick!" I whispered. "He followed us here?"

"He has been following us since we left the station house. He and his hairless cohort, the diminutive *Gospodin* Plešec, have wandered through all of Venice with us; they sat upon the steps of the Basilica di San Marco this afternoon while we enjoyed our drinks in the *piazzetta*."

"What should we do?"

His eyes remained closed, his expression serene. He hadn't a care in the world. "Nothing."

What was the matter with him? *Rurick is the real brute, a bloody, soulless predator*, Arkwright had said. Warthrop must have thought we were safe inside this pathetic dive, but we could not stay ensconced here forever.

"That's two old friends accounted for," the doctor said. "Rurick is in front, so Plešec must be watching the back." He opened his eyes and sat up straight. Bits of plaster from the crumbling wall rained to the floor behind his chair.

"And here comes the third!" He leaned forward, resting his forearms on his knees. His eyes gleamed in the shivery flicker of the gas jets.

A man in a wrinkled white shirt and black vest emerged from the doorway beside the stage, dipped slightly at the waist toward the meager audience, and sat down at the piano. He raised his hands high over the keys, held them suspended there for a dramatic moment, and then brought them smashing down, launching into a rollicking rendition of "A Wand'ring Minstrel I" from *The Mikado*. The instrument was badly out of tune, and the man's technique was horrible, but he was a very physical musician, throwing his entire body into the effort. His buttocks popped up and down in rhythm on the rickety stool while he swayed in time, a human metronome, a man who played the piano as if *it* played *him*.

Abruptly, with no bridge whatsoever, he switched to Violetta's aria from *La Traviata*, and a woman emerged from the doorway dressed in a faded red gown, her long dark hair flowing freely over her bare shoulders. Her face was heavy with stage paint; still, she was a striking woman, on the cusp of her middle years, I guessed, with sparkling chocolate-colored eyes that, like those of so many Italian women, bespoke of promise as well as danger. I cannot say her voice rose to the level of her looks. In fact, it wasn't very good at all. I glanced at the monstrumologist, who was listening in a state of complete rapture. I wondered what so entranced him; it could not have been her singing.

He pounded on the table at the conclusion of the song, shouting "Bravo! *Bravissimo!*" while the other patrons politely clapped and then turned back quickly to their bottles. The woman skipped lightly from the stage and swept straight toward us.

"Pellinore! Dear, dear, Pellinore!" She kissed him lightly on both cheeks. "*Ciao, amore mio. Mi sei mancato tanto.*" She ran her hand over his whiskered cheek and added, "But what is this?"

"Don't you like it? I think it makes me look distinguished. Veronica, this is Will Henry, James's son, and my latest *acquisizione.*"

"*Acquisizione!*" Her brown eyes danced with delight. "*Ciao*, Will Henry, *come sta?* I knew your father well. *E 'molto triste. Molto triste!* But, Pellinore, *perché sei qui a Venezia? Lavoro o piacere?*" she asked, sliding into the chair beside him. At that moment our waiter came back with the doctor's *spritz.* Veronica snapped her fingers at him, and he left, returning a moment later with a glass of wine.

"It is always a pleasure to be in Venice," the monstrumologist answered. He lifted his glass to salute her but did not take a sip.

She turned those laughing eyes back to me and said, "The looks of a *farabutto*, the words of a *politico!*"

"Veronica is saying she likes my new whiskers," the doctor said in response to my baffled expression.

"They make you look old and tired," she opined with a sniff.

"Perhaps it isn't the beard," Warthrop returned. "Perhaps I *am* old and tired."

"Tired, *sì*. Old, never! You have not aged a day, not an hour since I saw you last. How long has it been? Three years?"

"Six," he answered.

"No! As long as that? It is no wonder, then, why I have been so lonely!" She turned to me. "You will tell me, yes? What brings the great Pellinore Warthrop all the way to Venice? He is in trouble, isn't he?" And then to the doctor: "Who is it this time, Pellinore? The Germans?"

"Actually, it's the Russians."

She stared at him for a moment before dissolving into laughter.

"And the British," Warthrop added, raising his voice slightly. "Though I've managed to put them off, for a while at least."

"Sidorov?" she asked.

He shrugged. "Probably somewhere in the mix."

"So it is business, then. You did not come to see me."

"Signorina Soranzo, how could I come all this way and *not* see you? To me, you *are* Venice."

Her eyes narrowed; the compliment did not sit well.

"I suppose you could say I am in a bit of trouble," he

hurriedly continued. "The problem being twofold. The first part is very large, heavily armed, and loitering outside on the Calle de Canonica. The second, I think, is in the alleyway behind us. He is not so large but carries a knife that is. My problem is compounded by the fact that my train is scheduled to depart in an hour."

"So?" she asked. "*Perché pensi di avere un problema?* Kill them." She said it casually, like she was advising him on how to treat a headache.

"I'm afraid that would further compound my problem. My business is difficult enough without becoming a fugitive on top of everything else."

She slapped him across the cheek. He kept himself very still; he took care not to look away.

"*Bastardo,*" she said. "When I walk out and see you sitting there, my heart, it . . . *Sono stupido,* I should have known. For six years I do not see you. I do not receive a single letter. Until I think you must be dead. Why else would you not come? Why else would you not write? You are in the business of death, I think; you must be dead!"

"I never pretended to be something that I am not," the monstrumologist replied stiffly. "I was very honest with you, Veronica."

"You sneak out of Venice without even saying good-bye, no note, no nothing, like a thief in the night. You call this honest?" She tilted her chin in his direction. "*Sei un cardardo,* Pellinore Warthrop. You are a not a man; you are a coward."

"Ask Will Henry. It is how I say all my good-byes," he said.

"I am married," she announced suddenly. "To Bartolomeo."

"Who is Bartolomeo?"

"The piano player."

The doctor couldn't decide whether to be relieved or hurt. "Really? Well, he seems very . . . energetic."

"He is *here*," she snapped.

"As am I. Which brings us back to my problem."

"Exactly! *Il problema*. I wish the Russian with the knife luck to find your heart!"

She spun from the chair in a dramatic flourish, allowing him to catch her by the wrist before she could escape. He pulled her close and whispered urgently into her ear. She listened with head bowed, her eyes fixed upon the floor. Her heart was clearly torn. Once drawn into the Warthropian orbit, even the strongest of hearts—and women possess the strongest of any—find it hard to break free. She hated him and loved him, longed for him and loathed him, and cursed herself for feeling anything at all. Her love demanded she save him, her hate that she destroy him.

The cruelest aspect of love, the monstrumologist had said, *is its inviolable integrity.*

Veronica and Bartolomeo lived directly above the nightclub, in a cramped, sparsely furnished apartment that she had labored to brighten with fresh flowers and colorful throws and art poster prints. There was a small balcony in the front that overlooked the Calle de Canonica. The balcony doors were open when we came in; the white curtains undulated in the balmy wind, and I could hear the sound of the Venetian street life below.

Bartolomeo joined us, his shirtfront saturated in sweat, his eyes possessing that distracted, otherworldly stare universal to artists—and to madmen. He embraced Warthrop as if he were a long-lost friend and asked him how he liked his playing. The doctor replied that a musician of his caliber deserved a better instrument, and Bartolomeo threw his arms around him and kissed him sloppily on the cheek.

The monstrumologist explained our predicament and his idea to resolve it. Bartolomeo embraced the plan with the same ferocity he had just employed upon the doctor, but worried that the difference in their height could pose a problem.

"We'll extinguish the light in here," Warthrop said. "And Veronica will station herself between you and the street. It won't be a perfect disguise, but it should buy us the time we need."

The doctor retired to the bedroom to undress; Bartolomeo stripped right where he stood, smiling all the while, amused, perhaps, by my astonishment at his decidedly un-Victorian lack of modesty.

The bedroom door opened, and Veronica emerged with the doctor's clothes, fussed in Italian at her husband, returned to the bedroom, and slammed shut the door. Bartolomeo shrugged and said to me, "*La signora è una tigre, ma lei è la mia tigre.*" The monstrumologist's clothes were too big for him—Bartolomeo was not a tall man—but from the street, at night, in dim lighting . . . I prayed the doctor was right.

After several more minutes the bedroom door came open again and Veronica came out, followed by another woman—or anyway a womanish creature akin to something Mr. P. T. Barnum might include in his sideshow attraction, wearing the same faded red gown that had, just a few moments before, adorned the decidely more curvaceous form of Veronica Soranzo. Bartolomeo burst out laughing at this ludicrous mockery of all things feminine, from the hastily applied makeup to the doctor's bare heels hanging over the back of his wife's shoes.

"The lady, I think, needs a shave," he teased.

"There isn't time," Warthrop replied seriously. "I will need a hat."

"Something with gold," Bartolomeo suggested. "To bring out the color in your eyes."

He held out the doctor's revolver, which he had found in the jacket pocket.

"Give it to Will Henry; I've nowhere to put it."

"If you carried a smaller weapon, you could stick it in your garter."

"I like your husband," the monstrumologist told Veronica as she pushed a wide-brimmed hat onto his head.

"He is an idiot," she said, and Bartolomeo laughed. "Do you see? I insult him and he laughs."

"That's what makes me a good husband," Bartolomeo said.

Veronica hissed something under her breath, grabbed her husband by the wrist, and dragged him toward the balcony.

"You don't say nothing, understand? You stand by the door and lower your head, and I do all the talking."

"I thought you said there would be acting involved."

She peeked through the curtains to the street below. "I don't see this man you describe, Pellinore."

"He's there," Warthrop assured her, adjusting his hat in the mirror.

She started outside, stopped, turned back, and then abandoned her husband in his baggy clothes, the monstrumologist in miniature, to return to the doctor's side.

"I will never see you again," she said.

"We cannot know that."

She shook her head. "*Non si capisce*. You are an idiot like him. All men are idiots. I say *I* will never see you again. Never come here again. Thanks to you, every time I see my husband, I will see the man who he is not."

She kissed him: the love. Then she slapped him: the hate. Bartolomeo watched all of it, smiling. What did he care? Warthrop might have her heart, but he, Bartolomeo, had *her*.

They went onto the balcony. Her voice, trained to project itself in large, open spaces, rang out, saying, "How dare you come back here now, after all these years! I am married now, to Bartolomeo. I cannot leave, Pellinore. I cannot leave! What is that? What is that you say, Pellinore Warthrop? *Amore!* You speak of love?" She laughed cruelly. "I will never love you, Pellinore Warthrop! I will never love another man again!"

"Well, Will Henry." My master-cum-mistress sighed. "I think that is enough; we'd better go."

We left through the front door, Warthrop's hand resting protectively upon my shoulder, a (very tall and overdressed) governess with her charge, walking as fast as the doctor's wobbly gait would allow, down the Calle de Canonica toward the canal. The doctor kept his head down, but I could not resist and glanced about for the Russian assassin. I spied him lounging in an archway across the street, pretending not to listen to Veronica's performance overhead. Her acting was only slightly better than her singing; still, it seemed to be doing the trick. Rurick did not abandon his post.

Reaching the Rio di Palazzo unmolested, we climbed aboard a gondola whose pilot was a model of discretion. He made no comment or reacted in any noticeable way to this very homely woman—or very strange man—stepping into his craft. He even asked, with a perfectly straight face, if his passengers would like to hear a song.

The sounds of the street faded. The dark water glittered like the star-encrusted heavens as we passed with but a whispery ripple beneath a limestone bridge shining bone white in the glow of the quarter-moon.

"The Ponte dei Sospiri," the monstrumologist said in a quiet voice. "The Bridge of Sighs. See the bars over the windows, Will Henry? Through them prisoners would have their last view of the beauty of *Venezia*. They say lovers will be blessed if they kiss beneath the Ponte dei Sospiri."

"*Sì*, signor—signorina . . . *sì*. That is what they say," acknowledged our slightly confused gondolier.

"I might have kissed her here," said Pellinore Warthrop to himself—the fugitive, the prisoner. "I do not remember."

TWENTY-NINE

"Before You Were, I Was"

The hunt for the Faceless One resumed, with us, the hunters, now hunted ourselves. The doctor adjusted better to this change of fortune than his young apprentice, who could not rid his thoughts of the cold fire in his pursuer's eyes, so similar to the one that burned in his master's, the ancient, unquenchable flame that blazes in the eyes of all predators, the flinty remnants of the primordial conflagration. With each tick of the clock, with every passing mile, the fire in the monstrumologist's eye grew colder and brighter. That which drove him was older than he. It was as old as life and just as inexorable. It burned in him and it consumed him. He was the predator; he was the prey.

"How did they find us?" I wondered aloud that night as we readied for bed.

"I think they never 'lost' us," he answered. "They have been on this train since Calais, or at least since Lucerne. They followed us into Venice because it was their first and best opportunity."

"Opportunity to do what?"

"To say hello and catch up on old times. *Really*, Will Henry."

"If they let you go before, why do they want to kill you now?"

"They did not let me go, as you recall. Unless you consider throwing someone into a lunatic asylum letting him go."

"But why would they want to kill you if they think you don't know where the *magnificum* is?"

"For the same reason they wanted to kill me when they didn't know what I thought." He lay back in his bunk and said, "They've had months to consider my little trick in the sewer, long enough for even a man of Rurick's limited mental agility to come to the conclusion that I might have been lying. Or it could just be they think I'm better off dead." He gave a dry little laugh. "And they are not alone in that!"

"Who is she, Dr. Warthrop? Who is Veronica Soranzo?"

"Someone I do not wish to talk about."

"Were the two of you . . ." I did not know the word I should use.

He apparently did, for he answered, "Yes . . . and no. And what does it matter?"

"It doesn't."

THE ISLE OF BLOOD 551

"Then, why did you bring it up?" he asked testily, flopping onto his side and fussily snapping the sheet.

"I just never thought . . ."

"Yes? What did you never think? There are so many possibilities; don't make me guess. What? That I might have had a life before you came into it? I did not spring into existence upon your entrance, Will Henry. Before you were, I was, and for a good while too. Veronica Soranzo belongs to what was, and I try to concern myself with what is and what will be. Now, please, give me some peace. I must think."

When I woke several hours later, for a disoriented instant I thought I was back in my little loft on Harrington Lane, shaken from a deep sleep by his desperate cries beckoning me to his bedside. The doctor had drawn the blinds, the little compartment was as black as pitch, and I found him by the sound of his choked sobs. I reached for him. His body jerked at the touch of my hand.

"Dr. Warthrop?"

"It is nothing. Nothing. A dream, that's all. Nothing. Go back to sleep."

"Are you sure?" I asked. It did not seem like nothing to me. I'd never heard him sound so terrified.

"What if he killed her, Will Henry?" he cried. "When he discovered our charade, he would have confronted her, don't you think? Yes, yes. He would be furious; he would express his rage upon her. Oh, what have I done, Will Henry? What have I done?"

"Should we go back?"

"Go back? Go back for what? To bury her? Do you *ever* listen to what I say? Do you ever listen to what *you* say? I have offered her up in my stead, Will Henry. I have killed her!"

"You don't know that, sir. You *can't* know that." His terror was infectious. I wrapped the covers around my quivering shoulders. Suddenly the compartment was very cold and very small. I could not see his face; he was an insubstantial shade against the darker gray.

"Look not into my eyes," he muttered feverishly. "For I am the basilisk. Fear my touch, for I am the Midas of annihilation." He sought out my hand in the dark, for comfort, I thought, but I was wrong. It was for proof. "James and Mary, Erasmus and Malachi, John and Muriel, Damien and Thomas and Jacob and Veronica, and the ones whose names I have forgotten and the ones whose names I never knew . . ." He pressed the spot where my finger should have been. "And you, Will Henry. You have given yourself in service to *ha-Mashchit*, the destroyer, the angel of death whom God created on the first day, the same day he said, 'Let there be light.'

"And when I step upon the shore of the Isle of Blood to plant the conqueror's flag, when I attain the summit of the abyss, when I find the thing that all of us fear and all of us seek, when I turn to face the Faceless One, whose face will I see?"

In the darkness he raised my hand and pressed it against his cheek.

His face is beatific when I picture it now, frozen in an attitude of godlike serenity, like a Greek statue of an ancient hero—Hercules, perhaps—or the bust of Caesar Augustus in the Musei Capitolini. The face of the living Warthrop has petrified in my memory, and his eyes, like those of a statue, are blank, devoid of detail, devoid of sight. It isn't a failure of memory—how well I remember those eyes! It is the mercy I grant myself. And it is my gift to him—the absolution of blindness.

He fell silent. I do not think he spoke more than three words to me between Venice and Brindisi. He broke the verbal drought once, while we were standing in the ticket line at the P&O offices to secure our berths for the passage to Port Said.

"We are a few hours ahead of them, Will Henry. Barring the unexpected delay, we may expect to arrive at Aden long before they do. But there they may catch up to us. I don't know how long it will take to arrange our passage to Socotra."

He looked down at me. "Unless you wish to turn back."

"Turn back?" I thought I must have been hallucinating. The monstrumologist was seriously thinking about giving up? It was so uncharacteristic a remark that I wondered if he had lost his mind—if Arkwright had jumped the gun by four months when he'd brought him to Hanwell.

"I can wire von Helrung to meet you in London."

"And leave you alone? No, Dr. Warthrop."

He shook his head ruefully. "I don't think you understand what your no is saying yes to."

"It's never stopped me before," I replied. "Not understanding the yes in 'no.'"

The monstrumologist laughed.

For the first few hours of the Mediterranean leg of our seven-thousand-mile journey, I feared that the mal de mer I'd suffered in the Atlantic crossing would return, like an unpleasant relative who arrives unexpectedly for dinner. You loathe his company, but you cannot turn him away. The monstrumologist forbade me from remaining belowdecks, saying the atmosphere was foul with coal dust and "the effluvia of four continents," meaning, I guessed, the other passengers. He brought me up to the forecastle and pointed straight ahead.

"Keep your eyes on the horizon, Will Henry. It's the only trick that works. Works for almost every ailment, when you think about it."

"Dr. von Helrung said I should dance."

The doctor nodded seriously. "Dancing isn't a bad idea either."

He leaned his arms upon the rail. The southerly wind whipped his long dark hair back, turned his jacket into a snapping semaphore flag. He closed his eyes and raised his face into the wind. "Not yet, not yet," he murmured. He looked down at my puzzled expression and explained, "Africa. You can smell it, you know."

"What does it smell like?"

"I cannot tell you. It would be like trying to describe the color blue to a man blind from birth." And then, because he was Pellinore Warthrop, he proceeded to try. "Old. Africa smells . . . old. Not old in the sense of something rotten or gone sour; old in the best sense—old because we've yet to make it 'new.' 'Old' meaning the world as it was before we recast it in our image, before we scarred the land with our plows and cut down the forests with our axes, before we dammed the rivers and drilled great holes into the earth, before we learned to take more than what we needed, before we stood upright, that kind of old, which is another way of saying that Africa smells *new*."

He turned again toward the horizon. "On those days when I am at my lowest, when it is all I can do to raise my head from my pillow, and all the world seems black and life itself the idiot's tale, I think of Africa. And the dark tide as if in fear recedes—it has no answer for Africa."

"'The dark tide'?"

He shook his head sharply. He seemed chagrinned to have brought it up.

"My name for something that can't be named, Will Henry. Or that I am too frightened to name. A part of me and somehow not. It is not unlike a tide—it withdraws gently, it roars back in. Yet not predictable like the tides. Governed, though, as the moon guides the tides . . ." He shook his head in frustration; the monstrumologist was not accustomed to inarticulateness. "On my better days I am able to drive back the dark tide. On my worst, I am overwhelmed—*it* drives *me*. I would flee from it, but it is a part of me, and so where might I run? Oh, never mind. It is impossible to say exactly what I mean."

"That's all right, sir. I think I understand."

I closed my eyes and lifted my nose to the hot Mediterranean wind. I wanted very badly to know the smell of Africa.

Our stopover in Port Said, at the northern terminus of the Suez Canal, would be brief—two hours for the ship to take on coal and supplies and transfers. The maelstrom that was a steamer's coaling operation was enough to drive most passengers ashore for the duration, my master and I among them, though his goal was not so much to escape than to arrange a rescue.

We stopped at the telegraph office first, where Warthrop sent this curt missive to von Helrung:

ARRIVED EGYPT. SHOULD ARRIVE
ADEN BY THE 19TH, INSTANT. WIRE
THERE IF NEWS.

And then this, to the one who had saved him in Venice:

RESPOND TO PORT AUTHORITY
OFFICE ADEN WHEN YOU RECEIVE
THIS. PELLINORE.

The office was hot and stuffy and crowded, mostly with Europeans (the telegraph operator himself was German), and most of them were on their way home from India, already having had their continental fill of exotic lands and the romance of foreign travel. We went outside, where it was not quite as stuffy and crowded but was much hotter, a blast-furnace heat to which I, a boy from New England, was wholly unaccustomed. It felt as if my lungs were being slowly crushed.

"Where is your hat, Will Henry?" the doctor asked. "You can't go anywhere in Africa without a hat."

"I left it on the boat, sir," I gasped.

"Come along, then, but we must hurry. There is someone I must see before we depart."

He led me down a series of narrow, winding streets, a confusion of intersecting lanes hardly wider than forest paths, except here the trees were thin-trunked and branchless, and the dust puffed and boiled beneath our feet.

We turned a corner and came into an open-air market called a *souq*, a kind of bazaar where one might find practically anything—candies and curiosities (I saw more than one vendor hawking shrunken heads), liquor, tobacco, coffee, and clothing—including a variety of boater hats, though we could not find one that wasn't at least three sizes too big for me. There was some comment made that the sun must have boiled all the moisture from my head. I didn't care. The brim rested on my eyebrows, and the thing jiggled annoyingly when I made the slightest movement, but it blocked the hateful sun.

We left the market and retraced our steps to a smoky café not far from the docks. The patrons—they were all male— sat about in small groups, smoking *sisha*, a fruit-flavored tobacco, from ornate water pipes. Upon seeing my master, the proprietor rushed forward, clapping his hands furiously and shouting the name "Mihos! Mihos!" He wrapped the doctor in a tremendous rib-cracking hug.

"Look what the wind has blown in from the desert! Hullo, hullo, my old friend!" the man cried in nearly unaccented English.

"Fadil, it is good to see you again," returned Warthrop warmly. "How is business?"

"About the same."

"As bad as that?"

"Worse! It is terrible! But it is always terrible, so what can I complain? But who is this hiding under the big white umbrella?"

"This is Will Henry," replied the monstrumologist.

"Henry! James's boy? But where is James?"

"Gone."

"Gone?"

"Dead," I put in.

"Dead! Oh, but that is terrible! Terrible!" Tears welled in his mud-colored eyes. "When? How? And you are his son?"

I nodded, and the hat bounced back and forth upon my heat-shrunken head.

"And now you take his place. Very large shoes to fill, little William Henry. Very large indeed!"

"Yes," said Warthrop. "Fadil, my ship leaves in less than an hour, and there is something I must—"

"Oh, but that is terrible! You will come to my house for dinner, Mihos; take the next boat. Say yes; you will wound my feelings if you say no."

"Then, I'm afraid I must wound them. Perhaps when— or if—I return . . ."

"*If* you return? *If?* What does this mean, *if?*"

The doctor peered about in the fragrant haze. Fadil's customers seemed oblivious to our presence. Still . . .

"I will explain everything—in private."

We followed him into the back room, a kind of gambling hall in miniature, where a very fat man was conducting a game of dice with two anxious, sweating, clearly overextended Belgians. They plunked down their silver, watched the dice tumble from the fat man's wooden box, and then watched their silver disappear. Warthrop grunted in disapproval; Fadil waved his objection away.

"They're *Belgians*, Mihos; they don't care for nothing.

Sit; sit, in the corner there, where we cannot hear their cries of pain and sorrow. But this is terrible; where has my mind gone? I will bring you some tea—I have Darjeeling!—and a *lassi* for William."

"I've really no time for tea, Fadil," said my master politely.

"What? No time for tea? *You*, Mihos? Then, your business in Egypt, like mine, must be truly terrible."

The monstrumologist nodded. "In nearly every aspect."

"What is it this time? Smugglers again? I told you to stay away from those scum, Mihos."

"My trouble has to do with scum from an entirely different pond, Fadil. Okhranka, the czar's secret police."

"Russians? But this is terrible! What have you done to the czar?"

Warthrop smiled. "Let us say my interests conflict with his."

"Oh, that is not good—for the czar! Ha!" He leaned his forearms on the table; his eyes glimmered eagerly. "What can Fadil do for his good friend Mihos?

"There are two of them," the doctor replied. He described Rurick and Plešec. "I managed to avoid them in London and Venice, but they can't be more than a few hours behind me."

"And their boat will stop here to take on coal and supplies." Fadil was nodding grimly. "Leave everything to me, Mihos. These two have seen their last sunrise!"

"I don't want you to kill them."

"You don't want me to kill them?"

"Killing them would only bring you more trouble. In a week Port Said would be drowning in a plague of Ruricks and Plešecs."

Fadil snorted and smacked his fist into his open palm, an Arabic gesture of contempt. "Let them come. I have no fear of Russians."

"You've not met these Russians. They are sons of Sekhmet the destroyer."

"And you are Mihos the lion, guardian of the horizon, and I am Menthu, god of war!" He turned his sparkling brown eyes upon me. "Who shall you be, son of James Henry? Your father was Anubis, weigher of men's hearts. Shall you be Ophois, his son, who opens the way to victory?"

Warthrop said, "What I need is time, Fadil. A fortnight would be good, a month would be better, four months would be poetic. Can you give me that time?"

"If you would let me kill them, I could give you eternity! But yes, I have friends in Port Said who have friends in Cairo who have friends in Tewfik's court. It could be arranged. It will not come cheap, Mihos."

"Von Helrung will wire you whatever's required." The monstrumologist checked his watch. "There is one more thing," he said briskly. "We are on our way to Aden, and I shall need transport from there to our final destination."

"What is your final destination?"

"I cannot say."

"What is this, you cannot say? This is me, Fadil!"

"I need someone who can be trusted to keep his mouth shut and who isn't afraid of a little risk. A fast ship would be helpful as well. Do you know anyone like that in Aden?"

"I know many people in Aden, though not very many I would trust. There is one man; he isn't so bad. He doesn't have a fast ship, but he will know someone who does. . . . What is it that you hunt that would interest the czar of Russia and that would keep you from trusting your old friend Fadil? What manner of monster is it this time?"

"I don't know," replied the doctor honestly. "But I intend to find out or die in the attempt."

Fadil insisted upon seeing us off, and it seemed everyone on the crowded streets knew him. Cries of "Fadil! Fadil!" followed us from the doorway of the café to the gangplank. The doctor flinched at every "Fadil!"—he had wanted his presence in Port Said to go unnoticed.

"When your terrible business is done at this place you cannot say, after your hunt for what you do not know is consummated, you will come back and tell me what the czar may know but Fadil may not! We shall feast on *fasieekh* and *kofta*, and I shall introduce my daughters to William—or should I say Ophois? Ha, ha!"

He clapped me hard on the back, glanced about furtively, and then pulled a small object from his trouser pocket. It was a scarab beetle carved from alabaster and fashioned into a necklace. He pressed the amulet into my hands, saying, "A *kheper*, my new young friend, from the Tenth Dynasty. In ancient Egyptian its name means 'to come into being.' It will bring you luck."

"And several years in prison if the authorities should catch you with it," added the doctor drily.

"It came to me honestly, in a game of hounds and jackals with a very drunk Hungarian viscount who had purchased it from a street urchin in Alexandria. Now, do not insult me by refusing my gift."

He embraced Warthrop, topped off the bear hug with a kiss—a sign of friendship in Egypt—and sent me off with one as well, right on the lips. He found my startled reaction extremely funny; his robust laughter followed us all the way up the gangplank and onto the ship.

"You should not have accepted it," Warthrop said to me, referring to the scarab. "Now you've taken his luck."

He smiled wanly. The remark, I think, was only partially in jest.

It took the French ten years to build the Suez Canal, and it seemed to take that long to traverse its hundred miles. We chugged along at a pace a snail would scoff at, and the scenery, if it could be called that, offered no pleasant distraction—desert to the left, desert to the right, and above a sky on fire, the sun an arm's length away. The only sign of life outside the boat were the flies, whose painful bites tormented us anytime we stepped on deck. The doctor overheard me cursing them, and said, "To the ancients these flies represented tenacity and viciousness in battle. They would be presented to victorious warriors as symbols of valor." It was a historical footnote that probably would have been more interesting in our parlor on Harrington Lane. In the moment, the flies seemed more symbols of madness than valor.

We fed the flies until sunset, when the sky changed from blue to yellow to orange to a velvety indigo blue and the first stars poked hesitantly through the firmament. Then a quick trip below to feed ourselves—quick because the heat above was nothing compared to the ovenlike temperatures achieved inside a coal steamer in the desert—then back on deck to revel in the cool night air. There were no settlements along the canal, no lights twinkling on the shore, no sound or sign of civilization anywhere. There were the stars and the water and the lifeless land we could not see, and the ship's bow slicing the wakeless surface, as silent as Charon's ferry in the stygian dark. A feeling of dread came over me, a vertiginous sensation of being acutely aware of every breath and yet feeling unmoored from my own body, a living ghost, a shade who has paid his silver to the ferryman for the passage to the underworld. I might have turned to the man beside me for comfort—as he had turned to me on the train to Brindisi, as he had turned countless times in the past, when swamped in what he called "the dark tide." I might have turned to him and said, "Dr. Warthrop, sir, I am afraid."

I did not, because I dared not. It wasn't his temper that stayed my confession. It wasn't that he might belittle or judge me. I had grown accustomed to the point of boredom to those things.

No, I held my tongue because I feared he would abandon me again.

The stars above. The water below. The lifeless land on either side. And, over the invisible horizon, its approach marked by each beat of our hearts, the thing we both longed for and feared—the *magnificum, das Ungeheuer,* the summit of the abyss.

THIRTY

'I Will Come for You'

There were two telegrams waiting for the doctor upon our arrival at Steamer Point in Aden. The first was from New York:

> ALL QUIET. JOHN BULL ASKED IF WE
> FOUND HIS LOST DOG. TOLD HIM
> TO ASK IVAN. EMILY SENDS HER
> LOVE. GODSPEED. A.V.H.

"John Bull?" I asked.

"The English," the monstrumologist translated. "The missing 'dog' is Arkwright. 'Ivan' is the Russians. Von Helrung must have had a visit from British intelligence, looking for their absent operative, and he has pinned the blame on Okhranka. But who is Emily, and why does she send her love?" He pulled on his bottom lip, puzzling over this, to him, enigmatic phrase.

"Emily is Mrs. Bates, sir, Dr. von Helrung's niece."

"That's odd. Why does she send her love to me? I've never even met the woman."

"I think, sir . . ." I cleared my throat. "I think she is sending it to me."

"To you!" He shook his head as if the notion baffled him. The second telegram was from Port Said:

NO SIGN OF SEKHMET'S SONS.
WILL KEEP DOOR OPEN FOR THEM.
MENTHU.

"Not what I expected, Will Henry," Warthrop confessed. "And I don't know whether to be heartened or troubled."

"Maybe they've given up."

He shook his head. "I've known men like Rurick; he is not the sort to give up. I suppose they could have been ordered back to Saint Petersburg or replaced after their failure in Venice. It's possible. Or they've taken an alternative route . . . or Fadil's men missed them somehow. . . . Well, there's no point in worrying about it. We will be vigilant and hope for the best."

He attempted a reassuring smile and achieved a Warthropian one; that is, a smile that hardly rose above the level of a grimace. He *was* troubled, clearly, by the telegram from Port Said that had been waiting for him and the one from Venice that had not. There'd been no reply from Veronica Soranzo.

We stepped outside the telegraph office. It was around ten in the morning, but already the day was stiflingly hot, nearly ninety degrees. (By that afternoon it would hover around one hundred.) The quayside was humming with activity—Somali porters and Yemeni hucksters, British colonialists and soldiers. The British controlled Aden; it was an important stopover and refueling point between Africa and their interests in India. Local boys dressed in *thobes*, traditional long-sleeved tunics, waited along the shore with donkeys to take passengers into the nearby town of Crater. Or, if you were a person of less modest means, you could hire a gharry, an Indian one-horse cab that resembled an American stagecoach.

The doctor picked neither donkey nor gharry, for our destination was within sight of the wharf. The man recommended by Fadil was staying at the Grand Hotel De L'Univers on Prince of Wales Crescent (named in honor of the royal visit in 1874), a street that curved gently away from the sea toward the barren dun-colored hills that brooded over the beach. It did not appear to be a long walk, but all walks are long in the cauldron heat of Aden. On our way we passed a huge coal depot, where scores of shirtless men, Somalis mostly, their ebony torsos shining like obsidian, heaved heavy sacks of coal to the discordant jangle of tambourines. Occasionally a man would drop out of line to roll upon the blackened planks, using the coal dust to soak up his sweat. What dust didn't coat the workers or the ground hung about the depot in a choking fog. The scene was hellish—like a purgatorial dream—and it was beautiful—the way the harsh sunlight cut through the spinning cloud of dust, the larger particles sparking and spitting golden light.

Beside me the monstrumologist murmured, "'I believe I am in hell, therefore I am there.'" He was tapping an envelope against his thigh as he walked, keeping time with the tambourine players, who used the thigh bones of calves to make their music. The envelope contained Fadil's letter of introduction to our contact in Aden. The monstrumologist had become very excited when Fadil had mentioned the man's name.

"I'd no idea he was back in Yemen," he'd exclaimed. "I thought he was running guns in Ethiopia."

"That did not work out so well for him," Fadil had replied. "In fact, it was terrible! He says King Menelik cheated him, left him with only six thousand francs to show for his trouble. He returned to Yemen—to Harad for the coffee and ivory trade. Though he makes frequent trips back and forth to Crater, where he should be now. If so, I'm certain you'll find him at the Grand Hotel De L'Univers. He always stays there when he is in town."

"I sincerely hope you're right, Fadil," my master had responded. "Besides needing his aid in a rather desperate humanitarian circumstance, it would give me enormous personal satisfaction to meet him."

The hotel was a long, low structure with stone archways and patios and lattice shutters on the windows, a common architectural style here and in India. We stepped inside, where the temperature dropped a minuscule two or three degrees. On our left was the hotel shop displaying exotic wares, animal furs from Africa and Asia, silk from Bombay, Arabic swords and daggers, as well as more mundane fare, postcards and stationery, pith sun hats and white cotton suits, the unofficial uniform of the colonist. The lobby itself had been designed to reflect its owners' pride in empire, all dark woods and rich velvet, but the heat and the humidity had warped and cracked the wood and eaten holes in the velvet, a portent of things to come.

"I have come to see Monsieur Arthur Rimbaud," the monstrumologist informed the desk clerk, an Arab whose white shirt had probably started out the day crisply starched but now had wilted in the heat, like the Queen of the Night desert flower. "Is he here?"

"Monsieur Rimbaud is staying with us," acknowledged the clerk. "May I tell him who is calling?"

"Dr. Pellinore Warthrop. I have a letter of introduction . . ."

The clerk held out his hand, but the doctor did not give him the letter. He insisted upon delivering it to Mr. Rimbaud personally. The clerk shrugged—it was too hot to make an issue of anything—and handed us off to a small boy who led us into the dining hall across the way from the gift shop. The room opened onto a terrace that overlooked the ocean; in the distance I could see Flint Island, a large, bare rock that the British used as a quarantine station during the frequent outbreaks of cholera.

Seated alone at one table was a slender man around Warthrop's age. His hair was dark, turning gray at the temples, and cut very short. He was wearing the ubiquitous white cotton suit. When he swung his head in our direction, I was immediately struck, as most who knew him were, by his eyes. At first I thought they were gray, but on further inspection determined they were the palest blue, like the color of moonstones, the gems that Indians called "dream stones," believing they produced beautiful night visions. His gaze was direct and disconcerting, like everything else about Jean Nicholas Arthur Rimbaud.

"Yes?" he asked. There was nothing pleasant in that "yes."

The doctor introduced himself quickly, and a touch breathlessly, the lowly peasant who suddenly finds himself in the company of royalty. He handed Fadil's letter to Rimbaud. We did not sit. We waited for Rimbaud to read the letter. It was not a long letter, but it seemed to take a good long while for the man to read it, as I stood there in the blistering Arabian heat with the sparkling ocean a tantalizing few hundred yards away. Rimbaud picked up a crystalline goblet filled with a liquid the color of green algae and sipped delicately.

"Fadil," he said softly. "I haven't seen Fadil in eight years or more. I am surprised he is not dead." He glanced up from the paper, perhaps expecting the doctor to do something interesting, make a witty retort, laugh at the joke (if it was a joke), tell him something he didn't know about Fadil. The doctor said nothing. Rimbaud flicked his free hand toward a chair, and we gratefully joined him at the table. He ordered another absinthe from the little Arab boy, who had been standing obediently out of the way, and asked the doctor if he wanted anything.

"Some tea would be wonderful."

"And for the boy?" Rimbaud inquired.

"Just some water, please," I croaked. My throat burned with every dry swallow.

"You don't want water," Rimbaud cautioned me. "They say they boil it, but . . ." He shrugged and ordered a ginger ale for me.

"Monsieur Rimbaud," Warthrop began, sitting forward in his chair and resting his forearms on his knees. "I must tell you what a pleasure it is to meet you, sir. Having dabbled in the craft in my youth, I—"

"Dabbled in what craft? The coffee business?"

"No, I mean—"

"For that is my craft, Dr. Warthrop, my raison d'être. I am a businessman."

"Just so!" cried the doctor, as if the Frenchman had pointed out another similarity. "That is how it played out for me. I abandoned poetry too, though it was for a very different sort of craft than yours."

"Oh? And what would be that very different sort of craft, Dr. Warthrop?"

"I am a scientist."

Rimbaud was lifting the glass to his lips. He froze at the word "scientist," and then slowly set the glass back down, the absinthe untouched.

"Fadil did not mention in his letter that you were a *scientific* sort of doctor. I had hoped you could have a look at my leg; it has been bothering me, and the doctors at Camp Aden . . . Well, they are all very *British*, if you do not mind my saying so."

Warthrop, who had just spent several months under the exclusive care of very British doctors, nodded emphatically, and said, "I understand completely, Monsieur Rimbaud."

The boy came back with our drinks. Rimbaud gulped the remainder of his first absinthe—if it was his first; I suspected it was not—before accepting the fresh one from the boy, as if Rimbaud were hurrying to catch up with the doctor, who had not even begun. *Show me a man who cannot control his appetites*, the monstrumologist had said, *and I will show a man living under a death sentence.*

Rimbaud sipped his new drink, decided he liked it better than the old one, and took another sip. His moonstone gaze fell upon my hand.

"What happened to your finger?"

I glanced at the doctor, who said, "An accident."

"See this? This is my 'accident.'" Rimbaud held out his wrist, displaying a bright red, puckered area of damaged flesh. "Shot by a dear friend. Also by 'accident.' My dear friend is in Europe. I am in Aden. And my wound is right here."

"I think my favorite line is from *Illuminations*," said my master, pressing on. He seemed annoyed by something. "'*Et j'ai senti un peu son immense corps.*' The juxtaposition of '*peu*' and '*immense*' . . . simply wonderful."

"I do not talk of my poetry, Dr. Warthrop."

"Really?" The doctor was stunned. "But . . ."

"It is . . . what? What are my poems? *Rinçures*—leavings, the dregs. The poet is dead. He died many years ago—drowned, at Bab-el-Mandeb, the Gate of Tears—and I took his body up into those mountains behind us, to the Tower of Silence in Crater, where I left it for the carrion, lest his corruption poison what little was left of my soul."

He smiled tightly, quite pleased with himself. Poets never die, I thought. They just fail in the end.

"Now what is this business that brings you to Aden?" demanded Rimbaud brusquely. "I am a very busy man, as you can see."

The doctor, his high spirits dampened by Rimbaud's dismissive attitude—the shoe being on the other foot, for once—explained our purpose in disturbing Rimbaud's important midmorning absinthian chore.

"I am sorry," Rimbaud interrupted him. "But you say you are desiring to go where?"

"Socotra."

"Socotra! Oh, you can't go to Socotra now."

"Why can't I?"

"Well, you *could*, but it would be the last place you'd want to go."

"And why is that, if I may ask, Monsieur Rimbaud?" The doctor waited nervously for the reply. Had word of the *magnificum* reached Aden?

"Because the monsoons have come. No sane person tries it now. You must wait till October."

"October!" The monstrumologist shook his head sharply, as if he were trying to clear his ears. "That is unacceptable, Monsieur Rimbaud."

Rimbaud shrugged. "I do not control the weather, Dr. Warthrop. Bring your complaint up with God."

Of course the monstrumologist, like the monster Rurick, was not one to give up so easily. He pressed Rimbaud. He pleaded with Rimbaud. He came just short of threatening Rimbaud. Rimbaud absorbed it all with a bemused expression. Perhaps he was thinking, *This Warthrop, he is so very American!* In the end, and after two more absinthes, the poet relented, saying, "Oh, very well. I can't stop you from committing suicide any more than I could stop you from writing poetry. Here." He scribbled an address on the back of his business card. "Give this to a *gharry-wallah*; he will know where it is. Ask for Monsieur Bardey. Tell him what you have told me, and if he doesn't laugh you out the door, you may get lucky."

Warthrop thanked him, rose, and beckoned me to rise, and then Rimbaud stood up and said, "But where are you going?"

"To see Monsieur Bardey," the doctor replied, puzzled.

"But it is not even ten thirty. He won't be in yet. Sit. You haven't finished your tea."

"The address is in Crater, yes? By the time I get there..."

"Oh, very well, but don't expect to be back anytime soon." He looked at me. "And you should not take the boy."

Warthrop stiffened and then told a lie—perhaps an inadvertent one, but it was still a lie. "I always take the boy."

"It is not a good part of town. There are men in Crater who would kill him for his fine shoes alone—or that very nice jacket, which is very fashionable but not very practical here in Aden. You should leave him with me."

"With you?" The doctor was thinking it over; I was shocked.

"I want to come with you, sir," I said.

"I would not advise it," Rimbaud cautioned. "But what business is it of mine? Do what you wish."

"Dr. Warthrop . . . ," I began. And finished weakly: "Please, sir."

"Rimbaud is right. You should stay here," the doctor decided. He drew me to one side and whispered, "It will be all right, Will Henry. I should be back well before sunset, and you will be safer here at the hotel. I don't know what I will find in town, and we still do not know the final disposition of Rurick and Plešec."

"I don't care. I swore I would never leave you again, Dr. Warthrop."

"Well, you aren't. *I* am leaving *you*. And Monsieur Rimbaud is being very generous in his offer to look after you." He lifted my chin with his forefinger and looked deeply into my eyes. "You came for me in England, Will Henry. I give you my word that I will come for you."

And with that, he left.

THIRTY-ONE

"Have You Been Abandoned?"

Rimbaud ordered another absinthe. I ordered another ginger ale. We drank and sweated. The air was breathless, the heat intense. Steamers pulled up to the quay. Others pulled out. The tambourines of the coal workers jangled faintly in the shimmering air. The boy came up and asked if we wanted anything for lunch. Rimbaud ordered a bowl of *saltah* and another absinthe. I said I wasn't hungry. Rimbaud shrugged and held up two fingers. The boy left.

"You have to eat," Rimbaud said matter-of-factly, his first words since the doctor had left. "In this climate if you don't eat—almost as bad as not drinking. Do you like Aden?"

I replied that I had not seen enough to form an opinion either way.

"I hate it," he said. "I despise it. I have always despised it.

Aden is a rock, a terrible rock without a single blade of grass or drop of good water. Half the tanks up in Crater stand empty. Have you seen the tanks?"

"Tanks?"

"Yes, the Tawila Tanks up above Crater, giant cisterns to capture water—very old, very deep, very dramatic. They keep the town from flooding, built around the time of King Solomon—or so they say. The British dug them out, polished them up, a *very* British thing to do, but they still don't keep the place from flooding. The local children go swimming up there in the summer and come back down with cholera. They cool off, and then they die."

He looked away. The sea was bluer than his eyes. Lilly's eyes were closer to the color of the sea, but hers were more beautiful. I wondered why Lilly had suddenly popped into my head.

"What is on Socotra?" he asked.

I nearly blurted it out: *Typhoeus magnificum*. I sipped my warm ginger ale to stall for time, frantically—or as frantically as I could in the horrendous heat—trying to think of an answer. Finally I said the only thing I could remember from the doctor's lecture in the hansom. "Dragon's Blood."

"Dragon's Blood? You mean the tree?"

I nodded. The ginger ale was flat, but it was wet and my mouth was very dry. "Dr. Warthrop is a botanist."

"Is he?"

"He is." I tried to sound firm.

"And if he is a botanist, what are you?"

"I am his . . . I am a junior botanist."

"Are you?"

"I am."

"Hmmm. And I am a poet."

The boy returned with two steaming bowls of stew and a plate of flatbread, called *khamira*, for us to use as a kind of edible spoon, Rimbaud explained. I looked at the brown, oily surface of the *saltah* and apologized; I had no appetite.

"Don't apologize to me," Rimbaud said with a shrug. He dove into the stew, his jaw grimly set. Perhaps he hated *saltah* like he hated Aden.

"If you despise it here, why don't you leave?" I asked him.

"Where would I go?"

"I don't know. Someplace else."

"That is very easy to say. And so ironic. That kind of thinking landed me here!"

He tore off a piece of *khamira* and stuffed it into his mouth, chomping with his mouth open, as if he wanted to inflict as much suffering as possible upon the incognizant staple of the land he despised.

"A junior botanist," he said. "Is that what happened to your hand? You were holding a tree limb and his axe slipped?"

I tore my eyes away from his disconcerting gaze. "Something like that."

"'Something like that.' I like it! I think I shall use it the next time someone asks what happened to my wrist.

'Something like that.'" He was smiling expectantly, waiting for me to ask. I didn't ask. He went on. "It happens. *C'est la vie*. So, would you like to see them?"

"See what?"

"The tanks! I will take you there."

"The doctor expects me to be here."

"The doctor expects you to be with me. If I go to the tanks, you cannot stay here."

"I've seen cisterns before."

"You haven't seen cisterns like these."

"I don't want to see them."

"You do not trust me? I won't push you in, I promise." He pushed his bowl away, mopped his lips with a piece of bread, and downed the last of his lime green drink. He stood up.

"Come. It will be worth the trip. I promise."

He strode off, going into the dining room without a backward glance—another man who assumed others would follow. I watched the terns fishing just beyond the surf and the ships passing Flint Island. I could hear someone singing, a woman or perhaps a young boy; I could not make out the words. If I was gone when he returned, the doctor would not be pleased, to put it mildly. I could picture the fury in his eyes—and that reminded me of another's eyes, the one who shared that ancient, cold fire, and I finished my ginger ale and went to find Monsieur Rimbaud.

I found him standing just outside the front doors. A gharry was pulled up in front of the hotel, and we ducked inside the cab, out of the sun but still very much in the heat, and Rimbaud told the Somali *gharry-wallah* where we were going, and we rattled toward the quay, riding on top of our shadow.

The road ran through a small fishing village of thatched-roof huts clustered along the shore, then turned inland and began to rise. Before us loomed a chaos of bare rocks and towering cliffs, the remnants of a volcano whose cataclysmic explosion had created the deep sea port of Aden—though the peninsula did not remind one so much of creation as it did its opposite. There were no trees, no shrubs, no flowers, no life to speak of anywhere, if you discounted donkeys and humans and carrion, or the occasional rat. The colors of Aden were gray and a brownish, rusty red—gray the rocky bones of the violated earth; red the hardened lava that had bled from it.

This was Aden, the land of blood and bones, a great, cauterized wound in the earth where the fist of God had slammed down, thrusting skyward heaps of shattered rock to make the mountains that brooded over the ruined landscape, sullen and lifeless and emptied of all color, except the gray of Gaia's broken bones and the rusty red of her dried blood.

Crater was the oldest and most populated settlement on the peninsula. Described by one writer as "the Devil's Punch Bowl," it wasn't just called Crater; it *was* a crater, the hollowed-out center of an extinct volcano, surrounded on three sides by jagged mountains. Camp Aden, the British garrison, was located here, along with a sizeable population of Arabs, Parsi, Somalis, Jews, Malaysians, and Indonesians.

It took more than an hour to cross the old Arab quarter of town. The narrow streets were crowded with donkey carts and gharries and villagers on foot—though there was none of the hustle and bustle that one finds in New York or London. In Crater there is much activity but little motion, for the town bakes in its punch bowl in the afternoon, when the sun fills the sky directly overhead and the shadows disappear, pinned down beneath your feet. The buildings were as drab as the surrounding countryside, tired-looking, even the newer colonial ones, slumping, it seemed to my eye, like painted gourds rotting in the sun.

We bounced along the hot, dusty street until the hot, dusty street came to an abrupt dead end. We had come to the head of Wadi Tawila, the Tawila Valley, where the volcanic heaps of hardened lava and ash reared high their bald heads toward the unforgiving sky. It was the end of civilization and of our gharry ride; we would hike up to the tanks along stone steps that snaked through a mountain defile. Our *gharry-wallah* said something to Rimbaud in French; I caught the word "*l'eau.*" Rimbaud shook his head and murmured, "*Nous serons bien. Merci.*"

"You see the problem," he gasped over his shoulder as I followed him up the steps. "Look behind you. Spread out below in all her infertile glory is the town of Crater. Aden can't get more than three inches of rainfall a year, but when it rains, it pours! The tanks were built to stop flooding, and to give the British something to do a thousand years later. Almost there. . . . Around this next bend . . ."

He stepped nimbly around an outcropping, stopped abruptly, and pointed down. We were standing on the lip of a large cone-shaped hole excavated from solid rock, fifty feet across at the top and at least as deep, shining brightly, like marble in the sun.

"Well, what do you think?" he asked. His face glistened with sweat, his shirtfront was soaked with it, and his cheeks were ablaze with either excitement or exertion.

"It's a hole."

"No, it's a very big hole. And a very old hole. See how it shines like marble? That is not marble, though; it's stucco."

"It's dry."

"It's the desert."

"I mean, there's no water in it."

"This is just one of them. There are dozens all around these hills."

"Are you going to show me all of them?"

He stared at me for a moment. In the sunlight his eyes appeared to have no color at all.

"Would you like to see my favorite spot in Aden?" he asked.

"Is it in the shade?"

"It isn't far, about two hundred meters, and there might be some shade."

"Shouldn't we be getting back to the hotel? The doctor will be worried about us."

"Why?"

"Because he expects to find us there."

"Are you afraid of him?"

"No."

"Does he beat you?"

"No. Never."

"I see. He just cuts off your fingers."

"I didn't say that."

"You said something like that."

"I think I'll go back to the hotel," I said, turning carefully around; I didn't want to tumble into the pit.

"Wait. I promise it isn't far, and we can rest there before hiking back down."

"What is it?"

"A holy place."

I narrowed my eyes at him suspiciously, and when I did, sweat dripped into my eyes and the world melted a little.

"A church?"

"Did I say that? No. I said 'a holy place.' Come, it is not far. I promise."

We climbed another series of steps that ran along a low stone wall. I looked to my left and saw Crater spread out below us, the white-washed buildings undulating in the blistering heat. At the end of the wall, Rimbaud turned right, and we continued to climb up a wide dirt path that rose steeply toward the cloudless sky. The crunch of our shoes in the volcanic dust, the heaving of air in and out of our lungs—that was the only sound as we labored to the top, where the end of the path met the pale, bled-out blue of the sky. Cresting the hill, we found ourselves at the base of a small plateau five hundred feet above the extinct crater. Another series of steps led up to the top.

"How much farther?" I asked Rimbaud.

"We are almost there."

We rested for a moment after this final ascent, in the slice of shade beneath an archway cut into a six-foot-high stone wall that curved out of sight in either direction, a barrier that encircled the holy place of sun and rock and silent sentinel stone, high above the sea.

We sat with our backs against the cool stone, and Rimbaud wrapped his lean arms around his upraised knees and stared dreamily down into the town nestled in the blasted guts of the dead volcano.

"So what do you think?" he asked. "The best view in Aden."

"Is that why you brought me up here, to show me the view?" I returned. I was weak from the climb, overheated and terribly thirsty. Why had I agreed to come with him? I should have stayed at the hotel.

"No, but I thought you'd like it," he said. "You are at the entrance to the Tour du Silence, the Tower of Silence, called

Dakhma by the Parsi. It is a holy place, as I told you, forbidden to outsiders."

"Then, why did you bring me here?"

"To show it to you," he said slowly, as if speaking to a simpleton.

"But we are outsiders."

He stood up. "I am outside nothing."

There were no sentries posted, no guards to man the entrance or patrol the grounds of the Dakhma. Dakhma did not belong to the living; we were the interlopers here. Our approach to the tower was noted only by the crows and kite hawks and several large white birds that glided effortlessly in the updrafts of superheated air.

"Are those eagles?" I asked.

"They are the white buzzards of Yemen," answered Rimbaud.

The Dakhma occupied the far end of the compound, at the highest spot on the plateau. It was a simple structure—three massive seven-foot-thick concentric stone circles, with a pit dug inside the smallest, innermost ring, and all of it open to the sky.

"This is the place where the Zoroastrians bring their dead," Rimbaud said quietly. "You cannot burn them. That would pollute the fire. You cannot bury them. That would defile the earth. The dead are *nasu*, unclean. So you bring them here. You lay them out on the stone, the men atop the outer circle, the women on the second, the children on the last, the one closest to the center, and you leave them to rot. And when their bones have been picked clean by the birds and bleached by the sun, you bring them to the ossuary at the bottom, until they are ground by the wind to a handful of dust. It is the *Dahkma-nashini*, the Zoroastrian burial of the dead."

He offered to take me inside for a look.

"There's no one about, and the dead won't care."

"I don't think I want to see them."

"You don't think you want to see them? Now, that is interesting to me, the way you said it, like you are not sure of your own mind."

"I don't want to see them."

A sudden breeze kissed our cheeks. The stench of death could not reach where we stood; it rose from the ledges twenty feet over our heads, swept away by the same wind that kissed our cheeks and bore the white buzzards and the kite hawks and the crows. Their shadows raced across the grassless rock.

"Why is this place your favorite?" I asked him.

"Because I am a wanderer, and after going to and fro on the earth and walking up and down on it, I came to this place at last, the part after which there is nothing. I came to the end, and that is why I love this place and why I despise it. There is nothing left when you reach the center of everything, just the pit of bones inside the innermost circle. This is the center of the earth, Monsieur Will Henry, and where can a man go once he's reached the center?"

I was certain the doctor would be waiting for us when we arrived back at the Grand Hotel De L'Univers. Certain too that he would be furious with me for taking off with the Frenchman without a word to anyone. *I* was angry at me for doing it and could not understand why I had. There was something about Arthur Rimbaud that brought out the irresponsible spirit, the amoral animus that says yes, when the Gypsy outside the tent urges us to "come and see."

But the monstrumologist was not waiting for us when we got back around three that afternoon. The clerk informed Rimbaud that he had not seen Warthrop either. We retired to the same table on the terrace outside the dining room (it appeared to be his favorite roosting spot), where the poet-turned-coffee-exporter ordered another absinthe and settled in to await the doctor's return.

"You see? You worried for nothing," he said.

"He should be back by now," I said.

"First you worry he will come back, and then you worry he won't."

"Where did he go?" I asked.

"Into town to arrange your passage to Socotra. Don't you remember? I tried to tell him it was too soon. Bardey never gets about till five or so. He is nocturnal, like a bat. You seem nervous. What's the matter? Is he in some kind of trouble?"

"You said it wasn't a good part of town."

"Because there is *no* good part of town, unless it's Camp Aden or the English quarter, and then it is, well, the *English* quarter."

"Should we go look for him?"

"We just got back, and I've just gotten my drink."

"You don't have to come."

"I apologize. When you said 'should we go look for him,' I understood you to mean 'should *we* go look for him.' You may do whatever you like. I am going to sit here and finish my drink, and then I am going up to my room for a nap. I am tired from our hike."

The afternoon tide came in. A pleasant sea breeze picked up. The sun slipped behind the Shamsan Mountains, and their shadows stretched over Crater and crawled toward us. Rimbaud finished his drink.

"I am going to lie down for a while," he told me. "What will you do?"

"I'll stay here and wait for the doctor."

"If he still isn't back when I get up, we will go into town to look for him."

He left me alone on the terrace with the breeze and the advancing shadows and the ever-present faraway jingling of the tambourines. The little Arab boy came out to fetch Rimbaud's empty glass and asked if I wanted another ginger ale. I ordered two and drank them both quickly, one right after the other, and was still thirsty afterward, as if this lifeless land had sucked every drop of moisture from my body.

Around five o'clock the door opened behind me and I turned around, expecting—*knowing*—it was the doctor.

Two men stepped outside. One was very large with a shock of bright red hair. His companion was much shorter and thinner and had no hair at all. Rurick took the chair on my right; Plešec sat down on my left.

"You will not run," Rurick said.

I nodded. I would not run.

THIRTY-TWO

"Give It to Will Henry"

"Where is Warthrop?" he asked.

The question eased some of my terror. It meant the doctor was still alive. How long he—and I—would stay that way was the issue. For a brief moment I wondered how they had found me, and then I decided it was a pointless speculation. The *how* did not matter, and the *why* I already knew. Would it be *if* or *when*? That was the salient point.

"I don't know," I answered.

Something sharp pressed against my stomach. Plešec was leaning toward me, his right hand hidden beneath the tabletop. When he smiled, I noticed that one of his front teeth was missing.

"I could gut you right here," Plešec said. "You think I won't?"

"You are staying at this hotel?" Rurick asked.

"No. Yes."

"I will explain rules to you now," Rurick said patiently. "Rule one: tell truth. Rule two: speak only when spoken to. You know these rules, yes? You are child. All children know these rules."

I nodded. "Yes, sir."

"Good boy. Very polite boy too. I like that. Now we start again. Where is Warthrop?"

"He's gone into town."

"But he comes back—for you."

"Yes. He will come back for me."

"When does he come back?"

"I don't know. He didn't say."

Rurick grunted. He looked at Plešec. Plešec nodded and put away his knife.

"We wait with you for him," Rurick decided. "It is nice here in the shade. Nice breeze, no smell of dead fish."

It was the best I could hope for in a nearly hopeless situation. Perhaps Rimbaud would wake up and come back downstairs. I thought about leaping from the table and hurdling the railing and chancing I could reach the quay without Rurick putting a bullet into the back of my head. I decided that chance was exceedingly slim. But if I didn't run, if I did nothing and Rimbaud did not get up before the doctor returned, Warthrop was doomed.

Two doors. Behind one, the lady. Behind the other, the tiger. Which should he choose?

As I watched, a tern dove into the surf and emerged with a shiny fish twisting in its beak. I looked farther out and saw the edge of the world, the line between sea and sky.

It is part and parcel of the business, Will Henry. Eventually the luck runs out.

A gull shot from its sentry post on the shore, its shadow long and fleeting on the sun-burnished sand. I remembered the shadows of the carrion birds upon the bare rock at the center of the world.

There is nothing left when you reach the center of everything, just the pit of bones inside the innermost circle.

"What is it?" asked Rurick. "Why do you cry?"

"I'm not waiting for him," I confessed. "He is waiting for me," I lied.

This is the time of the dead. The time of the Dahkma-nashini.

In the fourteenth hour, on the second day of the week, a boy dies of cholera in his mother's arms. Her tears are bitter; he is her only son.

His spirit hovers nearby, troubled by her tears. He calls to her, but she gives no answer.

She holds him until his body goes cold, and then she lays him down. She lays him down, for the time has come; the evil spirit approaches to take his body, and after that she will touch him no more.

The next Geh is begun. He is nasu *now, unclean. It is time for the Nassesalars. It is the sixteenth hour of the second day.*

"I do not understand," said Rurick. "Why does he meet you up there?"

"That's where he was meeting with Dr. Torrance."

"Who is Dr. Torrance?"

"Dr. Warthrop's friend. He's helping us."

"Helping you to do what?"

"Find a way to the island."

"What island?"

"The island of the *magnificum*."

He was struggling for breath. The way was steep; he was not used to the heat.

"For what are these pits?" he wondered aloud.

"To keep the town from flooding."

The dry tanks were flooded with deep shadows; they appeared to have no bottom. If you fell into one, you might fall forever.

The corpse bearers take the boy and bathe him in Taro, the urine of the white bull. They dress him in a Sudreh-Kusti, the garments of the dead. Only his face is left exposed. He is nasu, *unclean. The boy's spirit watches them and does not understand. It does not remember that this was its body. The spirit is an infant again; it has no memory. It is now the sixth hour of the third day.*

"How much farther?" Plešec asked.

"It's just over that next rise," I answered.

"You better not be lying to us."

"This is the place," I said.

"If you are lying to us, I will gut you. I will cut out your intestines and throw them down the mountain."

"This is the place," I said again.

It is the hour of the Geh-Sarna. The Dasturs pray the verses of the Avestan Mathras over the body, to strengthen his soul and help it along its journey. After the prayers the body is carried up and into the Dakhma, where it is laid upon the stone. It is now the twelfth hour of the third day.

"Something is not right," Rurick said. "This place, it is deserted."

"He told me to come here."

"Do you remember rule one?"

"He said he would be here."

"Here," Plešec repeated. "But where is 'here'? What is this place?"

"It's called a Dakhma," I answered.

Rurick pressed his hand to his mouth. "What is that smell?"

I decided Rurick had to be first. Rurick had the gun. I dropped my hand into my jacket pocket.

Give it to Will Henry; I've nowhere to put it.

If you carried a smaller weapon, you could stick it in your garter.

"Something is not right here," Plešec said. He turned to Rurick. "Something is not right."

There is the boy in the inner circle, above the pit in which lies the dry bones and the dust of the dry bones. He is for the sun now and the flies and the birds that take his sightless eyes first. It is the first hour of the fourth day, above the pit, at the summit of the abyss.

Rurick's eyes widened. His mouth came open. The last thing he saw before the bullet tore into his brain did not make sense. Having been a very self-assured man, he died very confused.

Plešec lunged forward; the knife blade flashed in the final, dying embers of daylight. His thrust tore into my shirtfront; the knife's tip struck Fadil's present that hung around my neck, the scarab to bring me good luck; and I fired pointblank into his stomach.

He fell face-first at my feet. I stumbled backward until I smacked against the white wall of the tower, and then my knees gave out and I sank onto the stony ground with Plešec, who was not dead but bleeding badly and crawling toward me, and his blood shone wetly on the bare rock, trailing behind his jerking legs.

I raised the doctor's revolver to the level of his eyes. I held the gun in both hands, but I still couldn't keep it steady.

He stopped. He rolled onto his side. He clutched his bleeding stomach with one hand and reached toward me with the other. I didn't move. He was *nasu*, unclean.

I looked past him, to the sea framed in the arched opening of the wall, to the line formed where the water met the sky. The world was not round, I realized. The world was a plate.

"Please," he whispered. "Don't."

Unlike Rurick, Plešec did not die confused.

The boy's spirit comes to the Chinvato-Peretu, *the bridge of sighs joining the two worlds. There he meets himself in the form of a beautiful maiden, his* Kainini-Keherpa, *who guides him to Mithra to be judged for what he has done and what he has left undone.*

I left them there for the flies and the birds and the sun and the wind. In the silence outside the Tour du Silence, I left them. Where the faceless dead faced the sky, I left them there at the center of the world.

FOLIO X

Τυφωεύς

WHAT IS THAT SOUND HIGH IN THE AIR
MURMUR OF MATERNAL LAMENTATION
WHO ARE THOSE HOODED HORDES SWARMING
OVER ENDLESS PLAINS, STUMBLING IN CRACKED EARTH
—T. S. ELIOT, "THE WASTE LAND"

THIRTY-THREE

"Our Only Hope for Success"

I discovered Arthur Rimbaud lounging on the front steps of the Grand Hotel De L'Univers, wearing a fresh shirt and an ironic smile.

"Well?" he asked.

"Well what?" I felt certain he could see it in my eyes, smell it rising from my being. The Zoroastrians believe the dead do not depart at first; for three days they circle around their abandoned bodies, lost and forlorn. They have been evicted, and they do not understand why.

"Has Dr. Warthrop returned?" I asked.

"Yes, but he is about to leave again—to look for you."

"Where is he?"

"There," he said, with a nod toward the lobby. I took the steps two at a time. "Better have something good to say. He has a few good things to say to *you*," he called after me.

The monstrumologist was standing in the middle of the room surrounded by several uniformed members of the British colonial police, as well as one or two armed sepoys. Warthrop, by far the most experienced hunter in the group, spotted me first. He shoved a man out of his way and strode over to greet me with a hard slap against the side of my head.

"Where have you been, Will Henry?" he cried. His face was contorted with fury and pent-up anxiety. I'd seen him that way before. *I will not suffer you to die!* He grabbed my shoulders and roughly shook me. "Tell me! Why did you wander off like that? Didn't I tell you to stay with Monsieur Rimbaud? Why didn't you wait for me? Well? Have you nothing to say for yourself? Speak!"

"I'm sorry, sir—"

"*Sorry?* You are *sorry?*" He shook his head with wonder. Keeping one hand on my shoulder—fearing, perhaps, I might fly away unless anchored—he turned to the search party, informed them that the lost little lamb had wandered home, and thanked them for their speedy response to his call for help. He said no more until they had gone, and then he said to me, "With no further halfhearted apologies, Will Henry, please explain why you snuck off without a word to anyone."

I avoided his eyes. "I went to look for you, sir."

"Will Henry . . ."

"I tried to get Monsieur Rimbaud to come with me, but he said he was tired and wanted to take a nap."

"And the reason you took it into your head to look for me?"

"I thought . . ." The words would not come.

"Yes, I am interested in hearing those—your thoughts. What were you thinking? And if you were thinking some ill fate had befallen me, why did you go off by yourself? Did it not occur to you to wake Rimbaud from his nap and at least *tell* him where you were going?"

"No, sir, it didn't."

"Hmmm." Some of the anger had drained from his face. "Well," he said, relaxing a bit. "The day seems to have been a success all around, Will Henry, for you have found me and I have found us passage to Socotra. We leave at first light for the Isle of Blood."

We were both tired and hungry, but the doctor insisted on walking down to the telegraph office before anything else, where he sent off a wire to von Helrung:

LEAVING TOMORROW FINAL
DESTINATION. PXW.

There was a message waiting for him. He read it and then slipped it into his pocket without showing it to me. I deduced from his concerned expression that it had not come from Venice. He was very quiet on the walk back.

We took a room at the hotel for the night, changed quickly for dinner—we were both ravenously hungry—and ended up sharing our table with Rimbaud, who kept mum about our sightseeing foray into the Shamsan Mountains above Crater. Instead he talked about his early days in Aden and the coffeehouse where he oversaw a "harem" of women workers preparing the beans for shipment to Europe. The doctor listened politely but spoke little. His mind was elsewhere.

Later that evening I woke from a light sleep to find myself alone. A shadow moved outside the window. I peeked between the wooden slats onto the veranda. Silhouetted against the silvery sea was the form of the monstrumologist facing east, looking toward Socotra.

He turned suddenly and peered down the beach toward the quay, his body stiffening, his right hand dropping into his coat pocket, searching for his revolver. He would not find it, I knew.

Tell him, a voice whispered inside my head. *You must tell him.*

I got out of bed and dressed in the semidarkness, shivering, though it was not cold. I'd never hidden anything from him—had never tried, because my faith in his ability to see through any lie was insurmountable.

I was pulling on my shoes when the floor creaked outside the door. In a panic—apparently my quick thinking was done for the night—I jumped back into bed and yanked the covers up to my chin.

Through half-open eyes I watched him cross the room to the chair where I had carelessly thrown my jacket. If he checked the revolver's chamber, I was done for. But what did it matter? I was going to confess, wasn't I?

He went to the same window through which I had spied on him and stood for a long while with his back to me before saying, "Will Henry." And again, with a sigh, "Will Henry, I know you are awake. Your nightshirt is on the floor and your shoes have gone missing."

I opened my eyes fully. "I saw you outside and—"

"And when you heard me coming back, you jumped into bed fully dressed."

I nodded.

"Do you think such behavior might strike someone as odd?" he asked.

"I didn't know what to do."

"So the most reasonable thing that occurred to you was jumping into bed and pretending to sleep?"

He turned to me and said, "I know why you left this afternoon."

I swallowed hard. My faith in his powers was not misplaced. He did not need my confession. He knew.

"Do you trust me, Will Henry?"

"Of course."

"Your actions today give lie to your words. Why did you think I wouldn't come back for you? I told you I would, and yet you left to look for me. And just now, finding me gone, you threw on your clothes to chase after me. It's New York, isn't it? You remember New York and you fear at any moment I may abandon you. Perhaps I need to point out the difference between New York and this afternoon. I made no promise in New York."

I was wrong. The monstrumologist had not discerned the truth. I felt the burden settle back upon my shoulders.

"I don't know what we will find on Socotra, Will Henry. Kearns and the Russians have beaten us to the treasure, and there is a possibility that once again the grail has slipped from our grasp. I hope not. I pray it is not too late. If it is not, then you and I must shoulder a burden greater than most men can carry. Our only hope for success lies not in the force of arms or in numbers, or even much in our wits. No, *this* is what will save us." He pulled my left hand into his and squeezed hard. "It saved you in America and it saved me in England, the thing in which I must now put absolute faith— the one thing I do not begin to understand! The thing that frightens me more than the abominations I pursue—the monster whose face I cannot bring myself to turn and face. We have been—we are—we must be—*indispensable* to each other, Will Henry, or both of us will fall. Do you understand what I mean?"

He let go of my wounded hand, rose, turned away.

"On the night you were born, your father drew me aside and with great solemnity—and tears in his eyes—told me your name would be Pellinore. He did not, I think, expect my reaction to this flattering gesture, of which I'm sure your mother was unaware. I unreservedly upbraided him, disavowing him of any notion that I was honored by the choice. My own anger confounded me. I did not understand why it enraged me, the thought of you carrying on my name. So many times we express our fear as anger, Will Henry, and now I think I wasn't angry at all but afraid. Terribly, terribly afraid."

It was time to confess. Were not my actions that day the indispensable proof that his faith in me was not misplaced? I tried. My mouth came open, but, like with Rurick's before I killed him, no sound came out. Though I had most likely saved both our lives, though I had chosen the only door through which our salvation lay, I remembered his quiet despair on the beach at Dover. *The very strange and ironic thing is that I left you behind so you wouldn't have to live on that plate with them.* If I confessed, there would be no absolution; I would still be *nasu*.

And so would he. He would be made unclean by my touch. My "success" at the Tower of Silence would be his failure, the fulfillment of his deepest fears. He would know beyond all doubt that by my saving him he had lost me forever.

THIRTY-FOUR

"The Best Stories Are Better Left Untold"

Captain Julius Russell, owner of the cargo clipper *Dagmar*, was a tall, flush-faced, one-eyed expatriate, a former officer in the British cavalry who'd retired from the army following the second Afghan campaign. He'd come to Aden in '84 to make his fortune in the coffee trade, plunking down his life savings on a retired packet steamer that in its day had been the fastest vessel of its class in the British fleet. He'd had trouble finding contracts, though—most of the coffee exporters used their own ships to transport their goods to Europe—and his hopes to undersell them by buying directly from the growers, thus cutting out the middlemen, had been dashed by the near monopoly held by companies like the one Rimbaud used to work for in Aden.

"It's the bloody heat," Russell told my master. "It melts the honor right out of a man. The customs officers are so corrupt they'd sell their mums for a sixpence and a bottle of *araq*."

Bankrupt and desperate, Russell turned to trading in a decidedly more lucrative commodity—diamonds. Twice a month he sailed the *Dagmar* down the African coast to Sofala, where he picked up the contraband from a corrupt Portuguese official for transport to brokers based in Port Said. The diamonds were hidden in coffee bags, not so much to fool customs officials as to provide reasonable cover for the inevitable raid of Somali and Egyptian pirates who prowled along the glittering corridor between Mozambique and the Bab-el-Mandab Strait, the Gate of Tears, where the Red Sea meets the Gulf of Aden, and where the poet in Arthur Rimbaud had died.

We met the captain and his first mate, a Somali of gargantuan proportions named Awaale, in the hotel dining hall for breakfast. Awaale took an immediate fancy to me, his landlubbing equivalent.

"What does your name mean?" He spoke perfect English.

"What does it mean?"

"Yes. I am Awaale; it means 'lucky' in my language. What does your name mean?"

"I don't know that it means anything."

"Oh, all names mean something. Why did your parents name you William?"

"I never asked them."

"But now you will, I think." His eyes danced and he broke into a wide smile.

I looked away. The doctor and Captain Russell were engaged in a rather heated conversation about the portage fee, the continuation of an argument that had taken up the majority of Warthrop's visit the day before. Russell wanted the entire amount up front, and the doctor, as tightfisted as ever, would agree to only half, with the remainder to be paid upon our safe return.

"What happened to your parents?" asked Awaale. He had read my reaction correctly.

"They were killed in a fire," I answered.

"Mine are gone too." He laid his huge hand over mine. "I was just a boy, like you. You are *walaalo*, little Will. Brother."

He glanced at Russell, whose naturally rosy countenance now burned a deep crimson, and smiled. "Do you know how Captain Julius lost his eye? He fell off his horse at Kandahar, and his gun misfired when he hit the ground. He missed the entire battle. He tells people he was wounded in a charge, which like many stories of war is true but also not quite!"

"I must cover my risk, Warthrop," Russell was insisting vehemently. "I've told you, no one attempts Socotra this time of year. The British won't bring even their biggest frigate within a hundred miles of the place until October. They shut down Hadibu during the monsoon, and Hadibu is the only decent deepwater port on the whole bloody island."

"Then, we make landing at Gishub or Steroh in the south."

"*You* can attempt a landing there. The currents in the south are treacherous, especially this time of year. I will remind you, Doctor, I did not promise you a stroll from deck onto shore."

Awaale leaned close to me and asked in a quiet voice, "Why do you go to Socotra, *walaalo*? That place is *xumaato*, evil ... cursed."

"The doctor has important business there," I whispered back.

"He is a *dhaktar*? They say there are many strange plants there. He is going to collect herbs for his medicines, then?"

"He is a *dhaktar*," I said.

We boarded the *Dagmar* at a quarter past eight, and for once I could not wait to put out to sea. The quay was swarming with British military police and soldiers; I expected to be pulled aside for questioning about the two bodies left for the carrion birds on the front porch of the world, for I was certain they had been discovered by now.

We would make excellent time, Russell promised my anxious master; our journey should take no more than five and a half days. The *Dagmar* had been recently refitted with new boilers (a wise investment if you are running diamonds), and her holds would be empty, which would nearly double her speed.

"That is the last thing I wanted to confirm with you," Warthrop said, casting his eyes about for eavesdroppers. "We are agreed as to the particulars for our return to Brindisi?"

Russell nodded. "I'll take you all the way to Brindisi,

Doctor. And port your special cargo for you, though it goes against my better judgment. I would hope we could trust each other, like gentlemen."

"Like yours, Captain Russell, my business is fraught more with scoundrels than gentlemen. You'll know soon enough the nature of my special cargo and will be well compensated for the risk of its transport, I promise you."

The monstrumologist and I walked forward as the *Dagmar* chugged through the harbor for the open sea. To our left were the towering rust-colored mountains of Aden, the roiling black dust of the coal depot, the graceful sweep of the Prince of Wales Crescent, and the tired-looking facade of the Grand Hotel De L'Univers, where I spied a man in a white suit sitting on the veranda, caressing a tumbler filled with a vile green liquid. Did I see him raise his glass in a mock toast?

"So, Will Henry," said the doctor, "what did you learn from the great Arthur Rimbaud?" He must have seen the same man.

There is nothing left when you reach the center of everything, just the pit of bones inside the innermost circle.

"What did I learn, sir?" The breeze was delicious upon my face. I could smell the sea. "I learned a poet doesn't stop being a poet simply because he stops writing poetry."

He thought that was very clever of me, for very complicated reasons. The monstrumologist clapped me on the back, and laughed.

First there was the land receding behind us, until the

horizon overcame the land. Then a bevy of ships, packets and cargo steamers, light passenger crafts filled with colonists escaping the heat, and Arab fishing dhows, their great triangular sails snapping angrily in the wind, until the horizon rose up to swallow them. The terns and gulls followed us for a while, until they gave up the chase and returned to their hunting grounds off Flint Island. Then it was the *Dagmar* and the sea beneath a cloudless sky and the sun that hurled her shadow upon the churning wake, and the empty horizon in all directions. There was the great rumbling of the ship's engines and the faint singing below of the coal-heavers and the laughter of the indolent crew lounging topside. Somalis all, and none who spoke a word of English, with the exception of Awaale. They had been told nothing about our mission and did not seem in the least curious. They were grateful for the respite from pirates and nosy customs officials; they laughed and joked like a group of schoolboys on holiday.

There were only two cabins on board. One was the captain's, of course, and the other belonged to Awaale, who cheerfully gave it up for the doctor, though there was room for only one.

"You shall sleep with me and my crew," Awaale informed me. "It will be grand! We'll swap stories of our adventures. I would know what you have seen of the world."

The doctor took me aside and cautioned, "I would be judicious in describing the parts I had seen, Will Henry. Sometimes the best stories are better left untold."

Situated near the boiler room, the crew's quarters was small, noisy, constantly hot, and therefore nearly always deserted in the summer months, when those not on the night watch slept on deck in a row of hammocks suspended midship. I did not get much sleep our first two nights at sea. I could not relax with the incessant sway and counter-sway of the hammock beneath me and the naked night sky refusing to stay still above me. Closing my eyes only made it worse. But by the third night I actually started to find it pleasant, swinging back and forth while the warm salty air caressed my cheeks and the dancing stars sang down from the inky firmament. I listened to Awaale beside me, weaving tall tales as intricate as a *nidus ex magnificum*.

On the third night he said to me, "Do you know why Captain Julius hired me to be his mate? Because I used to be a pirate and I knew their ways. It is true, *walaalo*. For six years I was a pirate, sailing up and down the coast. From the Cape of Good Hope to Madagascar, I was the scourge of the seven seas! Diamonds, gold, silks, mail packets, sometimes people . . . Yes, I even trucked in people. After my parents died, I signed on to a pirate ship, and when I had learned all I could from the captain of that ship, I snuck into his cabin one night and slit his throat. I killed him, and then I gathered the crew together and said, 'The captain is dead; all hail the new captain!' And the first thing I did as captain? Put a heavy lock upon the cabin door!" He chuckled. "I was all of seventeen. And in two years I was the most feared pirate on the Indian Ocean; Awaale the Terrible, they called me. Awaale the Devil.

"And I *was* a devil. The only ones who feared me more than my victims were my crew. I would shoot a man for hiccupping in my direction. I had everything, *walaalo*. Money, power, respect. Now all that is gone."

"What happened?" I asked.

He sighed, his spirit troubled by the memory. "My first mate brought a boy to me—a boy he vouched for, who wanted a berth—and like a fool I agreed. He was about the age I was when I began, also an orphan like me, and I took pity on him. He was very bright and very strong and very fearless—like another boy who decided he wanted to be a pirate. We became quite close. He was devoted to me, and I to him. I even started to think, if I ever became tired of it, I would quit the pirate's life and give the ship to him as my heir."

Then one day a member of the crew brought to Awaale troubling news. He had overheard the boy and the first mate, the man who had vouched for him, whispering one night about their captain's tyrannical rule and, most damning of all, his refusal to share fairly the ill-gotten spoils of their labors.

"He trusts you," the first mate told the boy. "He will not suspect the knife until the knife strikes home!"

Awaale did not hesitate. He seized the alleged conspirators immediately and confronted them. Both denied the plot and accused their accuser of scheming against them in order to curry favor and increase his share of the booty. Awaale's judgment was swift and ruthless: He killed all three of them, accuser and accused, including the boy he loved, though he admitted that had been hard—very hard. Then he decapitated them with his own hand, and hung their heads from the mizzenmast as a reminder to his crew that he was their lord and master.

"I don't understand," I said. "If the first man was telling the truth, why did you kill him? He warned you about the mutiny."

"I did not know if he was telling the truth, *walaalo*. I did not know who to believe."

"Then, you killed at least one innocent man."

"I had no choice," he cried in a voice broken with despair. "If I let the wrong one live, then I would die! Spill the blood of the innocent or have the guilty spill my own! You do not know, *walaalo*. You are a boy. You've never faced the faceless one."

"The faceless one?"

"That is my name for it. I wept when I plunged the dagger into his heart; I cried bitter tears for the boy whom I loved, while his blood, scalding hot, poured through my fingers. And crying, I laughed with a fierce, unconquerable joy! I laughed because I was free of something; I cried because I was bound to something. I was saved; I was damned. Bless you, *walaalo*, you have never had to face the faceless one; you do not know."

Freed and enslaved, Awaale did not remain a pirate long

after his impossible choice. He abandoned his ship at Dar es Salaam, whose name is a mangling of the Arabic *andar as-salām*, the "harbor of peace." Penniless and friendless in a foreign land, he wandered deep into the African interior until he reached Buganda, where he was taken in by a group of Anglican missionaries who taught him how to read and write English and prayed daily for his immortal soul. He prayed with them, for it seemed to him he shared a special kinship with their God.

"The spilling of innocent blood is nothing new to him— no, not to him!" said Awaale. "His own son he suffered to die a bloody death that I might live to worship him. This God I think understands the space between 'may' and 'must'; he's seen the face of the faceless one!"

I did not speak for some time. I watched the stars swing back and forth, left and right and back again; I listened to the slap of the sea against the clipper's bow; I felt the beat of my heart.

"I saw it too," I said finally. "I know that space." It existed between Warthrop and Kendall in the bedroom at Harrington Lane, between Torrance and Arkwright in the Monstrumarium, between Rurick and me in the place of silence at the center of the world.

"Where, *walaalo?*" He sounded incredulous. "Where did you see it?"

"It's here," I said, and pressed my hand to my chest.

THIRTY-FIVE

"The Fury of a Merciful God"

On the fourth day the horizon before us turned black and the seas rose, driven by a stiff wind that pushed against the *Dagmar* like a giant hand pressing upon her chest. Captain Russell turned the ship southward to skirt the worst of the storm, a decision that did not sit well with the monstrumologist, who ground his teeth and tugged on his bottom lip and paced the foredeck while the gale bent him nearly double and whipped his hair into a cyclonic confusion. I braved the elements to urge him inside, convinced he would be swept overboard at any moment by the tempestuous waves crashing furiously across the bow.

"You know what von Helrung would say!" he shouted above the whipping wind and pounding sea. "The fury of a merciful God! Well, *I* say let him loose his signs and wonders! Array the powers of heaven against me, and I will contend against them with every fiber of my being!"

The deck shuddered violently and then bounced upward, throwing me off my feet. The monstrumologist's hand shot out and grabbed my arm, yanking me back from the edge.

"You shouldn't be out here!" he screamed.

"Neither should you!" I hollered back.

"I will never sound the retreat! Never!"

He shoved me toward the stern and turned his back upon me, planting his legs wide for balance and spreading his arms as if inviting the fullness of God's wrath upon his head. A burst of lightning flashed, thunder shook the planks, and Warthrop laughed. The monstrumologist laughed, and his laughter overtook the wind and the lashing rain and the thunder itself, trampling the maelstrom under its unconquerable heels. Is it any wonder the power this man held over me—this man who did not run from his demons like most of us do, but embraced them as his own, clutching them to his heart in a choke hold grip. He did not try to escape them by denying them or drugging them or bargaining with them. He met them where they lived, in the secret place most of us keep hidden. Warthrop was Warthrop down to the marrow of his bones, for his demons defined him; they breathed the breath of life into him; and, without them, he would go down, as most of us do, into that purgatorial fog of a life unrealized.

You may call him mad. You may judge him vain and

selfish and arrogant and bereft of all normal human sentiment. You may dismiss him entirely as a fool blinded by his own ambition and pride. But you cannot say Pellinore Warthrop was not finally, fully, furiously *alive*.

I retreated to the safety of the bridge, where I could at least keep an eye on him, though the water splattering and streaming down the glass obscured my view, turning him into a maddened, wraithlike shadow against the lighter gray of the white-capped sea. As it happened, Awaale had taken the helm. His massive arms flexed and stiffened as he fought the wheel.

"What is he doing?" he wondered. "Does he wish to be blown out to sea?"

"He is anxious," I answered.

"Anxious for what?"

I said nothing. *To face the Faceless One*, I might have answered, but said naught.

The storm chased us well past nightfall, forcing the *Dagmar* miles off course, far south of the island, and putting her directly in the path of the monsoon winds driving down from the north. When the weather cleared, Russell planned a heading to bring us back to the west of Socotra; it was, he told the doctor, the only prudent course.

"We can't approach from the south, not with winds like these," he said.

"That would cost us at least a day," the monstrumologist

pointed out, his jaw tightening with barely suppressed ire.

"More than that," answered Russell grimly.

"How much more?"

"Two days, two and a half."

Warthrop slammed his hand down hard on the table. "Unacceptable!"

"No, Dr. Warthrop, *unavoidable*. I tried to tell you back in Aden. No one goes to Socotra this time of—"

"Then, why in God's name did you agree to it?" the doctor snarled.

Russell called upon all his English fortitude and said, in the calmest manner he could muster, "Coming from the west is our only hope of getting you close enough for a landing. Forcing our way north against this wind could take just as long and entail twice the risk."

Warthrop drew a deep breath to collect himself. "Of course I will defer to your judgment, Captain. But I hope you can understand the urgency of my mission."

"Well, I do not understand it. You've been marvelously obtuse about your purpose, Dr. Warthrop. Perhaps you could realize your hope by telling me what the bloody hell is so important on that desolate rock that you're willing to risk life and limb—*my* life and limb—for it."

The doctor said nothing for a moment. He stared at the floor, weighing something in his mind. Then he looked up and said, "I am not a botanist."

*

"I have seen some strange things in this dark part of the world," the captain confided at the conclusion of the doctor's confession. "But none as strange as those you describe, Warthrop. I'd heard of—what did you call it?—that foul jelly that brings madness and death, but never thought it to be real. I've also heard men speak of the so-called red rain, blood pouring from the sky like some biblical scourge, but I never put much stock in sailors' tales. You could very well be mad, which is of no concern to me, except when that madness threatens my ship and the safety of my crew."

"I assure you, Captain Russell, I am neither mad nor naïve. The stories are true, and I intend to show you the proof when you return for us. If, that is, we ever manage to get there!"

"I will get you there, Warthrop, but I must ask how you plan to prevail over a squadron of Russians *and* capture this monster of yours, both intent on killing you, with nothing more than this boy by your side and a revolver in your pocket."

Both Russell and I waited for his answer. I did not think he'd give the one he gave to me in Aden—*this is what will save us*—and he didn't.

"I will leave all things nautical to you, Captain Russell," he said. "If you will leave all things monstrumological to me."

"Did you hear, *walaalo?*" Awaale asked me later that night as we lay in our hammocks belowdecks. He had to raise his voice to be heard over the thrumming of the engines. "I am going with you."

I was stunned. "What do you mean?"

"Captain Julius asked me tonight what I thought about it. 'This damn Yank may be the biggest fool I've ever met,' he told me. 'He could very well be mad as a hatter, but I can't just drop him on the beach and be done with it.' He offered to double my pay and I said yes, but not for the money. I said yes for you, *walaalo*. I said yes for you and for the one whose life I took all those years ago. I think God has sent you to me that I might save my soul."

"I don't understand, Awaale."

"You are my redemption, the key to the prison of my sin. By saving you, I will save myself from judgment."

He stroked my arm in the dark. "You are his gift to me, my *walaalo*."

There are spirits in the deep. On this night, the last night in the long march of nights, you can hear their voices on the open water, in the sea spray and the wind and the *slap, slap* of the water breaking across the bow. Voices of the quick and the dead, like the sirens calling you to your doom. As you face that spot where the sea meets the sky, you hear their portentous lamentations. And then, before your startled eyes, the horizon breaks apart, thrusting up jagged shards of itself to blot out the stars.

And the voices speak to you.

Nullité! Nullité! Nullité! *That is all it is!*

In Sanskrit it is called Dvipa Sukhadhara, *the Isle of Bliss.*

This night is the last in the long march of nights. The night Mr. Kendall appeared at our door. The night the monstrumologist bound himself to me and cried, *I will not suffer you to die!* The night he abandoned me. The night I ran upon a river of fire and blood to save him. The night Jacob Torrance showed Thomas Arkwright two doors. The night of my master's despair—*You have given yourself in service to* ha-Mashchit, *the angel of death*—and the night of my own despair at the center of the world.

The island is black as it rises toward you, a rip in the sky through which only darkness pours, and the wind wails, pushing you back upon your heels, while the tear in the endless vista draws you ever closer, as if the sea is draining into the abyss, bearing you down with it. The mass of darkness slips off to your left as your boat swings south and east. For a moment it seems like you are still and it is the island that moves, a massive black barge silently cutting through the sea.

This is the home of Τυφωεύς the *magnificum*, the Lord of the Abyss, the most terrifying monster of all, who lives in that space between spaces, in that spot one ten-thousandth of an inch outside your range of vision. I understand you may wish to turn away. And you can, if you wish. That is your blessing.

The monstrumologist and I do not have that luxury. We labor in the dark that you might live in the light.

THIRTY-SIX

"Is It Not Wondrous?"

At Warthrop's insistence the *Dagmar* dropped anchor a half mile from the southern shore, the closest Russell dared bring his ship. The currents were treacherous this time of year, he told us; they swirled around Socotra with the fury of Charybdis; the beaches were littered with the rotting skeletons of ships that had ventured too close during the monsoon. In June the stratospheric winds from Africa are dragged down by the five-thousand-foot Hagghier Mountains and sent howling along the northern coastline. For three months without pause the winds rage at a nearly constant speed of sixty miles per hour, with gusts up to well over a hundred. June is also the month of the rains, torrential downpours that deluge the interior and the south, where we would attempt our landing.

The doctor and I followed Russell up to the forecastle, where he trained his spyglass north, looking for Gishub, a small fishing village that lay—or should have lain—due north and about a mile from our position. The captain was troubled. He knew we were in the right place, but no lights shone in the distance indicating Gishub's existence.

"Completely dark," he murmured. "That's odd. It appears to be deserted." He handed the spyglass to Warthrop, who swung it back and forth a few times before admitting he saw nothing but varying shades of gray rock.

"Look at twelve o'clock," Russell advised. "Find the fishing boats on the beach, then straight back. . . . The natives fashion their buildings from stone—there's precious little wood on the island—if they bother building anything at all. Quite a few, I hear, live in the caves at Moomi and Hoq."

"I don't . . . Yes, now I see them. You're correct, Captain. All the windows are dark, not a single candle lit or lamp burning."

"There's another little village called Steroh about ten miles to the east. I could bring the *Dagmar* down there."

"No," said Warthrop firmly. "This must be investigated, Captain. We shall go ashore here."

"You'll have an easier time of it in the morning, when the tide shifts," Russell said as we descended to the main deck.

"I prefer to go now," answered the monstrumologist. "Immediately."

The knots that bound the dinghy to the ship were loosed. The ropes that bore it were paid out. We sat clutching the sides of the little boat as it fell, jerked, fell again, then plopped with a teeth-jarring splash into the water. Captain Russell's face appeared over the quarter railing, his one eye shining in the glow of the lamp beside him.

"I'll see you in three weeks, Warthrop! And I expect my first mate to be returned in good working order!"

"Don't worry, Captain Julius," Awaale called back. "I'll keep them out of trouble!" He pushed against the *Dagmar*'s hull with the end of his oar and then set to with arms and shoulders bulging, swinging us round toward the looming, lightless shadow that was Socotra. The lights of the *Dagmar* receded into the night.

Warthrop leaned forward, every muscle tense, his eyes shining. Behind him the path lay strewn with bodies— the young sailor who had borne the *nidus* from the Isle of Blood and Bliss; Wymond Kendall, who had carried it to us; Thomas Arkwright, who had tasted its rot; Jacob Torrance, who had fed it to him; Pierre Lebroque and all the ones who had fallen in the quest for the Faceless One of a Thousand Faces. Before him the way was dark, the path unknown. *I am the one!* he had cried from the depths of his soul, the same fathomless well from which had risen, *Look not into my eyes, for I am the basilisk!* There was no difference, really. The monstrumologist's desire was Pellinore Warthrop's despair.

Beside me Awaale fought against the swift current that swept east to west, pushing us sideways as he labored to drive us forward. Our progress was nearly indiscernible. Warthrop slapped his hand upon the rail in frustration, and Awaale grunted, "I'm sorry, *dhaktar*. The current is very strong."

"Then, you must be stronger!" snapped Warthrop.

Awaale gritted his teeth and strained against the insistent sea. *It would keep us away*, I thought. *It doesn't want us here.* I imagined the behemoth ocean dragging us to the middle of its landless expanse where it would devour us. Socotra mocked us—drawing closer, pulling away again, while Warthrop cursed under his breath and Awaale prayed under his.

"Pull, damn you. *Pull!*" the monstrumologist shouted at him. He shoved Awaale aside, seized the oars, and strove against the tide, digging the oars furiously into the black, swirling water. With each thrust Warthrop roared, and Awaale gave me a look of grave concern. We'd not made landing, and already the doctor seemed on the edge of reason.

"Awaale is stronger, Dr. Warthrop," I said gently. "You should let him—"

"And you should keep your mouth shut," he growled. "I did not come all this way . . . I did not sacrifice what I have sacrificed . . . I did not endure that which I've endured . . ."

Awaale leapt from the boat a dozen yards from the beach, wrapped the rope around his powerful forearm, and pulled us the rest of the way, until the hull of the dinghy bumped against the bottom.

There was no rest upon our landing. There was no celebratory moment. Awaale hauled the boat out of the surf, and we quickly unloaded our supplies—the large rucksack containing the provisions and ammunition (Captain Russell had generously loaned Awaale his rifle), a lamp to light our way in the dark, and the doctor's field case, the latter two entrusted to me. We set off at once toward Gishub, a small collection of stone buildings clustered at the foot of the towering cliffs that marked the edge of the Diksam Plateau.

"Will Henry, walk a little in front and keep the light low," the doctor instructed. "Awaale, step carefully. If you see something that looks like a jellyfish, it probably isn't. When we reach the village, touch nothing—*nothing*—without putting on a pair of gloves first."

"Gloves, *dhaktar?*"

"Gishub has either been abandoned or overcome. I see no other possibility."

Awaale whispered to me, "Gloves, *walaalo?*"

"To protect you from the *pwdre ser*," I said.

"*Pwdre ser?*"

"The rot of stars," I answered.

"Death," the monstrumologist clarified.

The way became steep, the ground hard. Before we'd come within a hundred yards of the first building, I smelled it—Awaale did too. He covered his mouth and nose, shuddering with revulsion: Gishub had not been abandoned; it had been overcome.

"*Xumaato!*" came his muffled voice from behind his large hand. With the other he quickly crossed himself.

Warthrop suddenly rushed forward, toward a building on the western end of the little village, commanding me to follow closely with the light. Stones had been piled against the doorway, blocking the entrance. The smell of rotting flesh permeated the atmosphere around the barrier; it seeped through the cracks between the hastily stacked rocks. The monstrumologist donned a pair of gloves and tore into the rocks. When the makeshift wall was halfway down, Warthrop seized the lamp from my hand and swung it through the opening.

It had been a curing house for fish. The last catch still hung in rows from the low ceiling; the blank, dead eyes of the fish glowed ghastly yellow in the lamplight. Scattered about the floor were several corpses—I counted fourteen in all—in various stages of decomposition. No more a curing house, now it was a charnel house.

The doctor ordered me to put on gloves and bade me to follow him with the light.

"Stay out here," he ordered Awaale before we stepped inside. "Shoot anything that moves."

There was no question what had delivered these corpses to the makeshift tomb. While I held the light, the monstrumologist examined their eyes—those that still had eyes— and they stared sightlessly back at him with irises the size of dimes—*Oculus Dei*, the eyes of God inanimate. The same sharp-tipped bony growths that had erupted over the entirety of Mr. Kendall's body protruded through their pale papery skin. The same exposed, swollen muscles and yellowish rock-hard claws for nails. The doctor puzzled over several corpses whose bodies appeared to have blown apart, spraying the walls and ceiling with their pulverized innards. A woman who'd already given up her face to the progeny of the flies that swarmed around our heads, whose skull grinned wetly at the doctor as he bent to examine her—brushing the maggots away with his little finger—gave away her particular *causa mortis*. Her cheekbones had been shattered, her skull crushed, her chin broken in half. She had not perished from the *pwdre ser*; she had been beaten to death.

Beside her a man lay on his side holding a child to his chest. It was a touching tableau, until I saw the claws imbedded to their roots in the child's back and the stringy bits of its dried flesh hanging from the man's elongated incisors. The child exhibited no signs of exposure; she had been healthy when the man had pulled her into his arms.

"It is wondrous, Will Henry," breathed the monstrumologist over the maddening hum of the flies. "I feared we might be wrong—that Socotra was not the *locus ex magnificum*. But we have found it, haven't we? And is it not wondrous?"

I agreed with him. It was wondrous.

He insisted on inspecting the rest of the village, so house by house we went, with Awaale standing guard at the door of each. Some we found relatively undisturbed, as if the inhabitants had simply stepped out for a few moments and were expecting to return. Other houses displayed evidence of violent struggle—tables overturned, cookware shattered, clothing strewn across the floor, blood splashed upon the walls and splattered in cone-shaped patterns across the ceilings.

We came to one house that appeared abandoned, but as we turned to leave, a pile of rags in the corner quivered and a small hand emerged, clawing impotently in the direction of the lamp.

The doctor drew out his revolver. He motioned for me to stay back and eased toward the squirming pile. The little fingers undulated, fell to the floor, and commenced to scrape across the hard stone with a horrid, dry scratching sound. Standing as far back as possible, Warthrop leaned down and carefully unpacked the makeshift cocoon, until he revealed a child, a boy no more than five, I guessed, in the final stages of exposure, with huge black eyes, more marsupial than human, and a suppurating face split apart by dozens of thornlike growths. He was naked from the waist up; his trousers hung about him in tatters. Long lacerations ran down his chest, like the mauling marks of a tiger; the wounds wept with fresh blood, and his lips shone with it and his nails dripped with it, and I remembered what the doctor had told me and realized that the boy was the last of the living and he had turned upon himself; he was eating himself alive.

And when the light struck him, his body jerked violently, his mouth came open in a gargled scream, and he heaved up a mass of clotted blood mixed with a clear, viscous fluid. The boy lunged toward the light, but he was very weak; he collapsed upon his belly, clawing at the hard stone. His back arched, and the skin pulled taut over the protuberances growing from his spine and then split apart, from the base of his neck to his lower back, like a zipper coming open.

Awaale heard my cry of revulsion and rushed into the house in time to see the monstrumologist step up to the writhing body, level the revolver at the small head, and, with a quick squeeze of his finger, launch a saving bullet into what was left of the child's brain.

The former pirate (who had lost count of the number he had killed; Awaale the Devil, they had called him) stared at Warthrop uncomprehendingly for a long moment. Then he looked at the dead child by the doctor's feet. One of the tiny hands had fallen upon Warthrop's shoe and was clutching it tightly, as if it had been his favorite toy, and the blood from the wound spread out slowly beneath his small, round head, creating a half-moon shape that reminded me of a Byzantine painting of the Christ child.

Awaale backed out the open doorway without saying a word. The doctor's shoulders relaxed—Awaale's appearance had unnerved him more than shooting the child—and he asked for his instrument case.

"Just a sample or two—the first fresh one we've found. I won't need you for this, Will Henry. Perhaps you should keep watch with Awaale."

"Yes, sir."

"Oh, you had better take this." He dropped the revolver into my hands. "You aren't afraid to use it, are you?"

"No, sir."

"I didn't think so."

Awaale was sitting in the dirt just to the left of the doorway, pressing his back against the wall of the house, facing toward the sea. I sat beside him. We were only a mile from the ocean, but there was no breeze. The air was still and heavy with dust, and towering behind us, like a great gray battlement, the gray cliffs of the Diksam Plateau.

"Who is this man?" he asked me. "Who is this *dhaktar* you serve?"

"He is a monstrumologist."

"A strange name, *walaalo*. What does it mean?"

"Someone who studies monsters."

"What monsters?"

"The ones worth studying, I suppose."

"The one in there—who looked so very much like a child, a little boy—he was a monster?"

"He was sick, Awaale—very sick. The doctor did the only thing he could. He was . . . he was helping him."

"*Helping* him? What a very strange kind of medicine this

monstrumology is!" He looked at me. "And you have been with him how long?"

"Two years now." I could not meet his appraising stare. I kept my face toward the unseen sea.

"And such things"—he meant what had happened inside the little stone house—"they are not new to you?"

"No, Awaale," I said. "They are not new to me."

"Oh," he said. "Oh, *walaalo*." His huge hand engulfed mine. "I am sorry; I did not know. You *have* seen the face of the faceless one, haven't you?"

He closed his eyes and his lips moved, but he spoke no word. It took me an absurdly long time to realize that he was praying.

THIRTY-SEVEN

"We Are Not Too Late"

The doctor stepped outside, and Awaale and I scrambled to our feet. We both were anxious to quit Gishub. The village was *nasu*. The monstrumologist had a different idea.

"We will stay here for the night," he announced quietly. "By all accounts *magnificum* is a nocturnal hunter, and as *his* hunters, we should keep his hours, but there is great risk in that. Exposure to *pwdre ser* leads to extreme sensitivity to light as well as a ravenous appetite for human flesh. A brilliant adaptation, really, for by so infecting his prey he forces *them* to keep *his* hours. The survivors act as his scouts. *Oculus Dei* indeed!"

We chose one of the clean abandoned houses in which to spend the rest of the night. Awaale volunteered to take the first watch, but the doctor demurred; he was not tired. He would wake Awaale in four hours.

"I shall take the rifle. Will Henry, give the revolver to Awaale, and try to get some sleep! We have a long march ahead of us."

There were no beds, just sleeping mats that we rolled out onto the floor of hard-packed dirt. I saw the monstrumologist sit down in the open doorway. Anything that might want to get to us must first get past him.

"*Walaalo*," Awaale whispered. "What happened to your hand?"

I kept my voice very low, lest the doctor hear me. "It makes a nest, and it uses its spit—the *pwdre ser*—to hold it together, and if you touch it, you change into . . . into what you saw tonight."

"And that is what happened? You touched the nest?"

"No, I . . . Indirectly, yes, I touched it."

He was silent for a time. "*He* cut it off, didn't he? The *dhaktar*."

"Yes. To save me."

"Like he saved the child."

"It wasn't too late for me."

He was silent for a long time. "What is this thing, this *magnificum*?"

"No one knows. No one has seen it. That's why we've come."

"To see it?"

"Or kill one. Or capture it. I think the doctor would like a living one, if he can manage it."

"For what reason?"

"Because he's a monstrumologist. That's what he does."

We could see the doctor's still silhouette framed in the doorway. "This is very strange to me, *walaalo*," Awaale said. "Like a dream. As if before you came I was awake and now I am dreaming."

I thought of the woman standing in the kitchen and the tall glass of milk and the smell of warm apples.

"I know," I said.

They swapped places at some point during the night; I slept through that. I was dreaming I was the boy who had died of cholera and the *Nassesalars* had borne my swaddled body to the innermost wall of the circle, placing it with my exposed face to the cloud-barren sky. My soul was trapped inside the unclean flesh; it did not circle round like it should. It was trapped, and I could see the crows and white vultures land on the ledge beside me, their small eyes clever and shiny black, and I watched as their sharp beaks filled my frozen vision, when they lowered their heads to peck out my eyes.

Sometime before dawn a startled cry jolted me awake. A shadow raced past me toward the open doorway. It was the monstrumologist. Alarmed, I leapt up and ran after him. Awaale was several feet away from the building, standing beside a small fire he had made with no small effort from bits of driftwood that had littered the beach. He swung the rifle around at the doctor's approach and then shuffled backward as the monstrumologist attacked the fire, stomping on the glowing embers and grinding them into the sand.

"No light, do you understand?" he snarled into the larger man's startled face. "You'll draw every last stinking one of them down upon us."

"I understand, *dhaktar*," Awaale answered, holding up his hand. Perhaps he had begun to think he'd joined company with a madman.

"You have only seen the final stages of an exposure," the monstrumologist said. "They are very strong and very quick and mad with hunger before they succumb. Ask Will Henry if you doubt me."

He stamped on the lingering coals until the last red speck was black. He ordered me back into the house.

"I'll stay out here with Awaale," he said. "In case he is tempted to do some other foolish thing."

Like accompanying a monstrumologist on the hunt for the Father of Monsters, thought I.

We set out at first light, heading straight toward the rising sun, and our shadows stretched long and thin behind us on the rocky soil. To our right the land sloped gently to the sea. On our left were the cliffs, soaring more than a thousand feet straight up, their craggy faces inscrutable in the early morning sunlight. The wind hissed and whistled sharply high over

our heads as it rushed across the highland plains and over the jagged lip of the plateau. Below there was no wind, just the sound of the wind, and that sound was incessant. It hovered in the background like the voice of an unseen chorus.

Around ten o'clock we came upon a great gash in the rock face, carved out over the centuries by the flash floods of the monsoons. The rocks shone wetly in the defile, and water still trickled along the course that cut directly across our path as it made its way toward its birthplace, the sea. Along either side of the riverbed, strange pale-skinned plants clung to the rock, with bulbous trunks and skinny branches festooned with dark green waxy leaves. The monstrumologist pointed these out to me and said, "They grow nowhere else on earth, Will Henry, like so many species on Socotra. This is why the island is called the Galápagos of the East."

"Is that what you call it?" muttered Awaale under his breath.

The monstrumologist did not hear him, or chose to ignore him. He pointed to the winding path into the cliffs. "What do you think, gentlemen? Shall we break our fast here before we attempt the ascent?"

During our breakfast of cured beef and hardtack, Warthrop took a stick and drew a map of the island in the sand. "We are *here*, midway between Gishub and Steroh. Up *here* is Hadibu, about thirty miles to our north and west."

"Thirty miles?" said Awaale. "That isn't so bad."

"Thirty miles as the crow flies," the doctor said. "Between

us and Hadibu lies the Hagghier Mountains, nearly impassible this time of year—flash floods, high winds, rock slides. . . . No, we must head north first, past the mountains, and then turn west for Hadibu."

"That is where your monster is, then, in Hadibu?" asked Awaale.

The doctor shook his head. "I've no idea. It's the most logical place to start, though. Hadibu is the largest settlement on the island. If you would find the tiger, find first the antelope."

We hiked up to the plateau. The ground was steep and wet, and I slipped several times. Each time, Awaale grabbed whatever piece of me was closest at hand—a wrist, the back of my shirt—chuckling at my clumsiness.

"Perhaps I should carry you across my shoulders like a shepherd his lamb, *walaalo*," he teased me.

"Perhaps if you and Will Henry would talk less and focus more on the task at hand, we might make better time," the monstrumologist snapped. With each minute the unnerving fire in his eyes grew brighter and colder. He paused only once about halfway up, when a gust of wind came rushing down the defile. He lifted his head and allowed the wind to bathe his face, eyes closed, arms spread wide for balance. The wind died to a gentle trickle, and he resumed the climb at a quicker pace, as if he had smelled something promising in the wind.

At the top, with the vast heart of Socotra spread out before me, I saw little that I would deem promising. The central plateau was a flat, nearly featureless landscape, crisscrossed with lines of scrub and clusters of green-crowned trees that looked like giant umbrellas turned inside out. Their exposed, interwoven branches reminded me of wicker baskets at first, and then I decided, *No, they are more like the intricate weave of a* nidus ex magnificum. Two were clinging to the rocks above the riverbed, and we rested for a moment in their meager shade. The day had grown hot, though the dry wind still blew.

"Awaale," the doctor said. "Let me borrow your knife for a moment. I want to show Will Henry something."

Warthrop rammed the blade into the trunk of the tree and sliced downward, making a six-inch incision. Thick, bright red resin oozed from the tree's wound.

Awaale groaned softly. "Bleeding trees? How did I not guess?"

"This is Dragon's Blood, Will Henry," the doctor said, "from which Socotra derives one of her names. It was highly valued in antiquity. They say Cleopatra used it for lipstick. This particular species, like the one you saw earlier, grows nowhere else on earth."

"It does not look like any tree I have ever seen," said Awaale, carefully wiping the blade clean on his trousers. "But this island is full of things I've never seen, and I have seen many, many things."

Warthrop pointed to his right. "The Hagghier Mountains. And, on the other side, Hadibu."

In the distance the range undulated in the noonday heat. The tallest peaks reared their saw-toothed heads more than five thousand feet into the air and thrust them into the billowing clouds draped over their jagged shoulders. They puffed their broken cheeks and blew a flurry of wind that stirred the monstrumologist's dark hair.

"Hurry, gentlemen," he said. "I think there may be a storm coming."

The wind off the mountains played with our hair for a while and flicked at our collars. The wind was dry, though, the sky clear, the sun high and hot. After we'd traversed a mile or two, when the gigantic serrated teeth of Socotra sidled closer to our right, the wind grew tired of toying with us and began to prod and push, with an occasional thirty-mile-per-hour shove thrown in, testing our will to hold our northerly course. At one point a massive gust hurled me to the rocky ground. Awaale helped me up and said to the doctor, "If we walked in the gully, the wind could not reach us."

"If we walked in the gully, a flash flood could sweep us off the plateau and into the ocean," Warthrop answered testily. Both had to raise their voices to be heard. "But you are free to do as you wish."

"I think I am not so free, because my wish is to be off this accursed island!"

"I did not ask for you to come!" returned my master.

"I did not come for you, *dhaktar*. I came for—"

"Yes?" The monstrumologist whirled on him. "Tell me. What did you come for?"

Awaale glanced at me. "For the unspoiled beaches."

Warthrop stared at him for a long, awful moment. He started to say something, and when his mouth came open, the wind abruptly died. The sudden silence was deafening.

An object tumbled out of the sky and landed at the monstrumologist's feet. Thin and shriveled, yellowish gray and speckled with gore—a human finger.

We followed the doctor's thoughtful gaze upward. A shadow was descending from the cloudless sky, a whirling mass of blood and shattered bone and the blasted bits of a human carcass. The doctor was the first to react, and his reaction was to shove me as hard as he could with a panicked cry of "Run, Will Henry! Run!" In two strides he had outpaced Awaale and me, making for a tight grouping of Dragon's Blood trees clinging precariously to the lip of the three-foot-deep gully along which we'd been hiking. The big Somali scooped me up under his massive arm and followed, shouting in abject terror, "What is this? What is this?" as the bloody rain began to slap and spatter the hard ground, popping all around us. A large piece of an organ—probably a portion of a liver—fell directly in front of him, and Awaale hopped over it with that peculiar grace that is born of desperation. We joined the monstrumologist beneath the relative safety of the trees. He was tearing through the ruck-sack, looking for our ponchos.

"Did it strike either of you?" Warthrop asked breath-lessly. He did not wait for an answer. His eyes glowed with exultation. "Red rain! You understand what this means, don't you? We are not too late."

"It feels as if we are," Awaale shouted in his face before yanking on his poncho.

The monstrumologist laughed, and lifted his face toward the bleeding sky.

THIRTY-EIGHT

"The Faithful Scrivener of His Handiwork"

The red rain ended as abruptly as it had begun, and now a great shadow raced across the plain, the sky was engulfed, and the wind returned with a vengeful howl. Then the heavens split open in a furious cannonade. Like a gray curtain slamming down came the torrential rain, driven sideways by the wind, full of hate.

"Stay here!" the monstrumologist commanded, and he dove into the maelstrom and was quickly lost in the twisting sheets of gray. He returned after a moment and threw himself to the ground beside us with a great sigh of relief not altogether owing to the paucity of shelter offered by the trees.

"Well, the rain has washed away most of the evidence,

but I did manage to scoop this up," Warthrop said, opening his hand to show us the severed tip of a human finger. He dug into the instrument case for something to put it in. Awaale watched him impassively; it was impossible to tell what he was thinking. His stony expression unnerved me, though.

Not so the doctor of monstrumology. "Before you volunteer for an expedition with a practitioner of aberrant biology, perhaps you should educate yourself in what precisely constitutes aberrant biology," he said to Awaale.

"The missionaries who taught me must have overlooked that part of my education, *dhaktar*," returned Awaale dryly. The poncho was too small for him. The hood would not fit over his large head, and water coursed down his wide face and dripped from his chin. Fat drops splattered from above, filtered by the tangled arms of the Dragon's Blood trees.

"I am not surprised," Warthrop return. "It's not the sort of thing that God-fearing men like to think about."

"Now you will tell me that you do not fear God."

"I don't know enough about him to form a reasonable basis for fear."

The doctor wrapped his long arms around his upraised knees and looked to the east—the source of the storm and the gruesome shower that had preceded it.

"We must correct our course, gentlemen. The way lies due east of us."

"East?" Awaale asked. He glanced over his shoulder but

could not even see to the other side of the gully through the ruffling gray shroud of water. "But you said the mountains were impassible this time of year. Rock slides and wind and—"

"Well, I suppose we could send Will Henry ahead with a polite note for the *magnificum* to rendezvous with us in Hadibu?" The monstrumologist laughed harshly and humorlessly, and then spoke gravely. "Those remains were carried aloft by the winds coming down from the Hagghier Mountains, so it is to the Hagghier Mountains that I intend to go, with your charming company or without it!"

He turned to me, unable to restrain his childlike enthusiasm. "You understand what this means, Will Henry. Despite their best efforts to keep the prize from my grasp, the Russians have failed. The *magnificum* still roams free!"

"Russians?" asked Awaale. "What Russians?"

The doctor ignored him. "I suspect they put their trust in Sidorov, a terrible scientist who couldn't find the Statue of Liberty if you plunked him down on Bedloe's Island!" He tapped the container that held the severed digit. "Maybe this belongs to my former colleague—a fitting end to an ignominious career!"

Awaale was slowly shaking his head. In all his travels he'd never met a man like the monstrumologist, and Awaale, you will recall, had traveled with bloodthirsty pirates. Warthrop's particular brand of bloodlust was of a peculiar vintage, though, a taste that was wholly foreign to the Somali, like the difference between rotgut and fine wine.

The doctor dropped the specimen container into the instrument case and pulled himself to his feet, holding on to the trunk of the Dragon's Blood tree to keep from sliding down the muddy slope. He cocked his head, as if listening for something hidden in the tumult of the smashing rain. In the gully below, the trickle of water had swelled into a shallow stream merrily racing over the rocks.

"We have to cross," Warthrop said suddenly. He threw the instrument case over his shoulder and started down. "Now!"

We were nearly too late. A wall of water five feet high spun around the bend ahead, a churning debris-laden foaming mass that roared toward us like a runaway locomotive. Halfway across I slipped and pitched forward, my terrified cry smothered by the heavy throw of rain. Awaale, who had already reached the other side, turned and ran back for me, driving his legs furiously through the knee-deep water. He grabbed my arm and slung my body over his shoulders with the same fluid motion of a Steamer Point coal-heaver. With a mighty roar he hurled me up toward the doctor, who managed to grab hold of my collar before the slippery rocks shot me back down. I scrambled backward, like a scuttling crab up the slope, pushing my heels hard against the stone. Below me Awaale clutched and clawed at the rocks, while below him the muddy floodwaters churned and chewed along the course, bearing the effluvia of the mountains, their foul vomitus, to the sea.

Warthrop sensed it coming somehow—he must have, for we did not seek shelter upon reaching the summit of the opposite bank. He squatted on the lip of the gulch, pulled his hat low to shield the rain from his eyes, and waited. He raised his hand, one finger extended, and, as if on cue, a headless human torso came round the bend, turning lazily in the slowing current, its trunk split wide down the middle, its intestines trailing behind in the bloody froth.

More refuse followed. Some of the larger pieces were easily identifiable—a hand here, a head there. Others had been shredded past all recognition. The rain slackened; the current eased; the cosmic stage manager willed the pageant to slow to a stately pace befitting the solemnity of the occasion. The water went from muddy brown to rusty red—a river of blood coursing from the island's fractured heart.

The monstrumologist looked down upon the human tide, and was entranced.

He murmured. "'In this thou shalt know that I am the Lord: behold, I will smite with the rod that is in mine hand upon the waters which are in the river, and they shall be turned to blood.'"

"This does not belong to him," Awaale whispered back. There was no need to whisper, really, yet somehow there was every need. "You pervert his word."

"To the contrary," answered the monstrumologist. "I am his devoted servant, the faithful scrivener of his handiwork."

✳

His hour had come. The hour when all the blood and death in his wake would be justified, the ledger sheet would be balanced, the debt repaid. *James and Mary, Erasmus and Malachi, John and Muriel, Damien and Thomas and Jacob and Veronica, and the ones whose names I have forgotten and the ones whose names I never knew* . . . Finding the *magnificum* would redeem the time, would redeem the dream. It was the hour—*his* hour—the hour when desire met despair. I saw it in the icy, unquenchable fire within his eyes. What fueled that infernal flame? Was it desire or was it despair?

The rain had departed, but the scudding clouds remained; the day would die a premature death. The mountains loomed before us, their serrated teeth draped in mist and shadow, and the earth beneath our feet was broken and crumbling, like the bones in the *Dakhma*'s ossuary. Huge boulders littered the way, hurled down in ages past by angry gods long since dead. Deep, shadowed-filled fissures, some only inches across, others spanning six feet or more, fanned out from the mountains' feet like the tentacles of an enormous beast reaching for us. The ground rose and dipped in a frozen undulation, each hill a little higher, each valley a little shallower, and the wind dove down to test the monstrumologist's will. It barreled across the plain, a wall of wind against which Warthrop pushed us without pause. It snatched the breath from our lungs, trammeled our words to the ground, spat dust into our eyes, and still he strove against it, bending forward lest he be driven backward or knocked off his feet entirely, moving like a man wading in waist-deep water, each step forward a victory hardly won.

I tried to stay by his side, but little by little the wind wore me down, and I fell farther and farther behind. The doctor did not notice—or did not care—and kept walking, but Awaale came back for me, hollering to Warthrop that I needed to rest. The monstrumologist did not hear him—or did not care.

"Here, I will carry you, *walaalo*," Awaale shouted over the wind.

I shook my head. I would be no one's burden.

We did not halt until we'd reached the mountains' rock-strewn base. We threw down our packs and collapsed against an outcropping, while the wind whined and whistled through the rocks and the setting sun broke through the clouds, painting the plain below us golden, a breathtaking, starkly beautiful sight.

You'll swear the sun has fallen into the sea, for every tree on that island is a golden tree, and every leaf a golden leaf, and the leaves shine with a radiance all their own, so even in the darkest night the island seems to burn like a lighthouse beacon.

"Night is coming," Awaale said. "We must find some shelter."

The doctor did not argue with him. He may have been thinking, like I was, of iris-less eyes. Awaale rose, shouldered his rifle, and hiked farther up the trail, disappearing between two boulders that stood like mute sentries on either side of a narrow pass—the gateway to the lair of the *magnificum*.

"It's the most beautiful thing I have ever seen," the monstrumologist said, looking down upon the golden plain. "And I have seen many beautiful things. Did you ever dream of anything so lovely, Will Henry?"

I see it, Father! The Isle of Bliss. It burns like the sun in the black water.

"No, sir."

He looked at me, and I looked back at him, and his face shone in the golden light.

"Did I show you the telegram I received before we left Aden? I don't think I did." He pulled the crumpled form from his pocket and pressed it into my hand.

> TERRIBLE NEWS. FOOLS GOT IT
> WRONG. WERE LOOKING FOR TWO
> BALD MEN, ONE SHORT AND FAT
> THE OTHER TALL AND THIN. JUST
> NOW LEARNED. STAND GUARD,
> MIHOS. MENTHU

He watched my expression carefully. I was careful too. I said, "Rurick and Plešec?"

He nodded. "Apparently they slipped through Fadil's net."

He pulled out his revolver and held it loosely in his lap. The barrel glistened in the kiss of the dying sun.

"There are two bullets in this chamber. By my count, Will Henry, there should be five. Three missing bullets. Two missing Russians."

"I didn't have a choice, sir."

"Oh, Will Henry," he said. "Will Henry! Why didn't you tell me?"

"I don't know—"

"Stop that."

"I didn't know how—"

"*Stop that.*"

"I didn't want you to be . . . disappointed in me."

"Disappointed in you? I don't understand."

"I was afraid you'd leave me behind again."

"Why? Because you defended yourself against two soulless brutes who would have killed us both without batting an eye?"

"No, sir," I answered. "Because *I* killed *them* without batting an eye."

He nodded; he understood.

"Do you want to know how it happened?" I asked.

He shook his head. "The place may vary and the names may be different, but the crime is the same, Will Henry."

He scrubbed his hand across his whiskered chin, picked up a stick lying by his foot, and began drawing in the soft ground.

"Born under the same roof," he said pensively. "Perhaps it *is* like the mark of Cain." He lifted his face to the setting sun, tapping the end of the stick against the dirt. "Do you remember when you first came to live with me—how we would keep a bucket beside the necropsy table in the event you became ill? And you always became ill—in the beginning. I can't remember the last time the work made you sick."

He tossed the stick away; it tumbled down the decline toward the golden plain and was lost.

"It is a dark and dirty business, Will Henry. And you are well on your way." He patted my knee, not to congratulate, I think, but to console. His tone was sad and bitter. "You are well on your way."

Awaale returned and reported he'd found a suitable spot to spend the night. We shouldered our packs and followed him up the narrow trail, a steep, serpentine corridor that wound between two sheer rock walls. A lid of low, gray clouds spun restlessly overhead; and a river of wind funneled through the pass. After traversing a hundred yards or so, we came to a cleft in the cliff face, six feet across at the bottom and about that high, narrowing to a point at the top, a deep gash in the stone that could not be properly called a cave, but it would offer some protection from the elements. The shadows inside the cleft were deep, and the doctor peered anxiously inside.

"It is safe," Awaale assured him. "A scorpion or two, but I took care of them." His smile was bright. He was proud of his accomplishment.

Exhausted, I threw myself upon the ground and refused

to get up, though Awaale tried to entice me with some food. I rolled up my poncho to make a pillow and closed my eyes. Their voices floated over me—some discussion about who would take the first watch. Outside, the clouds sent down the wind and the wind blew out the light, and darkness lighted upon the trail like a great black bird of prey. Someone lay down next to me, and a warm hand pressed briefly upon my brow—Awaale.

I fell into the lightest of dozes, and then light shot into the space, and I sat up—Awaale, too, and then we stood up.

"*Dhaktar?*" Awaale called softly. "You said no light!"

We could see him standing just outside the opening, holding the lantern in one hand and the revolver in the other, peering off into the gloom.

"There is something out there, on the other side of those rocks," he said. "Awaale."

He motioned with the gun. Awaale picked up his rifle and stepped outside. The two men remained motionless for some time.

"There!" whispered Warthrop. "Did you hear it?"

Awaale slowly shook his head. "I hear the wind."

"There it is again! Stay here."

The doctor eased up the path, disappearing from view. I scooted forward; Awaale waved me back. He raised his rifle. The doctor's light faded, and the dark washed over Awaale, swallowing him whole.

"Awaale," I called to him quietly. "Do you see him?"

The light returned, throwing jittery shadows as it came, flowing over Awaale and then illuminating the entrance to the cleft. Awaale slung his rifle over his shoulder and accepted the lamp from the doctor, who needed both hands to keep his burden upright.

Leaning against the monstrumologist was a young woman, her clothes hanging in tatters, her long hair matted and encrusted with filth, her bare feet leaving bloody tattoos on the rock. He brought her inside, eased her down carefully, and motioned for Awaale to hand me the lamp. I saw then the woman was not alone: She was clutching a sleeping baby to her breast.

She said something. The doctor shook his head; he did not understand. She repeated it, her eyes wide and frightened.

"What is she saying?" Warthrop asked Awaale.

"I don't know."

The doctor looked sharply at him. "What do you mean? You speak their language."

"I speak Somali and English and a little French. I do not know the language on Socotra."

"You don't . . ." Warthrop was staring at him as if he'd just confessed to murder. "Captain Russell told me that you did."

The woman pulled on Warthrop's sleeve, pointed outside, and jabbered something hysterically. The doctor's focus, however, was on poor Awaale.

"It was the only reason I allowed you to come with us! Why did you lie to me?"

"I didn't lie to you. Captain Julius lied to you."

"To what purpose?"

"So you would let me come? I don't know. You should ask him."

"And I will, if I live long enough!" He turned to me. "My instrument case, Will Henry." He turned back to the woman. "I am doctor. *Doctor*. Do you understand?" He tried it in French. Awaale tried it in Somali. The monstrumologist tested Arabic next. Nothing. He pulled the stethoscope from the case and held it up. "See? Doctor."

She nodded emphatically and broke into a smile. Her teeth were dazzling white against the backdrop of her smudged face. She calmed down considerably, shaking her head with wonder at her good fortune—a doctor, here, of all places! She meekly submitted to the examination—heart, pulse, breathing, and last, her eyes, while I shone the light. The doctor sighed, and pointed at the child. "I will need to examine him. Yes?" He gently slid his hands beneath the slumbering infant, and her eyes hardened; she shook her head violently and tightened her grip. Warthrop held up his hands, smiling reassuringly, and said, "All right, good mother. You may hold him." He pressed his fingers gently against the child's wrist. Listened to his heart. Peeled up one eyelid and stared for a very long time at the exposed orb. He smiled again at her, nodding as if to say, *He's fine*. He set down the lamp and backed out of the cleft, motioning for me to follow.

"She is in the early stages of exposure," he said.

Awaale gasped. "And the child?"

"The child is not infected."

Awaale wiped his hand across his mouth. He looked up and down the path, then back at the doctor.

"What must we do?"

"We must convince her somehow to give up the child," whispered the monstrumologist.

"And then . . . what? Kill her?"

Warthrop said nothing. In his eyes was something I rarely saw—the agony of the impossible choice.

"That is what you're thinking," Awaale said. "We must kill her."

"She is doomed," my master said hoarsely. "She will die anyway, and not before infecting her own child."

"So we must kill them both."

"Is that what I said? Listen to me! She has hours. The child could have years, if we can get him away from her in time."

"I will get him away," Awaale said grimly. "I will save him, and then you do what you will do." He stepped into the opening.

"No!" Warthrop grabbed his arm and pulled him back. "If you try to take him now, you risk her inadvertently infecting him—or yourself. It takes but the slightest scratch."

"Then, what do you suggest?" snapped Awaale. He'd reached the end of his endurance.

"I don't . . . I don't know." As if winded, the monstrumologist was struggling to catch his breath. "Probably . . . if I can get close enough, a quick shot to the head . . ."

"Your hands are shaking," Awaale pointed out. And they were, badly. "I will do it."

"You won't be able to get close enough," the doctor argued. "Besides, it's me she trusts," he added bitterly.

"I'll do it, Dr. Warthrop."

The men started. I think they'd forgotten I was standing there. Warthrop looked stunned at my offer, Awaale horrified. I held out my hand for the gun. Unlike the monstrumologist's, my hands did not shake.

"It's the only way to save him," I said.

"No. No, I won't allow it, Will Henry."

"Why?"

"Because to shoot someone in self-defense is one thing. This is something entirely different."

"How?" I demanded. "We can't let her live. We can't let him die. I'm just a boy; she won't suspect anything."

"I can do it," the monstrumologist said, sounding more firm than he looked. "It should be me." He laid his hand upon my shoulder. "Stay here with Awaale, Will Henry."

He ducked inside the wound in the mountainside. Awaale turned away. I turned to watch.

In the lamplight she looked very young, still in her teens, I guessed, and despite being covered head to toe in dirt, she was beautiful, in the first full flush of womanhood. She smiled trustingly at the doctor as he knelt beside her. He touched her cheek, the heel of his left hand dangerously close to her mouth, while dropping his right hand into his pocket. He spoke softly to her, using his eyes and his tone to lull her. And the gun came out. He held it against his leg outside her range of vision. *Now, I thought. Do it now.*

I could not see his face. I do not know what she saw there, but she continued to smile and he continued to talk softly, stroking her cheek, and I wondered what he was saying. He could have been saying anything, anything at all, because she couldn't understand him. He could be saying, "For your child, I must do this. For your child . . ." Or: "My name is *ha-Mashchit*, and the Lord God created me on the first day . . ."

His hand fell from her cheek. The other did not rise. Then he fell away entirely, scooting backward until he hit the opposite wall, and there he stayed, his back pressed against the rock, head bowed, arms hanging uselessly by his sides. I started toward him, and he held up his empty hand. *Stay.*

"What is he doing?" whispered Awaale over his shoulder. He refused to turn and see.

"He can't do it," I murmured in reply.

Awaale grunted. "Maybe he's wrong. Maybe she isn't sick."

"No. Her eyes—I saw it."

"You saw what in her eyes?"

"*Oculus Dei*, the eyes of God."

"I do not understand, *walaalo*. What are the eyes of God?"

Within the cleft the monstrumologist raised his head.

His dark eyes shone wetly in the lamplight. *What are the eyes of God?*

"I know," whispered Awaale. "He waits for her to sleep. And when she falls asleep . . ."

"I don't know what he's waiting for," I said. His hesitation in the necessity of the hour troubled me deeply. He'd never hesitated before. He hadn't in Gishub. He hadn't in the kitchen at Harrington Lane when he'd raised the butcher knife high over his head. The monstrumologist had always followed the dictates of his discipline. Jacob Torrance may have worn the Society's motto on his finger, but Pellinore Warthrop had it engraved upon his heart. He was, as Fadil had named him, *Mihos*, the lion, the guardian of the horizon. What stayed him? Was he clinging to something—or had he let something go?

"I do not understand this man you serve," Awaale said. "He seems to revel in death and fear it all at once. He chases after it like a rabid hound and then runs from it like a frightened rabbit. Why does a man like this hunt monsters?"

He plopped down beside the mouth of the crevice, holding his rifle upright between his knees, and leaned his head back against the rock.

"I am tired, *walaalo*," he sighed.

"You can sleep if you like," I said. "I'll stay awake."

"Ah, but you forget my bargain. I am the one who must watch over you."

"I don't need you to watch over me."

"It is not you I must answer to one day, *walaalo*," he returned gently.

I eased myself to the ground, facing Awaale so I could keep the doctor within my peripheral vision. He hadn't moved; neither had the mother and child. Maybe the doctor *was* wrong, I thought. Not about the woman but about the child. How could the mother be infected and the child not be? Better to end their suffering now. I did not raise this possibility to either of my companions, though. I sat with it, and thought, and waited, while the night grew deep around me and my companions nodded off. I watched the woman's eyes grow heavy, watched her head fall forward and then snap back as she fought her exhaustion. I was wide awake. I could have stayed awake for a thousand nights, so tightly wound was the thing inside me, *das Ungeheuer*, the *me/not-me*, the thing that whispered, *I AM*, and the thing that strove within me—and strives within *you*—to be free.

And while Mihos slept, Ophois rose.

There was the sigh of the wind and the crunch of the earth's shattered bones and the cold steel of the gun and the sleeping woman. There was the baby pressed against her naked breast and the soles of her bloody, rock-chewed feet and the top of her head pointed toward me as if in offering. I raised the gun. Brought it to within an inch of her scalp.

The world is not round. The horizon is the summit of the abyss; there is no crossing back.

My eyes dropped to the baby as I started to squeeze the trigger. Its eyes looked back at me. He was awake, and he was suckling on his mother's breast. My heart slammed against my ribs in panic. I dropped the gun and yanked him from her arms.

She snapped awake with a sharp cry and lunged forward, but I'd already backed out and turned up the path. There was no light to speak of to guide my way, and I didn't get very far before I tripped over a rock and pitched forward, spinning at the last second to protect the child. Her wraithlike shadow loomed over me for a long, awful instant, frozen in time, and in that space between the one second and the next, a shot rang out from above, and the mother fell dead at the feet of the one who had stolen all that mattered to her. I looked up, expecting to see the doctor or Awaale, and seeing neither, but the smiling face of the one who'd begun it, the reason I was in this place of blood and rock and shadow, holding a bawling infant in my arms, the face of John Kearns.

THIRTY-NINE

"What Does It Look Like?"

With a little laugh he jumped down from his perch, dropping his rifle immediately when he saw Awaale and the doctor running toward us with the light. He raised his hands into the air.

"Don't shoot; I'm clean!" he called in that distinctive leonine purr of a voice. "My!" he said, sizing up Awaale. "You're a tall African!"

"Cover him, Awaale," said my master. "If he moves, kill him."

He knelt before Kearns's victim. She had been shot cleanly through the back of the head.

"Are you hurt?" Warthrop asked me anxiously. I shook my head. He quickly examined the baby, and then pulled it from my arms.

"I saved your life once again, Master Will Henry!" Kearns said teasingly. "Not that I'm keeping score. Warthrop, I thought you were dead—or mad, or both—so I am halfway right—or wrong. Like everything else, it's all in how you look at it. Is this very tall African going to shoot me for saving your assistant's life?"

"Who is this man?" demanded Awaale.

"Jack Kearns, that name will do, or you may call me by my African name, *Khasiis*. And you are Awaale, which means 'lucky,' I believe."

Awaale nodded. "And I know what your name means, *Khasiis* Jack Kearns."

"Good. And now that we've been properly introduced, I suggest we extinguish that light and find cover as quickly as possible. The light draws them like moths to the flame; you must know that, Pellinore."

The doctor did know. He directed me to pick up the surrendered rifle and ordered Kearns forward, followed closely by Awaale, back to our little hideout. Warthrop and I followed, the child twisting and whimpering in his arms. His little face was streaked with dirt and tears, and his mouth was glimmering with his dead mother's milk. When we reached the cleft in the stone, the monstrumologist extinguished the lamp.

"I can still see you," Awaale warned the Englishman.

"Really? Then, you have the eyes of a cat—or of a rotter."

"Where are your friends, Kearns?" demanded the doctor.

"What friends? Oh, you mean the Russians. Dead. Except Sidorov. He might not be dead . . . yet. Not the eyes of a cat, but certainly the lives!"

"So it was to Sidorov that you offered the *magnificum*."

"The *magnificum*? Well, I suppose. I offered to take him to its nesting grounds—but the beast itself, that was up to him and his friend the czar."

"And?" Warthrop barked softly. "Did he find it?"

"Well, yes—or it found him."

The doctor hissed through his teeth. He had been beaten to the prize, and by the worst possible rival, a disgraced and disbarred monstrumologist, a scientific charlatan who would take all the glory of being the first to lay eyes upon the Father of Monsters.

Kearns read the doctor's reaction, and said, "Now, don't be angry with me, Pellinore. I did send you the *nidus*, after all."

"Why did you send it to me, Kearns? Wouldn't you need that to convince Sidorov you were telling the truth?"

"Oh, the truth," Kearns said dismissively.

"You knew I would come looking for you."

"Well, it did occur to me that you might. And to Sidorov. He wasn't too happy when I told him I had sent it to you for safekeeping. 'Not *him*,' he said. 'Not *Warthrop*.'" Kearns's Russian accent was impeccable. "And I said, 'Oh, Warthrop's a good enough bloke, a fine fellow for a scientist and bloody moralist.'"

"That explains Rurick and Plešec."

Kearns laughed. "Oh, *good*. Those two fairly scream for an explanation."

"But not Arkwright."

"Who is Arkwright?"

"You don't know Arkwright?"

"Should I know Arkwright?"

"You offered the *locus ex magnificum* to the British."

"I don't think I should comment on that, except to say I am a loyal servant of Her Majesty the queen." He raised his voice: "God save the queen!"

"When you are finished with him," Awaale said to Warthrop, "I would like to kill him."

"Well, aren't you a bloodthirsty African! Wherever did you find him, Pellinore? Did you kidnap him from a pirate ship?"

"How did you know I was a pirate?" demanded Awaale.

"Enough, Awaale," Warthrop said. "It's best not to parlay with the devil, if you can avoid it."

"That's the trick, yes," agreed Kearns cheerfully. "Avoiding it."

"Where is it, Kearns?" growled the monstrumologist. "Where is the *magnificum*?"

John Kearns took his time in answering. My eyes had adjusted to the dark; still, I could see only the barest outline of the man, a shade of lighter gray against the black backdrop of the mountain. The voice issuing from that shadow was a low thrum, like the sound of a fly's wings beating the air.

"Where is the *magnificum*? It is right above you. It is right beside you. It is behind you and before you. It is in that space one ten-thousandth of an inch outside your range of vision. Look no farther than the length of your nose and you'll find it, Pellinore."

Beside me the doctor huffed in frustration. I could feel his body tense, as if at any moment he might launch himself at Kearns and choke the life out of him. The whimpering child cradled in his arms probably saved Kearns.

"I don't have the stomach for this, Jack. I have suffered too much to suffer your riddles, too."

"And not just you, I'd guess! I saw little Willy's hand. Curiosity got the better of him, hmmm?"

Warthrop ignored the jibe and snarled, "*Where is the magnificum?*"

"You really want to see it? All right, I'll take you to it. Not now, though. His children are about at night, and they are very protective of him, as my Russian friends discovered and you probably already know."

He asked for some water, and then emptied Warthrop's canteen. He announced he was ravenously hungry, and then tore into our provisions, cramming food into his mouth as fast as he could pluck it from the bag.

"Been hunting that one for days," he said around a mouthful of hardtack. "All the way from Moomi. They exile the infected ones, you know—throw them out of the caves to fend for themselves, but I was waiting for the beast to take full hold of her—much better sport that way. The females are much harder than the males. The males come at you head-on, no stealth or subtlety about them, but the females are very clever. They'll lure you into dead-end traps, lead you round in circles, sit statue-still for hours to ambush you. I'll take a male as big and strong as Awaale here over a rotter like *her* any day."

"You knew we were here," Warthrop said. It was not a question.

"Saw your light. Knew you took her in. Didn't know quite what to do; thought you'd take care of her yourself, Warthrop. Why didn't you?"

The doctor looked down at the infant against his chest. The child had fallen asleep, its fat lips wrapped around its tiny thumb.

"You'll have to do it, you know," Kearns said.

The monstrumologist looked up. "What?"

"Kill it."

"It has not been infected."

"Impossible."

"I've examined it."

"It's been sucking on its mother's teat. How could it not be infected?"

Warthrop chewed on his bottom lip for a moment. "It has no symptoms," he argued stubbornly. I wondered who he was trying to convince, Kearns or himself.

"Well, do what you like, then. Let it starve out here."

"We'll bring it with us."

"I thought we were going to see the *magnificum*."

The doctor was rocking the child gently as it slept. "Awaale will remain here to watch him," he decided.

"I will?" asked Awaale.

"And when the tyke gets hungry, he'll stick its little mouth on his big black nipple?"

"Where is the nearest settlement?"

"With living people in it? Probably the caves over in Hoq."

"He will deliver the child to Hoq, then."

"For what? It's been exposed; they'll just kill it. Should do it now and save you and them all the time and trouble."

"I can't kill it," the doctor said. "I *won't* kill it."

"Oh. Do you want me to do it?"

Warthrop instinctively pulled the child closer to his chest and changed the subject. "What happened to your Russian friends?"

"The same thing that happened to the girl out there— that happens to anyone who touches the rot of stars. It started out well enough. Mating season had just begun, and the casualties were limited; the sultan had it quite under control, contained to a couple remote villages. They isolate the plague, you see, rather like a smallpox outbreak, and let it burn itself out. Sidorov and company traced the nexus to the birthing grounds, deep in the belly of the mountains, and then one of the fools got strung up by his vanity. He literally put his foot in it—stepped in a fresh puddle of the *pwdre ser*—and then insisted on cleaning his boots! The rot burned through the entire company after that. I barely escaped. Been hunted—and hunting—ever since."

"And Sidorov?"

"Oh, it got him, too. What day is this? Tuesday? Isn't it funny how unimportant the days of the week become? Anyway, I think it was Thursday last that it took him."

"Took him?"

Kearns nodded. "To the nesting grounds, where I'm taking you. If you still want to go."

"What does it look like?" Warthrop asked. He did not wish to ask John Kearns that question—he wasn't confident he'd get a straight answer—but he couldn't help himself. The dead in his wake compelled him. He'd sacrificed them to know the face of the Faceless One.

"Well, it's quite large," Kearns replied in a serious tone. "Huge, actually. Been around as long as us, hopping from island to island to roost before going back into hiding for a generation or two. The males aren't very bright, rather indolent, I would say, like a lion, sitting back and letting the females bring home the spoils."

"But what is their appearance? Are they reptilian? Avian? Or are they more closely related to the flying mammals, like bats?"

"Well, their brains are quite small, like a lizard's or a bird's, but they don't have wings. They're covered in thorns—like a rose!—and their hides are very pale and thin, their claws sharp, and their digits are quite dexterous. Well, we all know the intricacy of their nests."

"So they lay eggs, like a bird or reptile."

Kearns shrugged, smiled. "Haven't seen an egg—wouldn't want to. Can't imagine how that might happen."

"How many are there?"

"Here on Socotra? Hundreds, I would guess."

"Hundreds?" The monstrumologist seemed shocked.

"In the world, I would say thousands. Hundreds of thousands. Millions. As many as there are grains of sand on this blessed island's beach. Look up, Pellinore. How many stars are there in the sky? That's how many *magnificum* there are, and that's the number of faces they have."

My master realized that he was wasting his time. He fell silent, and Kearns fell silent, and then there was the sound of the wind and no other sound for some time.

"If this is one of your tricks, I will kill you. Do you understand?" the doctor said at last.

"Oh, really, Pellinore. I *want* you to find it. Why do you think I sent the *nidus* to you in the first place?"

He asked for his rifle back. Warthrop refused.

"They'll be here soon, and I'd rather be armed," Kearns argued. "*You* would rather I'd be armed."

"Who?" demanded Awaale. "Who will be here soon?"

"The rotters," Kearns answered. "The children of *Typhoeus*. The blood draws them. They can smell it for miles, especially in this wind. May I please have my gun back?"

"I do not trust this man," Awaale said. "His name is true. He is *Khasiis*, the evil one."

"If I wanted to kill you, I had my chance hours ago," returned Kearns reasonably.

"Will Henry," the doctor said. "Return Dr. Kearns's gun to him."

Awaale muttered something under his breath. Kearns laughed softly. Warthrop rocked the baby in his arms, his expression as troubled as the baby's was serene.

And thus we waited for the children of *Typhoeus* to come.

FORTY

"I Stand Upright"

Warthrop decided to entrust the child to me.

"If the worst should happen, take him back the way we came," he instructed me. "Down the path and out of the mountains. Make your way south, back to the sea. Gishub should be relatively safe until the *Dagmar* returns."

"Let Awaale take it," I protested. "I want to stay with you."

"You are fierce, Will Henry," he acknowledged. "More Torrance-fierce than Kearns-fierce, I hope, but . . ."

"It is all right," Awaale put in. "*Walaalo* has his own bargains to keep. But your master is right, at least in this. Do not worry. I will protect him with my life."

Kearns was loitering near the opening of the cleft, staring into the dark where the body of the woman lay crumpled upon the stone.

"It's a perfect spot. Perfect!" he breathed. "We could not have arranged it better, Pellinore. I shall take my old roost there, on that ledge on the eastern face. You can take the northern approach, and Awaale the other end, at those boulders marking the trailhead. Oh, that devil Minotaur. I shall have his head yet!"

"Minotaur?" echoed the doctor.

"My name for him. A big brute, almost as big as our pirate here. Been after that one for days. He's not a mindless animal like the others. He's very clever, probably was a leader in his village, and he's very, very strong. You can't miss him—has a long spike growing right out the middle of his forehead—the stag of the herd, as it were. Travels in a pack of them, four or five the last time I counted, but they fall fast from the *pwdre ser*, as you know, Pellinore. So they may be down one or two unless a straggler's joined the cause. A single bullet won't take him down. He's carrying around three of mine and still shows no sign of slowing. The last time I shot him—now, that was quite interesting. The wound bled a good deal, and usually it's the blood that sets off the frenzy, but with the Minotaur the rest gathered around the spot and one by one gave it this kind of sycophantic lick, a rotter pledge of fealty. It was poignant, really, given that their lifetimes can now be measured in weeks."

He raised his head, and we listened with him—but I heard nothing but the wind rubbing on stone.

"Something is coming," he whispered. "I suggest we take

our positions, gentlemen. Don't fire until my signal or unless you have no choice. Best to wait till they're distracted with the bait; then it's rather like shooting fish in a barrel. Watch out for my friend the Minotaur!"

He scrambled up the trail; Warthrop followed a few steps behind. Awaale patted my shoulder, picked up his rifle, and took off in the opposite direction. I eased to the very back of the cut and hunkered down, holding the child awkwardly in my lap and thinking how stupid I was to be pressed into a corner like this with no means of escape and no way to defend myself. My fate—and that of the child—was completely in the hands of a psychopathic killer who liked to go by the Somali name for "the evil one."

The baby whimpered in its sleep. I ran my fingertips lightly over his face, brushing across closed eyelids, his stubby little nose, his soft cheeks. There was another child, not so long ago, whom I had stepped over in a filthy tenement hallway, whom I had abandoned, when it had been in my power to save him, whom I later found floating in pieces in a basement flooded in raw sewage. *You are my redemption, the key to the prison of my sin*, Awaale had said. *By saving you, I will save myself from judgment.* At the time, I will confess, I had a distinctly Warthropian reaction to those words. An illogical leap, I thought, from a chance meeting to divine intervention. But are not all leaps of faith by their nature illogical? *Redeem the time*, the stars had sung down to me. I thought of their song while I caressed the child's face.

Redeem the time. If it came to it, I decided, I would leave him here and try to draw them away—an abandonment that this time would not doom but deliver, that would not damn but redeem.

The north wind brought a sound down from the peaks, a high-pitched squeal I can only liken to that of a pig in the slaughterhouse, an ear-piercing shriek that did not strike me as human, and for a terrifying moment I was convinced it was not *Typhoeus's* children, but *Typhoeus* himself who was coming for Kearns's "bait." I pictured the *magnificum* descending the mountainside, pale flesh glistening and covered in wickedly sharp spines, slathering maw agape and dripping shining globs of *pwdre ser*, a black behemoth with twice the reach of a man and three times the height, and a face that was utterly blank, a face that was not a face, the faceless face that caused Pierre Lebroque to cry in the agony of perfect recognition, "*Nullité!* That is all it is! Nothing, nothing, nothing!"

That first shrill call was answered by another, and then another, each from a different direction, and they were drawing closer, the calls coming quicker but in shorter duration, until they resembled the short, hysterical bursts of hyenas on the hunt. Then, abruptly, nothing but the wind. It was terrible sitting there, not knowing what was happening outside. For all I knew, they could have been just outside, waiting for some signal before they sprang. I dropped one hand to the ground and groped about for a rock, a stick, anything I might use as a weapon. In my mind's eye I saw Mr. Kendall leaping down the stairs, his black eyes filling my vision.

And then I heard, very distinctly, a ripping sound and a loud crunch, the way the leg bone of a chicken sounds when you rip it from the carcass. Something—well, more than one *thing*—was sobbing, a horrible, snuffling, hic-cupping kind of wail—the tears of damnation, the bitter despair of the pit, and I knew that they were eating her, tearing her to pieces and stuffing the dripping offal into their mouths, gnashing with fury, chomping with such desperate hunger that more than one had already chewed their own tongues in half. And from his mountain throne *Typhoeus magnificum*, the magnificent father, looked down upon his children, and smiled.

Kearns cried down from his post, giving the waited for signal. I heard only six shots, two from Kearns's rifle, the rest from Warthrop's revolver, but their echoes scampered and skittered along the pass, chasing one another down to the bottom. I cried out softly when a large shadow flitted across the opening, and then I realized it was Awaale, running toward the site of the slaughter. I stood up and went outside. I felt no fear now, only the familiar, sickening curiosity to see what should not be seen, what most would not *want* to see, but what I *had* to see.

There were four bodies where before there had been one, all of them draped over one another in a confusing jumble of limbs. I had to step over a rivulet of blood worming its way down the slope.

"Very nice work, Warthrop," John Kearns was saying. "Four to my two. I'd no idea you were such a fine shot."

"But how can this be?" Awaale said, his voice shaking with revulsion and wonder. "This woman is very old, yet she is heavy with child."

"It isn't a child she's heavy with," said Kearns with a smile. "Stand back, gentlemen, and I will show you."

He pulled a bowie knife from his boot and bent over the old woman, who lay curled on her side, blood pooling beneath her mat of steel gray hair. Kearns did not stab her. He made a quick, shallow incision in her abdomen and then hopped back. The cut pulsed once, and then her stomach blew open with a loud *pop!* spewing a fine, clear mist and a foul-smelling soup of watery blood and atrophied entrails. Kearns laughed heartily and said, "You see? She isn't pregnant. She's just got a terrible case of the winds!"

Awaale turned away in disgust, but Warthrop seemed fascinated by the phenomenon, comparing it to the cases of beached whales whose decomposing bodies fill up with gases produced by certain bacteria in their guts, causing them to literally explode. It explained the blasted-open stomachs and bloody walls and ceiling of the death house in Gishub.

"Either some substance contained in the *pwdre ser* or the body's reaction to the exposure . . . ," Warthrop mused.

"I thought you'd like it. Remember the Russian I told

you about with the obsession with shiny shoes? Happened to him. Hosed down two men while Sidorov was examining him."

The doctor nodded absently. "I don't see your Minotaur."

"No." Kearns sighed. "He escapes my clutches once again. But I'm not finished with him yet. Before this is over, I shall have his head mounted on my study wall, I can assure you of that!"

There followed a lengthy debate between the monstrumologist and Kearns about what we should do next. We were all exhausted and desperately in need of sleep, but Kearns insisted we should quit the scene immediately. He knew of at least one more troop of "rotters" in the general vicinity, and he worried our luck—or our ammunition—might run out. Warthrop reminded Kearns that he had called it "the perfect spot," and the monstrumologist said it was better to lay a trap than risk an ambush.

"There is a cave higher up, about a mile from here," Kearns allowed. "I suppose we could make for that. But it's really best to keep their hours—sleep during the day and hunt at night."

"I understand," Warthrop said. "But we won't make much of the latter if we don't get some of the former! Here, Will Henry, I'll take the child now. Fetch our pack and my instrument case. Kearns and I will take the lead; Will Henry and Awaale in the rear. Quietly now, and quickly."

And that is how we proceeded deeper into the heart of the mountains. The way was not easy, littered with rocks—some as large as a brougham carriage—riven with deep fissures, at times so narrow we were forced to turn sideways and shuffle with our backs against the sheer cliff face while our toes dangled over the crumbly edge a thousand feet above the jagged ground. The air grew thin and cold. The wind pressed down from above and bit harshly at our cheeks. I felt my face grow numb.

"There is an old saying in my country, *walaalo*," Awaale said at one point. "'Do not walk into the snake pit with your eyes open.' I used to puzzle over that proverb. No more!" He laughed softly. "Do you think this viper Kearns may have been sent by God?"

The notion was so absurd, I laughed in spite of myself. "What are you talking about?" I asked.

"The child! Kearns chases him down to where we are, and now I am to bring him safely back to his people."

"Except he said those people would kill him."

Awaale cursed softly, but he was smiling. "I am only saying God might have sent me for the little one—not for you."

"That makes more sense," I replied. "I was going to kill her, Awaale. The gun was an inch from her head and I was pulling the trigger . . ."

"But you did not."

"No. I saw he was feeding, and I panicked."

"Ah. You mean *you* were meant to save him."

"I'm not meant to save anyone!" I snapped. I was suddenly very angry. "I'm here to serve the doctor, who's here to serve . . . to serve science, and that's all. That's *all*."

"Oh, *walaalo*." He sighed. "You are more a pirate than I ever was."

Kearns's cave was actually a warren of small chambers connected by tunnels bored into the rock by a million years of monsoon rains eating their way through tiny cracks in the rocks. Nature is anything but impatient. The deepest chamber was also the largest and probably the safest, but Kearns warned us against bunking there, for it was home to thousands of bats, and their guano was a foot deep on the chamber floor.

It was the bats that woke me the next morning, fluttering over our heads in a dizzying ballet of black and brown, squealing excitedly as they made for their roosts. I was the last to rise, finding the doctor and Awaale sitting outside the cave, the foundling squirming listlessly in Warthrop's lap.

"Where is Dr. Kearns?" I asked.

"Scouting the trail, or at least that's what he said he was going off to do."

"How is the baby?" I asked.

"Hungry," he answered. "And very weak." The child was gnawing on the monstrumologist's knuckle. "But he has no symptoms, and certainly he was exposed through his mother's milk. It suggests he may have some kind of natural immunity." He nodded toward the instrument case beside him. "I have taken samples of his blood. If nothing else comes of this, we may be able to find a cure for the rot of stars, Will Henry."

Kearns returned a few minutes later, carrying his rifle and a small leather satchel. He dug through his small stash of supplies inside the cave and returned with a bundle of rags, which he arranged carefully into a conical pile before setting it on fire. The rags burned hot and bright at first, and then settled into a smoldering mound.

"There's no decent wood in these mountains for a proper fire," he said. He dug into his satchel and removed three dead spiders—the largest I had ever seen, bigger than Awaale's enormous hand—and dropped them into the middle of the smoking ashes. "Solifugae—camel spiders. You must try one, Pellinore. I've developed somewhat of a taste for them."

"How far is it to the nesting grounds?" asked my master, ignoring Kearns's suggestion.

"Not far. Half a day if we don't stop to rest and the mountain is in a good mood. It has moods, you know. Yesterday it was very angry, stomping and puffing its stony cheeks. He is very prideful, and quick to anger. Not unlike a certain scientist I know."

"The child is starving," Awaale said, his patience with Kearns wilting. "I must leave at once for Hoq. Do you know the way?"

"I do." Kearns stabbed one of the spiders with the tip

of his knife and crammed the entire blackened wad into his mouth. A bit of greenish-yellow juice rolled down his chin. He wiped it away with the back of his hand, chewing thoughtfully. "But I wish you'd reconsider. Your services would be much more valuable to us, and as I've said, the villagers' first duty is to protect themselves from potential carriers. They will kill the child . . . and probably anyone who bears it."

Awaale stiffened and stuck out his huge chest. "Do you think I am afraid?"

"No, I think you're stupid."

"Hope is not stupid. Faith is not stupid."

"You left out charity," Kearns said with a wicked smile.

"That is enough, Kearns," said the monstrumologist wearily. "I am in agreement with Awaale. It is true; the child may be doomed. It is also true that without Awaale we may be doomed. But the alternative is worse. It is no alternative, really."

Warthrop rose to his feet. He seemed to tower over us, as tall and impregnable as the soaring peaks encircling the camp, a colossus hewn from flesh and blood, against which the mighty bones of the earth seemed puny.

"You may have fallen long ago over the edge of the world, John, but I have not. Not yet anyway. To show mercy is not naïve. To hold out against the end of hope is not stupidity or madness. It is fundamentally human. Of course the child is doomed. We are all doomed; we are all poisoned from our birth by the rot of stars. That does not mean we should succumb like you to the seductive fallacy of despair, the dark tide that would drown us. You may think I'm stupid, you may call me a madman and a fool, but at least I stand upright in a fallen world. At least I have yet, like you, to fall off the edge into the abyss.

"Now bring me to it, so I might confess with my lips what I have seen with my eyes. The time has come to redeem the time, so bring me to it, damn you. Bring me to the *magnificum*."

FORTY-ONE

"The Angel of Death"

Awaale and the child parted our company not long thereafter, with nothing more than one day's rations and ammunition for the rifle. "If you hurry, you might make it to the caves
before nightfall," Kearns told him. He sketched out a crude
map on a slip of paper and handed it to the Somali. "But if
night catches you and you run across my Minotaur, remember that I am Theseus in this little drama and you are . . .
Well, I'm not sure who you are."

"Shut up," Awaale said.

"You're a dead man," Kearns returned cheerfully. "On a
fool's errand."

"And you are a fool with a dead man's heart," Awaale
retorted. He drew me aside and said, "I have something
for you, *walaalo*." He pulled out his long knife and pressed

it into my hand. "I will not tell you that it will bring you luck—it is the knife I used to sacrifice the one I loved—but who knows? You may redeem its blade with the blood of the wicked." He glowered at Kearns. "No, no, you must keep it. I cannot leave without giving you a present, *walaalo*. I will see you in Gishub before long, so I will not say good-bye!"

He turned to Warthrop, who said simply, "Don't fail."

"You are hard man, *dhaktar* Pellinore Warthrop. Hard to understand and harder still to like. I will not fail."

He shouldered his rifle, accepted Warthrop's burden— the baby looked impossibly small in his massive arms— and headed up the trail. We watched him until he stepped around the bend and was gone.

To the top John Kearns led us now, to the very summit of the abyss, over deep drops and shadow-stuffed ravines, up craggy edifices where every handhold was precarious and every step fraught with peril, around heaps of shattered stone and deep pools of crystalline water reflecting back the empty sky, along terraced ledges thrust out like balconies overlooking the Diksam Plateau, an empty, featureless land-scape two thousand feet beneath us. It was cold, and the air plunged into our lungs like the sharp blade of Awaale's knife.

The clouds arrived at midmorning, swallowing the mountaintops, sliding swiftly and silently a hundred feet over our heads like a great white door slamming closed. And still higher we climbed, until I could reach up with my hand

and touch the misty belly of the clouds. We came to a level spot in the trail, and there Kearns abruptly stopped, hands on his hips, head bowed, pulling hard for air.

"What is it?" Warthrop demanded. "Are you lost?"

Kearns shook his head. "Tired. I have to rest."

He sank to the ground and fished about in his sack for a canteen. Warthrop could hardly contain himself. He paced the area, at times coming dangerously close to stepping over the edge and tumbling into the empty air.

"How much farther?" he asked.

"Five hundred feet . . . six?" Kearns shook his head. "Still haven't figured out *how* the poor bastards do it, much less *why*."

"Who? How they do what?"

"The rotters. Some protohuman instinct, I suppose. Get to the highest point before you pop . . ." He shrugged.

Warthrop was shaking his head. "I don't understand."

Kearns looked up at him and said in a voice drained of all playfulness, "You will."

We entered the clouds, and the world dissolved into a spinning white nothingness, the complete abnegation of color, and we but wraithlike shades, shapes without substance, forms without dimensions. I walked very close to the doctor; another foot or two between us and I would have lost him in the void. The wind whipped around the mountain and slammed into our backs. I was terrified it would push me right off the edge. I lost all sense of time. Time did not exist here at the summit of the abyss. A million years was the same as a minute.

An eight-foot-high rock wall rose out of the mist directly in front of us. We had come to the end, the doorstep of the Magnificent Father's abode, the nesting grounds of the *magnificum*.

The moment my master had longed for and dreaded had come. The monstrumologist rushed forward. I've no doubt that if Kearns—or even I—had tried to stop him, he would have flung him over the side of the mountain. He paused only long enough to don a fresh pair of gloves before slapping his hands over the top of the wall and heaving himself up with a kick against the side. He disappeared into the fog.

"Well?" Kearns said softly to me. "Aren't you going up?"

"Dr. Kearns," I whispered. "What is the *magnificum*?"

"You're a very sharp lad, Will. Surely you've discerned his face by now."

I flinched when he touched me lightly on the cheek. His gray eyes sparkled.

"They may be a different color, but we've the same eyes, Master William Henry, you and I. *Oculus Dei*—the eyes that are not afraid to look, that see where others are blind."

I pulled away. "I don't know what you're talking about."

"Do you not? In the beginning man made God in his image, and God saw that it was good. You agreed with me about the child. Don't deny it; I saw it in your eyes. Your eyes have come open, haven't they? It's why he keeps you with him, because you see in the dark places where he is afraid to look. So don't ask me what is the *magnificum*. The question insults my intelligence."

He knelt before me and held out his cupped hands.

"Come on, then; I'll give you a boost. He is in a dark place and he needs you to be his eyes."

I stepped into Kearns's hands and he lifted me up and over the wall.

I was standing upon the rim of a vast cave whose roof and walls had given way after a millennium of rain and wind and earthquakes. Gigantic slabs of the collapsed chamber littered the ground. Interspersed among the boulders were the remains of stalagmites, polished to a glimmering finish by the monsoons, some worn down by the relentless wind to foot-high nubs, others rising to twice my height, their tips as sharp as their bases were wide. They reminded me of the bony spikes erupting from Mr. Kendall's face.

I did not see the doctor. He was hidden in the swirling white. I saw the mountain's glittering teeth and its broken bones, and then a few feet farther in I came across the first body, badly decayed and picked over by scavengers, its gut blown apart, the cavity like a great black yawning mouth. Half of its face had been stripped away, and in one empty eye socket a scorpion snuggly nestled. A gust of wind tugged at the remnants of the papery flesh that still clung to its bones, and a few pieces tore away, rocketing aloft, like hot ash in the superheated air of a fire.

Behind me I heard Kearns say, "This is his mouth. When *Typhoeus*'s children sense the end has come, they drag their rotting, bloated bodies to this spot at the top of the world, where they explode—some after they've died, some before. I have seen the breathing corpses of his children blow apart with the force of a grenade. . . . And the winds come down. They scoop up the bloody viscera and carry it for miles until it falls as red rain from a clear, blue sky."

He drew me forward, the curtain of mist pulled back, and I saw hundreds of bodies frozen in the agony of death, crumpled between the rocks, strewn around the shining, sharp columns, growing more numerous as we went, until it was nearly impossible not to step on them. We picked our way carefully through the *magnificum*'s bountiful harvest, and the thin air was heavy with the rich smell of rot rising from the threshing floor.

We came to a shallow indention in the earth, the remains of an ancient cavernous pond. Kearns pointed out the kneeling, bent-backed shapes of the still living scattered throughout the dry lake bed, each sitting beside a dead brethren, all worrying with something cradled in their laps. Kearns pressed a finger against his lips to signal for silence. He crouched down, motioned for me to follow suit, and proceeded to lead me along the shore of the sterile pit. He brought me close— but not too close—to a kneeling man whose face had been smashed apart by the horns of bone growing from his skull, whose black eyes lacked any white in them, whose mouth hung open to reveal a bewildering profusion of thorn-like growths, and whose suppurating fingers picked and plucked with exquisite delicacy at the exquisitely delicate object resting between his legs. I did not know it then, but this human wreckage had once been a man named Anton Sidorov.

"These are his hands," Kearns murmured into my ear. "The hands of the *magnificum*. It's very curious to me; I don't understand what compels them to build the *nidus*, but they'll work for days without rest, until the moment they succumb."

The maker of the *nidus* was crying. From deep in his throat there issued a whimpering, an inarticulate, protest-ing whine, as if the irresistible force that drove him also repulsed him, and the tension between them—the *him* and *not-him*—could break a world in half.

"Do you hear it, Will?" whispered Kearns excitedly. "That is the voice of the *magnificum*, the last sound at the end of the world."

The once-Sidorov reached down to the desecrated body curled at his side and pulled its lifeless left hand to his chest. With an anguished sob the un-Sidorov snapped off the index finger. It pulled free from the corpse's hand with a soft crunch. He bent down again to incorporate the digit into the "nest."

The kneeling child of *Typhoeus* grunted sharply, his back arched, his mouth yawned open, and a viscous stream of clear fluid erupted from his mouth and poured onto his work. Not the rot of stars. Not the spit of monsters. Not *pwdre ser* but *pwdre ddynoliaeth*—the rot of humanity.

And John Kearns whispered into my ear: "Do you see it now? *You* are the nest. *You* are the hatchling. *You* are the chrysalis. *You* are the progeny. *You* are the rot that falls from stars. All of us—you and I and poor, dear Pellinore. Behold the face of the *magnificum*, child. And despair."

Though I was sickened by the sight, I looked. In the bower of the beast at the top of the world, I beheld the face of the *magnificum*, and I did not turn away.

Behind us a gunshot rang out, the retort no louder than a popgun's in the thin air. We whirled around. In the drifting mist I made out the shape of a tall man striding across the lake bed. He walked up to one of the kneeling figures and shot it point-blank in the back of the head. Then he walked on, stepping over the fallen as he went, till he reached the next one, whom he executed in the same manner. The monstrumologist paused only once in his rounds—to reload the revolver. He worked his way around the entire cavity, his actions methodical and eerily unhesitant—walk over to the kneeling victim, stop, blast apart his head, move on to the next.

You have given yourself in service to ha-Mashchit, *the destroyer, the angel of death.*

I stood up when Sidorov's turn came, but Warthrop said nothing as he passed. He walked straight to the mindless artisan, raised the gun, and put a bullet into what was left of his brain.

He walked back to us, and the fog melted before him, burned away by the cold fire that roared in his eyes. I did not recognize him, this man with the tangled beard and long, wind-teased hair and eyes whose icy flame could freeze the sun. I do not know how to refer to the man who now strode toward us. I cannot call him Pellinore Warthrop or "the monstrumologist" or "the doctor," for he was not the same man who had attained the summit of the abyss, the *locus ex magnificum*, the beating heart of the nameless unwinding thing one ten-thousandth of an inch outside our range of vision.

The stranger seized Kearns by the collar and said, "Where is it? Where is the *magnificum*?"

"Have you not eyes? Open them, and see."

I heard a sharp click—the hammer drawing back. I saw a flash of black—the barrel coming round.

Kearns barely flinched. "Pull that trigger, and you'll never get out of these mountains alive."

"*Where is it?*" Finger quivering on the trigger.

"Ask Will Henry. He's just a boy, and he sees it. You're the monstrumologist; how is it that you cannot? Look at it, Pellinore. Turn and see! The Faceless One. The *Faceless* One. You have been pursuing something that has been right in front of you since the beginning. There is no monster. There are only men."

He might have killed John Kearns then. He had come to that place—the same place, here at the top of the world, where, at its center, I had stood. I will tell you honestly that it is not very hard to kill a man in that place. It takes hardly any thought at all. It is the place of the unwinding, the place where hunter meets monster and sees in its face his own reflected. It is the place where desire meets despair.

I had to stop him. I said, "He's right, sir. We need him."

He did not look at me. Though I stood right next to him, he was alone in that place. I pulled on his arm; it felt like iron beneath my fingers.

"Dr. Warthrop, please, listen. You can't. You can't."

"You're lying," he shouted into Kearns's face. "This is another of your damnable tricks. You think it's funny to make a fool of me—"

"Oh, you don't need my help for *that*," Kearns responded, laughing. "Of course I would love to take the credit for our penchant to put a monster's face on all things monstrous. It's comforting, in a way, to think a big dragon drags us up into the sky and rips us to shreds or that some gigantic spider weaves her nest from our leavings. If we're going to be put in our place in the grand scheme of things, why, it had better damn well be from something *impressive*."

The doctor's hand had begun to shake. I was afraid he might pull the trigger accidently.

"There is . . . nothing," Warthrop said hesitantly, echoing the anguished *Nullité!* of Pierre Lebroque.

"Nothing!" cried Kearns in mock astonishment. "Tell that to poor Sidorov, or to that shredded-up piece of clay beside him. Tell it to those poor buggers in Gishub or the mother who lost her child or the child who lost his mother! Tell it to the czar and those of his ilk who would tame the *magnificum* to subdue the world! Really, Pellinore, what sort of monstrumologist are you? A contagion with the potential to wipe out the entire human species—and you call it *nothing!*"

Warthrop's hand fell away. He sank to the ground, overwhelmed by the enormity of his folly. The dark tide swept over him and bore him down to its crushing, lightless depths. Kearns was right. The signs had been all around the doctor since the beginning—from the jelly-filled sacks in Mr. Kendall's stomach to the blasted-open corpses in Gishub—but he had turned away. He had not forced himself to look upon the true face of the *magnificum*, and now the blood of those who had sacrificed their lives upon the altar of his ambition cried to heaven against him.

I knelt beside him. "Dr. Warthrop? Dr. Warthrop, sir, we can't stay here."

"Why not?" he cried. "It's good enough for *them*." He swept his arm across the blasted mountaintop. He looked up at me, and I saw nothing but ashes in his eyes; the cold fire had gone out. "You said it yourself at Harrington Lane. What they are I am inside. I am their brother, Will Henry. I am their brother, and I will not leave them."

FORTY-TWO
"Fundamentally Human"

There was no moving him. I begged, I coaxed, I appealed to his reason, the one thing to which he always clung, no matter how strongly the dark tide pulled him down. He would not budge—or, I should say, the dark unwinding thing in his heart would not loosen its grip. He did not seem to hear me, or perhaps my words sounded to him like mere gibberish, incoherent ranting that made no more sense than the cackling of a chimpanzee. I looked around for Kearns, thinking our situation must be desperate that I would turn to *him* for help, but Kearns had vanished into the mist. Gently, so as not to startle the doctor, I eased the gun from his trembling hand; I was afraid he might discharge it and blow off his foot.

The swirling white cloud had grown thick around us. I could see no more than a few feet in any direction, and I heard no sound but the wind whistling between the mountain's broken teeth, and my own ragged breath. I stood up, unnerved and disoriented, turning in a slow circle, a panicky voice whispering inside my head, *Where is Kearns? Where did he go? Why did he go?* as my finger caressed the trigger. What was that in the mist? Was it a stalagmite or the shape of a once-human child of *Typhoeus*, looming out of the blurring white? I pointed the gun at it and called out Kearns's name.

Something a ten-thousandth of an inch outside my range of vision rocketed toward me, slamming into the middle of my back and hurling me head over heels toward the shallow bowl in the center of *Typhoeus's* ruined throne. The impact knocked the wind out of my lungs, and the doctor's gun out of my hand. I landed on my back and rolled over, coming up to face the leering, desiccated remains of a living corpse, a human sack of poison, its gut filled with star rot, its explosion of thorny teeth glistening in the anemic light of a suffocated sun. I scrambled backward as it lunged forward, my cries of terror and its cries of rage warring with the high-pitched grinding of the wind against the ageless stone. I jammed my hand into my jacket pocket for Awaale's knife. The cold steel sliced open my palm as I fumbled for the handle. The monster's mouth yawned wide when it smelled my blood; I could see my reflection captured in its black, unblinking eyes.

I retreated; it came on. The knife was in my hand now, and its wooden handle was slippery with my blood. I could feel the blood weeping from the wound to the rhythm of my galloping heart. Time itself began to jiggle and come apart, and we slipped into the space between spaces, the child of *Typhoeus* and I, skittering together upon the precipice while on either side was the depthless divide, the pit without bottom, *das Ungeheuer*. Its mouth stretched so wide, the hinges of its jaws tore apart. The tendons ripped with a wet *pop!*, and then the entire lower half of its face fell off and was trammeled beneath its shuffling feet. It reached for me, flexing its fingers, its sharp yellow nails clicking. I swung wildly at what was left of its face; the knife, slick with blood, flew from my grip; and then the thing was upon me.

I reacted without thinking. For more than two years I had stood by the monstrumologist's side at the necropsy table. Human anatomy was as familiar to me as the lines on my master's face. I knew precisely where to find the organ that powered the mortal engine. I could see it now, pounding furiously against the thin covering of decaying skin, and it beat in time with my own, in that space between spaces, upon that dizzying precipice above the abyss.

I punched my hand into its torso with all the force I could muster, just below the rib cage, and forced my fist deep into the center of the beast, my four outspread fingers digging up past the liver and between the laboring lungs until I was elbow-deep in its guts and my clawing hand found its heart.

And I crushed it with my bare hand. My fingers burst through the chambers of its heart. The beast's weight came down upon me. We sank to our knees together, its black eyes

boring into mine as its blood poured out the cavity I had made. I yanked my arm free with a disgusted sob and rolled away from it. Its hand slapped at the earth, once, twice, and was still.

I was crying hysterically, scrambling about for the knife, my right hand coated in my blood, my left in its, thinking, *Done, done, done, you've done it now. You've poisoned yourself with it; the* pwdre ser, *it's all over you. Done, done, done.*

I found the knife, stood up, and called the doctor's name, but the words were caught in my throat, and what little sound I made was snatched by the wind and whipped away like the blasted remains of the *magnificum*'s victims scattered all around me. I had lost all sense of direction in the fog. It seemed the ancient lake bed spread out to infinity; there was no horizon for Mihos to guard.

And then I turned and saw them shambling toward me, dozens of them, black shadows against the spinning white, their screeches of pain and rage akin to those of animals in the slaughterhouse. *The blood draws them,* Kearns had said. *They can smell it for miles.* If I stood my ground, I would be overrun. If I ran, the blood would lead them right to me.

For an eternity I stood in indecisive torment. There was no fighting it; there was no running from it. It was already in me; I was already one of *them.* Better to let them take me here, from without, than to allow *it* to devour me from within.

I stood upon the shore of a dead sea, and there were two doors before me. Behind one, a savage beast that would rip me to shreds. Behind the other, a monster of a thousand faces that would make my face one of his. That is the *magnificum*. Ours is the face of the beast.

Nil timendum est. "Fear nothing." The motto of my master could be interpreted two ways. There was Jacob Torrance's interpretation, and then there was Pierre Lebroque's. But we are more than the sum of our fears. We are greater than the gravity of the abyss. I had come to that terrible place for one reason and only one reason:

Why the devil are you going again?

To save the doctor.

Save him from what?

Whatever he needs saving from. I'm his apprentice.

I tore through the roiling mist, screaming his name, and the teeth sprung up from the ground, and the broken bones crunched beneath my feet, and the mist spat them out, the once-human hands and teeth of the *magnificum*, their arms opened wide to receive me, their new brother. I thought I heard gunfire off to my right and stumbled toward the sound, thrashing my arms as if I could wave away the fog. And then I stepped into empty air; I had come back to the ledge, the eight-foot-high wall at the end of the path leading to the *magnificum*'s roost. For an awful instant I teetered upon the edge, flailing my arms uselessly to regain my balance, before gravity took me down.

I tucked my shoulder instinctively and hit the ground below in a roll. I rose with a cry of frustrated rage and leapt at the wall, but it was too high. I heard my pursuers then, their screams a deeper, throatier echo of my own, and I backed away, holding the knife with both hands in front of me and slicing it back and forth. Oh, what a ridiculous and pitiful sight I must have been!

And this voice, agreeing: *What are you doing, Will Henry? You can't go back for him. You are* nasu. *You will give the infection to him—or hand him over to the beasts chasing you. It is too late for you. But not for him.*

I cried out his name once more before I fled down the path, taking the contagion with me, away from him.

I emerged from the clouds and beheld the world laid out before me, brown and black and shades of gray, and I prayed that the living corpses would follow the blood-smell that rose from my skin. I prayed that they would follow me down, their unclean brother, to their fate. The path diverged; I choose the steepest, thinking it would bring me down quicker to the plain. I had a vague idea I would lead them to Gishub, the city of the dead by the sea. It was not the way we had ascended, and at spots the path was nearly impassable, littered with huge boulders that left barely enough room for me to squeeze past. The wound in my right hand throbbed horribly, the bleeding would not stop, and my left hand was growing numb. *That's how it starts*, I thought, remembering the doctor's lecture to Mr. Kendall. First the numbness, then the aches in the joints, then the eyes, then . . .

I came to a sharp bend in the path. I turned the corner

and stopped, for the way was blocked by a large pool of the clearest water I'd ever seen. Protected from the wind by the soaring peaks surrounding it, the water's surface was unperturbed by the slightest ripple, reflecting back to the brooding clouds their own gray faces.

I was exhausted. I was at the end of it, the end of all of it, and I wept by the water's edge.

And the clouds raced across the sky above the undefiled water.

And I raised up my head and peered into the mirror, and there was my face looking back at me.

Without thinking I stood up and tore off my jacket. I stripped off my shirt. I strode into the water.

I walked until the water lapped against my chest, and then I kept walking until it kissed the underside of my jaw. I was surprised how cold it was. I closed my eyes and ducked beneath the surface. There was the wind and the clouds and the pure pool and the boy beneath its unsettled surface, and the blood, the boy's and the monster's, defiling the pool.

I am nasu *now.*

I came out of the water and threw myself back upon the ground. I was shivering uncontrollably; I had no feeling in my left arm. My neck was stiff and my eyes felt very dry. The hour was late.

The day was dying, and so was I.

To hold out against the end of hope is not stupidity or madness, the monstrumologist had said. *It is fundamentally human.*

I sat with my back against the mountain, Awaale's knife cradled in my lap.

The knife was very sharp. Its edge was stained with my blood.

I will not tell you that it will bring you luck—it is the knife I used to sacrifice the one I loved—but who knows? You may redeem its blade with the blood of the wicked.

Two doors: I might wait for death to come in its own time—or I could choose the time. I could perish a monster or I could die as a human being.

We are the sons of Adam. It is in our nature to turn and face the faceless thing.

The day was dying, and yet the world seemed dazzlingly bright, and my eyes gathered in the smallest detail with astounding clarity.

It is called Oculus Dei . . . *the eyes of God.*

It had found me out at last, *Typhoeus*, the Faceless One of a Thousand Faces.

I was the nest.

I was the hatchling.

I was the rot that falls from stars.

Now you understand what I mean.

Night fell upon the Isle of Blood, but no darkness crowded my eyes. Mine were the eyes of God now, and nothing was hidden from me, not the smallest speck of matter. I could see through the mountains. I could see clear through to the burning heart of the earth. The wind drove the clouds away, and the stars were an arm's length away; if I wanted, I could reach up and pluck them from the sky. I was numb; there was nothing I did not feel. I felt the contagion worming into the walls of my cells, taking residence in the synapses of my brain. There was no sound I did not hear. I heard the beating of a butterfly's wing in an English meadow and the soft singing of Mrs. Bates to her son.

I still held the knife. I would not wait for the moment that the doctor had said would come—*When everyone else is dead or has run off, he turns upon himself and feeds from his own body....*

"I'm sorry, Dr. Warthrop," I whimpered. "I'm sorry, sir."

I had failed him and I had saved him. I had gone down to the darkness that he might live in the light.

I think you are lonely a great deal of the time.

I set down the knife and dug into my pocket for her photograph.

It's for luck, she had said, *and for when you get lonely.*

I eased it out of my pocket; it had gotten wet, and the paper was soft. The last time I had seen Lilly, I'd had the urge to kiss her. Some of us never learn the difference between urge and inspiration.

I picked up the knife again. In one hand Awaale's gift, and Lilly's in the other.

I think you are lonely a great deal of the time.

I heard them coming long before I saw them. I heard the
bones of the earth snap and crunch beneath their feet, and I
heard their labored breath and I heard their anxious hearts
in the spaces between their ribs. I turned my head and saw
Kearns first, and his voice was the width of a fingernail from
my ear, "Here, Pellinore; I found him!" He slung his rifle
over his shoulder and hurried over, and then I saw the doctor racing past the water's edge, and his hand shot out and
shoved Kearns out of the way.

"Don't touch me!" I cried. "It's too late, Doctor, too late,
don't touch me, too late!"

"I told you one of the buggers got him," Kearns said, and
the monstrumologist cursed him and told him to be quiet.

He opened his instrument case, donned a pair of gloves,
murmuring to me all the while, telling me to relax, to stay
calm, he was here now, and he had not forgotten his promise,
and I wondered what promise he was talking about as he
felt my pulse and shined a light into my eyes. My lips drew
back in a snarl of pain and anger when the light struck. With
shaking hands Warthrop carefully withdrew a vial of blood
from his case. It was one of the samples he had extracted
from the baby. The yellowish-white serum had separated
out from the coagulated blood and now floated on top, suspended above the deep crimson. The doctor pressed the vial

into Kearns's hand and instructed him to hold it very still while he loaded the syringe.

"What the devil are you doing?" Kearns asked.

"I am attempting to slay a dragon," answered the monstrumologist, and then he plunged the needle into my arm.

FORTY-THREE

"Lessons of the Unintended Kind"

Throughout the night he remained by my side, the man I kept human, battling to keep me human. He did not sleep that night or for the two that followed. Occasionally I would fall into a fitful, feverish doze, and when I woke, there he would be, watching over me. My dreams were terrible, filled with shadows and blood, and he would literally pull me out of them, shaking me roughly and saying, "Snap to, Will Henry. It was a dream. Only a dream."

My symptoms did not immediately disappear. For two days the light scorched my eyes, and he would prepare compresses soaked in the cold lake water to lay over them. While the numbness in my other extremities slowly faded, my left arm had lost all sensitivity. He forced me to drink copiously, though the tiniest morsels made my stomach heave in protest.

Once I gave in to despair. It was too late. The serum was not working. I had seen the face of the Faceless One, and it was *my* face.

To which the monstrumologist replied fiercely, "Do you remember what I told you in Aden, Will Henry? Not by numbers or force of arms." He seized my hand and squeezed it. "By this . . . by *this*."

On the morning of the third day I was able to open my eyes a little, though tears of protest streaked down my cheeks, and I actually had an appetite. While my delighted caretaker dug into our bag of provisions, I looked about for Kearns. I could not remember seeing much of him.

"Where is Dr. Kearns?" I asked.

The doctor waved his hand toward the mountaintop. "Playing Theseus, looking for his Minotaur. He's become quite obsessed with it. It offends his estimation of himself as a tracker par excellence."

"Are we . . . Is it safe here, Dr. Warthrop?"

"Safe?" He was frowning. "Well, that is always a matter of degree, Will Henry. Is it as safe as *Meister* Abram's brownstone? Probably not. But the worst is over, I would say. There may be a few of the infected still wandering about up here, though I doubt any are left in the plains or coastal regions. The natives are well acquainted with *Typhoeus*, and when an outbreak occurs, they isolate the infected villages and take to the caves until it burns itself out. *Pwdre ser* loses its potency over time, as I think I've told you, and the monsoon rains wash the remnants to the sea. I suspect the contagion emerged in Gishub and spread from there. Kearns informed me it was a fisherman—a boy around your age, actually—who was first exposed, probably on one of the smaller islands, and he gave—or, mostly likely, sold—his gruesome discovery to Yeoman Stowe."

"So there is no monster," I said. "There never was."

"Really, Will Henry? What do you want in a monster, anyway?" he asked. "Size? The *magnificum* was the size of Socotra with the potential to grow as large as the world. An insatiable appetite for human flesh? You have experienced firsthand how ravenous it is. A grotesque appearance? Name something—anything!—more grotesque than what we have seen on this island. No, the *magnificum* is worthy of the name—a dragon by function, though, not—as we'd supposed—by design." He patted his instrument case, where he had carefully packed the remaining samples of the baby's blood. "And I have it in my power to slay it."

He rose and walked the few steps to the water's edge, and the man in the glassy surface gazed upward into the monstrumologist's eyes.

"It nearly undid me," he said pensively. It struck me as an exceedingly odd thing to say to the one recuperating from its terrible bite. I did not realize he was referring to an entirely different monster.

"My ambition bore me up like the wings of Icarus," he

said. "And when the truth of the *magnificum* burned those wings away, I fell. I fell very far. And I did not fall alone."

He turned to me. "When you were attacked and I lost you in the melee, it . . . broke something in me. As if I'd been rudely shaken from a deep sleep. In short . . ." He noisily cleared his throat and looked away. "It reminded me of why I became a monstrumologist in the first place."

"Why did you?" I asked.

"Why do you think?" he returned testily. "To save the world, of course. And then, at some point, as with most self-appointed saviors, it became about saving myself. Neither goal is entirely realistic. I cannot save the world, and I don't care much anymore about saving me . . . but I do care very much about . . ."

He returned to sit beside me. I saw something in his hand. It was Lilly's photograph.

"And now I must ask you about this," he said. His tone was grave.

"It's nothing," I said, reaching for it. He held it just beyond my grasp.

"*Nullité?*" he asked. "Nothing?"

"Yes. It's . . . She gave it to me . . ."

"Who gave it to you? When?"

"Lilly. Lilly Bates, Dr. von Helrung's great-niece. Before I left for London."

"And why did she give it to you?"

"I don't know."

"You don't know?"

"She said it would bring me luck."

"Ah. Luck. Then, you *did* know why she gave it to you."

"I don't like her very much."

"Oh, no. Of course not."

"Can I have it back now?" I asked.

"You mean '*May* I have it back now.'"

"May I?"

"Have you fallen in love, Will Henry?"

"That's stupid."

"What is? Love or my question?"

"I don't know."

"You don't know? You've tried that trick once. Why do you suppose it will work better the second time?"

"I don't love her. She bothers me."

"You have just defined the very thing you denied."

He stared at her face in the photograph with a curious expression, the naturalist stumbling upon a strange new species.

"Well, she is pretty, I suppose," he said. "And you are getting older, and there are some contagions for which we will never find a cure."

He handed the photograph back to me. "I told you once never to fall in love. Do you think that was wise advice or self-serving manipulation?"

"I don't know."

He nodded. "I don't either."

Kearns returned at dusk with a fresh catch of camel spiders and a chip on his shoulder. For Kearns, he was downright sullen.

"Bagged only three today," he said. "This isn't a hunt; it's a turkey shoot."

"Except they are not turkeys and we are not hunting them," replied the doctor. "We are ending their agony and preventing the spread of a deadly disease."

"Oh, you're always desperate to be so bloody *noble*." Kearns glanced at me. "Are you cured?"

"It appears so," Warthrop answered for me. He preferred to limit Kearns's interaction with me, as if he feared an altogether different sort of contagion.

"Then, shouldn't we be using what you have to cure them and not be slaughtering them like cows?"

"Human beings are not cows," retorted the doctor, echoing his old master. "I've only two vials of sera. These vials must be preserved in order to replicate the antidote."

"You realize you are talking out of both sides of your mouth, Pellinore. You didn't worry about preserving the antidote when it came to your assistant here."

"And you really should avoid mimicking the voice of conscience, Kearns. It rings hollow, like someone attempting to speak in a language he does not understand."

Smiling mischievously, Kearns stuffed a whole spider into his mouth. The monstrumologist turned his head away in disgust.

✳

The doctor had designed a brutally efficient protocol to finish the grisly work of eradicating the *magnificum* from the island. We set up camp at a spot that provided good cover and some shelter from the elements, a few hundred feet below the clouds that enveloped the nesting grounds. We kept our quarry's hours, sleeping by day and luring them into the killing zone by night.

Fire was our bait. It drew them in, and Warthrop and Kearns would hide behind an outcropping or a boulder and pick them off as they crept into the circle of light. The bodies from the night before were used for fuel for the next night's fire.

It was grim, grisly work. There was no thrill of the chase, no near brushes with death. There was just death.

This was the somber side of monstrumology, heroism of the grittiest kind, the labor in darkness that the rest might live in the light. It began to take its toll on my master. He stopped eating. He slept only a few minutes at a stretch, and then would be up again, staring into the distance with eyes that had taken on a desperate, haunted look, like a man caught between two unthinkable alternatives.

Kearns was not faring much better. He complained constantly that he still had not found his Minotaur and this was far from the epic quest he had envisioned.

"Come now, Pellinore. Surely we could make this more fun," he said late one night. Not a single victim had wandered into our trap. "We could split up—make a game of it. Whoever bags the most wins the prize."

"Leave us if you like, Kearns," Warthrop said wearily. "In fact, I wish you would."

"You're being very unfair, Pellinore. It isn't my fault, you know. I didn't invent the myth of the *magnificum*."

"No, you just used it to turn a profit."

"And you would have used it to profit your reputation and take revenge upon your rivals. All hail the great scientist, the self-righteous knight who brought home the grail to Christendom, Pellinore the Pure, Pellinore the Proud, Pellinore the Magnificent!'" He laughed merrily. "As motives go, mine was by far the most pure."

"Leave him alone!" I snapped at him. I wanted to take Awaale's knife and slice off that insufferable smirk. "It's *your* fault—all of it! He almost died because of you!"

"What are you talking about, boy? The Russians? I didn't tell the Russians to kill Pellinore. That was their idea."

"You sent him the *nidus*."

"For safekeeping, and you should thank me that I did it."

"I should kill you, is what I should do!"

His eyebrows rose in surprise. "Well! Aren't we the bloodthirsty little savage? What have you been teaching this child, Pellinore?"

The monstrumologist shook his head ruefully. "Lessons of the unintended kind."

For a week we labored in the vineyards of the dead. After two nights without a sighting, Kearns began to talk of returning to Gishub, where we would await the arrival of the *Dagmar*.

"I suppose I must give up on my Minotaur." He pouted. "But all things—even the best of things—must eventually come to an end."

A troubled look passed over the doctor's face. He pulled me out of Kearns's earshot and whispered, "I have made a terrible mistake, Will Henry."

"No, you didn't," I whispered back. "Everyone thought the *magnificum* was real—"

"Shhh! I'm not talking about the *magnificum*." He glanced toward the ledge upon which Kearns lay hidden. "I don't know what he's waiting for. Perhaps his mind is divided; perhaps he still retains some vestige of his humanity, though I'm hard-pressed to see much evidence of that. Most likely the opportune moment simply has yet to present itself."

He smiled grimly at my startled expression. "He has to kill me. Well, you too, of course—both of us. What choice does he have? He's trapped here until the end of the monsoon, and even then he will find it difficult to escape. To whom can he turn for help? The only port on the island is controlled by the British, but he's wanted by them for murder and treason. The Russians? They will hold him accountable for the expedition's debacle and will seek retribution. Stay and be hunted—or risk escape and be arrested."

"But that's why he won't kill us," I argued. "He needs us to escape."

"Does he? He knows when and where we will be rendezvousing with the *Dagmar*. That was my terrible mistake, telling him that. All he has to do is inform Captain Russell that you and I were lost or killed on the hunt. And then John Kearns is free to go anywhere he wants, become anyone he wants. He will melt back into the human family with his human mask—and life—intact."

I was quiet for a moment, thinking it through, worrying with it, trying to poke holes in his argument. I decided it was useless and focused instead on finding a solution.

"We could hit him over the head, knock him out, tie him up. . . . Or wait till he falls asleep . . ."

The doctor was nodding. "Yes, of course. It's the only way. He has to sleep sometime. . . ." His voice trailed off. The haunted look of the past few days flitted across his countenance. "Well, we can't tie him up. That would be a death sentence, and a particularly cruel one at that."

"Then, we hit him over the head and take his rifle."

"Why do you insist on hitting him over the head? We merely have to wait for him to fall asleep to take his rifle."

"Then, that's what we do. Wait till he falls asleep and take his rifle."

"And then . . . what? Take him prisoner?" he asked.

"We can turn him over to the British."

"Who will then question him about Arkwright, and

you will be arrested for complicity in his murder—von Helrung, too."

"He said he didn't know Arkwright."

Warthrop gave me a withering look. "Why is it, Will Henry, that at the precise moment when I begin to think you might actually have a head on your shoulders, you say something like that?"

"Then, we don't turn him over to anyone. We hold him until we board the *Dagmar*, and then we leave him here."

The monstrumologist was nodding, but he still seemed troubled. "Yes. It's the only acceptable alternative. When our work is finished, we'll spring the trap."

I did not ask, *The only acceptable alternative to what?* I did not need to.

It was close to dawn on the last night of our bitter harvest, and so far only one of the stricken had stumbled into our trap. Kearns shot him, and then pushed the body onto its back and stared down with disappointment at its face.

"Where *is* he?" he wondered aloud. "Where is my Minotaur?"

"Dead, I'd guess," answered Warthrop.

"Oh, don't say that! Should I fail to take him, I would feel the entire enterprise was for naught."

"What, not enough death for you, Kearns?"

"That's the wonderful thing about life," retorted Kearns heartily. "It's just chock-full of all the death you can handle!"

"I hope you get your fill, then, before the *Dagmar* returns tomorrow."

"It's tomorrow? Then we *must* find my Minotaur tonight. Perhaps we should return to the locus. He might be up there, ready to pop."

"You see the condition of this one," replied Warthrop, referring to the victim at their feet. "If the uninfected populace has isolated itself safely, the contagion has nearly run its course. The odds are he has already 'popped.'"

Kearns was not willing to let it go easily, however. He decided to bleed the latest victim instead of burning him, hoping the smell of blood would succeed where the fire had failed. Then he shooed us away. "Have a good rest. We've quite a hike down to the sea in the morning. I won't abandon you, I promise."

"Perhaps that is his plan," mused the doctor after we had retired to our shelter. "Sneak off and trust we won't find our way out in time."

I thought my master was being naïve. A man like John Kearns did not leave such things to chance.

"We should do it now," I said. "He thinks we've gone to sleep. I'll do it, if you'd like."

"You will do 'it'? What is 'it'?"

"Hit him over the head."

"Again, I understand the appeal of such an act . . ."

"You heard him, sir. He won't go to sleep today, and today we are going to Gishub to meet the *Dagmar*."

"We could wait till he quits for the night," he proposed. "He'll have to lay his rifle down at some point."

"Why would he do that?" I felt myself losing patience with him. Me, with Pellinore Warthrop! "He plans to kill us today, as soon as the sun rises."

"Yes. Yes, of course you're right, Will Henry. That must be his plan. And he must suspect ours, so he will be on his guard. How do we lower it?"

I told him my idea. He raised several objections to it, the chief of which being the most obvious—Kearns might smell a rat.

"And if he does," the monstrumologist said, "most certainly you will pay the ultimate price."

But he could think of nothing better. We needed to act quickly; at any moment Kearns might decide our time had come.

Before we parted, he touched my shoulder and looked deeply into my eyes. I saw a question in his. I repeated what I'd said to him at Dover: "I am not afraid, sir."

"I know that," he said gravely. "And that makes me afraid."

There is no monster, John Kearns had said. *There are only men.*

He heard my approach long before I reached his hiding place, and he whirled to face me as he brought the rifle round. I drew up at once and called to him softly, "Dr. Kearns! Dr. Kearns!"

"What is it?" he called back softly. "Where is Warthrop?"

"We heard something . . . back there." I pointed down the path. "He went to see what it was."

"He went . . . Why did he do that, Will?"

I stepped closer. He did not lower the rifle. That gave it away. If he had lowered the rifle, I might have thought the doctor and I were indulging in a paranoid delusion. But he did not lower the rifle; he kept it trained at the exact center of my chest.

"To see what it might be," I answered.

"Then he has lost his mind. All he had to do was join me here and wait for it to come to us."

"It was very close to the cave," I said in a quivery voice. "Just on the other side of the boulders. He didn't want to chance it. It was very close, sir, and he's been gone too long. I'm afraid . . ."

"Are you?" he asked. "Are you?"

He stepped down from his perch and walked slowly over to stand before me.

"Are you?" he asked again. His gray eyes shone hard in the firelight. His expression was uncharacteristically serious.

"Can we go find him, please?" I whimpered. There was the familiar tightening in my chest, the compacting force that could break the world in half, and the doctor's voice in Aden, saying, *We must be indispensable to each other.*

"Well, of course. We'll go together, Will. Strength in numbers, yes?"

He broke out his Kearns-ish grin, shifted the rifle into

the crook of his arm, and patted me kindly on the head, the way an uncle might a beloved nephew.

"There is no need to be afraid," he said.

I lifted up my eyes—*Oculus Dei*, Kearns had called them—and looked directly into his, and he recognized in them his own, but too late, too late, and before he could raise the gun or pull away, Awaale's long knife came whistling around and buried itself in his neck.

He sank to his knees, his eyes wide in astonishment. He started to raise the rifle. I kicked it out of his hands. He brought them up toward the gushing wound in his neck— the blood pulsed with the rhythm of his dying heart—while he looked up at me with wonder. And then he toppled over, reaching for me with bloody hands, but I was too far. I was beyond his grasp.

I went over to the rifle, picked it up, brought it back to where his body lay. I shoved it under him. Then I lifted his right hand and forced his finger through the trigger guard. I stepped back to examine my handiwork.

There are no monsters. There are only men.

I scooped up the knife and ran to fetch the doctor.

FORTY-FOUR
"A Fallen Star"

"Tell me again," the doctor said.

I did without hesitation, my gaze, like my story, unwavering. Kearns had indeed smelled a rat and had given me no choice but to defend myself.

"He was going to shoot you point-blank," the monstrumologist said dubiously. "With a Winchester rifle."

"Yes, Doctor. He pointed it right at my chest and told me he was sorry but he didn't have a choice."

"Like you. No choice."

"Yes, sir."

"So you stabbed him in the neck. While he held a rifle to your chest."

"Yes, sir."

"How did you manage it? To get close enough with the barrel of a Winchester between you?" He was having a hard time picturing it.

"I knocked it away with my left hand and swung with my right."

"You knocked it away?"

"I mean I shoved it away. He never let go of it."

"And he didn't notice you were holding a knife the whole time?"

"I was hiding it behind my back."

"So when he brought the rifle up to shoot you," he said slowly, "you whipped your right hand behind your back, knocked the gun away with your left, and at the same instant pulled out the knife with the other and swung it around to stab him in the neck?"

"Yes."

"Yes?"

"Yes, sir."

He scratched the underside of his chin thoughtfully. "That was quick thinking."

"Yes, sir. I mean, thank you, sir."

"And even quicker reflexes. You must demonstrate it to me sometime."

"I had to kill him, Dr. Warthrop."

"Hmm. Yes. I suppose you did, Will Henry. Self-preservation is your inalienable right."

"I had to," I insisted. "For both of us."

"I liked the plan better when it entailed luring him down the path so I could bop him over the head."

"I didn't plan it. It just . . . happened."

"Did I say that you planned it, Will Henry? Now, that would be a different animal altogether. It wasn't like what happened in Aden. There was no need to kill John Kearns."

"It's better that he's dead, though."

He frowned. His eyes sought out mine, and still I did not look away.

"How so, Will Henry?"

"If we had just left him here, he might have found a way off the island. I think he *would* have somehow, because he's . . . he's John Kearns."

"So? What does that matter as long as we escape?"

"It matters, sir, because you'd still be a threat to him. You know too much. You've seen too much."

A silence came between us. He looked at me, and I looked back at him, as the last stars faded gently from the sky.

"I think we both have, Will," he said, breaking the silence between us but not the thing that lay in silence between us.

On the tenth hour of our last day on the Isle of Blood, the great arms of the mountains opened before us, and we saw the plain stretching toward the sea. The day was bright and hot and nearly windless, and I saw several brilliantly colored lizards sunning themselves on the rocks. A butterfly fluttered by upon wings of iridescent blue. The monstrumologist pointed it out and said, "Look at him. Not a flower for miles. He must be lost."

A hulking figure appeared below us, between the two boulders marking the trailhead. At first my heart rose. *It must be Awaale,* I thought. I quickened my pace; the monstrumologist grabbed my shoulder and pulled me back. We stood and watched the huge figure shuffle painfully toward us. Rags hung from its massive frame. Its feet were bare and lacerated by the sharp stones, and left bloody footprints in its wake. Its mouth hung open; its eyes were black and unblinking; its hands were large and caked in blood. A large horn protruded from its wide forehead. We had found the Minotaur.

I raised Kearns's rifle. Beside me the monstrumologist made a soft, protesting sound, and he reached over and forced the barrel down.

The child of *Typhoeus* lifted its ponderous head, and its mouth curled into a snarl of agonized rage, the blood-flecked drool of *pwdre ser* glimmering in the midmorning sun. It stumbled toward us, too weak to run, and lost its footing. It fell. With a shudder of its huge shoulders, it pushed against the rocky ground, tears of *pwdre ser* streaming down its wasted face, and the light penetrated the translucent flesh and I could see clear down to its bones. It rose, swayed, fell again. The head reared back; the black eyes regarded the unalloyed sky and wept.

"'Seek a fallen star,'" said the monstrumologist, "'and thou shalt only light on some foul jelly, which, in shooting through the horizon, has assumed for a moment an appearance of splendour.'"

Tears of pity shone in his eyes. They both were crying, the monster and the man, the fallen star and the seeker of it.

And when I step upon the shore of the Isle of Blood to plant the conqueror's flag, when I attain the summit of the abyss, when I find the thing that all of us fear and all of us seek, when I turn to face the Faceless One, whose face will I see?

The man lifted his gun to the level of the monster's eyes.

We found Gishub as we'd left it, abandoned, a city of the dead. Years would pass before life returned. The fallen would be burned, their ashes returned to the earth from whence they'd come, the houses cleared and cleaned, and another generation would take to the sea for the harvest. Life would return. It always does.

We waited for Awaale. I had no doubt he would come. All names mean something, he had told me. We sat in the lengthening shade of a Dragon's Blood tree, and the sun fattened toward the horizon and the air was suffused with golden light. The light danced upon the leaves singing softly over my head. I looked down the slope to the sea and saw balanced upon the edge of the world a ship of a thousand sails. My father had found a way to keep his promise, through the unlikeliest of men.

That man's arm slid around my shoulders. His voice spoke into my ear.

"I will never leave you again, Will Henry. I will never abandon you. As long as I live, I will watch over you. As you brought me out of the darkness, I will keep the darkness from you. And if the tide should overwhelm me, I will raise you upon my shoulders; I will not suffer you to drown."

It was his moment of triumph. The moment when he'd turned to face the thing that all of us fear and all of us seek.

I could almost hear it, the conqueror's flag, snapping in the breeze.

At dusk we walked down to the shore. The *Dagmar* lay anchored between the wet sand and the horizon, and between us and the *Dagmar* a dinghy rode the incoming current to take us home.

"Awaale?" I said.

"He may not come, Will," said the doctor. "Kearns may have been right."

I thought of a man standing like the colossus in a fallen world, cradling a child in his arms, saying with a voice like the thunder's, *To show mercy is not naïve. To hold out against the end of hope is not stupidity or madness. It is fundamentally human.*

"No," I said. "*You* were right, Doctor."

I pointed to the east, where a man walked barefoot in the crash of the surf, a giant of a man whose dark skin shone in the last rays of a dying sun. Even from a distance I could see his wide smile. I knew what that smile meant. And he, the murderous pirate, his heart no longer burdened, raised his hand and waved with childlike joy.

From Socotra to Aden, then from Aden to Port Said, where Fadil kept his promise, providing a feast of *fasieekh* and *kofta* and introducing me to his twin daughters, Astarte and Dendera. He told them they could do worse than marrying Ophois, the ward of Mihos, guardian of the horizon. I may have left Port Said engaged to one of them; I am not certain.

Warthrop sent a cable to New York before we boarded the steamer for Brindisi:

THE MAGNIFICUM IS OURS.

"'The *magnificum* is ours'?" I echoed. I was afraid my master had lost hold of his reason.

"Well, it certainly doesn't belong to the Russians!" he said with a smile. "We have 'defanged' the terrible beast." He patted his instrument case. "I hope you can appreciate the irony of it, Will Henry. A healthy sense of the ironic is the best way to remain sane in a world that often isn't; I highly recommend it. But there will be no hero's welcome, no rewards or parades in our honor. Our victory over *Typhoeus* will go unheralded and unsung. A defeat for Pellinore Warthrop. A triumph for monstrumology." Then he corrected himself. "No. For humanity."

Across the Mediterranean to Brindisi, where we boarded the train for Venice. The doctor sent me on a special errand, one that proved quite challenging for a thirteen-year-old boy. "Don't bother with the first-class passengers. Go straight to the third-class. Money has a way of curdling the milk of human kindness, Will Henry." I finally managed to borrow the sought for item from an Indian emigrating from Bombay.

"I don't normally subscribe to superstition, but it may bring me good luck," Warthrop confessed as he sat down. He loosened his collar and lifted his chin. He eyed the razor gleaming in my hand. "Steady now. If you nick me, I shall be very angry and send you to bed without any supper."

He examined my handiwork in the mirror and pronounced it fairly executed.

"Should I find a barber in Venice?" he wondered aloud, running his fingers through his shoulder-length locks. Then he shrugged. "I shouldn't press it, should I?"

It was well past nine in the evening when we arrived in Venice. The dark waters of the canals glittered like diamond necklaces, and the air was moist with coming rain. I recognized the same people in the club that I had seen weeks before, as if they had never left, as if time stood still in Venice.

Perhaps it did. The doctor ordered a drink from the same basset-hound-faced little waiter; Bartolomeo came out and sat at the piano, wearing the same black vest and white shirt soaked in sweat; the door beside the stage came open and Veronica Soranzo emerged in a faded red gown identical to

the one she had given my master. Bartolomeo played ener-
getically, Veronica sang badly, and Pellinore watched, enrapt.
At the end of the song, she came to our table, slapped his
freshly shaven cheek in greeting, calling him *bastardo* and *idi-
ota*, and from the stage Bartolomeo laughed.

"You never answered my cable," the doctor said to her.

"How many of my letters did you not answer?" she
retorted.

"I thought you might be dead."

"I feared you might be alive."

"Have patience."

She laughed in spite of herself.

"What do you want, Pellinore?" she asked. "What monster are you chasing now?"

He whispered something into her ear. I saw her blush
beneath the heavy makeup.

"But why, Pellinore?" she asked.

"Why not?" he returned with a laugh. "While I am
here—and while you are here—but most important, while
we both still can!"

The monstrumologist swept her into his arms.
Bartolomeo took the cue and began to play a waltz. The
patrons sitting at the tables lifted their glasses and paid
no attention. Bartolomeo was not watching either; he was
absorbed in the music. I was the only one who watched them
dance in the smoky yellow light, as outside the rain kissed
the cobblestones of the Calle De Canonica. There was the

woman in red and the lonely man who danced with her and the boy who watched, alone.

The world is large, and it is easy to forget how very small we are. Like the rot of stars, time consumes us. He had thought the quest would bring him immortality, a triumph that would outlast his brief appearance upon the stage. He was wrong. Pellinore Warthrop would pass into oblivion, his noble work unrecognized, his sacrifice overshadowed by the deeds of lesser men. He could have wallowed in despair; he might have chewed upon the dry bones of bitterness and regret.

Instead he came to Venice, and he danced.

We are hunters all. We are, all of us, monstrumologists. And Pellinore Warthrop was the best of us, for he had found the courage to turn and face the most terrifying monster of all.

EPILOGUE

The morning after I finished reading the tenth folio, I called my friend, the director of the facility where Will Henry had ended his 131 years on earth.

"Was he missing a finger on his left hand?" I asked, and held my breath.

"Why, yes he was, the index finger," the director replied. "Did you find out why?"

I started to say yes. Then it occurred to me that that answer was a bit misleading. Like so many things in the journals, there were the facts and then there were Will Henry's explanations for them—not unlike the story of the *magnificum*, attributing circumstantial evidence of a monster to a monster that did not exist, a phenomenon that might fairly be called Warthrop's Folly.

"He wrote about it," I said. I told him I had just finished with the tenth notebook.

"Any more name-dropping?" he asked. He found that aspect of the journals the most intriguing.

"President McKinley; Arthur Conan Doyle, the creator of Sherlock Holmes; and Arthur Rimbaud."

"Rimbaud? Never heard of him."

"He was a French poet from the period. Still considered pretty important. I read somewhere that Bob Dylan was influenced by his work."

"Did Will Henry know Bob Dylan, too?"

I laughed. "Well, I haven't finished with the journals yet. Maybe."

"Anything more about Lilly?"

There was. I had found the article in the Auburn newspaper reporting the fire in 1952 that had destroyed Will and Lilly's house. I'd also obtained a copy of Lilly's obituary that had run two years before the fire. Lillian Bates Henry had been born in New York City, the daughter of Nathaniel Bates, a prominent investment banker, and Emily Bates, an influential figure in the women's suffrage movement at the turn of the century. Lillian had served on the boards of several charitable organizations, devoting her life, the article stated, to the service of others. She was survived by nieces and nephews on her brother Reginald's side of the family, and by her beloved spouse of thirty-eight years, William J. Henry.

"Thirty-eight years," the director said. "Means they must have gotten married in . . ."

"1912," I finished for him. "In 1912 Warthrop would have been fifty-nine years old."

"Warthrop?"

"If there ever was a Warthrop. If there was, then by 1912 he was dead."

"Why do you think that?"

"Will writes that he was Warthrop's constant companion till he died. I can't imagine them getting married and moving Pellinore Warthrop in with them."

"But do you really think there ever was a Pellinore Warthrop?" I could detect a smile in his voice. Will Henry's words popped into my head at the question. *I was pursuing the one I had lost.*

"I'm beginning to think there's some underlying allegory here," I said carefully. "At the very beginning of the diary, Will Henry says Warthrop has been dead for forty years. If Warthrop 'died' around 1912, that means Will began the journals around the same time the house in Auburn burned down, right after he lost everything—not just his sole companion in life but everything he had. Maybe the journals are some weird way of dealing with all that."

"So he invents a past populated by monsters to understand the monsters of his past?"

"Well, it's just a theory. I'm no psychiatrist."

"Maybe we need to get one involved."

For whom? I wondered silently. *Will Henry or me?*

I lay awake in bed that night, thinking of fire—the first fire that had yanked his parents away from him and the second fire that had claimed everything else. *Fire destroys,* he had written, *but it also purifies.* Here was a man who had lost everything—not once but twice, if that element of the journal was to be believed. He must have questioned, like John Kearns, if our colossal human error was in praying to the wrong god. Perhaps the folios were his attempt at making sense of the senseless, the unseen monster that is always there, the Faceless One that lurks one ten-thousandth of an inch outside our range of vision.

While I pondered that possibility, my heart began to race, and I was suddenly overwhelmed by a desire to simply turn away . . . to not finish the three remaining journals . . . to return all of them to the director and drop my investigation, or whatever you wanted to call it. A little voice warned me I was heading down a path where I did not want to go, where I *should* not go. I had the sensation of something coming unwound inside me, something that was an intimate part of me and yet somehow totally foreign and unrecognizable, and those two parts pulled against each other with enough force to break the world in half. Will Henry had called it *das Ungeheuer,* the monster, and he had promised me I would come to understand what he meant.

He had kept his promise.